Amy Myers was born in Kent. After taking a degree in English literature, she was director of a London publishing company, and is now a freelance editor and writer. She is married to an American and they live in a Kentish village on the North Downs. She also writes under the name of Laura Daniels.

Praise for Amy Myers' previous books featuring Auguste Didier, also available from Headline:

'Wittily written and intricately plotted with some fine characterisation. Perfection' *Best*

'Reading like a cross between Hercule Poirot and Mrs Beeton ... this feast of entertainment is packed with splendid late-Victorian detail' *Evening Standard*

'What a marvellous tale of Victorian mores and murders this is – an entertaining whodunnit that whets the appetite of mystery lovers and foodies alike' *Kent Today*

'Delightfully written, light, amusing and witty. I look forward to Auguste Didier's next banquet of delights' *Eastern Daily Press*

'Plenty of fun, along with murder and mystery ... as brilliantly coloured as a picture postcard' *Dartmouth Chronicle*

'Classically murderous' *Woman's Own*

'An amusing Victorian whodunnit' Netta Martin, *Annabel*

'Impossible to put down' *Kent Messenger*

'An intriguing Victorian whodunnit' *Daily Examiner*

# Murder
# at the
# Music Hall

**Amy Myers**

**HEADLINE**

First published in 1995
by HEADLINE BOOK PUBLISHING

First published in paperback in 1996
by HEADLINE BOOK PUBLISHING

10 9 8 7 6 5 4 3 2 1

ISBN 0 7472 4843 5

Printed and bound in Great Britain by
Cox & Wyman Ltd, Reading, Berkshire

HEADLINE BOOK PUBLISHING
A division of Hodder Headline PLC
338 Euston Road
London NW1 3BH

For Richard and Barbara
with love

# Prologue

Rain plopped down the collar of Chief Inspector Egbert Rose's ulster, despite the umbrella. Changing its tactics with the gusting wind through the dock, it assaulted his face and mocked his eyes. He was far from happy.

'We've missed the boat, sir.' There was no glimmer of a smile on Inspector Grey's face, whether he was conscious of his pun or not. Rose regarded Grey without enthusiasm.

'The boat's missed *you*, Grey,' he retorted grimly. 'Six o'clock you told me the *Lisboa* was due to leave. It's six now, and she sailed two hours ago.' The North Quay of London Docks was no place to spend a Saturday, even a wet dismal September afternoon. He thought of Edith cosily taking toasted crumpets and seed cake at Highbury, and compared her lot to his.

'To catch the tide, sir.' Grey's reply had the desperation of the cornered rat. 'She'll dock again in two weeks.'

'Think she'll come steaming back with the loot still tucked under the captain's arm? Any chance of the river boats catching her?'

Grey shook his head. 'She'll be outside territorial waters. It would be piracy. Unless you think we'd be

1

justified . . .' He broke off, as his companion's umbrella jerked irritably.

'Much as I'd like to don eye patch and broadsword, it ain't precisely going to soothe Portuguese prickles, is it? There's been enough fuss over this cross; there'll be more when it comes out it's been nicked from Windsor Castle. What's His Majesty going to say if the Stepney police and Scotland Yard start dancing around like the pirates of Penzance, eh?'

'In Stepney,' Grey replied stolidly, 'we have more to think about than His Majesty's embarrassment.'

Rose envied him. It was no joke to be summoned to Buckingham Palace at Saturday luncheon time by an irate monarch ordering him to track down a missing relic of incalculable value, before it left the country for good; an event, His Majesty informed him, that would ensure not only the severing of diplomatic relations with England's oldest ally, but probably his own enforced abdication, a mere month or so after his coronation. Every coastal and dockyard police force from Harwich to Plymouth had been alerted with descriptions of the two villains. In the Thames, the most obvious departure point, the dockyard police had orders to detain every piece of shipping with any connection with Portugal till cleared. Then at three-thirty, surprisingly, Special Branch had come up with a name, the *Lisboa*. Unfortunately the *Lisboa* was now in mid-ocean, ploughing its way home, in all likelihood taking Prince Henry the Navigator's cross with it. And what the press would do with that, Rose preferred not to imagine. Half of them delicately, and sometimes not so delicately, had been suggesting that Portugal ought to have the cross back anyway, and the other half had foretold the end of the monarchy if it did. Now he had to report failure to His Britannic Majesty King Edward VII, and very little imagination was required to foresee the results of that conversation. Crumpets retreated to the same odds as a castle in Spain – or Portugal.

Around them loomed the tall forbidding rain-swept warehouses of the London Docks, their cranes idle now, but stretching out threatening dark arms towards their prey; before them were moored steamers from unknown ports, their crews hurrying in the twilight towards the excitement of Saturday night in the pubs, gin palaces and less savoury institutions eagerly awaiting them. At least it was no longer Rose's job to mop up the resulting mess. As a raw newcomer to the force, his beat had taken in the docks, not to mention the nearby St George's Street; the latter might be more salubrious than he remembered it, but off it still lay some of the poorest slums in London.

'Sir.' A wet Dock Police constable materialised from the gloom at Grey's side. From underneath his helmet, two scared eyes peered out, torn between relief at the presence of two superior-ranking officers, and anxiety since neither belonged to his own force.

'What is it, Constable?' Grey barked irritably.

'A body, sir. In Nightingale Lane. Been there an hour or two, I reckon. Sucking the monkey, I reckon.'

'What monkey?'

'Dock talk, sir. Siphoning port wine with a tube through the bung-hole of the cask. Strong stuff.'

'Then most likely he's drunk, you fool,' Grey snarled.

The constable held firm. 'Dead, sir.'

'Nightingale Lane, you say?' Rose's attention was suddenly diverted from the absent *Lisboa*, as he was mentally catapulted back from the autumn of 1902 to the 1870s. So Nightingale Lane hadn't changed. Hardly surprising, he supposed. You'd have to burn it down and plant a rose garden before you could make Nightingale Lane respectable – and even then the roses would smell of sewers. 'Show me.'

'There's no need—' Grey began.

'Let's go.' His tone of voice made it clear Rose was going anyway, if only to make Grey squirm.

They squelched in the constable's wake through the labyrinth of warehouses on the western boundary of the docks, through a locked and barred gateway into the narrow winding lane that had probably seen more murders than any other London thoroughfare. There was no sign to Rose's eyes that anything had changed. Here the rain made no difference, for the sun was shy of the high wall of St Katherine's Dock on the one side and the tall warehouses of London Docks facing it. The bends and twists of the lane made it an admirable place for the disposal of grudges. The police torch shone in the puddles, as the constable flashed it in a narrow entrance between two of the dock buildings. There, half-hidden behind a pile of rotting rubbish, overflowing and burying the zinc pail it was aimed at, was the body, its shape indistinct in the gloom. For a moment the only sound was the pelting rain.

'Another of them casuals,' Grey then said disgustedly, lifting the body up slightly with one foot and letting it drop again.

'Not from the pubs round here, sir, I know 'em all.'

4

Grey regarded the constable with dislike. Unknowns might mean trouble. 'A casual's what we call them,' he told Rose loudly. 'They hang around the pubs waiting for odd jobs, carrying and fetching from the docks, and don't mind too much if they get 'em or not.'

Rose knew what a casual was all right, but he disapproved of Grey's boot. A casual was a man, with a name, even if he alone knew it. 'Nothing strikes you as odd?' He squatted down by the body, and lifted it again.

A pause. 'Not in this neighbourhood.'

'He's been stabbed. Knifed. Not much blood, because the knife's still in it, driven in deep.'

The young constable flushed red, and seeing it, Rose added kindly: 'You did right not to move the body, and there was no seeing without doing that.'

Overwhelmed with gratitude, the constable's young face brightened. 'I found this, sir, by his hand in a puddle. I took it for safe keeping.'

Rose looked at the small piece of shaped dark-red glass, examining it carefully. 'Could be nothing, or it could be a garnet.'

'He's a thief then,' Grey was impatient to be away. 'Or a fence's runner. I'll take it. Valuable, is it?'

'Not in itself.' Rose replied absently. He was remembering this morning's interview.

*Can you describe the cross, Your Majesty?*

*Silver with ivory, studded with precious stones.*

*What kind of precious stones, sir?*

*Mainly garnets,* the King had replied promptly.

'I'll take it to the Yard.' Rose scribbled a receipt. It was probably coincidence, but it might possibly be the tarragon in the sauce. He remembered Auguste once saying that of an apparently insignificant detail. He shivered. There were smells in this narrow corridor that were far removed from an Auguste Didier kitchen. Smells of decay and death, that remained uncleansed by the rain still steadily beating down. And smells stirring in his mind as well – and those he didn't like.

# Chapter One

'Is this a dagger which I see before me?'

The little man broke off. He looked perplexedly at his audience. 'I ask you, you'd think he could *see* it was a dagger. "The handle toward my hand." Now, is that poetry? No, that is a – ' he wildly searched for the right word – 'a *perlice* report.'

The dancing dagger pranced along its invisible wire, as Will Lamb made valiant attempts to grasp it, leaping around the stage in increasing desperation as each time the dagger jerked out of his reach. 'Come, let me clutch thee,' he pleaded to it in vain. He appealed to his audience. 'Now, if that was his old woman there I could understand it, but a dagger, well, I ask you, who'd want to clutch a dagger? Nasty unfriendly things. No, if you ask me,' shaking his head sadly, 'this Shakespeare fellow's got it wrong.'

The literary context was familiar to him, but even if it had not been the comedy was irresistible and universal. Auguste Didier laughed helplessly in his private box at the back of the Empire Theatre's grand circle.

Lamb's anxious eyes bore the bewildered expression

of Everyman faced with a world of inanimate objects beyond his control. 'Downright dangerous, I call it.'

'Horrible, terrible,' shouted out a jovial member of his audience.

The theatre rocked with laughter, as Lamb, peering anxiously round, made one final desperate glance of appeal to his audience, then plunged after his elusive quarry, and promptly tripped over, falling flat on the dagger, which had condescended to rest on the ground point upwards.

'He is superb,' Auguste cried enthusiastically to his companion. 'He is another Grimaldi, a true clown.'

'And a nice man, too.' Gwendolen, Lady Westland, alias the former Magnificent Masher, the toast of the halls until her marriage, commented apparently casually. Auguste glanced at her, catching something odd in her tone, though she was laughing as hard as he. Was it just his imagination or could it be that the company of Auguste Didier was not the sole reason for her last-minute invitation to escort her this evening? Perhaps he longed too much for something just a little out of the ordinary to happen, and was seeing bears where only bushes existed. High society into which he had perforce been catapulted on his marriage provided a constrained life, and Tatiana had so far been more ingenious than he in squirreling out escape routes. She had her School of Motoring for Ladies, whereas his ten-volume work, *Dining with Didier*, was proving insufficient to satisfy his restlessness.

The troupe of brightly and lightly clad pierrots who concluded the first half of the programme were greeted with the polite but unrapturous applause to which they were resigned, after the final chorus of the song that larded Lamb's patter: 'So I said to the Bard . . .'

As Auguste escorted Lady Westland through the notorious Promenade to the select champagne bar, his eyes strayed a trifle wistfully to right and left where soft birds of paradise sparkled in jewels and allure in search of custom for later this evening. Wistfully? He caught himself guiltily. He was a happily married man, he reminded himself, then cheered up as he reflected that to appreciate the aroma of the soup was not the same as sipping it.

The sight of the Veuve Cliquot awaiting them, as he advanced behind his hostess's ample purple-satined posterior, cheered him even more, and it was well into the second glass before he ventured to put voice to his suspicions.

'It is indeed a pleasure to be here, Lady Westland—'

'But you want to know why, is that it?' Gwendolen cut in cheerfully.

He nodded, relieved. After all, he hardly knew her. He had only met her once, and then only partially. He had visited Tatiana's School of Motoring (an elegant title that discreetly failed to mention the motor garage, complete with engineering workshop, also on the premises), to discover his wife clad in hideous bloomers lying underneath a motor-car with someone in a similar state of dress. His wife emerged, Lady Westland had remained mostly hidden, as it appeared repairs were at a critical point. In her fifties now, Lady Westland had retired from the music-hall stage over twenty years ago. As the Magnificent Masher, she had stormed the music halls of the late seventies and eighties with her male impersonations and comic abilities. Auguste suspected the comic potential of her life had seriously declined, and that she missed it in her present role of Magnificent Peeress.

'Dear Tatiana asked me to entertain you while she was away.'

'And why else, Lady Westland?' he asked politely.

'Nettie Turner's got a job for you.'

Auguste had of course seen Nettie Turner on stage before – one could hardly avoid it. She was the darling of the halls in East and West Ends alike, and he seemed to remember hearing that it had been Lady Westland who had first spotted and encouraged her talent. Her warmth and vitality seemed to increase with the years, and she was well over forty now. How quickly magical illusion could vanish, however. As they went into her dressing-room after the performance, Auguste saw merely a middle-aged, tired woman, her face lined with more creases than laughter had provided, sitting in a room as plush and crowded with mementoes as any parlour. Where was the bewitching creature who had just held three and a half thousand people in the palm of her hand as she teased them, laughed with them, enchanted them? The innuendoes and movements accompanying her songs were carefully toned down for this audience, as she thrust her personality over the footlights, but Auguste had seen her in less refined halls. For Auguste, it was like meeting Sarah Bernhardt, but with her coster's costume given way to a rather dull cream silk evening dress which emphasised the sallowness of a skin newly cleansed from greasepaint,

Nettie looked disappointingly ordinary – until she smiled at them. Immediately her face came alive, the warmth came back into her eyes and he saw then the strength of personality was just resting, not vanished. 'Gwennie, me old dear. How's the Gold Plate? Still keeping you on a ball and chain?'

'Randolph is well, thank you, Nettie.' Gwendolen correctly translated Plate as Mate. She ignored the jibe. 'May I introduce Mr Auguste Didier, Nettie?'

For an instant, Auguste was aware of being appraised by the sharpest eyes he'd seen since he first met Egbert Rose, then the impression vanished, as she asked conventionally, 'Enjoy the show, did you, Mr Didier?'

'Who could not, with you topping the bill?'

'*Will* and me.'

'Has he waited for us?' asked Gwendolen.

'We're playing the Empire, Gwennie, not five halls a night. 'Course he's still here. Have you met Will, Mr Didier?'

'No, and I'd very much like to. He is a great artiste.'

'There aren't many nice people around in music hall,' Nettie said soberly. 'Many of us start out nice, and the higher we get on the bill the less nice we become. Will's the exception. He'll always do anyone a good turn. Money flows into one hand and jumps out of his other. He's a bloody marvel. Most of us depend on a whole troupe of agents, writers, publishers, to prop us up. Not Will. He's got an agent who looks after the business side, but as for the rest, he needs no one but himself. He writes his own material, the patter, the song, the whole act. His head's full of music. He's always scribbling; if he don't want the stuff for himself, he'll give it away. He let me have my Donkey Song, the one

I did tonight.' She winked, wriggling her body suggestively in her chair, bursting out with 'Everybody pats me, everybody strokes me, oh give me a carrot, oh do.'

Auguste blushed, and seeing this she roared with laughter. 'That's how I do it down East. But you didn't blush out front tonight, did you?'

He laughed. 'I did not.'

'That's better,' Nettie said, relieved. 'You'd better get used to our ways.'

'Why?' Auguste had a sudden foreboding.

'You're going to be Will's personal detective.'

For a moment Auguste thought he'd misheard, but from the way in which he appeared to be the cynosure of both Nettie's and Gwendolen's eyes, he was greatly afraid he hadn't. 'I have had some success in solving crime,' he began firmly, 'but—'

Nettie blithely disregarded him. 'Ever heard of the Old King Cole?'

Auguste racked his memory. Something came back to him, something Egbert Rose had once said, and not a polite something. 'A music hall in the East End?' he inquired cautiously.

'Right. In St George's Street, Wapping, down near the docks. Will and I both started our careers there. The owner's an old rogue who sees bailiffs round every corner and no wonder. Percy Jowitt he's called. This time he's really in a bad way, and looks as if they'll get him this time. He asked if we'd go back there for a week's run to save him from the workhouse a bit longer. Will being a generous soul, too bloody generous this time, if you ask me, agreed.'

12

'That was indeed kind of him,' Auguste said.

'In this instance, not so bloomin' kind, in fact. There's an attraction who sat in the scales to add weight to Percy Jowitt's arguments – he sent her to do his dirty business for him. A lady called Mariella Gomez. An auburn-haired English beauty married to a Portuguese juggler.'

'She too is an artiste?'

Gwendolen caught Nettie's eye and burst out laughing. 'Adorable little doggies in frilly collars, sliding down a chute into a water tank.'

'Come on, Gwennie. You're not being fair,' Nettie roared. 'She's a serio-vocalist.' She relapsed into her stage persona as she piped out mockingly:

'What's a poor mermaid to do
When she's only got a tail?'

'She'd find out soon enough,' Gwendolen snorted.

'Provided it's not with Will.' Nettie sobered down. 'He was crazy about her ten years ago, at the Old King Cole, but he was a four-foot-nine no one then, so she chose Miguel. She might have made the right choice in some ways – ' she caught Gwendolen's eye in unspoken understanding – 'but not the way Mariella chiefly cares about. Money.'

'And that is why he needs a nursemaid?' Auguste was appalled.

'No.' Nettie instantly sobered. 'He's convinced someone's going to murder him.'

Will Lamb's dressing-room was a stark contrast to

Nettie's, a plain working room with not a personal object to be seen. Yet the room didn't seem empty, not with the nervous energy and personality of Will Lamb in it. He was sitting staring into the mirror, removing the last of the greasepaint from his eyebrows, but even at this mundane task he had the air of a bouncing ball merely awaiting the slightest touch to be back in play.

Nettie sailed in, wasting no time. 'Will, I've brought your personal detective.'

Will leapt up, hurried towards Auguste, and pumped his hand warmly. 'That's really very generous of you, Mr Didier, very kind.' He beamed.

'I have explained, Mr Lamb, I am a chef,' Auguste tried to protest, 'and though I have experience of detection, I do not feel I am the right person to protect you.'

The two women exchanged a look, and Gwendolen grinned. 'You could cook,' Nettie said brightly. 'We've arranged all that.'

Panic was replaced with cautious interest. 'Cook?'

'The Old King Cole serves food in its bar – quite a famous local eating-house it's become,' Nettie said airily. 'They need a cook, and Will needs someone to protect him.'

Auguste looked at her suspiciously. 'But how can I do both?'

'There'll be staff there, of course, Percy says. I'll see Will to the theatre, then you nip backstage and keep an eye on him. You can watch the acts if you like. Rubbish, most of it. The regular turns Percy can afford to put on don't keep him in bangers and mash.'

Will looked anxious. 'Harry?' he murmured.

14

'Oh yes.' Nettie roared. 'Harry Pickles. He's my husband, not that you'd notice. We don't see much of each other. Fancy your remembering, Will. Husband number three,' she explained to Auguste. 'I told him if he don't keep his name clean, he'll be out and Will here can be number four.'

'That will be nice, Nettie,' Will said valiantly.

'Don't worry, old cock. I'm too fond of you to wish that on you.'

For a moment Auguste glimpsed the pain behind the bravado. It was common knowledge. None of Nettie's marriages had given her happiness. 'Mr Lamb, why do you think someone wishes to murder you?' Auguste asked firmly, getting back to the heart of the matter.

Will looked anxious. 'Dreamed it,' he told Auguste apologetically.

'Dreams are not real.' Auguste said with relief.

'Will's are,' Nettie remarked glumly.

It was then he remembered that Will Lamb had had several breakdowns and was always in fragile health. Yet after all, there could be nothing to a mere dream, so the job of protecting Will would not be onerous, and the temporary job of cook would be an *adventure*. He was not sure Tatiana would approve of either task, let alone His Majesty, but after all, neither, he told himself, would ever know.

'He dreamed of Bill Terriss. He was a friend of his,' Nettie explained sombrely.

Auguste understood immediately. The murder of the famous actor William Terriss a few years ago, at the stage door of the Adelphi, committed by a crazy super who imagined his path from crowd scenes to leading man had been blighted by Terriss, had shocked the theatre world and public alike. Who in their right mind would want to murder Terriss – or Will Lamb?

As if following his thoughts, Nettie said robustly, 'I've told him it's ridiculous – isn't it, Will?'

'No.' Will Lamb's large eyes looked dolefully at them. 'On the morning of the day Bill died, his understudy told me he'd had a dream the previous night of dear old Bill lying on the stairs with a group of people round him, one of whom was his leading lady. He died. And that evening his dream was re-enacted in real life. So you see, dreams *can* be warnings.'

Perhaps, Auguste thought to himself, but even if recognised, how can they be acted upon? But aloud he spoke briskly. 'Then please do not go to Wapping, Mr Lamb. Let Miss Turner go alone.'

Will Lamb stared at him blankly. 'Oh no, I must go. I must. Don't you see?'

'No, I don't, Will,' Nettie said forthrightly. 'If it's just because of that woman, then arrange to meet her somewhere else, for cripes' sake.'

'No, Nettie,' Will said gently. 'I have promised, you see. You don't understand. We—' He broke off, but his face was as excited as a child's watching the curtain rise on a pantomime.

'These dreams are your only evidence?' Auguste asked gently, curiosity aroused by that sudden excitement. A child – but a child with a secret.

Will shook his head sadly. 'No.'

'And what else has happened?' Auguste's spirits sank.

'Communications.' Will fished in the pocket of his overcoat, and produced a crumpled piece of paper with letters cut out from some form of print and stuck on. Its message was stark.

'Keep away from the Old King Cole.' And it was signed, 'The Raven.'

'I've had one every day this week,' Will told him dolefully.

'And when did you have your dream?' Auguste asked carefully.

'Tuesday, or perhaps it was Wednesday. Yes, it must have been Wednesday because of the pickled egg. Tuesday's my night for caviar, or is it oysters, at any rate my cook won't give me pickled egg and oysters, so it must have been Wednesday,' Will informed him brightly.

'I see.' Auguste was quite sure he did. 'So the dream could have been sparked off by the letters.'

'You mean Bill wrote the letters?' Will was puzzled.

'No, you associated Bill's murder with the threat to murder you.'

'But he was here tonight.'

'Who was?'

'Bill.'

Auguste glanced at Nettie, who came to his aid.

'Will, old chum, you've been on the beer.'

'No, no, he *was* here. You heard him, you must have done.' Will looked appealingly from one to the other. 'I heard him calling out, "Horrible, terrible," that's what he said. That's what poor Bill said to his wife a few days before he was killed, he said it about being killed with a knife. And he *was*.'

'But, Mr Lamb, that is mere coincidence,' Auguste soothed.

'And the letters?' Will asked anxiously, eager to be convinced.

'Warning from a friend,' Gwendolen said heartily. 'Reminding you that Percy's an old rogue. Or someone jealous of you.'

'Signed "The Raven"?' Auguste asked. If there was cause for concern, then Will should be on his guard, not lulled into false security.

Will pumped Auguste's hand again. 'I like you, Mr Didier,' he assured him earnestly.

' "The raven himself is hoarse",' Auguste quoted almost to himself, as three pairs of eyes fixed on him in horror. 'From *Macbeth*,' he explained, startled. 'It's a reference to your act.'

'You *quoted*!' Nettie's voice was grim.

'Of course, you're French, Mr Didier,' Gwendolen said kindly. 'You cannot know there's a superstition that it is very bad luck to quote from or even name that play offstage in a theatre.'

'Don't worry, Mr Didier,' Will reassured him gaily. 'It reverses the curse to say it backwards. You see? *Esraoh si flesmih nevar eht*. Never ate? Now what a foolish thing. No wonder the poor bird feels a little cross. Talking of which . . .' He chattered on, giving Auguste time to recover, then picked up his stage dagger with its retractable blade. 'I'm armed, you see, and now you have agreed to be my detective and cook, I defy any murderous chop to get past this. Chop meet dagger, dagger meet chop.'

Had he agreed? Even as he laughed, Auguste reflected, he couldn't remember doing so. Yet after all, it offered great possibilities. What could he cook? How

could he educate an entirely new and receptive clientele
in the joys of dining with Didier? He would offer them
such delights as they had never tasted before. Just as
Alexis Soyer had both cooked and set down his recipes
for all men, whether rich or poor, so now would he. A
whole new area of cuisine might be revealed to him.
True, His Majesty had forbidden him to cook for profit,
after his marriage last year, but this job could be said
to be a form of charity, and even if it wasn't, it was
unlikely Buckingham Palace would ever hear about his
adventures in Wapping. Excitement welled up inside
him. Tatiana would not be returning for at least ten
days from her road race in France, and the boredom of
ten days without her was banished. He could *cook*.

True, he had also to ensure that nobody murdered
Will Lamb, but this, he managed to convince himself,
was a simple task. Somehow those communications did
not have the ring of a serious intent to murder. Indeed,
given Will's disposition, they might even have been
composed by Will himself to give substance to his
dreams. Splendid though Workers' Educational Classes
were, it was unlikely that anyone at the Old King Cole
would be up to quoting from Shakespeare. Auguste
managed in his optimism to ignore two facts. Firstly,
that since Will's most famous songs and lines of patter
were based on Shakespeare, the notes were, to say the
least, relevant. And secondly, that St George's Street,
where the Old King Cole was situated, was a name only
a few decades old. Before that, the street had another
name, the Ratcliffe Highway, at one time notorious for
murder.

* * *

19

An anonymous figure in cap and rough jacket threaded his way through the costers' stalls of Whitehorse Street, having emerged from the London and Blackwall railway into the Commercial Road. Egbert Rose whistled thoughtfully as he made his way towards St Dunstan's Church and Stepney Green; then, having ensured no interested eyes watched his progress, plunged off to the right, into a network of narrow streets, alleys and courts. Some of them appeared in dark blue or black in Mr Booth's poverty map of London. That had been charted in 1889, but the colours hadn't changed much in thirteen years to his way of thinking, as he got deeper into the warren. Still pretty nearly as bad as you could get, whole families in one stinking room in some of these places.

He crossed Eastfield Street and strolled past the identical small houses, controlling his impulse to look down to see what he was walking in. He needed his eyes on the level. He was observed all right, by children playing in the gutters, by women glaring at him from doorsteps. Strangers were noticed and remembered. He clutched his battered suitcase, the passport for his presence. He dived off through one of the alleyways and when he emerged, walked quickly back the way he had come, and then into one of the small courts that peppered the street. He had arrived.

'Morning, Ma,' he roared. The damp heat was immense, and steam curled under an inner door. As Ma Bisley waddled through, it hissed then billowed in triumph round the hitched-up serge skirt and curled itself around the broad beaming face.

'Yer oughta know better than to come here on a

Monday morning. Boiler time. I got a living to make,' she told him amiably.

He shook his head firmly. 'Too much at stake not to, Ma, even for the sake of your washing.' Around him were ticketed bundles, the mangle, washing boards and flat irons arranged in orderly fashion, the paraphernalia of her business. One of her businesses, in fact; the other was providing information to him through a team of runners, within strictly observed guidelines.

'What is it this time?'

'I don't know yet, Ma. May be nothing, may be a can of stinking worms.'

His Majesty had taken the bad news of the disappearing *Lisboa* surprisingly philosophically for him. Rose had emerged with his head, and even his job, which was more than he had expected. The British ambassador to Portugal would be informed, the Portuguese ambassador to Britain would be informed, and, somewhat less enthusiastically, the British public would be informed that the cross had disappeared without trace, and that it was unlikely in the extreme that the Portuguese royal family were in any way involved, since the theft from Windsor Castle had been carried out by bogus representatives of their government who were doubtless anarchists in disguise. Staff had been reprimanded for not checking credentials, and the Metropolitan Police for failing to apprehend the villains.

Rose had inwardly seethed, and commented mildly that Special Branch might wish to be more actively involved if anarchists were the villains; he had earned himself a glare and the ruling that 'politics were politics, but property was property'. In his relief at still finding himself employed, it was not until Sunday that he had realised he was smelling something unsatisfactory – and that it was not for once Edith's burnt roast beef. He had foregone his evening glass of ale at the Queen's Arms in order to eradicate the smell. 'Any news on that corpse?' he shouted through the telephone at the unfortunate Grey.

'Yes, sir. As I said, he was a casual, a villain by the name of Jack Knight, place of loitering the Three Tars in Limehouse. Employment putting away as many pints of porter as he could. Time of death between three and four.'

'Far off his usual beat, wasn't he?'

'They take what's offered, that sort.'

Rose knew. *That* sort of casual (as opposed to those of their more energetic brothers who stormed the dock gates daily hoping for the odd day's work) loafed in pubs waiting for work to come to them. Never sought it out. They fetched and carried merchandise, legal or illegal, to the ships, and never asked questions. For that reason, most were 'safe'. Yet this one got murdered, and not on his usual beat.

As if reading his thoughts, Grey told him: 'We've checked the pubs round Nightingale Lane, if you're thinking he might have got into a fight after spending his dosh.'

'Nice job, carrying jewels,' Rose said thoughtfully. 'Must have paid him well.'

'Might have been Auntie Maisie's engagement ring. Or Uncle Sam Fence's runner. We're working on that.'

'Family?'

'Casuals don't have 'em.'

'They don't come out of nowhere. He didn't look like he slept out at nights, so he laid his weary head somewhere. Even if it's only Medland Hall.' He thought of the nearby lodging house for the destitute, and the long dreary queues that formed there waiting hopefully and hopelessly for the seven o'clock opening time.

'No one's come forward. I don't waste my men's time. I've got witnesses he was given a job around two-thirty. Someone remembers him buying a pie to take with him. That any help? If you need to know the name of his board school teacher, let me know.'

If Grey meant this sarcastically, he was disappointed. Rose thanked him cordially, and hung the receiver up. He was a happy man. He could still smell something fishy, and he knew the fish was distinctly off.

'Corpse in Nightingale Lane, Ma,' he said now.

'What's a nice Chief Inspector from Scotland Yard doing in the likes of Nightingale Lane?'

'Ship called the *Lisboa* sailed on Saturday. A silver cross with garnets belonging to Prince Henry the Navigator. Either of them mean anything to you?'

'Not a tin farthing.'

Ma could not read, and however heated, the discussion of the newspapers, society or intelligentsia passed her by. Ask her whether Jimmy Longtooth had been up to his old tricks, or another Charlie Peace or Kate Webster appeared in her territory, and she was as informed on her subject as Mycroft Holmes himself.

'The cross was stolen from Windsor Castle Saturday morning, and I was tipped off it was leaving on the

*Lisboa*. The *Lisboa* left two hours early and before I got there. There was a corpse in Nightingale Alley.'

'As dirty as a dock casual's long johns.'

'They don't wear 'em, do they?'

'Not often.'

He took her point and considered it. Then he shook his head. 'Just because the King's involved, that don't mean I'm smelling rats where there's only pure roses, Ma. There was a small garnet lying by the corpse.'

She looked at him sharply. 'Think this cross was pinched from him, do you?'

'Yes. Why kill him if he'd already delivered the cross?'

'Stop him from talking?'

'Then why employ him in the first place? He came from Limehouse, so someone took care over this. I don't like it, Ma. Could you ask around – urgently?'

'With the afternoon collection. Now, give me that laundry of yours. It'll be at your desk seven prompt.'

The battered suitcase having been duly ticketed took its place amidst its even humbler fellows.

Rose stared out from his high, small office overlooking the river below. By rights he should have surrendered this office to Twitch on his promotion and moved into the more accessible room on the first floor. He'd refused to. Accessibility was not one of his objectives. If people needed him, they'd come; if they couldn't be bothered to climb a few stairs, they could stay away and solve their own problems. A simple method but it worked, and he still had his view of the Thames. It helped him. The Thames flowed into London, it flowed out again to the sea. It didn't care whether it was passing the House of Lords or Limehouse Basin; it carried its corpses and secrets on regardless.

The only snag about retaining his old room was that Twitch had magnanimously decided to make the same gesture and did not accept the room elsewhere to which his promotion to Inspector entitled him. He was still next door, the faithful terrier that waited for bones. Rose had found his loyalty, somewhat to his surprise, strangely moving. He firmly buried such emotion and replaced it for daily use with his usual sharp irritation.

There was one good thing about Inspector Stitch (Twitch was Rose's not so private name for him); he delivered the goods. Unlike Grey, who let them sail down the river out of sight.

'You wanted me, sir?' Stitch was still under the impression he owed grateful thanks to Rose for not blocking his promotion. Correctly, in fact. Better the devil you knew was Rose's guiding principle.

'Yes. That post mortem on the docks' corpse arrived yet?'

'Yes, sir. I've just read it.'

'Bring it in, there's a good chap.'

Pink in the cheeks at this unaccustomed courtesy, Twitch vanished and reappeared with the alacrity of the devil in a pantomime. Rose read through the brief report. 'Late thirties, died between three and four as Grey said.' Very helpful. That meant he might or might not have delivered his package. 'Remains of undigested meal . . .'

'What interests you, sir?'

'Probably nothing, if His Majesty wasn't mixed up with it – in a manner of speaking.'

'If this chap came from Limehouse to London Docks to deliver a package, why should the body turn up in Nightingale Lane?' Stitch asked portentously.

'Perhaps he had a notion to choose his own execution place,' Rose said scathingly.

'Perhaps that's where he handed the package over, sir. If it was a secret mission, he wouldn't want to go up to the ship.'

'A rendezvous, eh? Sometimes, Stitch, you excel yourself.'

'I know, sir,' Stitch murmured, flustered. 'And then,' driven to new heights of endeavour, 'the captain or contact on the ship murdered him as per instructions.'

Rose looked at him. 'No reason why not, I suppose,' he grunted. 'Or he was murdered on the way to the ship and the cross was stolen? In the fight a garnet dropped out.'

'Why go by Nightingale Lane? That's the far side of the docks from Limehouse.'

'Perhaps he came by railway, Stitch,' Rose suggested mildly.

Twitch looked crestfallen, and relenting Rose added: 'If the cross was stolen before it reached the *Lisboa* it's still in this country.'

'Why, sir?'

Rose stared at him. 'Because—' He stopped. 'I'm going off it, Stitch. We need to go back to our muttons. If it's straight theft, why plan to steal a cross that isn't worth much in its materials and gems? It's *what* it is that makes it special.'

'Your laundry from Stepney, sir.' An impassive

sergeant, puffing reproachfully, entered to hand over the battered suitcase.

Rose's eyes gleamed. 'Did you pay him?'

'Yes, sir. Six shillings.'

Rose calmly counted out this fortune, while Stitch watched, dumbfounded. He made a mental note to tell the Chief about Postlethwaites of Clapham who'd do it for tuppence.

Still the Chief had his idiosyncrasies and if a Chinese laundry was one of them, it was harmless enough. Catch his Martha asking any Chinese men to do his laundry. She'd wash it all again. He tried to imagine Martha married to Egbert Rose and shuddered on her behalf. Thank goodness she had him, Alfred Stitch.

Once the glory that was Twitch had departed, Rose opened the suitcase. Inside was the same pair of socks he had sent, now washed, and with one other benefit. Tucked inside one of them was a piece of paper, which he eagerly extracted. It was an advance programme for a music hall, the Old King Cole. He ran his eye down it: Nettie Turner and her Donkey Song, Will Lamb plays Macbeth, Our Pickles sings . . . All at the Old King Cole.

He grinned. He remembered it, for it was one of the halls on his old beat. He picked up the telephone, and shouted amiably at the operator. A few moments later Inspector Grey's querulous voice was all attention. 'Ah, Grey,' Rose told him agreeably, 'I expect you remember that ship which unfortunately left early. I need to make a few more inquiries. No objection, have you?'

Grey had not, especially if they did not rebound on his head.

* * *

The Old King Cole was not quite the Empire. Auguste looked round aghast at his new, thankfully temporary, domain. And its 'restaurant' moreover was far from Escoffier's Carlton. He tried to remind himself he should be grateful for the opportunity to be able to cook at all, but his first sight suggested some prices were too high to pay. He had chosen to walk from the Tower of London to the theatre in order to acquaint himself with the area, and counted himself lucky to arrive. True, no snarling bandits had leapt out on him, but despite the most valiant efforts of the local council to improve the image of the road, the high dockland warehouses on his right, and the rows of uninviting-looking shops, and pubs, with the ill-smelling alleyways and lanes leading off, suggested the efforts had merely resulted in the tide of murky humanity being swept back off the main thoroughfare and forcibly held there, while it bided its time to leap out on the unsuspecting. Like Auguste Didier. Groups of sailors and dockers huddled outside the pubs, watching him curiously, and he was glad to reach the music hall.

The Old King Cole, not far from St George's-in-the-East church, had once been a humble pub, a wayside inn outside Shadwell, and no better, no worse than its fellows. Then an ambitious publican in the mid-nineteenth century had coincided with the decision to improve the murky image of the Ratcliffe Highway by renaming it. What better improvement than to expand his old ale-house of dubious reputation into a music hall? Consequently he built out to the rear an ornate and, he vowed, high-class music hall with a circle, gallery, *fauteuils* and sedate atmosphere. Unfortunately, he forgot to mention this desire for social betterment to his clientele, which remained identical to that which had provided his ale-house with its reputation. When LCC regulations first discouraged, then banished, the serving of food and drink in the auditorium, he gave up the struggle for respectability. The new owner, Percy Jowitt, also had ambitions, and turned the long bar on the ground floor into a grill-room, which degenerated quickly into a common eating house. Nevertheless little by little, by raising the prices, his clientele did improve to the point where respectable loving husbands were able to bring wives, even daughters. Jowitt glowed with satisfaction – though not for long. Wives and daughters, he discovered, rarely drank as much as their menfolk, and his ownership of the Old King Cole had degenerated into a constant struggle to retain such brilliant newcomers as he discovered, and to persuade his regulars to support his ageing regular turns which he shared with half a dozen or so similar institutions within a radius of three miles. Jowitt was now in his sixties, a dapper, dark-haired, anxious man, ever torn between stark reality and a Micawber-like hopefulness of the infinite possibilities of the future.

Auguste stood at the doorway and surveyed the smoky, smelly hell which he had fondly imagined a paradise. He summoned his strength. If Alexis Soyer could cook on the top of Pyramids, or in the Crimea, surely he, Auguste Didier, could transform this den into something approaching a place fit for food. The smell of stale food and plates wafted towards him, increasing the nearer he approached to the bar.

'Most of the cooking is done downstairs on the

gridirons and ovens,' Jowitt told him reassuringly. 'You keep it hot up here, and the potato cans are outside.'

This largely passed over Auguste's head, as he peered into a foul-smelling hot dish.

'Faggots and mustard pickle,' Jowitt told him proudly.

'I beg your pardon?'

'That's the Monday Special. You heat it up for the evening crowd. Penny hot, three-farthings cold. And in the evenings you have the whole splendid range. Herrings, savelorys, pease pudding, currant pudding, lobscouse—'

Auguste pricked up his ears, and his spirits cautiously halted awhile in their downward progress. Lobscouse? He had never heard of the dish, but no doubt it had to do with lobster. Some local dialect word, perhaps. He could produce lobscouse thermidor, lobscouse salad—

'And eels,' Jowitt was saying.

'A *matelote à la Parisienne?*'

'A what?'

'In a delicious casserole with white wine, oysters, crayfish butter and a little nutmeg?'

Percy evidently decided this was a joke, and after the required roar of laughter, amplified kindly: 'Collared or jellied.'

Auguste gazed at him nonplussed.

Jowitt did not notice. 'Mostly they take the ha'porth and ha'porth though.'

Auguste searched his vast store of culinary knowledge, but could not recollect such a dish. 'Is this a local name for fish?' he asked doubtfully.

Percy blinked. 'Fish and potatoes. Ha'porth of fish,

ha'porth of spuds.' He began to wonder if this cook knew his onions.

'*À la lyonnaise?*' Auguste stopped, in quiet desperation. There was no common ground. He was on his own. 'I cannot cook and serve all by myself,' he said firmly. 'And serve the drink as well.'

'Of course not, my dear fellow,' Percy reassured him hastily, glad there was something he could answer. 'Wouldn't expect it. Full staff at your beck and call. There's the girl.'

'What girl?'

'*The* girl.'

'Her name?'

'Can't bring it to mind. I expect she has one,' Percy told him somewhat apologetically, smoothing down suspiciously black hair. 'And old Jacob does the drink. You don't have to lift a finger there.'

'You must remember I am here for another reason too,' Auguste said firmly, unconvinced.

'Keeping the bailiffs away. I know. Very good of you.'

'*Quoi?*' This was no time for politeness.

'When Nettie offered me your services, I was truly grateful, my dear man. They mean to get me this time.'

'But—' Auguste broke off. What was the point? He fulminated against women, not so much for their deviousness, but for their blithe disregard of minor details . . . like informing those most concerned of what was going on.

'Might I ask if you are expecting many bailiffs at the moment?'

'You never *expect* bailiffs,' Percy explained reasonably. 'If they came when they were expected, you'd make yourself and your goods scarce, wouldn't you?'

Auguste had never been in the unfortunate position of discovering the truth of this statement, though in his apprentice days he had come close to it. He could see the logic of Jowitt's argument. Nevertheless it seemed he was expected to cook for numberless hordes, help quench their never-ending need for beer, keep the bailiffs from troubling Mr Jowitt, and, as a mere extra, prevent a possible foul murder by being a constant shadow to Will Lamb. Fortunately it was only for a week.

'Imeretrelpyer.'

'*Je m'excuse?*' Startled, Auguste glanced down at the source of this squeak.

Roughly level with his chest was the dirtiest white cap he'd ever seen, crammed over long unkempt greasy hair, atop a broomhandle, or, on second glance, the skinniest girl he'd ever seen. Her boots were cracked, her too-short skirts revealed bony bare ankles, her print gown was covered by a dirty white apron. The latter was unnecessary since the dress was dirty enough in its own right. The face stared confidingly and gap-toothed up at him, then cracked in a large grin.

'I'm Lizzie.'

'You're a waitress, Miss Eliza?' he asked faintly.

'Nah. I'm yer cook.'

If ever there was a time to prove Auguste Didier was a man of resolution, this was it. He took out his pocket watch. Three-thirty. Happily providence had brought him here early. Will Lamb would not be arriving at the Old King Cole in the care of Nettie Turner until this evening and whatever culinary fate might be in store for the lucky diners tonight was presumably already stacked up, probably in some verminous outhouse. Meanwhile, garnish could do much to disguise even the worst of culinary disasters, he told himself.

'Lizzie, kindly call a cab for us.'

'You're not leaving?' wailed Jowitt.

'And taking this young lady with me. Merely for an hour, Mr Jowitt. Should any bailiffs call, kindly lock them in the cellar.'

Lizzie looked scared. 'There ain't no cabs round here.'

'An omnibus then, Lizzie. Any mode of transport.'

'Ma don't like me going out with strange men.'

'How old are you, Lizzie?'

'Sixteen.'

Auguste choked. He'd put her down as ten, and promptly abandoned his original instinct to remove her to the nearest tin bath, strip her and immerse her in a bath of disinfectant. He executed all his considerable charm. 'Lizzie, please take me to the nearest outfitters.'

'Commercial Road's the best,' Lizzie said doubtfully.

Bond Street it was not, and there were none of the new horseless buses here, but they had emerged an hour later from an outfitters of sorts, a large parcel tucked firmly under Lizzie's arm, from which she would not be parted.

'For me?' Lizzie asked in wonder for the twentieth time.

'Only after a visit to the Public Baths, *ma fille.*'

He handed Lizzie plus parcel, twopence, and a threepenny tip over to the attendant. Half an hour later a Lizzie of totally different hue shyly emerged. She was bright red from the scrubbing, and much of her hair had vanished. What there was left made her look like a hopeful hedgehog.

'My dad will take a strap to me, looking like a tart.'

'The only tart you resemble, Lizzie, is a strawberry one.'

She eyed him doubtfully. 'I don't look like a tart, then?'

Auguste studied the most visible of the new clothes, the new brown print gown, fitting over the young breasts and modestly sinking beneath stocking-clad ankles. He compared her briefly with the ladies who strolled the Empire Promenade. 'No,' he said. Then, ominously, 'What is that bundle under your arm, Lizzie?'

'Me working clothes, of course,' she said in surprise. 'I can't work togged up like this, can I?'

None too gently he wrested the package from her, and threw it in a zinc bin destined for the adjoining wash-house.

'What you doing?' she howled in anguish.

'Lizzie,' he said, 'cook for me, watch for me, *help* me, and you shall have enough to buy yourself twenty such dresses. Will you do that?'

Lizzie considered, rather too long to please Auguste entirely. 'Yus,' she told him eventually.

'Excellent, *ma petite*.' So pleased was he at this non-acrimonious agreement, so filled with dreams as to what he could teach this young disciple, and then so taken with the wares of the elderly woman at the kerbside selling hot pig's trotters, that he failed to notice Lizzie had reclaimed her precious bundle, as she dutifully climbed up after him to the open-air deck of the bus.

'You enjoy your work, *ma fille*?'

Enjoy? Lizzie looked at him blankly, and he tried another tack.

'The Old King Cole is a happy place?'

'Old Jowitt's a rum cove.'

'That I see, but the artistes? You like them?' He perceived from the blank expression that he was getting nowhere. The Lizzies of this world had no time for reflecting on their lot. He changed tack. 'Tell me about them, those that come to the eating-room.'

'Mist'rill.'

Auguste's turn to look blank.

'Max Hill,' she repeated, 'old cove. Does impersonations. Eats chops.' She peeped at him to see if this was what he wanted and encouraged, swept on: 'Mr Brodie, big he is. Jolly. Pats me bum, beefsteak man, hates Harry Pickles, he's a one. Eels and bangers, don't like Brodie, Brodie don't like him. Miguel, he's a juggler, smarmy, thinks he's a swell, but he ain't, 'cos he eats his eels jellied and whelks. Mariella's pretty – and don't she know it.' She giggled. 'You'll be meeting her,' she added mysteriously.

'You like her?' Auguste inquired, interested at the mention of Will Lamb's former love. Seeing her look of doubt, he added hastily, 'And what does she eat?'

'She won't eat nothing of ours,' Lizzie said crossly. 'But I reckons she'd be a shrimps-and-pie lady.'

Auguste regarded her in wonder. '*Ma petite*, you have the makings of a true connoisseur of cuisine.' To find someone after his own heart in such a place cheered him immensely.

'Garn,' snorted Lizzie, not understanding a word.

* * *

35

A brief reconnoitre backstage told Auguste much about the financial state of the Old King Cole. It looked and smelled of failure. There were two large dressing-rooms at the rear of the building next to the stage door, and a series of cubby-holes opposite the cramped wings and backstage area, two of which, according to hastily pinned notices, had been allotted to Nettie and Will; the others spilled ancient props and lighting paraphernalia out of their doors. The performers, he understood, arrived in most cases only for their particular turns and for the moment he had the place to himself. Or so he thought.

'Ah. How good of you, my dear chap, to keep a look-out for bailiffs.' Percy Jowitt descended on him, beaming.

Auguste surrendered. 'Could any bailiffs get in here undetected?' he asked.

Jowitt looked nonplussed. 'People come and go,' he said vaguely.

'Is the stage door kept locked?'

'No. But bailiffs get in anywhere, you know.'

Auguste abandoned bailiffs. 'Was it your idea to ask Will Lamb to play here?'

'Certainly.'

'The idea stemmed from you.'

'Naturally. I am the proprietor.' Percy puffed out his chest.

'What put the idea in your head?'

'Do you know, I really can't say. It might,' Percy acknowledged, 'have been Pickles.'

'You mean faggots and pickles?'

'No, no. Our loveable Cockney chappie, Harry Pickles.

Nettie Turner's husband. Rather surprised me when he suggested it because he doesn't like Will Lamb. Jealous, I think. But then all my regulars have the good of the Old King Cole at heart,' he explained complacently.

'Does everyone here wish it well?'

'Good heavens, yes,' Percy declared. 'They all love the place. And each other.' He paused. 'Mostly, that is.'

# Chapter Two

Heat hit him like the full force of Jem Mace's heavyweight fist. Auguste observed that the hell that had the presumption to call itself a kitchen did have outlets to the outside world, but it felt to him like a sealed Turkish bath. The idea of murder within these steaming walls did not seem so preposterous now. He remembered Will would be arriving with Nettie just before or soon after the performance started. Time was running short, with only two hours to sum up what he was dealing with, and *whom* he was dealing with. At the moment the 'what' was taking precedence. He recalled the London particular, the thick fog through which he'd once battled his way, only to find murder awaiting him at the end. Heat was like fog. It confused, it drummed in upon you, numbing the senses. He listened to Lizzie's monologue as she rushed hither and thither from stove to gridiron. 'I got the pies, mutton and eel. I done the pickled eels and faggots . . . I fries the fish, you broils yer chops.' You? *Him! He* was the chef in this nightmare surrounding him and in half an hour's time the customers would be pouring through the door.

Panic spurred him to action, as he raced through the furnace of the underground kitchen after the quicksilver Lizzie, averting his eyes from the grease, crumbs and vegetable detritus that liberally gave witness of her endeavours during the day.

'What is this horrible mess on the floor, Lizzie?' A white gooey mess that looked like frozen porridge.

''Ere's yer faggots, Mr D. Cockroaches.'

This was hell indeed. 'You serve cockroaches here?' he asked faintly. 'Soup, perhaps?'

Lizzie stared at him. 'That what you do in France, is it? I kills 'em here. That's what the white stuff's for. Oatmeal and Plaster of Paris.'

Auguste opened his mouth and shut it again. Time enough for hygiene tomorrow. Tonight he must survive as best he could under Lizzie's mercurial management; he needed all his antennae trained on Will Lamb.

At least, *nearly* all his antennae. One must be spared for this horrible astringent smell from one of the cooking pots.

'*What* is that, if you please, Miss Lizzie?'

'Pickle for tomorrow's eels. Want to see 'em?' She led the way to a larder, and flung open the door with pride. Hanging in rows from hooks were what appeared to be a dozen ladies' stockinged legs.

'Eels boiled in cloth,' Lizzie said proudly. 'And there's your faggots too. Good, ain't they? Pig's caul and liver.'

He duly praised her. These were the delicacies of which he had heard so much? He tried hard to ignore a murmur of protest in his stomach. After all, was not much of the exquisite charcuterie of France the result of similar cooking processes? It was merely the

unfamiliar made these appear so unappetising. This is
what his brain told him, but his stomach began to
contradict it vigorously, and with Lizzie in anxious
pursuit, he hurried back to the upper floor in the hope
he might track down the last few gulps of oxygen
available before customers began to arrive. There would
then be, so he had understood, a brisk trade in pies and
potatoes. *Potatoes!* Where were they?

Even as the thought rushed through his mind, Lizzie,
faithfully on his heels, cried, 'Where you bin, Fred?'

Auguste glanced up from his frantic inspection. At
the window he saw faces pressed to the glass like Oliver
Twist's in the workhouse. Through the door loped a
skeleton in ragged evening dress, which had obviously
started in Jermyn Street and found the journey to the
East End hard in the extreme. On top of the skeleton's
six-foot frame was a top-hat which it raised politely.

'Good evening, Miss Lizzie,' it replied humbly in a
hoarse voice. 'Business detained me, for I am performing
my tasks on the cans to which I must speedily return.'

'Fred's a sword-swallower for the queues outside, Mr
Didier,' Lizzie informed him, 'but he does the spuds as
well. He's a dab hand at 'em.'

Of course, Auguste thought resignedly, what more
natural than to have a sword-swallower as an assistant
cook?

'He cooks 'em on the spikes over the fires in the cans
– and we keep 'em hot here.' She indicated the filthy
range.

Auguste did not doubt it – what he doubted was if
anything in this hell-hole could be kept cool.

Mr Frederick Wolf regarded his new temporary

superior apologetically. 'I fear there is little profit in sword-swallowing nowadays. I entertain the queue with my act, for it is my duty, but the rewards for my art are insufficient for my continued survival,' he informed Auguste gravely. 'I trust, sir, you have no objection to my continuing my tasks here? I assure you I turn a most delightful floury potato, it positively floats to the plate beneath, so light and airy is its nature. And I am most judicious in my seasoning. I am also dexterous with a poached egg,' he added hopefully.

'I am delighted to welcome you to my staff.' Auguste meant it.

Another burden was lifted from him. He wondered idly whether those potatoes might be improved upon . . . a little cheese or cream adorned with a pickled nasturtium seed perhaps? There might be avenues to be explored here.

But not now. In the next half an hour his stomach was put to the severe test of ordeal by piles of fatty mutton chops and, to his horrified eye, tough steaks and tired herrings destined for the gridirons. He reflected on the nearness of Smithfield Market with relief. Here was one instant improvement he could make. Whoever was responsible for the provision of these horrors would be subjected to a series of lectures on the art of choosing meat and fish. Huge canisters of pease pudding stood steaming on the range, side by side with dishes of saveloys and fish. Fresh fish, kippers and herrings, with a dish of something that might conceivably in the siege of Paris have passed for batter, stood by a heap of dull grey haddock. He eyed them unenthusiastically. There was, he gathered, a fish market at nearby Shadwell. Sturgeon was in season, oysters – like Alexis Soyer he, Auguste Didier, would make a contribution to the noble cause of spreading knowledge of food, no matter what the pocket that sought it. A stirring of something that might possibly be professional interest replaced the queasiness in his stomach.

At five to seven the faces pressed to the glass began to disappear, as each straightened up on its body to prepare itself for the grand charge ahead. It was, Auguste realised with dread in his heart, time for his first customers. An aged gentleman who had apparently crept from the hearthside of one of Mr Dickens' novels, judging by his attire, had now taken his place at the bar – presumably the 'old Jacob' to whom Jowitt had referred. It was conceivable, Auguste supposed, that he might move with lightning dexterity when customers appeared, but improbable. There would be fewer now than later, he understood, for it was more important to secure and defend one's place than to feed one's stomach for those who had paid their shilling for a *fauteuil* or ninepenny seat in the circle. And at any moment from now, he realised to his horror, Will Lamb might be arriving at the stage door, where he could be greeted by a crazed assassin or by the ghost of William Terriss. The fever pitch of excitement in the queue communicated itself to him through the window: his stomach now lurched again with something he did not at first recognise. When he identified it, he would not fully acknowledge it, but he recognised it as fear.

Thomas Yapp prepared to haul himself from his slouched

position over the bar at the back of the grand circle, and to face up to his responsibilities as chairman of the evening's festivities. He pushed the second brandy aside. He needed all his wits about him tonight. It would be a full house, and keeping order was hard enough in the Old King Cole at the best of times. Audiences knew what they liked – and what they didn't like, and were far from shy about letting the artistes know their opinions. This happened frequently for Jowitt couldn't afford to pay the good acts, and had to rely on old stagers like Our Pickles and Max Hill – and, Thomas faced facts, his own wife Evangeline. Their one regular asset, Horace, the Great Brodie, had just told Jowitt he was going up West to the Alhambra. That was the last they'd see of him, even though it was the Old King Cole had made him. That was the way things went. One song caught the popular fancy, and the singer thought he was made. Horace had struck lucky with 'Don't Wait Up', so off he'd trot on the golden path of West End audiences, publication, agents, pantomime work, and he'd never look back. Or would he? He was a good sort at heart. Like Nettie Turner and Will Lamb: they started here and now *they* were coming back – though not for long, thank goodness. He slumped over the bar again. Perhaps he needed a drink after all. The thought of Will Lamb and Evangeline would make anyone turn to drink.

*Not to mention the Shadwell Mob!*

Panic-stricken, he drained the brandy at one gulp, as Evangeline swept through the door.

'Ah, Thomas, I've decided to render "I Dreamt that I Dwelt in Marble Halls".' She trilled happily and untunefully, her bosom heaving in passion. ' "That you loved me, you loved me still the same".' The top G missed, which was just as well. Thomas Yapp watched his brandy glass gloomily; he could swear it was shivering, and about to shatter. He sympathised. It did not escape his notice that Evangeline was wearing her red satin, choker and all. She looked enormous and undefiable. Yet as her husband he felt duty-bound to try.

Evangeline was built on generous proportions, five foot ten with a width to support it that left whalebone stays creaking in protest. Her voice, she claimed, demanded sustenance. Why she should have fallen for Will Lamb, a foot shorter than herself and half her width, when she already had a fine upstanding figure of a man in Thomas Yapp had left him puzzled. Will had fortunately departed ten years ago, *but tonight he was coming back*.

'Why not sing "The Lost Chord", my love?'

She peered at him. 'I do believe you're jealous,' she said archly.

'It's the Shadwell Mob!' he shouted, irritated beyond endurance.

'What of them?' Evangeline was scornful of pit and gallery.

'They're sending a chirruping mob.'

'My dear Thomas, a Hooligan gang! The police stopped that blackmail gambit years ago.'

'And the Shadwell Mob have revived it. They'll kill "Marble Halls" stone dead.' And the chairman too probably, he thought wildly.

Evangeline was used to barracking from those that

did not understand or appreciate her art, and Will had to be told her true feelings. 'Marble Halls' it was going to be. She'd sing 'The Lost Chord' over her dead body, she decided confusedly.

' "Marble Halls". *And*,' she added menacingly, 'I shall *not* sing directly after the interval. Move me!'

Yapp's heart sank even further. True, to play the turn after the interval was the most unpopular since people wandered back late or even stayed in the bars, and when Evangeline's number was put up on the boards nearly everyone stayed there. But didn't she realise if it wasn't for him, she wouldn't have a spot at all? Oh, the unfairness of it.

'Put young Orsini after the interval.'

'I can't,' he moaned.

'Oh, I think you *can*, Thomas,' she replied, disappointed. 'After all, it is for darling Will.'

Thomas's face went as white as his starched shirt front. Suppose she realised who had had this foolish idea of inviting Will Lamb back here? She would get entirely the wrong idea. No, the sooner Will disappeared, the better. 'I'll do my best,' he told Evangeline listlessly. He lurched to his feet and blindly staggered towards his position of torture for the evening.

Lizzie licked her thumb approvingly. 'I does a good custard,' she told Auguste proudly.

Auguste looked at the stagnant yellow pile in the canister, now minus one thumbful, and shuddered. No self-respecting egg had lent itself to that horror. Outside the last defiant wail of the tinny violin ground to a halt, and the tap-tap of the hornpipe dancer ceased as the queue for the hall vanished entirely. Frederick's raspy voice could be heard thanking his public for their valued custom and exhorting them to return tomorrow, and be further amazed and stupefied at his dangerous feats of sword-swallowing.

From his office upstairs, Percy Jowitt beamed as he saw the crowds vanishing into his beloved hall, and congratulated himself on being such a good employer that he could attract the likes of Nettie Turner and Will Lamb back to it. Even the threat of bailiffs ceased temporarily to worry him. Everything was lovely in his garden. He did not notice the Shadwell Mob staggering towards his kingdom.

'Ain't it exciting?' Lizzie shrieked blissfully to Auguste, eyes shining.

'This?' Auguste lifted his head from frying battered cod with one hand and grilling mutton chops with the other. 'Not precisely exciting. An experience.'

'Nah. Nettie Turner coming here. "Whoa, Nellie, don't you go too far . . ." That Donkey Song, I *luvs* it.' Lizzie wriggled her non-existent hips in a way that suggested the Old King Cole music hall was not above pirating songs on occasions, since Auguste doubted whether Lizzie had ever visited the Empire or the other West End halls.

A flying skeleton in the form of Frederick Wolf rushed in to take up his interior position on the potatoes. Chairs scraped against floor, mutton pies passed in an endless chain to two harassed barmen who doubled as waiters, or passed direct to the clutching hands of impatient diners, the smell of mutton chops on the gridiron intensified, mingling with the smell of cooking kippers.

Mutton chops and glasses of beer apparently flew through the air to their recipients with the same dexterity as the young man on the flying trapeze. Potatoes cascaded in white crumbly torrents on to plates. Tonight Auguste would dream of potatoes, wielded with the flashing dexterity of Frederick's hands as he first slit it open, lifted it high in one hand, the plate in the other and shot the contents of the first onto the second, turned it out in a mound of succulent crumbs. A lump of butter followed it, a dash of pepper . . . yes, tomorrow he would try spices, curry powder and cream perhaps, a dazed voice at the back of Auguste's mind promised, as he gazed down at the smelly ha'porth and ha'porth he'd just dished up from the unappetising pans.

A roar went up from the hall, which could be heard even over the racket in the eating-room.

'What's that?' Had something happened already? Surely Will had not yet arrived? Auguste dropped a chop in alarm, splashing grease on to his spotless apron.

'Old Yapp, the chairman, taking his place, I expect,' Lizzie replied offhandedly. 'I like 'im. He's a gentleman. He don't let old Jowitt get away without paying me. His wife don't like me, though. You wait till you see the size of her. She sings.' Lizzie paused briefly to evaluate the truth of her words, then bawled out: 'Come into the garden, Maud', meanwhile doing a passable imitation of a woman four times her width. 'Jowitt keeps them on because the crowd like him, and her because of him . . . But Yapp couldn't control a bunch of coconuts.' She giggled. 'Hear that?'

Auguste did. The roar was no longer friendly.

'Oh, it's going to be a good evening tonight,' Lizzie told him happily.

Auguste was not so confident, as he rushed from the eating-room to assume his duties as Will's protector.

Some fifteen minutes earlier Nettie Turner's carriage had drawn up outside the lodgings in Whitechapel where Will Lamb still lived, despite his fame and prosperity. No one cooked sausages like Mrs Jones.

'All set for the costers, Will?' she asked brightly as he climbed in beside her.

'Oh yes.' He beamed.

'You're a love, aren't you, Will? Don't matter to you whether we play the Empire or Hackney Coalhole just so long as you can make people laugh.' He grinned. 'Doesn't it worry you at all going back, Will?' she asked anxiously.

He shook his head vigorously. 'No.'

'I suppose not, with Mariella there.' Better to get it in the open, Nettie thought to herself. The red-headed bitch would cause trouble one way or another, that was for sure.

'Mariella,' Will repeated excitedly, drawing out each syllable.

'You're still fond of her, aren't you, Will?'

He said nothing, but even in the dim light she could see his blush.

'Like I used to be of Harry – once.' She laughed bitterly. 'Fools, weren't we? Mariella wouldn't marry you, because you were nobody. Harry was all too eager to marry me because I wasn't. We should have married each other, Will, and put an end to it. Are you still fond of her?'

For answer, he took her hand in his and squeezed it. His felt more like a child's than a man's, and perhaps that was just how he thought of her, as a mother figure. Nettie sighed. Marriage wouldn't have worked with Will, of course. She was vigorous, earthy, robust – and she liked a bit of fun. Will was an idealist, fragile, only half living in the real world; and as for sex, did he even know what it was? Sometimes she doubted it, though perhaps she was wrong. He wasn't very stable, and in her experience that sometimes put the old privates into a frenzy. There was a suppressed excitement about him tonight, like a kid going to a pantomime. Only Mariella wasn't a pantomime, from what she remembered of that young madam.

The carriage rattled over the streets towards the Old King Cole. Suddenly Will spoke. 'Will you miss me, Nettie?'

'What do you mean, Will?' she asked, startled. 'You don't really think you're going to get murdered, do you?'

'I don't know.' He giggled nervously.

'Don't go. *Please*,' she said urgently. 'I'll stop the carriage, take you home.'

'I *want* to go.' He set his lips stubbornly.

She said no more, but she was even more worried than before. There was a half-smile on his lips. The smile of a kid with a secret.

Our Pickles, or to give him his full name, Harry Pickles, Cockney *comique*, stood morosely in the wings, his mind divided between the moment when in response to old

Yapp's introduction and a flourish from the orchestra he would leap on to the stage, sweeping off his high stove hat and shout out 'Wot cher, pals!', and the fact that Nettie would soon be arriving at the Old King Cole. Not to mention Will. He wasn't looking forward to seeing either of them, especially together. Nettie because she would undoubtedly want to know what he needed extra dosh for so urgently when she made him an excellent allowance to stay away from her, and Will because he'd blasted well ruined his career. Him and Brodie. Will had taken all the laughs deliberately, so there'd been none to spare for when he came on. Will deliberately made him take that spot. He was as bad as the Great Horace Brodie. At least he'd soon be rid of him in the East End halls. Brodie had had it in for him ever since they'd started over ten years ago. He'd taken all the best *comique* songs and left him with the Cockney ones. The Great Brodie didn't like Lamb any more than he did, didn't want the glory being taken away from his act. Brodie reckoned he was the big star round here, and it was going to spike his guns to have Lamb back. Pickles smirked. That's why he'd suggested the idea to Jowitt. 'Why don't you ask Will Lamb back for a week?' 'Good idea, Harry,' Jowitt had said. '*And* Nettie, too . . .' Pickles had added. She'd come, of course she would, if Will was coming. Lamb was the reason for Nettie's staying away from him – must be. Why else would anyone want to leave Our Pickles, particularly an old hen like her? She said she was forty, but she must be pushing forty-five at least. He was handsome, thirty-four, five foot eight; Will was ugly, forty-five, four foot nothing and hadn't enough ammo in his gun to fire a shot. Not Nettie's usual style. There must be more to it. Meanwhile tonight he was going to show her what she was missing. He grinned. Some blasted coster done up to the nines with a moustache and apron on chose that moment to wander in. 'Piss off,' he snarled at a startled Auguste Didier.

'Our very own Pickles, our lovable Cockney chappie!' came Yapp's disembodied voice.

Pickles bounded on to the stage, down to the footlights, hands stuck in pockets. He slouched, he winked, he double-shuffled, he confided: 'I call her ball and chain . . . 'Cos she keeps the key of the door . . .'

The welcome was half-hearted, but he knew why. They were waiting for Will Lamb.

Violet and Marigold Pears were sitting tensely in their jolting four-wheeler and not just because they were running late for their turn as Number Two. They couldn't afford to hire their own carriage and driver to take them between engagements at the various halls during the evening; their turn at the Shadwell Grand had been running late, and then they couldn't find a hansom cab. They had their costumes already on underneath their dresses, but even so they doubted if they would get to the Old King Cole in time. But this was not the greatest of their worries. How were they going to break the news? Someone as grand as he was wouldn't want to marry them – since they were twins they automatically thought of themselves as 'them', though it was Marigold who had the major problem. Her problems were Violet's too of course, particularly since their turn depended on split-second timing by the

two of them, for they were acrobatic artistes. Soon
Marigold would not be able to play her part, and that
meant no money for either of them. Now they were
nearly thirty, that meant perhaps there never would
be again. It wasn't fair – *he* had plenty of money now.

Gentlemen, they had realised, were not really
interested in their artistry, only in their pink tights and
clinging costumes. Dear Mama had insisted they
performed in long pantaloons, but when the sisters
guiltily defied her edict they got more bookings. Dear
Mama couldn't even look after baby when it came,
because dear Mama was dead.

At least Will would be at the Old King Cole this
evening. They could try appealing to him. They jumped
down from the cab, threw money at the driver and rushed
into the theatre, tearing off their dresses as they went.
Willing hands helped them, and Horace Brodie's caressing
hand automatically patted Violet on to the stage.

Thomas Yapp in his mirror saw the board proclaiming
Number Three had quickly changed to Number Two
and sighed with relief. That should keep the Shadwell
Mob in the gallery quiet for a bit while they studied
their pink-hosed legs. 'Ladies and gentlemen, the
Tumbling Twins.'

'Who'd they tumble to?' a voice yelled back, to be
immediately followed by gusts of laughter and bawdy
comments, shushed from their marginally more
respectable fellow audience below.

In fact both of them had tumbled to the same man.

Shortly before Miguel and his wife Mariella had climbed
down from their hired carriage, in an atmosphere as

cold as a first turn on a wet night. It had not been a pleasant journey. If he remained as tense as this he would be dropping things all over the stage, and that would not be good for the reputation of Miguel, Continental Juggler. So far everything was going well; why then did he feel so angry? Then he realised the reason. Will Lamb was going to be there. True, this was going to prove extremely useful, but nevertheless he wished he could have been more certain of Mariella's co-operation. Who knew what she was thinking now, as she sat silently at his side? Will Lamb was a rich man now, he must be. Well, so shortly would he, Miguel, be able to send more money back to his parents in his beloved country, now their own juggling days were over. Mariella's act was not until the end of the show, but it was imperative she should be with him, especially tonight. Once he had let her hire her own carriage in order to take extra engagements, and what had happened? He had arrived at the Flagon to find her in the arms of the Marvellous McNaughten, illusionist. And *that* had been no illusion.

'Miguel, it's too risky. You know how jumpy Will is,' Mariella suddenly hissed. 'I'll tell him I've changed my mind.'

Miguel glared. 'No. *You* asked him. *You* are implicated. It is the plan. *My* plan,' to make his point even clearer.

'I won't do it.' Her disinclination was not on moral grounds, but for reasons of her own which she had no intention of sharing with her husband.

'You have no choice,' he replied simply. The threat was implied in his dark eyes.

'I'll tell him Fernando has discovered.'

The eyes blazed. 'No. You should not encourage Fernando so much, Mariella. He is dangerous.'

She shrugged. 'He adores me. He's got no more brains than a baby. Where's the harm?'

'The harm, sweet wife, is that he *has* no brains. Did you tell him Will Lamb was coming?'

'Yes. He didn't like it.'

'Not good. Leave things as they are, Mariella.' It was an order.

Mariella, to whom self-survival was a path perpetually brilliantly lit, fell silent, and began to consider other options. Others' survival, after all, was not of so much importance.

The Shadwell Mob was getting restless, eager to show muscle. The pink tights had vanished from sight and memory, and a continental juggler was too good an opportunity to pass up. The low hiss became louder, a well-aimed rotten egg joined the spinning plates and met its end bursting over their juggler's shoulder, and despite indignant howls from other parts of the house and Yapp's best efforts, the sound of 'Two Lovely Black Eyes' provided an accompaniment to Miguel's act which drowned the orchestra's best attempts at 'The Toreador's Song' from *Carmen*.

Backstage, anxiously awaiting the arrival of Will Lamb, Auguste heard the rumpus in alarm, both for the performers' sake and for his own. He did not relish the prospect of those healthy spirits descending in force on his eating-room in the interval. The proper place for rotten food was the rubbish bin, not adorning the person of a *maître* chef. At the sound of the stage door opening he hurried towards it hopefully. Standing guard over it was a gentleman of imposing build clad in a leopard skin, with a club clenched in one huge fist. Another personal detective? Before he had time to inquire, the new arrival entered. It was not Will Lamb, but a tall well-built man in his mid to late thirties, with a handsome, if florid, face and clad in Ascot gear. The new arrival, evidently already in role, raised his hat politely. 'The Great Brodie,' he announced.

'The Great Didier,' Auguste replied, flustered.

'You are a performer?' Horace Brodie looked puzzled. 'Your turn?'

'*Faisan truffé* and bailiff-hunting,' Auguste replied gravely.

Noise from the auditorium deflected the Great Brodie from pursuit of this red herring. 'A lively night,' he murmured. 'I see I am needed. Ah, Harry,' he stopped to raise his hat to Harry Pickles, still in costermonger costume, on his way out to his next engagement. 'A good house?'

'First-rate till you walked in.' Pickles slammed the door.

Horace sighed. 'Dear boy, but not a true performer. Jealous, alas.'

The Great Brodie, lion *comique*, puffed out his chest, took a deep breath and a statuesque stance in the wings, watching Miguel in some amusement at his inability to control his audience. He tweaked his lapel complacently. He wouldn't be here much longer now, and could afford to be generous.

He strolled nonchalantly on to the stage, adjusted his monocle and stared out at the audience. The noise stopped, and Yapp sank back in his seat with relief. That walk, that stare, were known everywhere, even at the Shadwell Grand. No one in their right mind would barrack or chirrup the Great Brodie's song. Out here in the East they were still privileged to its exclusive hearing; when the Great Brodie went up West and the song was published, every Tom, Dick and Harry would be whistling and caterwauling it. Tonight it was theirs alone. Even the Shadwell Mob thought that worth a breathless hush.

Miguel, casting his saviour a look of anything but thanks, scuttled off, defiantly juggling a few plates on the way. Two of them crashed and broke. The Great Brodie did not bother to turn his head. He held the audience in the silence of anticipation for a moment. He lightly adjusted his elegant cravat, his top-hat was pushed fractionally towards the rakish, his elegant cane was uplifted. He recounted in a bored voice:

'Romanos, Rules and the Ritz for me, Though I might call in to the Carlton for tea. I'm considered a lucky mascot, At Goodwood, Henley and Ascot . . .'

Auguste, despite his anxiety, crept back to the wings to listen, as the roar came up: 'So . . .!' The Great Brodie launched into his chorus:

> 'Don't wait up, don't wait up,
> Don't wait up tonight, love.
> Tonight I'm going out with the chaps,
> And I'll be back tomorrow perhaps.
> You never know how far they'll go . . .
> Perhaps they'll go as far as Flo . . .
> So don't wait up, have your tea,
> And don't wait up for me.'

There was a giggle. At his side had appeared a buxom girl of twenty-five or so with a kerchief round her shoulders, and her skirts bunched up over her petticoat, and a battered straw hat crammed on to her head. 'Wonderful, ain't he?'

'He is good, certainly,' Auguste agreed diplomatically. Will Lamb and Nettie Turner had artistry, though, that shone out over and above their material. He was not sure the same applied to this man, though he would not say so to the girl at his side who had a look in her eyes Auguste recognised. Devoted adoration, and not, alas, for Auguste Didier.

'He's going up West next week. To the Alhambra. He'll have to change the patter for them. I told him that.'

'Why?'

'More respectable audience. Can't be too careful,' she said knowledgeably. 'Look at me, now. Young girl up from country.' She saw his amazed look and giggled. 'Me songs, chum. All about vile seducers of young innocent lasses. Like me.' She winked. 'Like me and Horace, eh?'

'Who?'

'Him. The Great Brodie,' she said fondly.

Next week she'd be up with him in London, the Old King Cole left far behind. Out on stage, the lion *comique* was taking his bow, humbly and gratefully. She heaved up her yoke and milk pails.

Not long now, Brodie thought. On Saturday it was good-bye, Old King Cole. And good-bye, Dolly Dadd.

Percy Jowitt arrived in the wings, moaning agitatedly, as he saw Dolly taking her place centre stage amid a chorus of whistles. A well-aimed potato landed in one of the pails, and Percy groaned. He clutched his new cook like the Ancient Mariner without asking, fortunately, the reason for his presence.

'I'm too late,' he moaned. 'I was going to stop her and send Will on next. It's the only hope. They're getting ready for their big effort up in the gallery. She'll never hold them like Brodie or Lamb.'

'He's not here.'

Percy gazed at him in horror. 'Not here? What do you mean, not *here*?'

His words had seemed quite comprehensible to Auguste. 'He has not yet arrived.'

'Where is he?' This time the shriek must have been audible on stage for Dolly in the midst of her first chorus, 'I was the lamb and he was the wolf—' glared in the direction of the wings.

'I don't *know*,' Auguste hissed back.

'But there's only one more act to go.'

'Me.' The large leopardskin appeared between them, clothing the body of the enormous man whom Auguste had seen guarding the door. He must have been well over six foot, with muscles bulging through his tights, and arms and chest plentifully covered with hair.

'Oh, it's you, Fernando,' Percy said dismissively. 'Meet the new cook.'

Fernando grinned amiably, and gave Auguste a welcoming pat on the back that sent him stumbling forward, and almost precipitated his first stage music-hall appearance.

'Gentle as a lamb, he is,' Percy said reassuringly.

Fernando beamed, then frowned. 'Lamb?' he repeated slowly. 'Fernando not like Will Lamb.'

The winkles! He had forgotten to get the winkles and whelks ready for the interval. Yet how could he leave now before Will had even arrived? Anguished, Auguste watched Dolly Dadd take her bow and quickly run off the stage in relief. She had managed to hold the audience, but only just, and rumbles suggested the storm could not be far off. Fernando was about to take her place, apparently oblivious to anything unusual in the audience. But Auguste had no time to spare for what was on stage; at last, at last, he heard a carriage draw up, and, thanks be, the sound of Nettie's laughter – a trifle forced, he thought, as he rushed to open the stage door. As it opened, he saw Will descending after Nettie from the carriage, dwarfed by the driver. Will's face lit up as he saw Auguste – and then he screamed.

In the darkness a huge black shape hurtled over them in a clatter of wings, descending then swooped round twice more before flying away, black against the darkness of the sky. Will stood stock still, staring after it, until Nettie seized his arm and frog-marched him into the building, Auguste at their side. Will was shaking with terror.

'The raven,' he gibbered. 'The *raven*.'

Coincidence, was Auguste's immediate hope. Surely it was merely one of the Tower of London ravens strayed from its home territory? Then he realised with a chill of fear, that the window above the door was still slightly open. It might be no coincidence. Duncan had entered Macbeth's palace, the raven had spoken. It remained only to see if Duncan would be foolish enough to remain within these walls. Leaving Nettie to see Will into his dressing-room, Auguste rushed up the narrow steps to the next floor, part attic, part stage machinery, part props room. By the open window were several huge baskets, most with restless animal movement within. One stood empty. He thrust the window open, and in the branches of the tall tree opposite, a large black shape regarded him balefully.

On stage Fernando was standing bewildered. He was used to noise. He was used to being barracked. He just ignored it. But he was not used to being pelted with rotten vegetables and jeers. He liked approving roars, and gasps of amazement, as he performed his feats of strength. He growled and raised his club threateningly. The pit and gallery exploded into mirth. Puzzled, he decided to change the order of his act. He marched to the side of the stage, where the props table was prepared, and picked up six knives. Swiftly one after the other he threw them at the cloth dummy monkey swinging from the dummy tree against the jungle backcloth. Each one of them hit its target admirably. He lumbered up to reclaim them and faced his audience with a grin. There was a tentative clap after the sudden silence. So he began his feats of strength again.

'As bad as that?' Nettie asked. 'You really think Will's in danger?'

'I do,' Auguste replied gravely.

'Then you do have to leave, love. I'll do the work on my own,' Nettie informed Will robustly.

Will stood up, still shaking. 'Perhaps I should, Nettie.

Thank you, Mr Didier.' He took Auguste's arm and they walked to the door. But before they reached it, it opened. In came a young woman of about thirty, with hair of flaming red. She was still in her ordinary clothes, for her turn was not until near the end of the show, but it did not diminish her beauty. She smiled, and the light shone from her large blue eyes.

'Hallo, Will. Where are you off to?'

'He is indisposed, *madame*,' Auguste answered quickly for him. 'He must return home.'

'You're wrong, Mr Didier,' Will Lamb beamed. 'I'm not going anywhere. Hallo Mariella.'

Winkles, whelks and the approaching interval could not be ignored forever. His duty, now Will Lamb was well protected by others, lay in the eating-room. Outside the dressing-room, Auguste realised, the noise from the auditorium had resumed and redoubled. Fernando staggered towards him with tears rolling down his face. He threw himself into Auguste's arms, sending him back against the wall with his weight. The stage door once more opened and a small imperious figure swept towards them, attracted by the noise. She was young, she was fat, she had a very strong jaw.

'What's wrong with him?' she jabbed a finger at Fernando's heaving back.

'It is a noisy house this evening.'

'The Shadwell Mob, is it?' the ringleted phenomenon demanded.

'It is.'

'I'll settle them. Put me on next,' she yelled at the scared manager.

'Do it.' Percy appeared from nowhere, waving flustered despairing hands.

Six young ladies flitted from the dressing-room, attracted by their leader's voice, all dressed in pale blue frilly skirts and tights, and waving wands. They watched their young leader carefully; when she glared, they glared, a titter from her, a titter from them.

'Who are you?' the little girl demanded of Auguste.

Auguste now realised she was a matron of about thirteen, rather than the eight that her short pinafore dress and ringlets suggested. 'Auguste Didier, master chef,' he replied as best he could, half choked by Fernando's embrace.

'That's a stupid name. What's a master chef?'

'One who cooks better than anyone else.'

'Not better than my ma.'

'I can see that,' he replied politely, eyeing her podgy build.

It was not lost on her. 'I don't like you,' she announced, a gleam in her eye. 'Come on, fairies.'

From the auditorium he heard Thomas Yapp shouting with quavering voice: 'Little Emmeline and Her Fairies.' The roar that went up did not bode well for a mere child, and Auguste found it in his heart to be sorry for her.

Sometimes winkles and whelks sounded positively wonderful. He detached himself from Fernando, dashed to Will's dressing-room to check he was not alone, and then hurried back to the eating-room. As he did so, he heard the Shadwell Mob in full voice, highly delighted at such easy prey. Auguste wavered, decided he could not miss the downfall of Little Emmeline, and crept into the back of the pit. He saw the girl's stout figure in its white pinafore dress and black stockings. He saw it instantly change its stance as she fixed her beady eyes on the Shadwell Mob. A softer, gentler Emmeline materialised before his eyes. She cast her eyes up to her Maker – and the gallery. She quavered. 'Oh please, don't shout me down. My ma's sick and so's my baby brother, and Pa said he'd beat me if I don't come home with me money. Oh please . . .' She spread confiding little hands, as her trusting eyes appealed to her audience. There was a silence; the Shadwell Mob were temporarily shamed, but still suspicious. Little Emmeline squatted down to the conductor, carefully showing white frilly drawers, and whispered. A solitary violin began to play, and in a childish untuneful pipe Little Emmeline began to sing. Her fairies, used merely to their usual routine of dance, and their leader's monologues, hastily adapted themselves to a suitable mournful pose.

'Oh Father, dear Father, come home with me now . . .'

Auguste tore himself away from this fascinating scene, and returned to his true domain. Lizzie hardly seemed to notice he'd been absent, a fact that suggested more about his predecessor in the job than Auguste himself.

He found himself obediently whisking plates of shellfish and tubs of jellied eels onto tables at her command. One plate was dextrously commandeered by newcomers lurching into the eating-room.

'Lizzie, dear heart, come hither and let me chuck you under your chin.' The elder of the two, a man in his early sixties, slumped at the table. 'Beer, young man,' he ordered of Auguste. 'Gone are the days,' he observed sadly, 'when a dozen servants served my every whim.'

'Garn,' snorted Lizzie, as she dashed to the table plonking down pie and mash twice.

'It is true, Miss Lizzie. But pray tell me what has happened? Mine eyes dazzle, you're transformed. You glow. Have you fallen victim to this rich man's whim?' A glance at Auguste, who informed him grimly, 'She has not. I am temporary chef to this establishment. Auguste Didier.'

'*The* Auguste Didier?'

Auguste instantly warmed to him. Perhaps he had misjudged this character. 'The same.'

'He's bamboozling you,' Lizzie said indignantly. ''E's never heard of you, no more than I had.'

The man rose unsteadily to his feet. ''Tis true, I fear. Permit me to introduce myself, Mr Didier. I am Max Hill, character studies unlimited. My companion,' he waved a disparaging arm, 'is Clarence Bishop, illustrator, ventriloquist, and shoulder for aged actors to lean upon.'

Clarence, a willowy, wispy elderly young man, grinned. 'How do. What happened to old Beezer?'

'Gorn to the Savoy,' Lizzie told him happily.

'Ah, his prowess with soused herring, I presume.' Max paused. 'Is Will Lamb here yet?'

'He's on now,' Auguste told him.

'Ah.'

'You are on in the second half, Mr Hill?' Auguste asked, as he rushed over a second plate of whelks.

'No performance complete without the Magic Max,' Hill told him complacently, scooping another whelk from its shell with practised dexterity.

'The bells, the bells,' yelled Lizzie suddenly and

dramatically, clutching one hand to her bony chest. 'You should see 'is 'Enry Irving.'

'I shall make a point of it,' Auguste replied politely.

Clarence sniggered, commandeering the rest of the whelks.

'He follows Nettie Turner,' Lizzie commented.

'Sooner you than me,' Clarence said jovially.

Max looked sad. 'It is the way of the world as one grows old.'

'Then comes our Evangeline,' Clarence explained. 'Then 'tis I. 'Umble High.'

'No, you got it wrong. Orsini comes after Max. Evangeline's after the interval. Always is.'

'Not tonight,' Clarence said smugly. 'Sue put her foot down.'

'And a remarkably heavy foot it is,' Max said. 'Unfortunately Orsini's can be heavy too.'

Auguste listened to a torrent of information. A conjurer, a comic singer, a chorus of young ladies singing and dancing patriotic songs. And Mariella herself singing her famous Mermaid Song. Not to mention an animal act from Jamrach's just down the street.

'Animal act?' Auguste asked curiously.

'Jamrach's Emporium of Wild Animals. One of their fellers does this turn with 'em. Jack, his Talking Raven and Amazing Monkeys. Ever so good it is.'

Auguste swallowed. The now good-humoured roar from the hall suggested Will's act had ended. Reeking of shellfish and vinegar, and hoping his former *maître*, Auguste Escoffier, safe in the Carlton's kitchens, would never hear of this, Auguste made his way backstage again to check on Will's movements. Nettie was singing in the next but one spot after the interval, and after that she would escort Will home and his own duty – so far as being a personal detective was concerned – would be done. As to the very real threat he was now aware there was to Will, his task was only just beginning.

In the wings there was little camaraderie to be seen. On the contrary, a large woman in red satin was alternately shouting at and assaulting with her parasol a handsome but scared-looking young man of Latin looks. Two boards with numbers on them were being pulled back and forth out of the frantic stage manager's hands, until at last one board remained uncontested.

Alfredo Orsini, vocalist, had won the dubious honour of the post-interval turn. Remarkably few people were interested in 'The Miner's Dream of Home', but at the end of his act the audience swelled to full house. Nettie Turner was on next.

Usually the business of clearing up a kitchen after diners had departed could be enlivened by heart-warming memories of a soufflé well received, a delicate timbale appreciated, a daring combination of ingredients triumphantly rewarded. There was no such gratification to be found in the detritus of kippers and mutton chops, and Auguste saw no need to hurry back to it.

From the wings, keeping one eye on Will's dressing-room door, until he departed with Nettie, Auguste watched the rest of the performance, brought to a close by Mariella's clever act, which centred on her six performing dogs, a large fish tank, and her Mermaid

Song. He was curious to see Will's beloved in performance. She was as striking to look at on stage as off, especially poised with fishy tail atop a rock in the tank.

> 'Who's going to love a little mermaid
> When she's only got a tail . . .'

The dogs, who then slid down a chute into the tank and paddled feverishly towards their mistress, were succeeded by a group of dancers, who if they did not provide the excitements of the pink-hosed Tumbling Sisters at least supplied a decorative and unobjectionable finale. Up on the stage, grumbling and sweating hands were removing the tank, praying for the day when Mariella would tire of mermaids. His duty towards Will over, Auguste returned to the delights of kipper bones and cold pease pudding, still deeply troubled. There had been one hitch in the programme on stage. The act from Jamrach's had been cancelled owing to indisposition. Through inquiry, he discovered the indisposition was of one of the supporting cast rather than the human element. The talking bird had been indisposed to remain in the building, apparently preferring to lodge on the roof of St George's-in-the-East church. No doubt now that the threat to Will lay within these walls.

As for himself, home, Queen Anne's Gate, could not now, surely, be far removed in time. Frederick was valiantly plodding through the washing-up, but there was no sign of Lizzie. Auguste was too tired to speculate on this, assuming she had gone home, until a now familiar screech told him otherwise all too quickly.

Auguste rushed downstairs to the steaming underworld below, since the sound seemed to emanate from there, but there was no sign of her. Then sounds of altercation outside sent him hurling through a side door to the outside world, where amongst unappetising bins of rubbish he found Lizzie backing away from the open door of an outhouse, new print dress half on, half off, the old one draped over a bin.

'He leapt out at me, Mr Didier. Ooo-er!' She threw herself into his protective arms as the villain of the piece grimly stepped forward.

Auguste stared, stunned with shock, at the furious dirty face that glared in equal horror at him.

At the top of the flight of steps leading to the road level, Percy Jowitt peered down nervously. 'If you're the Shadwell Mob I advise you – my dear Mr Didier, I do apologise, I quite forgot to tell you. I took your advice while you were out and locked up that dastardly bailiff in the cellar. Pray do take care.'

'You may safely leave this villainous bailiff to me, Mr Jowitt. He will assault no more young ladies.' Jowitt promptly and eagerly disappeared, and Auguste's mouth began to twitch.

It was Egbert Rose.

Half an hour later Egbert had been somewhat mollified by a pint of ale and a mutton chop. Lizzie had been sent home in a cab and the glorious kitchens of the Old King Cole were devoid of life, save for themselves and the vermin which Auguste strongly suspected were enthusiastically planning their nightly assault at this very moment.

'I take it you've not taken leave of your senses, Auguste?' Egbert asked grimly, not yet prepared to yield completely, and looking pointedly at the smelly sack of fish bones.

'Nor you of yours, Egbert, I trust?' Auguste threw back at him, eyeing the cap and filthy jacket.

A pause. Then Egbert reluctantly grinned. 'There's good reason. You've heard of Prince Henry the Navigator's cross?'

'Who has not?' For years the warfare between those who felt the cross was Portuguese and those who firmly maintained it was English, had always been English, and by jingo, should remain English, had been desultory. Now its theft had been blazoned across the newspapers together with the news that Scotland Yard was baffled, it had reached fever pitch.

'Henry was the son of Philippa, daughter of John of Gaunt, Duke of Lancaster. Mean anything to you?'

'This royal throne of kings, this sceptre'd isle . . . This precious stone set in a silver sea,' Auguste declaimed. 'Shakespeare's *Richard II*.'

'There are even those who claim that last line is an oblique reference to the cross. Well, Philippa married the King of Portugal, and gave the cross to young Henry on her deathbed. He took it with him on his voyage to recapture Ceuta from the Muslims and that victory set Portugal off on its era of sea-going greatness and empire building. When Henry died, there was a battle royal, literally, as to who should have the cross, since Henry never married. The English crown was now in the hands of the Lancastrians, who said it should revert to them, the Portuguese claimed they should have it.

'We won of course, but every so often Portugal gets hot under the collar, and decides it represents their national honour. Unfortunately, there are powerful forces here who think just the same. It is made worse by the fact Portugal has got precious little left of Henry's, because everything disappeared in an earthquake a century or two later. The controversy has blown up again since Dom Carlos of Portugal is coming on an official visit here in two months' time and His Majesty King Bertie's going to return the compliment next April. There's going to be a lot of bad feeling if there's no news of that cross by November.'

'Not so much as if we refused to return it.' Auguste's head seemed to have a steak mallet thrashing inside and he longed only for bed. 'Besides, surely it is likely that the Portuguese have stolen it themselves?'

'Not as simple as that.' Egbert embarked on an explanation of the background. Accommodating him by listening seemed the quickest way to achieve his objective – home – so Auguste struggled hard. He fastened on what seemed to him the salient point.

'There is a murdered body, a missing cross, a ship that left early and a programme from this music hall. But you have no evidence any of these ingredients are linked to any of the others.'

Rose looked at him balefully. 'I can smell a connection as clearly as I smell bad herrings.' He chortled at Auguste's affronted look. 'You down here gathering a few tips on what to cook for His Majesty, then?'

Auguste stared at him coldly. 'Egbert, I have an excellent suggestion. If you are so convinced of the link, and you feel drawn to such a subtle disguise, I suggest you retain your present garb and remain here to investigate, in the position of—' He paused temptingly.

'What?'

'My mutton-chop broiler.'

A split second for Egbert to take this in. 'I don't cook,' he said flatly.

'Then I cannot detect.'

'Nobody asked you to.'

'You will, Egbert, you will.'

'Why?'

'I fear another murder.'

# Chapter Three

Perhaps he was wrong. Perhaps the fresh morning air would clarify the butter, distinguish fantasy from fact, and there was no menacing threat lurking in the shadows. Perhaps Egbert's quest to track down the missing cross would lead him far away from the Old King Cole. Perhaps he, Auguste, could be left quietly to enjoy the pleasures of the Shadwell riverside fish market at dawn. True, this was not one of those autumn mornings about which Keats had waxed so lyrical, but the air was full of early promise. Dockers and other workers hurried to their various destinations with a purposefulness lacking as days wore on, delivery boys were already cycling by with loaded baskets, and wayside vendors of toffee and watercress were zealously taking up their positions. In the market he was happy, surrounded by the wonders of the deep. Or, in this case, the Thames. Auguste eyed the silvery bodies of eels, no doubt fished from the river with forks by the urchins scooting around the fringes of this workplace. They seemed a vastly different species from the colourless grey flab that adorned the menu of the Old King Cole. Everywhere he looked lay the glories of river and sea.

Ah, what wonders of gastronomy he could show Lizzie if duty did not call. No doubt at this very moment she was plunging those ladies' legs into their pickling marinade, whereas a *matelote* . . . As soon as his choice was made, conscience hastened his step briskly back towards the Old King Cole.

Tatiana, after all, was away from home. When she was there, life crackled and sizzled like caramelising sugar. It bubbled with laughter like champagne. Without her it was as dull and flat as overcooked cod. On the other hand, the Old King Cole was not without its lighter side; after all, today he would be teaching Egbert to cook. Furthermore, he was here for only six days and for one of those at least Will had survived. Did that mean his fears were groundless? On the surface, the Old King Cole was what it seemed, yet at the very least the jovial image presented on stage and that backstage were markedly different. He had perceived no unity or warmth backstage, merely a group of performers going about their individual business. What heat there was was caused by jealousy and suspicion, not mutual admiration.

Fame was a double-headed monster: it attracted, it repelled. Moths danced round its bright light, but they were creatures of the night with all night's mysterious secrets. Will Lamb might have a simplicity that would take him like an arrow through life, but what might lie in wait in the undergrowth along his golden path?

Auguste laughed at himself for his high-flown sentiments, as Lizzie quickly brought him down to earth as soon as he walked in.

'I cooked him a negg,' she told Auguste with pride,

jerking her thumb at a slightly more human-looking Egbert, still clad in down-at-heel garb.

'A good 'un too,' Egbert commented approvingly, to Lizzie's gratification.

'Load of fish just arrived, Mr D,' she sang out, as she galloped down the stairs to her basement kingdom. 'Nearly slung it away,' came her now disembodied voice.

Surely a jest? Auguste rushed down to inspect his precious delivery. In their boxes, without the company of their fellows, he was forced to admit his prize purchases spoke a little less of ambrosia to come and a little more of hard work.

'What's this?' Lizzie came up to peer under his shoulder and poked curiously at a strange specimen. 'Cor, it's all slimy.'

'Slimy it may be, Lizzie, but it is a John Dory, distinguished by, legend says, St Peter's thumbprint, to which you have now added your own.'

'Who's John Dory?'

'It is said it derives from the Italian *janitore,* meaning the gatekeeper of heaven, St Peter. Or,' Auguste explained eagerly, anxious to instruct this keen new pupil, 'from a gentleman's name allotted to a fictitious plaintiff in a case of law.'

'How many fishes come up before the beak?'

'About as many as the paltry number of dishes we will produce at our present rate of working.'

Lizzie grinned, burst into 'Whoa, Nellie, don't you go too far' and plunged into a large tub of unappetising slime which he identified with difficulty as eel and onions.

Torn between the attractions of improving the cuisine

of Wapping and his rival duties to Egbert and Will
Lamb, it was with some reluctance that Auguste led
Egbert on a tour of the glories of the Old King Cole
music hall an hour later. Egbert had dutifully turned
up in his oldest suit, and a cap. Edith had not been
impressed. Auguste led the way to the rear door of the
eating-room that led into the entrance hall of the music
hall. He averted his eyes from tables that would have
to be hauled much further up the ladder towards
cleanliness before he would open the doors for custom.
Each should, he resolved, have a cloth laid on it, a *clean*
cloth. And suppose, he wondered, each table were to be
adorned with a dish of lemon catsup – no, not lemon,
*tomato*. His old *maître* Escoffier would throw up his
hands with horror at the abominable principle of any
food properly prepared requiring such additions, but
French cuisine was not English. Pungent tomato
catsups would spice even eel and onion pie, or mutton
chops, or faggots, or black pudding?

'Not quite the Galaxy, is it?' Egbert commented, faced
with the backstage delights of the music hall, and
remembering a similar tour years ago of the famous
Strand musical-comedy theatre.

'Nor its stars as fair as the Galaxy Girls,' Auguste
agreed. Still with its primitive gas lighting, and at the
moment dark, the working area backstage was bleak,
shorn even of the life provided by its constant stream of
hot sweaty bodies. To provide a dressing-room each for
Nettie and Will, two of the cubby-hole props rooms had
been unceremoniously stripped of their lumber and
provided with tables and shabby mirrors. A brave
attempt at welcome in each room had been made with

a Union Jack stuck in a coronation mug. The communal dressing-rooms at the back of the theatre were even starker. As Egbert peered in, his eye was met by a welter of old clothes, spare costumes, a few personal possessions and one small fireplace that gave no hint that it ever contained a fire, certainly not in late September.

'Of course,' Auguste said almost defensively, 'these are not dressing-rooms as in a theatre. Artistes with several engagements a night often come ready-costumed.'

Egbert ran his finger down the crack in the washing bowl. 'I don't see a silver cross hiding amongst this lot.'

'Nor I a murderer.'

'My cross and your mythical murderer, Auguste, have as much in common as herrings and mutton chops, that's my feeling. The cross was pinched last Saturday, and Will Lamb's threatening letters began over a week ago.'

'The theft too must have been planned, *mon ami*. There is as much link as between the dead body in Nightingale Lane and the cross.'

'I've got a garnet.' There was belligerence in Egbert's voice.

'And I a raven.'

Egbert stumbled over a coil of rope left lying in the wings, and cannoned into a flat depicting an Ascot race meeting. 'I misjudged you once before, Auguste, so I won't do it again, but sometimes a chop turns out to be a chop.'

Auguste could not resist temptation. 'When I have instructed you, you will realise a chop is a work of art.'

Then seeing Egbert's face, hurriedly returned to business: 'On what did Ma Bisley base her information?'

'I went to see her again to find out, since she can't write. No more than that the cross had something to do with the Old King Cole. Someone at the Three Tars thought he'd seen the chap who gave him his job and that it was at this music hall.'

'Performer or audience?'

'More likely to be performer, if he was recognised.'

'Why murder the man, after he has delivered the cross?'

'He could identify the villain.'

'The villain didn't seem anxious to conceal his identity when he and his companion walked into Windsor Castle and bluffed their way out with the cross.'

'Hell and Tommy.' It was strong language for Egbert, who had walked into another obstacle. This one had sharp corners.

'That's Mariella's fish tank.' Auguste hurried to steer him to safety. 'It's kept in this corner, I understand, wheeled on to the stage and re-filled weekly.'

'That's the woman you tell me Will Lamb's sweet on?'

'Yes. A very—' Auguste paused, 'seductive lady. With a Portuguese husband.'

'Oh-ho.'

'Perhaps oh-oh, Egbert, perhaps not. Thieves are not bound by national flags, as you know. They form a world-wide brotherhood.'

'Brotherhood or not, I'll start with a word with that gentleman.'

'Will he wish to have a word with a broiler of mutton chops?'

78

Egbert looked sourly at him, and then down at his scruffy attire, partly covered by an ancient apron provided by Lizzie from the previous cook's rag-bag.

'If he don't, I'll have to turn myself from frog to prince. It might put a spoke in your murderer's wheel too – if he exists.'

'But it would drive the cross far away, even if it is not on the *Lisboa*.'

'*If* it's still on the premises. But that's not likely, even if the villain's still here. Twitch is covering all the fences but I don't expect much from that. The cross couldn't be sold to the usual mob.'

'Maybe it will merely be suppressed to ensure it doesn't reach the Portuguese royal family.'

'You mean till after the King of Portugal has come and gone, and probably after our Edward's visit there next April. But then what? Send it back in a neat parcel done up with string and sealing wax to Windsor Castle?' Egbert shook his head. 'Unlikely.'

'Was His Majesty at the Castle when the cross was taken?'

Egbert snorted. 'A Saturday morning in September? Why be at Windsor, when he can be banging a gun at Sandringham? Oddly enough, he was at Buck Palace for once. It was one of the equerries got taken in by our villains, and I wouldn't give much for his having a job for life. Both these so-called representatives from the Portuguese court, incidentally, were bearded, one short, one tall, one on the young side, one a lot oldish.'

'It sounds like a scene from an E. Phillips Oppenheim novel,' Auguste observed. 'Egbert, does His Majesty know of your suspicions that the cross is still here?'

Rose fixed him with an eagle look. 'He does. I couldn't leave it till the *Lisboa* docks, could I, and then say, Oh yes, I forgot to tell you I found a corpse and deduced the cross might not be aboard after all.'

'Was he – er – put out?'

'He was.'

'Oh.' Auguste rapidly considered his own position, as cousin by marriage to His Majesty. A remote cousin, but not so remote that the royal eye was not carefully upon him.

Egbert grinned evilly.

Nettie Turner, in flowing tea-gown, sailed crossly into the drawing-room of her Islington home, summoned from her afternoon sleep by her housekeeper. She stopped short, far from pleased at the identity of the visitor awaiting her. 'What are you doing here, Harry?'

'Just visiting, Mrs Pickles. Looking round, as you might say. Nice place.' Harry Pickles did not bother to get up to greet his wife, remaining sprawled on the Chesterfield.

'Mrs Pickles!' she snorted. 'How did I land up with a name like that?'

'Very willingly, if I recall, darling.' He carefully lit the light in his eye in the old attractive way. It failed to attract her now. 'Heavy night last night, eh?'

'Play the fool on stage, Harry, not here.'

'It used to be me played your lead, not Will.'

'I was the fool then. No fool like an old fool, Harry, and you took the last laugh in the form of a hefty allowance. *To keep away.*'

'Most generous of you, darling. Mind you, I could do with more.'

'Push off.'

He came close to her, but she stood her ground. 'Why should I? Your chum Will ruined my life.'

'Some days Brodie did, some days Will did. You ruined your own life, Harry, by being too bone-idle to create one.'

'Poor old cuckolded husband. There'd be lots of sympathy for me, if I divorce you.'

'You're crazy.' There was a note of uncertainty in her voice though.

He caught it. 'Am I? Perhaps I don't want a divorce, eh? You're a fine woman still.' He ran his hand over her chiffon-covered bottom. She removed it. He caught both her hands savagely, bearing her down on the sofa.

'Get off me, Harry,' she said evenly.

He laughed in triumph. 'I'm your loving husband, Nettie. You can't stop me.'

'Loving?' She laughed in his face. 'You've got as much idea of love as a motor-car piston. In out, in out. Snore.'

His face darkened, strengthening his grip till it bruised her. 'Will Lamb's better, is he?'

'Will?' She didn't give an inch. 'Than a Sabbath to the devil.'

'The devil still has the best tunes, Nettie,' he leered. 'See how you like singing to this one.'

He yanked up her skirts, pinioning her arms with them, forcing her head into the corner of the sofa, lying sprawled across her. She wasn't going to shout for help, show fear, have the maids rushing in to rescue her. Not Nettie Turner, darling of the masses. So she endured it, the touch of him on her, in her, the smell of drink-sodden breath stifling her. When it was over and he relaxed his hold, she sent him sprawling on to the floor with one kick, pulled on her clothes again and fought for calmness.

'No more money, Harry. Not a penny. Blackmail me all you like.' But for all her brave words, her fears about the coming week doubled.

Egbert Rose opened the door of Wapping's Seamen's Rest pub. Behind the bar publican (and fence) James Higgins did not pause in his rapt contemplation of the beer glass he was studying at close quarters, as though cleanliness were his greatest preoccupation in life.

'What can I get you, sir?' he asked politely. Already his clientele, hardly fooled by Rose's clothes, began quietly to edge away. Fortunately Higgins was respected by both sides – up to a point.

'A silver—'

'It'll be a pleasure, sir,' Higgins cut smoothly across. 'Muriel,' he yelled stridently. 'Egbert wants a few words with us.'

'What have you been doing, love?' he asked loudly. Muriel, in battered blouse and black skirt, came sedately up the stairs from the cellar, and led the way to their private sanctum without a word.

'Handled any old relics recently, Higgins?'

'Only Muriel, sir,' was the jovial reply.

Muriel tittered. 'What had you in mind, Mr Rose?'

'A silver cross with ivory figure surrounded by precious stones, mainly garnets.'

'That does sound pretty,' Muriel observed. 'I don't

recall anyone wearing anything like that, do you, James? Mrs Fry, her from Number Eight, was wearing a nice one last week, mind you.'

'Ever heard of Miguel Gomez?'

'He's a juggler on the halls,' Muriel informed him, as if anxious to be of help.

'Ever met him?'

'Nah.' Higgins pulled his Newgate whiskers thoughtfully. 'Nor heard a whisper, if you takes my meaning.'

'I do, Higgins, I do. I'll make it worth your while.'

'Worth our while doing what?' Higgins appeared puzzled.

'Ah well, must have come to the wrong place,' Rose said loudly, as Higgins rose to open the door.

'Where may I reach you, sir?'

'The Old King Cole.'

Higgins guffawed. 'Oh dearie me. How are the mighty risen.'

'Come to the kitchen and complete your merriment.'

'It'll be a pleasure, sir.'


'You're here early, Will.' Mariella posed on the threshold of the small dressing-room. She had insisted to Miguel that they should be here before the performance started this evening. She needed to be ready.

'Nettie isn't very well. She's coming later. I came on my own,' Will told Mariella proudly, jumping up eagerly to greet her.

'Oh.' Mariella brushed this insignificant statement aside, as well as the lock of red hair that had conveniently fallen from its perch on her head. How he loved her hair, its softness, the way it gleamed. She was like the loveliest fairy on the Christmas tree. 'I've brought it, Will,' she breathed huskily, closing the door behind her, and coming close to him. Attar of roses filled his nostrils and happiness his entire body. She pushed the package into his hands.

'It's only a few days now, and then—'

'I know. We'll go over the hills and far away.' He put his arms round her adoringly, and she pushed her body, already costumed in its slight attire (apart from the mermaid's tail) against him to afford him the infinite pleasure of her whole shapely figure – though she doubted if he appreciated it.

'I'm so happy, Will,' she told him softly. 'Very, very happy. You'll look after me, won't you?'

'I will, Mariella. Words are funny, aren't they? I will . . . that's my name. I will.' He said it over to himself several times, lost in his other world.

'Where there's a will, there's a way, darling.' She smiled indulgently. 'That's another joke. You've always been so generous to me. You haven't changed your mind, have you? It's been a long time, and we haven't seen each other as often as I would have liked. I dared not. I *couldn't*. Miguel's so jealous. But now I've had enough of him. He wants to take all Auntie's jewellery away from me.'

'Nothing's changed, Mariella.'

'You won't tell Miguel what we're planning, will you? Or about the jewellery?'

She handed him the packet. 'You'll tell no one?'

'Of course not.'

'Where will you put it?'

Will looked bewildered. 'Home?' he offered eventually.

'No. Keep it here in this dressing-room. It's only for a few days.' Will nodded eagerly, anxious to please. 'How about in this props basket?' She threw open the top and lodged it between an assortment of old hats, cases and boxes. 'I made a mistake in choosing Miguel,' she sighed. 'You're so clever, Will.'

'Yes,' he agreed humbly.

She put her arms round him and hugged him. It was like hugging a child, she thought, disengaging herself, until he grabbed her again and this time put his lips to hers. There was nothing of the child in that greedy painful kiss. She hastily pulled herself away and wagged her finger at him. 'Naughty. Not till Saturday, Will.'

Little Emmeline, listening avidly at the door, backed away hastily as Mariella put her hand on it, and danced off into the dressing-room to see how many fairies had arrived. She was in a very good mood and only slapped one of them. She was in such a good mood it entirely slipped her mind that she'd seen someone going into the main props room next door to Will Lamb's dressing-room, whom she didn't see reappear. It meant nothing to Emmeline, for she didn't know there was a grille in the connecting wall, even better for eavesdropping than doors. And much more private.

Auguste, appalled to hear Will had arrived early, was relieved to find him beaming happily at himself in the small mirror, applying greasepaint to his eyebrows.

'You're early tonight, Mr Lamb.' He tried to keep the scolding note out of his voice. After all, no harm was done.

'Can we speak to you for a moment, Will?' The Tumbling Twins, promoted to further down the bill at the Shadwell Grand, followed him in. It appeared unlikely that Violet and Marigold Pears were assassins, but nevertheless Auguste ignored all meaningful glances indicating privacy would be welcome.

'Mr Didier, this is Miss Pears, Miss Marigold Pears and Miss Violet Pears. Mixed them together for Compote of Pears, that's compost of pears in English. Two pears make one pair, you see.' The patter, good or bad, seemed to pour out of Will Lamb automatically and unchecked. Perhaps, Auguste thought, it provided some kind of release – or even a refuge for him. What could he have on his mind that he needed to escape from? 'Pray do sit down, Misses Pears,' Will invited them.

They hesitated, as Auguste made it clear he had no intention of moving.

'Marigold would like to talk to you, Will,' Violet said sweetly, 'and *I* shall talk to Mr Didier – outside.' She took his arm as he looked questioningly at Will.

'I shall like that,' Will said haplessly, but he showed no signs of fear, so Auguste reluctantly acquiesced. Not that he had much choice without a physical wrangle, as Violet had him in something closely resembling the letter 'X' arrest demonstrated to him by Egbert.

'Marigold has no evil designs on poor Will,' Violet said gaily, as she led him out of the dressing-room. From the sounds on the far side of the shabby curtain, the audience was beginning to liven up in readiness for the evening, and on the stage a mysterious green light, that would do little to enhance complexions, seemed beyond the ability of the gasman to remove. The hit-and-miss approach to staging and lighting was far from the ordered precision Auguste remembered at the Galaxy. Wapping was a long way from the Strand.

'You're the new cook, aren't you?' Violet smiled brightly.

'Yes.'

'You're very handsome for a cook.' She eyed him appreciatively, making him feel like a plump *poussin*.

Marigold could charm this silly man in a moment, Violet was thinking eagerly, and marry him in two. These foreigners were all the same. She wondered how much cooks earned.

'Thank you, Miss Violet,' Auguste replied cautiously.

'What were you doing in Will's room if you're a cook?' Without waiting for an answer, the beautiful blue eyes narrowed, then flew wide open. 'Aren't you the cook who does the detective work?' she cried indignantly.

'I am.'

'What are you doing here?' Fear entered her voice, and she re-examined her early diagnosis. 'I read about you in *The Lady*. You're practically royal. And you're *married*,' she added indignantly. 'Where is your wife?'

'She is away.'

'So you come here to philander. To prey upon us innocent women. Like all men.'

'No, indeed,' he replied, somewhat annoyed. 'Someone has been threatening Mr Lamb, and I am here to protect him.' No harm in telling her; it could only do good.

'Threatening him? What with?'

'Murder.' She said nothing. Perhaps she had not understood. 'I hope by my presence to prevent any harm coming to him,' he added.

To his horror the blue eyes filled with tears, and she threw herself into his arms, clinging to him like a glaze to a piecrust. 'It's not me,' she sobbed obscurely. 'We just want to talk to him. Gentlemen like pink tights but they don't want to marry them.'

'There, there, *ma petite*,' he said soothingly, calming her, stroking her hair in a way that had never failed yet.

It appeared to be failing this time. 'You don't realise,' she hiccuped.

'What?'

'We're nearly *thirty*.'

'Well over,' a female voice announced scornfully. Mariella, coming to check that nobody had absconded with her fish tank, rather than to appreciate her husband's performance, had strolled towards them unnoticed. As Violet shrieked her indignation, she sized Auguste up. After all this was over, she wouldn't mind helping herself to one of this new cook's chops herself. An armful of Violet was but small beer compared with an armful of Mariella. 'Yapp's in full spate out here. You're on first. Pickles hasn't shown up.'

Violet shrieked, rushing back into the dressing-room to find Marigold.

Mariella smirked. Every spangle glistened as she eyed her prey. 'First time I've ever seen one without the other. And no wonder.' She looked him up and down. Oddly, instead of feeling like a *poussin* in the market, he now felt more like one recently roasted, and reminded himself hurriedly of his married state.

'Marigold is talking to Will Lamb.'

'What about?' she asked sharply.

'I have no idea.' Even in the darkness he could see she was annoyed.

Mariella quite forgot she had been bent on seducing him but a moment before. She had her mind very firmly set on other, more urgent, matters now.

Will appeared from his dressing-room in the wake of the flying figures of the Tumbling Twins. He looked preoccupied, but greeted Auguste cheerfully enough. 'I'm going to watch the show from the wings, like I used to,' he said happily. 'Marigold said I should.'

'The twins were here ten years ago when you first came here?'

'Oh my goodness, yes. They've never left. I'm going to look after them, you know. They deserve it. Both of them.' He trotted into the wings, and Auguste followed, watching the twins take their brief nervous bow just as the gasman managed to switch the green light for a softer hue. Then he watched Miguel, as he juggled what seemed to be an entire dinner service in the air. Auguste disapproved. There were better uses for dinner plates. There was a sense of purpose to the wings now, as dim shapes of stage hands and performers gathered one by one to wait their turn.

The smart-suited figure of the Great Brodie sauntered up to them. 'Good to see you, Will.' There was some condescension in his voice. 'Supporting your old mates, eh?'

'I like to watch everyone. And particularly those I used to know. The Misses Pears asked me to.'

'Doesn't it put them off?' Horace said dismissively. 'Does me.'

'Does it?' Will asked anxiously. 'I'm sorry, Horace.' He glanced on to the stage where Miguel was taking a bow, just as the remains of a baked potato sailed over his head.

'Suit yourself, Will. We're honoured to have you.'

He didn't sound very honoured, Auguste thought. Rather the contrary.

Miguel exited, clearly relieved to have escaped with one such tribute. There was no Shadwell Mob this evening, and the audience was disposed to be generous while waiting for Will Lamb.

'Evening, Miguel,' the Great Brodie greeted him. 'Don't worry. I'll get them going.'

'Going home, perhaps,' snarled Miguel, hurrying away.

Horace Brodie shrugged and laughed. 'Jealous!'

So much for comradely support offstage, Auguste thought.

Horace straightened up, adjusted his waistcoat, and strolled to the curtains, as Yapp's voice could be heard proclaiming: 'Our very own lion *comique* . . .' He vanished on to the stage, and launched into 'Don't Wait Up'. Dolly Dadd stood admiringly at Auguste's side, though the admiration was all directed on to the stage.

The next arrival in the wings, towards the end of Horace's act, was a rebellious assistant cook, Egbert Rose.

'I've left the washing-up to your sword-swallower, Auguste. I'm more interested in what's going on here. Evening, Mr Lamb.'

Will took no notice. He was talking to Percy Jowitt, who was making his ritual five-minute visit to encourage his troops, and it was Percy who, with a strangled yelp, broke his own rules about noise, gave a startled yelp and pointed a quivering finger at Egbert Rose. 'He's here *again*.'

Auguste grinned at the sight of Egbert's furious face. 'Ah, yes, Mr Jowitt,' he whispered blandly. 'I find the best thing to do with bailiffs is to feed them and set them to work.'

'Me? Employ a bailiff? Never, over my dead body.'

'I hope not,' Egbert replied unforgivingly. 'I'm with the Yard.'

'Scrap?'

'Scotland.'

Jowitt gazed at him, as he slowly absorbed his meaning. 'Scotland Yard is in debt to that extent?'

'I'm *not* a bailiff,' Egbert said through gritted teeth.

'Then why say you were?' Percy asked, reasonably enough in his view.

Not in Egbert's. As the Great Brodie roared into his final chorus, Egbert took Jowitt firmly by the arm and marched him off protestingly for a quiet chat. Horace strode offstage and Dolly replaced him. Auguste joined Will, who to his concern he noticed was looking strained.

'Are you all right, Mr Lamb?' he asked, alarmed.

Will managed to smile. 'Perfectly, thank you.' As if hypnotised, he stared at the stage where Dolly was bursting into song. She clasped her hands before her. 'A pretty maid up from the country, A vile seducer he . . .' Her face was innocently confiding to the audience, but inside was turmoil.

'That new cook is a *detective*,' Mariella hissed at Miguel

outside the stage door, on his way to find a cab to take him to the next engagement.

'*What*? How did he get here?' her husband demanded sharply. 'Have you been talking?'

'No.'

'You're coming with me.'

'I can't. I've got my turn to do here.'

'You can come back again. You must not be with him.'

'He's rather handsome.'

Miguel glowed with rage. 'If he is sniffing after you, I will—' He made an elegant gesture across the throat. '*His*.' To make it quite clear.

'I'm terrified,' she said scornfully.

'You had better be,' he told her slowly.

She stopped. She'd gone too far. When Miguel got that look in his eye, he was dangerous.

'I've done all you asked,' she said sullenly.

'I do not trust you, Mariella.'

'But I'm your wife.' She appeared hurt.

'That's why I *know* I can't trust you. You don't have any ideas about putting our plan into practice, do you?'

She lifted her large eyes to his. 'Of course not.'

Miguel decided to make sure someone kept an eye on her. He couldn't afford not to know exactly what Mariella was up to. Max perhaps, or better still, Fernando.

Max was at that moment lolling on a chair in the eating-room, an empty plate and half-empty glass before him. 'A mutton chop, if you please.' He waved a lordly hand towards Egbert Rose, who had decided he'd learn as much at his unofficial post as elsewhere – and not all about the art of broiling, either.

Egbert flipped the chop dexterously over on the hot-plate to give it a last warm. Nothing to this cooking game. Nice bit of mutton suet, and there you were. Typical of Auguste to spend half an hour lecturing him on gridiron heat, smoke, angle to fire and where you stick the fork. You put it on and you took it off, and that was that. 'Don't you have to go on stage, Mr Hill?'

'Mr Hill never goes on stage. *I* go on stage as Will Lamb, as Horace Brodie, as Nettie Turner, as our Gracious King himself. Mariella is a trifle beyond my range, I fear, but as for any other characters in this blessed isle of ours, Max is your man.' He gulped loudly, draining his glass. 'Let me introduce you, my dear sir, to your new employer, Mr Didier.'

He stood up, a trifle unsteadily. Then twenty years slipped from him.

'*Ah non, merde,*' he cried. He danced up and down in self-approval. 'Zis mutton chop it is great art, naturally for eet ees cooked by me, Auguste Didier, the Brillat-Savarin of 1902.' He pored lovingly over an imaginary stove, peered anxiously into pots, tasted non-existent soup in ecstatic bliss. Then eyes flashed dangerously. 'What is *zis*?' he cried ominously, hands waving vigorously. 'Eet is—' He stopped. 'Ah, Auguste, my dear chap,' he greeted the unexpected arrival genially.

Auguste was mystified. Who was this self-important Frenchman he was mocking? A terrible thought came into his head. Could it be—

'And let me do an impression of an inspector of Scotland Yard,' roared Max.

Egbert slung down the implements of his new-found

trade. 'You've been inside, haven't you?' he said grimly. 'Stir.'

'In my youth,' Max told him grandly. 'I am a reformed character, you might say. Evil I forswore many years ago.'

'You can always tell.'

'As I can tell the Old Bill, my dear sir. I have this one advantage over you, however, I am no longer one of the criminal classes, but you will remain indelibly identifiable as a copper for ever – even if cooking my chop?' The query in his voice went unanswered.

'Max!' Miguel came into the eating-room and stopped, seeing the assembled group. He smiled deprecatingly. 'Forgive me, gentlemen, a word with my fellow artiste, if I might.' What he had to say was nothing about their art, however.

It had all seemed a great adventure with a fairy-tale ending about to come true. Like a fairy-tale there was a wicked witch in the form of dreams and the raven, but surely that meant everything was going to be even more wonderful than he'd imagined, Will told himself stoutly. He remembered the first time he'd seen Mariella. She'd been plain Mary Elizabeth Pigg then, and eighteen years old, with great soft eyes and face and hair. So sweet, and she hadn't changed at all. Nor had he. She was just as loving, just as gentle. When she was eighteen she hadn't loved him, but now she did. Just like a fairy-tale. He hadn't had any more dreams either. So that must mean William Terriss was happy that everything was all right. Everything except . . . But that was such a little thing, though he did like everything being *tidy* in life, and he didn't like to feel he'd been take advantage of. Old Jowitt, for instance, had been eager enough to ask him to come here and he'd willingly accepted because he owed him a lot. But he hadn't forgotten how ten years ago Jowitt, having given him the chance, was willing to abandon him at the first sign of difficulties from the Shadwell Mob of the day. Nettie had saved him, darling Nettie.

The stage manager self-importantly popped his head round the door. 'Board's going up, Mr Lamb.'

Will heard the roar of the audience, he heard Yapp's voice . . . 'The lion lies down with the lamb at the Old King Cole. You've had the lion, the Great Brodie, now for the Great Lamb.' How he loved it. It wasn't that his vanity needed to be fed, it was more than it propelled him into that queer fantasy world of his, into which he leapt when the real one presented problems, both nice and nasty. Like now.

By the time he reached the stage he was beaming, oblivious of anything save his audience and the need to make them happy. He checked his stage dagger was correctly dancing on is wires in the flies. That dagger had travelled a long way with him. He launched himself at the stage, waiting to be swallowed up in the warmth he was giving and receiving, rushed to the footlights, towards *them*, his public; he took them into his confidence and his heart. 'So I met this bard, and he said, why not come along? I've got a part for you. A part of what, I asked . . .'

From the front, seated importantly near her husband, Evangeline watched as her beloved Will leapt on to the stage. He was playing for *her* alone. She knew it. What an artiste he was. He needed her loving care though, that was obvious. So far she had had no chance of purveying this important news to him, since someone or other always seemed to be hanging round his dressing-room. With some pleasure she suspected Thomas might be arranging this, since naturally he was jealous of her affection for Will. She was almost sure it was his voice she'd overheard talking to Will. She watched proudly and proprietorially as Will tumbled and twisted, the patter never faltering. It was never the same patter twice, but it always came back to the fixed point of the *Macbeth* speech. They were both artistes. Oh, how she understood the problems and triumphs of the artiste in a way Thomas could never appreciate.

'Thomas,' she hissed. 'I am going backstage.'

'Keep away from Will Lamb,' he pleaded desperately. Even Percy Jowitt had warned him to keep her here, and the chairman could hardly abandon his post to dash out of the hall after his wife.

But he was looking at an empty space, the large empty space where his wife had been sitting. He decided to try not to worry. After all, Will had seemed pleased to see him, and they'd had a nice talk. Furthermore, there was nothing he could do to avert any catastrophe that might fall, so he tried bravely to smile in the face of disaster, however fast it might be rushing towards them.

Leaving the capable (in her own inimitable way) Lizzie in charge, Auguste hurried back to his post to greet

Will as he came offstage. How much he would have preferred to stay tutoring his raw assistant than to pursue a probably imaginary death threat, or hunt a wild-goose in the form of a probably non-present missing cross.

He reached the dressing-room only to be physically swept aside at the door by a large lady in crimson whom he identified as Evangeline Yapp.

'I beg your pardon,' she said coldly. 'I believe I was here first.'

In fact, it was merely her corseted bosom and outstretched arm that had arrived first but in any case both were immaterial.

'I beg your pardon, madam, but I must be present.' He gently pushed the arm aside and opened the door.

Alarm leapt into Will's face as he saw who was behind his guardian. 'No,' he cried, leaping up and backing away.

'I regret, madam—' Auguste turned to Mrs Yapp.

'Nonsense,' she said briskly, advancing so that Auguste could only go backwards, sandwiched between Will and her, or sidestep. In defence of duty he chose the former course. 'Don't you remember, Will, how well we got on?' she asked soulfully. 'Don't you remember the props room at the Grand at Wigan?'

'Happy memories, Evangeline,' Will managed to stutter.

'We shared our love and our art.'

'Did we?' Will clutched pleadingly at Auguste.

'Mr Lamb is not well at present.' Auguste began firmly to push forward, colliding with the S-bend corset, and forcing her to retreat backwards. With Will still clutching behind, he felt he was engaged in some exotic dance.

'I have,' she announced with dignity over Auguste's shoulder, 'cherished your memory.'

'And I yours,' Will gabbled, seeing the door within Auguste's reach.

A shriek of delight from Evangeline and Auguste was pushed bodily to one side, stumbling over the chair. 'Oh, Will, I knew it. You care for me yet.'

She threw her arms around him, pressing him to her chest. Regaining balance, Auguste rushed in to separate them and found himself enveloped into a galloping threesome as Evangeline tried to reach Will once more.

'I love Mariella,' Will wailed desperately.

The flailing arms dropped. 'Mariella?' she repeated flatly.

'She smells nice and she sings to me,' Will explained happily, seeing a possible end once again in sight.

'I can sing to you too,' Evangeline offered hopelessly.

'She has nice little dogs too,' Will said eagerly. 'I like little dogs. Not to eat of course, and not the bloodhound type, but little yappy things.'

Evangeline left the room quietly, apparently defeated, and Auguste almost felt sorry for her. In fact she was seething with anger and planning her next move.

'We are not yet open,' Auguste cried, agonised at the banging on the door at a quite unreasonable hour on the Wednesday morning.

'Mr Didier, you disappoint me. You really do.'

A familiar voice. Auguste opened the door, and James Higgins strolled in.

'This is an honour,' Auguste greeted him somewhat cautiously, remembering his profession and other character traits from their previous meetings on a matter of Fabergé eggs.

'Likewise, I'm sure. Fancy your remembering me, Mr Didier. You get around, Cannes one time, Wapping the next. Mr Rose anywhere to be found?'

'Not until this afternoon.'

'Give him a message, then. Tell him he's sniffing at the wrong tree. No dolly-shops. Jewellers is what he's after. Restorers, repairers.' This was accompanied by a heavy wink. 'See what I mean?'

'Not precisely, Mr Higgins.'

Higgins sighed. 'I do have to spell it out for you youngsters. Fakers, Mr D, makers of fakes.'

'The Portuguese Embassy has suddenly got interested, Auguste,' Egbert told him, now clad once more in his usual business suit. Edith had been much relieved. 'Chatty, they were. And you know why? Because the cross hadn't turned up at Lisbon. Not that that's a surprise to us. The ship's captain said the parcel never arrived – mind you, that's what he would say if he decided to stab the courier and pinch the thing for himself. According to him, he was expecting it at three-thirty.'

'Does His Majesty know yet?'

Egbert fixed him with a look. 'Solicitous, aren't you, about His Majesty's welfare?'

Auguste went pink.

'He took it badly,' Egbert continued. 'He was more upset than about losing it in the first place, if you ask me. I get the blame. Incompetence, he calls it, whereas the theft itself was an unfortunate mishap. At least on the *Lisboa*, he says, he would have known it was steaming back to safe hands, even if Portuguese. Now it could be in Petticoat Lane or the Winter Palace for all we *know*. The embassy have been *told* the cross was stolen, but was on its way to Portugal, was delayed, and will be with them soon. His Majesty orders me to stop it reaching them. Just like that.'

'Told by whom?'

'Sources, they say. It strikes me the Monarchist Trade Unionist, Dom Carlos and our Gracious Majesty, are getting ready to stick together and blame the police.'

'You don't think the cross will reach Portugal?'

'It may reach Portugal, but not necessarily the King. The embassy admitted with some reluctance that there's a group of powerful folk over in Portugal in favour of doing away with the monarchy by whatever means, and declaring a republic. The movement's been growing quietly, and it isn't going to go away. It would do a lot of good to their cause if they had Prince Henry's cross. When it comes to making their big blow for power, to have the honour of Portugal in their tiny hands would be a help for popular support. If you ask me, that's what's put the wind up His Majesty – and what he meant by "anarchists" being behind the theft.'

'But if, as you imply, the Republicans have stolen the cross, how did they come to know about the Royalist plan to steal the cross?'

Egbert shrugged. 'Double agents, probably.'

'Then your task is hopeless, Egbert. The cross could be in Portugal by now. Think of all the shipping in the

Limehouse basin alone which comes and goes with few questions asked.'

'They may prefer to keep the cross safely in England if they aren't in a position to strike for power for some years.'

'Do you have a list of such people living here?'

'Stitch is working on it. My money is still on this place. My nose tells me so – when it can get away from the stink of those blasted herrings.'

'Our resident juggler?' Auguste ignored the slight to the hand-picked fish he'd selected from Shadwell market.

'Yes. Whatever the Assistant Commissioner says, I'm moving in on him.'

'What *did* he say?' Auguste asked, curiously.

'He wouldn't let me search this place, or the Gomez home.' He frowned. 'Too much of a political hot potato, he said. Too afraid they'd explode, you might say, like that lot.' By their side was Frederick's pile ready for the cans.

'Higgins came here this morning. He gave you a lead. Fakers, he suggested.'

Egbert's eyes gleamed. 'Royalists wouldn't need a fake, nor would a straightforward thief. What does that tell us?'

'The Republicans stole it, hoping to palm off the fake on Dom Carlos and keep the genuine one themselves?'

'Right. You can do without your broilerman tonight, Auguste. I've other fish to fry.'

'Egbert, have you mentioned my presence here to His Majesty?' Auguste tried to sound as offhand as he could.

Egbert eyed him in gleeful amusement. 'Going to be

a bit of family upset, is there? No, I didn't.' He paused. 'Not yet.'

Auguste glared. Strictly speaking he was within the terms of his arrangement with his royal relative by marriage, since he was not being paid for his service as cook at the Old King Cole. Somehow, however, he felt His Majesty would not be pleased that Cousin Tatiana's husband was cooking eel pies for the Shadwell Mob.

'And,' Egbert picked up his thoughts, 'he might not like to think you willingly chose to get mixed up with another murder.'

# Chapter Four

Two nights survived, only four to go. Never had Saturday seemed such a long way off. Even the hope of the brave new world Auguste had envisaged, in introducing the less fortunate to a finer cuisine, had evaporated. The delights of eel were beginning to pall. Two nights at the Old King Cole had convinced him that change was not what was required. Mutton chops, herrings, and faggots were, and tempting sauces (save for his brilliant idea of placing tomato catsup at the tables) were eyed with suspicion and ignored. The smell of the frying was ingrained in his skin. No matter what he did, he greeted it in the morning on his arrival, it clung to him as a friend, and then accompanied him home to Queen Anne's Gate – where it was ignominiously received by his staff to whom Auguste suspected he was an object of derision. It seemed to him that, despite the best endeavours of their new bath, the smell clung to his sheets and was there once more as faithful companion when he reawoke the next morning.

Wednesday did not bode any fairer than its two predecessors. He had stoically endured his chef's idea of breakfast, in the interest of his late dinner. When he summoned John to discuss this important subject, their thoughts had not run along the same lines.

'I could leave out cold pie, sir.'

'No doubt you could,' Auguste had replied amiably, 'but pies, John, are perhaps not your forte.' This showed admirable restraint on his part. John's pies were his own version of cannon-balls that sped to Auguste's stomach and lodged there, awaiting surgical removal.

'The Duke of Davenport praised my pies.'

'I am not the Duke of Davenport.'

'No, sir,' John agreed, wholeheartedly.

'My soup *de Crécy*, John. Then a *fricassée*. A—'

'That's foreign. I do English.'

'Alas, not very well.'

Battlelines had been drawn. Both sides smouldered. Auguste's temper was not improved by the fact that the postcard he had expected from Tatiana had not arrived. She too was working, he reminded himself, although a sneaking voice inside him suggested that a week's work at the Old King Cole could hardly be compared with a ten-day motoring event in France. One's dedication to one's art could only go so far.

There was more to Auguste's restlessness, however, than Tatiana's absence. Although two nights had passed without incident, save for the raven, he could not rid himself of the knowledge that backstage old emotions had been stirred up by Will and Nettie's return and that they were proving a catalyst to stirring dormant fires. Yet he felt powerless. In the eating-room a fog of war seemed to descend on him, making it difficult to think and difficult to act.

Today Egbert was doggedly visiting, with Stitch's help, as many of the East London fakers as he knew of, a task in which he could hardly expect Higgins' active participation. He, Auguste, had been left to the delights of organising fish, meat and Lizzie. The latter too was proving more difficult a task than he had imagined.

'I purchased lobster at the market this morning,' he told her innocently. 'I thought you might instruct me in lobscouse. It sounds a most fascinating dish.'

Lizzie paused fractionally in her flying circuits of cellar and stoves. 'Ere,' she shouted, disappearing into the nether regions.

'Where?' Auguste hurried downstairs, expectant of seeing delightful pink lobsters newly emerged from cooking pots.

'On the kitchener.'

No pink lobsters. No fresh smell of fish. Cautiously he dipped in and tasted a spoonful. Baron Liebig's product greeted him like an old familiar friend.

'Lizzie, what *is* this, if you please?'

She appeared proudly at his side. 'Lobscouse, Mr D. Meat and vegetable mash. Good, ain't it?'

'Delightful in its way,' he murmured grimly. 'But it is hardly lobster. Furthermore, Lizzie, tomorrow I teach you to make a *bourguignon*,' he promised. 'Meat stew,' he added firmly.

'Cor,' she said dutifully, but he suspected she was unimpressed. She whipped off her apron, and headed for the door.

'Where are you going?' he asked in surprise. Surely he had not offended her so quickly.

'Get me pies, of course.'

'Can't they deliver?'

'Mrs Jolly don't need to deliver.' With this cryptic utterance, she dashed outside, leaving Auguste to contemplate this other world of cooking. He had not yet tasted these pies, assuming they were Lizzie's own work, but he could imagine all too fearfully their taste. They probably came from the same source as the abominations that adorned the cafés of London railway stations. Or perhaps John supplied them? He would show Lizzie what a real pie could taste like . . .

At five-thirty, Auguste reluctantly abandoned his emergency transformation of kitchens and cuisine and took up his duties as Will's protector. The backstage area was still deserted. He walked up the steps to the upper floor. Again, deserted, nothing but the stale smell of scenery and disused props. Near the window above the stage door, an indignant rustle reminded him that though human beings might not be present, the area was hardly devoid of life. In the large basket the beady eyes of the raven watched him. Its trainer, he had learned, left it here on his way home to tea from Jamrach's, and came back in time for his turn. The raven and monkeys were spared the mad dash from hall to hall.

'The raven himself is hoarse . . .' No, it would surely have been no accident that the bird escaped at the very moment that Will was entering the Old King Cole. Someone had crept up here, opened the window, and unlocked the cage, all to warn Will Lamb. Ghosts, ravens, letters – someone was going to a lot of trouble to *prevent* Will Lamb from coming to harm. And with that good wish, Auguste was entirely in agreement, for after two days at the Old King Cole, murder did not seem as unlikely as it had at the Empire, Leicester Square.

'You look tired,' Nettie said bluntly, as Will climbed into the carriage. 'Why did you want to come early?'

'I've someone to see,' he replied simply. 'I'm not a bit tired, Nettie, really.'

'Mariella, I suppose. Oh, Will, you are a fool.'

He flushed and she was annoyed at having gone too far. She put her hand on his. 'Don't mind me, Will. I've got a lot on my mind.'

'You're not ill, Nettie?' he asked anxiously. 'I wouldn't like that.'

'Chronic disease, Will. Harry.'

'Pickles?'

'Our Pickles himself,' she continued bitterly. 'I've stopped his allowance, Will, so he's not pleased with me.' She tried to laugh, but failed.

'Money,' he agreed succinctly.

'They all want it,' she continued. 'They never realise how hard we had to work for it, do they? Remember you told me you had to earn farthings doing the double shuffle to queues before I met you?'

Will giggled, and kicked his feet appreciatively on the carriage floor.

'And there was me wasting my and the audience's time burbling about fairies in fairyland, till I realised what's really wanted.'

'What is that, Nettie?' he asked curiously.

'Me, me old darling. They want to devour me whole.

107

Never satisfied.' Her face was very serious. 'And when they've gnawed away at me long enough, they'll turn to someone else.'

He looked despondent.

'Not you, Will,' she reassured him. 'You're different. But me, I'm a woman. Replaceable. Others will always come along. Dolly, for instance. She'll do well when she stops being an innocent maid from the country and finds out what she's really made of. By that time, I'll be torn to bits between the audience and Our Loveable Pickles.' She grimaced.

'Don't you love him any more, Nettie?'

'*Love* him?' she burst out, caught unawares. 'Yesterday he forced himself in on me, half strangled me, tore off my clothes and put his cock in me, Will. What do you think? Would you do that to Mariella? 'Course not. An old hen like me doesn't matter, he says.'

The instant she'd spoken she regretted it. Will had nothing to do with that kind of talk; he didn't understand the kind of life it came from. She looked at him to see if she'd upset him. His eyes were blank for a moment. Perhaps he hadn't understood what she meant, she thought hopefully. Then he opened his mouth to speak. What's he going to say? Panic swept through her at the thought she might have pushed him over the edge again.

But Will seemed to speak quite normally: 'I usually get my pies from Mrs Scrawny Todd. Do you know Mrs Scrawny? You'd certainly know her pies again. She puts a lot in her pies, does Mrs Scrawny. I don't know what Jack Sprat would have done, that's his secret. I've got a secret too, I *think* it's a secret anyway, it's a nice one. About Mariella and me, Nettie.'

Nettie went cold. What had that bitch been up to now? It had been a mistake to come back to the Old King Cole. She'd known it would be, and she'd been proved right. She should have talked Will out of it.

'Not a nasty one,' he was saying. 'Not like you and Pickles. I don't think I like Pickles now. I'll tell him so when I see him, Nettie. Perhaps I'll even tell him about Bill—'

'Bill?' she asked uncertainly.

'Bill Terriss,' he explained, surprised she could have forgotten. 'Oh yes, I dreamed about him last night. Or did I see him? I forget. I went to lunch at Gatti's today and he was there. Dressed in grey, as usual. Be careful, Will, said his voice. At least I think it was, or did I dream it? Oh I will, said Will, I will have only three dozen oysters, so I will. Moderation will prevail. I think it *must* have been a dream, for Mrs Jones said she cooked sausages for luncheon. But I'm so sure I did see him, Nettie. And heard him.'

The carriage stopped outside the stage door of the Old King Cole. This time Nettie got out first – just in case. No raven appeared, nor the ghost of William Terriss, but Nettie shivered all the same. Auguste heard the carriage and came to the door to meet them. He saw Nettie, pale and trembling. Will was smiling happily, in a world of his own. Auguste sympathised here; he too was beginning not to know which was fantasy and which was fact. As Will came into the building though, his expression changed. He clung to

Nettie's arm, and when he glanced at Auguste there was deep fear on his face.

'I've arrived. Come here.' The stage door went back with a crash. Auguste, standing at the doorway of Will's room, was privileged to see the arrival of Little Emmeline and all six fluttering fairies (albeit prosaically clad in button-through wool skirts). He did not obey the summons.

A gleam appeared in Little Emmeline's eye. She marched over to him, but not in a spirit of defeat. 'I'm hungry. I want a chop.'

'When I return to the kitchens, I will ask my assistant to bring you one.'

'Now.'

'No.'

'*Now.*'

'*Non.*' He folded his arms.

Emmeline eyed him. 'You,' she whirled on a fairy. 'Go and get me a chop.'

'Tell Miss Lizzie, mademoiselle, that Miss Emmeline requires a most succulent, dainty chop, fit for an artiste. And that I, Auguste Didier, say so.'

The fairy scuttled off, Auguste went into Will's room and closed the door.

Emmeline smarted. It was not a good day. Her mother had forbidden her to buy that nice red corset on the grounds that her public expected her to be a little girl, and a little girl in a corded bodice she should be. Her parents were determined to milk the golden goose that had so unexpectedly fallen their way. Emmeline was commercially minded enough to appreciate this argument, young enough to kick and scream as a result.

She had failed to kick Auguste, so she looked around for someone else. Her fairies did not answer this need for they did not dare kick back. Where, oh where, would she find someone who would? Grumpily she changed into her fairy-queen costume, pouting anew at the straining bodice, and emerged in search of a worthy opponent. Fate was kind. She crept up and tapped Mariella on the behind with the point of her wand. The point was sharp and Mariella's costume was not thick.

'If you do that again, you little cow, I'll give you a good spanking.'

Little Emmeline was delighted, especially as she remembered the interesting scene she had overheard yesterday. 'You wouldn't dare.' Scorn dripped from every syllable.

'Wouldn't I? Better still, I'll get Fernando to do it.'

Little Emmeline grinned maliciously. 'I'll tell Miguel of you.'

'What about?' Mariella asked sharply.

'What I heard yesterday, that's what.'

Mariella relaxed a little, then panic began to set in. *Where* had she heard her? 'You didn't hear anything. It was your imagination,' she replied offhandedly.

This was a mistake, for she had played into Emmeline's hands. 'I'm going to tell Miguel about how you're leaving with Will Lamb at the end of the week.'

'Nonsense.' Mariella eyed her warily. This might be serious.

'*And* about something else.'

Worse. 'What?'

'You know what.'

Mariella wondered why this monster had not been

111

strangled at birth, or exposed on a hillside. 'I'll give you a sovereign if you won't tell. At the end of the week,' she added prudently.

'Don't want money.'

'There must be something you'd like.'

Emmeline considered. Imagination roved, hovered, centred. 'As a matter of fact, I want a red corset.'

'What?' Mariella giggled.

'You heard,' Emmeline snapped frostily.

'I'll get you a corset for tomorrow night,' Mariella agreed hastily, rapidly sizing the monster up physically and mentally.

'All right. Then I won't tell Miguel you-know-what.'

'You'd better not,' Mariella said viciously.

'I won't,' said Emmeline meekly. The fairies could have warned Mariella that Emmeline was never meek without a purpose. The purpose this time was that she hadn't promised not to tell anyone else.


'There is no need to stay, Mr Didier. I shall be quite all right.' And as Auguste showed no signs of moving, 'There is someone I have to see before the curtain rises.'

'Someone you trust?'

'Oh yes.' Will looked surprised. 'After all, Bill Terriss was killed on his way in to the theatre, not inside it.'

'But that does not mean to say someone might not plan to harm you inside the theatre,' Auguste pointed out baldly.

' "If it be not now it will be to come",' Will quoted softly. 'I will knock on Nettie's wall every five minutes. Will that make you happy, Mr Didier?'

'It is certainly better,' Auguste conceded, 'but I would like to—'

'There, you see?' Will cut across him firmly. 'Always a solution somewhere, even under the darkest bush.'

Defeated, Auguste went to report to Nettie, who nodded absently when he told her Will's plan.

'Is anything wrong, Miss Turner?' he asked hesitantly, noticing that she seemed preoccupied.

'Quite a lot, chum, but nothing you can do.' She sighed.

'I can listen,' he offered.

She glanced at him. 'That's good of you. Tomorrow, perhaps? What was it you were saying about Will?'

'He will knock on the wall every five minutes to let you know he's safe. He is expecting a visitor.'

'Daft old fool he is,' she said softly. 'Mariella, that's for sure. Anybody other than Will, and they'd want a quick curtain-raiser. Will just wants to hold her hand. She knows what she wants, that young lady. She's planning something with Will, I don't know what it is, but I don't like it. He's excited and worried at the same time. Still, I suppose there's no need to worry. She's not going to bump off the golden goose, is she? He's safe enough in that way. She'll guard his life like a coster his pennies.'

True enough, but his uneasiness did not evaporate. Lizzie must cope by herself. He would stay here, in the backstage area, watching Will's door. Though there were other more insidious ways of entry, it occurred to him. 'What about poison, Miss Turner? Could anyone harm Mr Lamb that way?'

She shook her head. 'He only takes water at a

performance, and I had some from his flask earlier on.'

'And his props?'

She thought for a moment. 'There's only the dagger, and he guards that like a baby. The stage manager comes for it before the performance starts, and takes it up to be flown.'

'And the windows?'

She snorted. 'Doubt if these windows have been opened since the coronation. Victoria's. Look at 'em.' He agreed she was right. They seemed welded shut by greasy dirt.

From the noise, the doors to the hall had opened and the rush for seats was beginning. The noise was not all good-humoured. A knock at the door, and Fernando filled the threshold, trousers and waistcoat donned over his leopardskin.

'Me front of house.'

'You do that, Fernando,' Nettie approved. 'It's going to be one of those nights,' she said as he went. 'He doubles as thrower-outer.'

'I must leave too, Nettie.' Auguste was uneasy. True, it was unlikely harm could come to Will in a dressing-room so politically situated, and with so little time to spare. But for the first time in his life, he almost regretted that he was a cook, as he turned back to his post to check preparations for the interval rush.

'My dear fellow,' Horace said, apparently pained, as he appeared in the wings to find Pickles gazing in terror at the curtain buckling with the weight of thrown missiles. All too shortly it would be drawn to reveal him.

'I'm merely offering to let you have the best position on the programme, and take this somewhat venturesome one myself.'

'Why are you so big-hearted all of a sudden?' snarled Pickles.

'I've explained. This is my last week. My timing of my turn at the Lyle cuts it extremely fine after my own turn here is over. I'm prepared to change places, that's all.'

'Like when you did me out of my place on the bill at the Ratcliffe Metropole.'

Brodie shrugged. 'The best man won in a straight race.'

'You set that chirruping mob on me. Ruined my career.'

'Last week I understood you to say Will Lamb had had that honour.'

At this affecting moment, Little Emmeline arrived sparkling in pink satin and sequins. She saw her opportunity. 'You'll be safe now, Mr Pickles. He's leaving.'

The two men broke off and gazed at her plump confident face.

Brodie cleared his throat. 'I shall merely be here for a few more days, Miss Emmeline,' he said agreeably, 'but Mr Pickles will be far from safe when I have departed. He will not have me to rescue the performance from disaster after his turn.'

'Not you,' Emmeline said impatiently, forestalling Pickles' outburst. 'Old Lamb, Mr Mutton himself.' She giggled at her joke.

'Push off, nipper,' Pickles told her rudely. 'Don't you think I bloody know Lamb's only here for a week?'

'He's going away for good,' Emmeline shrieked in temper. '*With* someone. A lady.'

'Who?' Brodie asked, interest captured.

'My lips are sealed,' Emmeline announced importantly. After all, she hadn't received her corset yet.

'Mariella?' Brodie demanded.

'Bet you he's got his eyes on Nettie, Horace,' Pickles exploded momentarily, overlooking his feud with Brodie. 'Bloody man ruined my career, now he ruins my life.' Tears of self-pity ran down his cheeks. 'Nettie,' he moaned. 'My Nettie.' He meant 'my allowance'.

'Why don't you stop it?' Brodie appeared amused.

'Stop it? How?'

'Put your foot down,' Brodie explained kindly. 'Insist on your husbandly rights and on keeping your allowance or you'll sue her for divorce, and drag both their names through the mud.'

Pickles gazed at Brodie. 'Horace, you're my friend. It's him, that Lamb, that's evil. I want you to know I'll not forget this, old mate.'

'Splendid,' murmured Brodie. 'Now, shall I go on or will you?'

Beyond the curtain the noise level was rising.

Apart from finding his assistant cook eating a mutton chop at a table rather than preparing to cook for others, all seemed to be in order, Auguste found.

'Oh, Mr D,' Lizzie shouted, pink with excitement. 'I put a touch of sage in the gravy, just like you said.'

'Did I?' His mind went blank, but if it pleased Lizzie . . . 'Splendid, *ma fille*. Perhaps tomorrow, rosemary.'

'When you've a moment, Auguste,' Egbert remarked somewhat caustically, 'not that I'd want to interfere with the course of true cuisine.'

'I thought, Egbert, you were growing interested in the art yourself.'

'I've resigned.'

Auguste sat down opposite Egbert, averting his eyes from the slapdash arrangement of cutlery and plates that was acceptable in the Old King Cole, despite his best endeavours to build Rome in a day.

'Shall I do yer an 'erring, Mr D?' Lizzie sang out.

'Thank you, no.' A little soup when he reached home, the *fricassée* perhaps, but nothing, *nothing* here. There was the *potage de Crécy* he had made yesterday when John was absent . . . A faint interest in food revived – but not in herrings. Perhaps one of his own pies, however. The faint interest grew stronger and he hurried to get one for himself. This, as he bit into it, *this* was what a mutton pie should taste like.

'We paid a visit to young Miguel's home today. Quite upset he was.' Egbert ploughed on with his chop.

'What did you find?'

'Not a thing. Professes himself a true follower of the Portuguese crown, but too busy working to have time for politics. Besides, he's British, he claims, now he has a British wife.'

'And the fakers Monsieur Higgins recommended?'

'Twitch was busy all the afternoon, but so far nothing. All regular customers – he had to tread carefully, you understand. The only special order was one by Sir Henry Irving. But it was a cross.'

'Somehow I don't see Sir Henry being involved in

stealing relics from Windsor Castle.'

'Very perspicacious of you, Auguste. He said he was playing Thomas à Becket, apparently. On the whole, my money's still on our Miguel. Sometimes, as I said, a chop is really a chop.' Egbert gazed irritably down at his plate with its unprepossessing remains. 'Who bought this meat? I reckon Edith's Mr Pinpole could do better.'

Smarting at this slur on his meat-purchasing abilities, Auguste hurried to his other post once more. Having refused to let his good friend Horace risk his own reputation, Pickles was in full voice on stage. So unfortunately was the audience; for once regulars and Shadwell Mob were of like mood. The Tumbling Twins, awaiting their turn, paled.

'Perhaps we should take our tights off?' Violet whispered hopefully but audibly to Marigold.

Auguste's immediate reaction was that even this drastic measure would have no effect tonight. It sounded bad out there.

'Would you like me to go on before you, ladies?' the Great Brodie inquired generously. 'I would suggest your asking Mr Lamb, but he, alas, is too overcome by love to be sensible to others' needs.'

'What *do* you mean, Horace?' the girls cried in unison with some excitement, his generous offer side-tracked for the moment.

'I have it on good authority that he is leaving with his loved one at the end of the week.' He looked at them archly. 'Is one of you the happy lady, I wonder?'

By the look on their faces it was not.

'I am happy to take your turn, ladies, if it would assist you,' he hastily reverted to his first subject.

'Yes, please, Horace,' Marigold accepted coolly.

'No need, no need. I am here to help.'

Evangeline, smug in bright green silk, bore down upon them. All three regarded her with dismay. 'I have told the accompanist at the piano I shall render "The Lost Chord". That will silence the ruffians.'

'Not for long,' Brodie muttered, as Pickles escaped his stage torment, cast a look of hatred at Horace, remembered he was his friend, and managed a weak grin.

'I shall go.' Evangeline prepared to sally forth.

'By George, you shall not, madam.' Horace's words might have had no effect, did not the twins' forceful pinioning of her arms succeed in persuading her, not in the interests of the Old King Cole, but in the hope there would still be an audience of sorts to perform to once they ventured forth themselves.

Sheer surprise stopped the Shadwell Mob. Horace strode on and tipped his top hat nonchalantly in their direction. No one had informed the stage manager that the Tumbling Twins announced on the board was turning into a lion *comique*. The belated strains of 'Don't Wait Up' hastily switched from the *Mikado*'s 'Three Little Girls from School Are We', temporarily appeased the mob. Unfortunately it mystified, then enraged Miguel, who arrived panic-stricken in the wings. He clutched Evangeline. 'I have missed my turn,' he moaned. 'Never, never before.'

'No, you haven't.' Evangeline rather enjoyed being closely clutched by a young man of such romantic ancestry. 'Horace changed places with the twins.'

'Then I'm running *late*.' He gazed at her, hypnotised.

119

'How *dare* he? He has upset everything.' Miguel's evening had been carefully timed, and it did not allow for *this*. Everything would have to be planned again.

'It is *his* fault,' hissed the lady, glaring at the stage. 'He has come between me and my dearest Will. Will will not hear me sing for him now. He will already have left the theatre before my turn.'

'Why should he want to listen to your caterwauling?' Mariella smirked, fresh from her delivery of one red corset to that repulsive child, and joining the group in the wings.

Marigold giggled, earning a reproachful look from Evangeline. 'Will likes younger ladies, doesn't he, Violet?'

Miguel looked darkly from Violet to Mariella, who seemed to be concentrating on her fingernails. 'Which lady in particular?' he muttered.

'Me,' said Evangeline, Violet and Marigold in unison. Mariella laughed outright.

Auguste, one eye on the stage manager emerging from Will's room with the precious dagger, wondered how a simple man of forty-odd like Will Lamb could attract such feminine devotion. Yet how far did Will's simplicity go, Auguste wondered? He was rich by his own talents, he wrote his own songs, he sold the publishing rights, largely organised his own business affairs, save for a booking agent. He remained an enigma enclosed in a circle of admirers. As he went to knock on Will's door, the Great Brodie strode offstage into the wings, and the twins, emboldened by his success, insisted on adhering to the original programme order, despite Miguel's fury.

'Do come in, Mr Didier,' Will said, as Auguste opened the door. 'I am still alive, as you see.'

Alive yes, but he looked ill. He was pale, his eyes despondent, and he was slumped in his chair, not yet made up.

'Are you feeling ill, Mr Lamb? Let me fetch you some tea, camomile perhaps.'

'No, thank you, Mr Didier.' He hesitated. 'Perhaps a dose of Nettie might help.'

Nettie was with him in a moment after Auguste's summons. She shut the door politely but firmly on Auguste. 'Some things,' she said, 'are better done by a woman. Even when she's not a chef.'

Little Emmeline twirled round, hugging her parcel. Where should she hide it till tonight so no one found it? Suddenly she had a brilliant idea. Who was on stage now? She could hide it, and be back ready for her turn. It would fit in very neatly. She pranced out of the dressing room gleefully, expecting to hear the Great Brodie on stage. Instead, to her surprise, Miguel was throwing his silly plates around, and only Fernando was watching in the wings. That meant Will was still in his dressing-room and she would have to talk to Fernando. She was a little wary of Fernando. There had been one occasion when she had removed his leopardskin from the gentlemen's dressing-room and the resounding thwack when he discovered it adorning one of Mariella's dogs had lingered for a long time. She had complained to her father, but the result had been disappointing. He had been oddly unwilling to tell Fernando what he thought of him. Fortunately Miguel came offstage at that moment, colliding with Dolly who had belatedly heard the news of the change of order. Another brilliant idea struck her: with her booty clutched in her arms, she could make further capital out of her secret.

'Hallo, Miguel,' she smirked. 'I know something you don't know.'

'I am sure you do.' He tried to smile, but it came out as a grimace. He was still smarting over the ruin of all his careful planning.

'About Will Lamb,' she added temptingly. This time she succeeded in gaining his attention. 'He's going away with a lady at the end of the week.'

A moment's dead silence. 'Mrs Turner?' inquired Miguel.

'No. And far, far away,' she emphasised. 'And she has red hair.'

'You are mistaken, I think,' Miguel said pleasantly.

Fernando was taking her seriously. He took a plod onwards, and she retreated involuntarily as she saw the expression on his face. 'Red?' he repeated heavily.

'It's a secret,' Emmeline said, delighted with the result of her bait.

'Mariella!' Fernando grunted.

'Nonsense!' There was fear in Miguel's face, and he dropped the juggling balls. One rolled back on to the stage to the alarm of poor Dolly.

Emmeline grinned happily, as Miguel dived after the ones that were retrievable. 'And there's another secret too,' she added.

'What is that, Little Emmeline?' Miguel hissed.

'I don't know,' she said truthfully, but unconvincingly.

'I am sure you do, my little one. Something to do with the lady and Mr Lamb, perhaps?'

'Yes.'

'She was hiding something?'

'Perhaps.' Emmeline perceived she was going too fast too quickly.

Fernando was still way back in the conversation. 'Mariella is leaving with Will Lamb?'

'No.' Miguel nimbly leapt between the girl and the advancing strong man. 'It's someone else, isn't it, Emmeline?'

'Yes,' she cried gratefully, having seen Fernando's expression.

Fernando stopped and thought this out. 'I will ask him.' He lumbered towards the dressing-room.

'And there's nothing else to tell me, dear Emmeline?' Miguel's voice was silky sweet.

'There may be,' Emmeline said brightly, regaining confidence, 'but I don't remember it now.'

'I could give you a present.'

More corsets? No, what did she want? Emmeline thought quickly. 'I'll let you know, Mr Gomez,' she promised grandly.

Fernando believed in the quickest solution for any problem. The dressing-room door was thrown open with a crash.

'Good evening, Fernando.' Will greeted him pleasantly, but with an effort, and Auguste, sensing trouble, edged forward.

'You, Mariella,' Fernando said. 'True you go?'

Will clung to the image of Mariella. She was the only

good thing in his life, his hope, his salvation. 'Yes,' he replied, sure Fernando would share his joy. 'Isn't that nice? I hope Miguel won't mind.'

Fernando did not seem to agree it was nice. He turned, and blindly strode out again as Dolly ran offstage. He was intent on strangling the entire Shadwell Mob from the look on his face, Auguste thought, alarmed. From now on he would not leave Will's side.

Will too seemed nervous. Auguste looked at the trembling hands and the anxious eyes, and wondered how troubled his mind was. Enough to push him over the brink? He seemed perilously close.

'I have to go on stage,' Will explained carefully. 'They want me. I can hear them.'

What he could hear was in fact the Shadwell Mob wreaking its fury on Fernando in order to earn a respite while Will was on.

Will stopped at the door, and clung to it for support. 'I suppose I shall have to see my solicitor,' he said forlornly and inconsequentially. He shook his head in a kind of daze, until the pull of the stage overtook him and he slipped into character.

Auguste accompanied him into the wings, and found not only Emmeline but, surprisingly, Miguel there watching. Emmeline greeted him enthusiastically. She had decided she liked Auguste. When she wore her new corset he would stop thinking of her as a little girl. She'd wear a long dress, thin stockings, and she'd drop the Little. Just Emmeline and her fairies. Then he'd love her. And she would scorn him, just like Mariella did to men who liked her. Meanwhile she nestled up to him. Auguste promptly decided to go through to one of the boxes to get a better view of the stage. There was nothing he could to do protect Will there, and he was worrying unnecessarily about that dagger. It had been in the stage manager's, then the flymen's care since the beginning of the performance. In the box he found Nettie who greeted him abstractedly, eyes fixed on the stage. She too looked worried.

On stage, Will's preoccupations dropped away, as he launched into patter. 'Romeo, I ask you, what a name. He killed Tybalt, you know. With a dagger. Shakespeare was like that. Saved on props. Mean, I call it. Same dagger as in that Scottish play. Is this a dagger that I see before me? Now, you all know what a Scottish play is, I'm sure. Of course. It's a tale about playing bagpipes. Bonnie Prince Macbeth goes over the sea to Skye. Is this his dagger? Now I ask you, why doesn't the fellow *know*? Overrated is Shakespeare. Will Shakespeare – that's my name too. Not the Shakespeare. Lamb. Will Lamb. Lamb's tales from Shakespeare.

'There's that dagger again. I can see it, *you* can see it. Why can't this fellow Macbeth? I mean, a playwright has to be realistic, or he gets nowhere. But what else can you expect from a dead author? They're not around to grumble at.'

Despite himself, Auguste found himself laughing with the audience. The Mob suspended animosity for the duration of Will's act, and were noisily guffawing with a different kind of laughter in their own testament to Will, as the dagger danced merrily on the end of its string.

Auguste watched Will's antics until he could not see for tears running from his eyes. He drew out his handkerchief, impatient not to miss anything. Through the mist of his eyes, he saw Will Lamb's lunge towards the dagger, saw him miss it. Will looked wildly round at the audience, his hand outflung and drawn back again. He turned his back in high disdain: 'Who wants a silly old dagger anyway?' The dagger promptly danced above his head, retreated bashfully once more as Will went to grasp it, then dropped to the floor, hovering there, just as Will stumbled, tripped, and fell upon it.

The applause rang out, but Will did not get up to receive it. Auguste registered first the silence, the moment's stillness when there should be the beginnings of movement. Did he shout then, or not until he saw the red splash, realised the curious curve of Will's body? His shout brought footsteps running from the wings, and even as he himself jumped up, the curtain fell. With leaden feet, as in a dream, he rushed backstage followed by Nettie. Someone called for a doctor, even as Auguste, pushing onlookers away, stared down at Miguel crouched over the body. Miguel looked up at him. 'I fear he is dead.'

But the lips moved, and Miguel dropped his head to listen, blocking Auguste's view. By the time he too was on his knees, Will Lamb was indeed dead, and only Miguel could have heard his last words.

# Chapter Five

Someone screamed. The sound died in the appalled silence.

Behind the hastily dropped curtain even the Shadwell Mob were quiet, and the audience shifted restlessly at this abrupt change of mood, still not convinced that the clown would not get up to take his bow. By the body, Auguste slowly rose to his feet, pulling Miguel after him. There was no doubt in his mind now. Will Lamb was dead. Nettie, kept back with the others, pulled herself free, and ran to them. He could hear her stage coster costume rustling. She looked down expressionlessly at the body of her friend, and then at Auguste.

'The dagger?'

'Yes.'

'But it couldn't be.' The stage manager, spearheading his small band of four backstage staff, hurried to defend his own. 'It was nothing to do with us,' he gabbled wildly.

'Calm yourself, monsieur,' Auguste said gently. 'You must talk to the police.' Egbert would be here soon enough, the news would have reached him by now.

These words may have calmed the stage manager, but they had the opposite effect on Percy Jowitt whose paper-white face peered over Nettie's shoulder. 'Police? But it must have been an accident – the blade must have stuck, not retreated back into the sheath?' There was desperate appeal in his eyes, but no one reassured him. Least of all Egbert Rose, now hurrying from the wings towards the group.

'This is not your department, Inspector,' Percy moaned. 'We are beyond such matters as debt collection, I fear.'

Rose ignored him. 'Off the stage please, everyone but Mr Didier.' It was a vain hope as more of the Old King Cole company arrived led by Evangeline, rushing in importantly.

'My husband wishes to know what is hap— he's still there! Oh . . .' The sight of Will's motionless body sent her into a scream that hit the top G more effectively than her rendering of 'Marble Halls'. Emmeline, all her sobbing fairies, the twins and Fernando peered curiously at the body. The fairies and the twins promptly burst into tears, but Emmeline and Fernando kept silent. Apart from them, standing by herself, was Nettie, her body rigid, her face expressionless – or so Auguste thought until he caught her eye by chance and saw there just for a second the private woman, never suspected on stage, but who gave her the strength to fight the world, and who was grieving for a beloved friend.

'Do you have a telephone here?' Egbert demanded of Jowitt.

'I'm not sure.'

'You're not *sure*?'

'Bailiffs, you know.' Jowitt trembled. 'A misunderstanding over payment. So unfair.'

'Then let's find out. Now, Mr Didier, stay here, if you please. Everyone else into the dressing-rooms, please. Miss Turner, Mr Jowitt, see to it, will you?'

Nettie said nothing, but instantly set about obeying, with only Emmeline resisting.

'Why?' She stuck her hands truculently on her plump hips.

'Because, miss, I'll arrest you if you don't.'

'You're only a cook.'

Egbert gazed at her, nonplussed. 'I'm a Chief Inspector of Scotland Yard.' His tone of voice did not invite contradiction.

'What have you been doing here, then?' There was hostility in Evangeline's voice, and in the faces of all around.

'Yard business.' Not theirs, he implied. 'This is going to be part of it.' He looked quietly down at Will's body.

Was it part of it? Auguste was left with the softly hissing gas lights, and the hunched horror at his feet. There was nothing to connect the Navigator's cross with Will's death, yet two major but independent crimes in one week both connected with the Old King Cole seemed unlikely. But then unlikely things did occur. Someone had wished Will dead, and despite efforts to keep him away, that someone had succeeded. The life of a generous, talented man had been snuffed out, and he, Auguste Didier, had been unable to prevent it. In the last resort, he tried to reason, murder would always find its way to its victim, if it were determined enough. No obstacle put in its way could ultimately prevent it. But here, alone, he wept that it should be so.

'I'm letting the audience go home, Auguste.' Egbert was quickly back. 'Just as soon as Grey's men get here. They can take names and addresses – if those ruffians out there part with them – but I can't see I'm justified in holding the whole audience.' He grinned slightly. 'I told old Jowitt they ought to have their money back. He's not too keen on the idea.'

'Grey?'

'Stepney Division. Stitch is on his way too.'

'Good.'

Egbert raised an eyebrow. 'Get you a badge, shall I? KOT? Keen on Twitch?'

'Inspector Stitch can be an asset,' Auguste replied with dignity. 'For certain tasks,' he qualified.

'Mr Rose, this geezer says he wants to see yer.' Lizzie, eyes shining, hurried across the stage, dragging a youth with a shock of red curls underneath his ancient cap. She gave him a friendly dig in the ribs with her elbow. He grinned, then his eyes widened, and he tore off his cap as he looked down at the floor of the stage. Lizzie looked down too. 'Oo-er! He's dead,' she whispered.

Auguste turned to her, but the youth forestalled her, putting his arm round her waist.

'It's Mr Lamb. I never realised,' she wailed. 'How'd he do that, poor old blighter? Git that arm orf.'

It was removed.

'I regret it looks as if someone did it for him, Lizzie.'

'What do you want, lad?' Egbert asked impatiently.

'Laundry.'

Egbert's eyes sharpened. 'Ma Bisley?'

'Yus. I'm Joe. Here.' He handed over a small bag.

Egbert Rose eyed him thoughtfully. 'Right, Joe.' He frogmarched him to the wings. 'See that door?' He pointed to Will's dressing-room. 'Stand guard over it. No one goes in, *no one*.'

'Yessir.' Joe glanced back. 'Tomorrow, miss?' he whispered mysteriously to Lizzie.

Lizzie tossed her slight figure in something that in another might have been coquettishly. 'After I done the kippers.'

'Back to the kitchen, Lizzie,' Auguste commanded gently. 'This is no place for you.'

She hesitated. 'I could help yer find 'im.'

'Who?'

'The geezer wot dun this. Ain't right.'

'It might have been an accident, Lizzie.'

'Garn. That's why you're 'ere, ain't it? I could tell you wasn't a cook.'

Auguste blenched. 'Indeed?'

'Never made a mutton pie in yer life. I tasted one of them you did today. Mind you, you got the makings.'

'Off!' Egbert interposed, seeing Auguste struggling for words.

Lizzie saluted smartly – and obeyed.

Rose gave all his attention hastily to Ma Bisley's bag. It contained no laundry, merely a sketch. A sketch of a pin man – with what appeared to be a sword of Damocles hanging perilously over his head.

The dressing-rooms were oddly quiet, when Auguste, at Egbert's bidding, went to check the company was still assembled there. In the women's room fairies sat disconsolately on the floor, Mariella perched on a table, Nettie sat in state like a gaoler at the door, and Dolly sobbed quietly in one corner with Evangeline's arm round her. The twins forlornly held hands. The men's dressing-room contained Miguel, who stood, arms crossed, while Fernando watched him with a puzzled expression. Orsini and Clarence Bishop had arrived early for their second-half appearances, and clearly wished they hadn't. It was too early for Max to have arrived. The stage manager and his gallant band of helpers stayed apart from the performers, as unwritten etiquette required.

'Mr Brodie and Mr Pickles?' Auguste asked Jowitt.

'Already left,' Percy said uninterestedly. 'Mr Pickles has an engagement at the Ratcliffe Metropole and Mr Brodie at the Lyle.'

Not helpful, Auguste reasoned. While those that appeared in the second half could reasonably be exonerated from having tampered with the dagger, those in the first half most certainly could not – unless the tampering had taken place last night.

Outside, he could hear the arrival of new voices, voices attached to heavy boots, what's more. He hurried out, to see whether it was Grey's men or Twitch's. It turned out to be both.

Twitch's face fell at this double blow after encountering Grey in the street outside. 'Evening, Mr Didier,' he said viciously. This French chap was always turning up on his patch. The man with him, who fixed Auguste with a baleful eye, must be Inspector Grey, Auguste realised, wondering why he was ignoring him; then he realised that with his cook's apron he was probably being taken for a part of a music-hall turn.

'Evening, Grey,' Rose greeted him, as Auguste led them through to the stage. 'Another body for you, and this one's no casual. I take it you've no objection to my taking over? Jointly, of course.'

Objections Grey had in plenty at seeing the crown of glory so expertly whisked away. He opened his mouth to express them.

'Be a pity if it turned out to be linked to that other matter,' Rose continued. 'The Palace would not be happy with any of us.'

Grey closed his mouth again. The Palace was one thing, but the Section Superintendent, who would undoubtedly be on the side of Majesty, was quite another.

Auguste quietly returned to the dressing-rooms after a word with Joe, still guarding Will's dressing-room as though the whole of the Shadwell Mob armed with knobkerries were about to batter it down. The Stepney and Scotland Yard men were taking over now. He had officially nothing to do. Doctors and photographers would be hard at work, while Rose and Grey conferred. What he *could* do was ask that burning question that remained still to be answered. He made his way to the dressing-rooms but he was not to be allowed to ask it, for Rose noticed his absence.

'Mr Didier,' he yelled.

Auguste rushed guiltily back.

'I want the stage manager and flymen now.'

Auguste flew back to the dressing-room to summon

them, whence three men, the stage manager and two
flymen, emerged as if expecting instant execution.

'Stop that!' barked Rose as the doctor appeared to be
about to remove the dagger.

Grey looked alert. 'Fingerprints?'

'Mine will be on it,' bleated the stage manager and
underlings almost in unison. The *Strand Magazine* had
made everyone aware of the infinite possibilities of
medical scientific evidence.

Will now lay face upwards, eyes staring in reproach at
his would-be protector, or so it seemed to Auguste.
Less than an hour earlier he had been helplessly
laughing at the man whose corpse now lay before
him. Where were those laughs now? He jerked himself
back to practical matters. There was the only way to help
Will now.

'This dagger.' Egbert held the dagger, now wrapped
in a handkerchief, by its handle, and detached from its
two wires. 'Show me how it works.'

The stage manager approached nervously. 'I didn't
do it.'

'Do what?'

'Do him in.'

'Then you've nothing to worry about, have you?
Except helping me,' Rose said firmly.

Thus emboldened, the stage manager set out to be
helpful. 'Mr Lamb insisted on looking after this dagger
himself. He took it home at night; it was his lucky
dagger, he said –' he avoided looking down at the corpse
'– and brought it back the next day. He would keep it in
the dressing-room, he told me, and I could call for it
just before the performance started.'

'You didn't this evening,' Auguste pointed out. 'I saw you collect it during one of the turns.'

'He told me he'd be busy,' gabbled the stage manager, 'and I could collect it after the curtain was up. So I did,' he finished defiantly.

'Did you check the mechanism was working correctly?'

The stage manager hesitated, caught out. 'There was no need, was there? Mr Lamb always checked it himself, so he told me.'

'Then what happened to it?'

'Len here fixes it straightaway on its wires.'

Len shrank back. 'Yes, I did. But it were Bill here looks after it during the show.'

Rose studied the third man, who was trying hard to look invisible.

'Bill does odd jobs like this while he's up on the bridge, don't you, Bill?'

'It were an accident,' Bill offered hopefully. 'These things happen.'

'They do, but not generally in the very week someone is *expecting* to be murdered.' Carefully Rose detached the dagger from the wires to which it was hooked at either end.

'Murder? In the Old King Cole?' the stage manager gasped. He made the hall sound like a convent school. 'He must have been imagining things.'

'Apparently not.' Rose looked down at the corpse. 'Look at this.' He partly unwrapped the dagger gingerly. 'The blade's been stuck, so it doesn't retreat. Glue, probably.'

'But Mr Lamb checked it,' Bill wailed.

'Does it have a sheath?' The three men looked at each other. 'Well, does it?' Rose repeated sharply.

'Yes. I take the sheath off and stick it in the flies, till the interval.' The flyman's voice trembled.

'So you wouldn't notice anything odd unless you peered at the dagger closely on the bridge up there?' Auguste said.

'No,' agreed the stage manager, weak with relief at the intervention from this unlikely source.

'It's dark up there. I don't notice nothing.' Bill's voice rose to a squeak.

'I suppose I'd better take a look.' Rose sounded unenthusiastic, and Auguste remembered he had been equally unenthusiastic about climbing up to the flies when, in their early acquaintance, murder had stalked the Galaxy musical comedy theatre in the Strand, where his dear Maisie had been a chorus girl.

Nervously Len and Bill scuttled into the wings, where a narrow staircase led up to the lower flies, roughly parallel with the upper floor which Auguste had explored in his search for the raven. Here there were ropes, cables, chairs, capstans and the Old King Cole's entire sound-effects department, it seemed – one sheet of copper for making thunder. A ladder led up to the higher range of flies, Len and Bill's domain. Here, above the battens, intense heat made the air a cauldron, and gave them a worm's eye view of the audience and of the stage beneath; it was from the bridge crossing the stage, Bill explained, that Will's dagger had been controlled. Sandwiching Egbert between Bill and Len, Auguste brought up the rear, reminding himself that he had survived the Galaxy's far higher, hotter upper levels. This, he instructed himself, was simple in comparison.

'Here!' Len reached out to them from the flies. 'This is the sheath.'

'You carry it down,' Egbert said thickly to Auguste. Then to Bill: 'You controlled the dagger on its wires, did you?'

'Yes. The wires are attached to this board, see?' Bill leaned over so far that even Auguste felt sick. 'Mr Lamb showed me how – it's quite easy, provided you watch 'im. Just the end bit—' He broke off, looking at them with frightened face. 'He said, soon as you see me stumble, jerk the wire and up it'll come. It did,' he added forlornly. 'The handle's weighted, you see.'

'Even so, you'd think the weight of his body would knock it sideways,' Auguste commented, puzzled.

'Sometimes it used to, he told me; it didn't matter much unless he knocked it too far and ruined the sketch, so he—' he stopped.

'He what?' asked Auguste gently.

'He used to fall so the audience couldn't see him grabbing the dagger with the hand furthest from them, and steadying it, as he fell over it.'

They stared down at the stage. The corpse had gone now, but in their imagination the scene was only too vivid. The hand reaching out – to ensure his own death.

'Hell's bells, I'm going to puke,' Bill choked.

Hastily Auguste clambered down with Egbert following in rapid pursuit. From sounds up above, Bill appeared to have fulfilled his prophecy.

Percy Jowitt watched the remains of his hopes for the rescue of the Old King Cole vanishing on a stretcher from the stage door. His task as guardian of the men's dressing-room had now been taken over by a policeman and he was free to ponder, wringing his hands like Lady Macbeth, over his fate.

'When that body gets to the mortuary,' Rose remarked to Grey as he regained terra firma with relief, 'we're going to have every newspaper in town descending on us.' He pondered on whether this was help or hindrance to what had been and might still be his main inquiry.

Jowitt, overhearing, brightened amidst his gloom, as the commercial prospects for the Old King Cole dramatically improved. Until he remembered the unfortunate fact that he had a major gap in his cast. Suppose Miss Turner too withdrew her services – not, he hoped, in the same way as Will, but the result would be the same? He clutched Auguste's arm, seeing him as his saviour from bailiffs and all other ills that might affect his beloved theatre. 'I've had to give back the box-office money for tonight. I face ruin, Mr Didier, now Mr Lamb has deserted me.'

'Percy, can't you give a thought to poor old Will for once?' Nettie cried, irritated. She had had enough of being cooped up with Evangeline Yapp, and had come to see for herself what was going on. Her formidable personality had dismissed a mere constable without problem. 'He did his best for you out of the kindness of his heart, and all you can think about it is your blooming theatre.'

'Yes, yes, you are right, Nettie,' Jowitt admitted eagerly. 'I am ungrateful. But you will continue the week here, will you not, Nettie?'

Nettie managed to laugh at that. 'You, Percy, are an old reprobate. Yes, if the police let us carry on.'

'Thank you,' Jowitt said humbly.

'But not for your sake,' she continued.

'Naturally not,' he agreed hastily. 'For your public's.'

'No. For Will's. I'm going to make sure whoever did this gets what they deserve, and I'm staying around here till they get it.'

'What the bloomin' heck's going on?' Max Hill came in on the late side for his second-half turn, and regarded them in astonishment. 'Been an accident, 'as there, Nettie? Saw a body being loaded.'

'Not an accident, Max. A murder.'

''Ere? Cripes. Who?'

'Will.'

He stared at her, his face turning pale. 'Will?' he repeated stupidly. '*Murdered*? Are you sure?'

She shrugged. 'Ask the Chief there.' She nodded towards Rose.

'True, Chief?'

'Looks like it. Where have you been?'

'Having a drink. I come here for my turn and walk into this lot.' A quaver in his voice belied his bravado. 'This what you were down here for, then?'

'No.' Rose firmly ushered Max and Nettie towards their fellow artistes. 'Run through the order of those turns, Auguste.' Rose commandeered Nettie's dressing-room in preference to Percy's office; he wasn't going to budge too far from the dressing-rooms.

'There was a change tonight. Usually Our Pickles is first, then the Tumbling Twins, followed by Miguel Gomez—'

'He was first to reach the body, wasn't he?'

'Yes. Before me. And I think Will may have said something before he died which I couldn't hear.'

'Did he indeed? Who's after him?'

'Usually the Great Brodie, lion *comique*, Dolly Dadd, the country girl singer, then Fernando the strong man, followed by Will Lamb and then Little Emmeline. But tonight Pickles went on first, and then Brodie. The twins followed him, and Gomez had to wait till they'd finished.'

'Why the change?'

'I think because the audience was rowdy, and Brodie had the best chance of silencing them.'

'He still here?'

'No, he and Pickles have left for engagements in other halls. They sometimes have three or four engagements an evening.'

'We'll get them back.'

Auguste's heart sank. It was going to be a long night. 'Is that necessary, Egbert?'

Rose regarded him in some amazement. 'Assuming Lamb didn't bung up his own dagger with glue, someone did it for him. Perhaps his landlady did, but being practical, someone went to his dressing-room and did it here. It wouldn't take long, even if Lamb were there, provided his attention was distracted for a minute or two.'

'I saw all those that went there after the curtain rose,' Auguste told him.

'And before?'

'There was half an hour or so before the performance started, when I returned to the kitchens.'

'More important than guarding Lamb, was it?'

'You do me an injustice, Egbert.' Auguste was hurt. 'Will told me he was expecting a visitor, and did not want me present. He promised to bang on the wall for Miss Turner next door to reassure her he was all right. Every five minutes. And he *did*.'

Egbert had the grace to blush. 'My apologies, Auguste. Don't know what's got into me. It's always the same in these cases where royalty's hovering over you.'

'So you believe Will's death is connected?'

'I do. I know you think otherwise, but I don't like coincidences. And that's why I'm going to talk to Miguel Gomez first.' He paused. 'Want to stay?'

Auguste brightened, relieved he was not being banished.

Miguel arrived, looking extremely sulky.

'We meet again, Mr Gomez,' Rose said cheerfully with a remarkable *volte face* from a few minutes before. 'Now perhaps you'll tell me what you were still doing in the theatre. You'd finished your turn. Don't you have another theatre to go on to?'

'Yes, but tonight I stay *here*.'

'Why's that? What was so special about tonight?'

'It is Mariella's birthday. I wish to stay with her.'

'Very conjugal of you, Mr Gomez, I'm sure. So why were you standing in the wings and not with her?'

'I wanted to see Will Lamb's performance,' he said disarmingly. 'He is – was, alas – a great artiste.'

'Afraid he'd found out something about you?' Rose asked gently. 'About your outside activities, perhaps?'

'No,' shouted Miguel. 'This is persecution. First you come to my house, you search it. Now you want to blame murder on me. No, no, *no*. I liked dear Will.'

'Although he was in love with your wife?' Auguste inquired.

'Mere gossip.'

'What was it he said to you before he died?'

'Nothing!'

'Mr Didier saw Mr Lamb say something.'

'Nothing of importance,' Miguel amended sullenly.

'We'll be the judge of that,' Egbert said firmly.

'It was silly. He just said "ghost".' He looked from one to the other triumphantly. 'You see, it was nothing.'

'No, not nothing,' Auguste said. 'I told you, Inspector, that Will believed that the ghost of William Terriss was haunting him; it was one of the reasons he believed that his life was threatened.'

'By the *ghost*?'

'He thought it had come to warn him.'

'All right, Mr Gomez, you can go – for the moment,' Egbert told him, to his visible relief.

'Do *you* believe in ghosts, Auguste?' he asked after Miguel had departed.

'*Will* did. That is the point. With many people such a ghost would have had a very practical explanation, but Will was so finely balanced between this world and his own that I think perhaps he might indeed have believed there was a presence.'

'Or seen a reality and deduced a ghost?'

'It is possible. Remember the raven, however.'

'Coincidence.'

'And the warning letters?'

'Ghosts don't write letters.'

'Would-be murderers might.'

'You think the same person that killed him also tried to warn him off?'

'If so, it follows that it was not that someone did not

want Will Lamb alive at all, but that someone did not want him alive and *here*.'

'Back to Miguel, then. You said Will was in love with his red-headed wife.'

'That is true, but Will's idea of love is not perhaps every man's. Miguel must have realised that, surely.'

'Nothing physical, you mean?'

'I would think not.'

'Jealous men don't think.'

There was a knock on the door but it was thrust open before Auguste could reach it. Inspector Grey glanced at him, but otherwise ignored him.

'Ah, Grey, this is Mr Didier, helping me on this case.'

Auguste received a reluctant nod. He didn't mind. In the course of the last few years he'd met a lot of Grey's men, so busy climbing their ladder they never bothered to choose the best position.

'Come and look at this.' There was pride in Grey's voice, as he threw open the door of Will's dressing-room.

Rose whistled. 'Your men been making a mess of things, have they?'

The room's contents were chaotically strewn around; greasepaint, costumes, the few personal belongings, lay in heaps where they had been randomly thrown.

'Not my men,' Grey retorted with dignity. 'This was done when we arrived. *Your* chap, perhaps.'

'Joe?' Egbert remembered the red-headed lad. 'I doubt it. This was done earlier. Somebody wanted something badly.'

'Not so badly, in fact.' Grey announced his coup. 'Look at this.' He went to the costume chest, now half emptied of its contents. He plucked out an old stove hat and thrust it beneath their noses. Inside was a roughly packed brown-paper parcel. 'That's how we found it,' Grey said smugly. 'Now look what's in it.' He took the parcel and unwrapped it. There, in his large hands, was a silver cross, with dark red stones set around the ivory body of Christ.

'Here of all places,' said Rose slowly.

'Will wouldn't have had anything to do with this,' exclaimed Auguste.

'Perhaps he forgot to mention it to you, Mr Didier,' Grey gloated in his triumph.

Perhaps, but Auguste liked things to make sense, and this did not. 'Surely Will could not be involved in pretending to be a Portuguese ambassador, in order to defraud His Majesty out of this relic,' he exploded.

'He *is* involved,' Grey said shortly. 'Look at this.'

'A plant,' said Auguste desperately.

Grey ignored him. 'He was being blackmailed, you see.'

'You deduce that, do you? Over what?' asked Rose. 'A woman?'

'No. His tastes lay in other directions. He had some rather embarrassing items tucked away. Queer sort of cove, wasn't he? One of them cross-dressers.'

'You're pulling my leg, Grey.'

'Look, sir.' Grey was greatly injured. He never pulled legs. He took out a paper bag from the chest where the cross had been found. Inside was an object of female clothing. 'His size, wouldn't you say?'

It was a red silk corset.

'I'm going to enjoy reporting this to the Palace,' Egbert

Rose said in satisfaction after Grey had gone.

'Will's odd taste in clothing?' Auguste was still puzzled.

Egbert fixed him with a withering look. 'No,' he explained patiently. '*This*. The cross. Remember?' He wrapped the paper round it lovingly. 'I'm going to enjoy returning it. Perhaps I'll get on to Special Branch right away.' Somewhat cheered, he went to Jowitt's office to carry out this pleasant mission.

Nettie had had enough of playing wardress, and had no hesitation in informing the policeman outside the dressing-room of the fact. She strode over to Auguste who had been about to seize the opportunity to see what might be happening in 'his' kitchens.

'What's happening?' she demanded.

What could he say? 'The police will find whoever did it, Miss Turner.'

She brushed aside this placebo. 'Don't call me that. I'm Nettie. We're on the same side.'

'Even though I failed to protect him?' Auguste asked quietly. It had been preying on his mind.

'No more than I did, letting him come here. It was *his* choice, and *his* decision to come, remember. We're human beings, not some kind of magic genie leaping out of a lamp to save him.' She paused. 'And I've been thinking. It must have been when you went back to the kitchens that the dagger was messed around with. That was what happened, wasn't it?'

'Yes. It might have been accident, they can't know for sure yet.'

'No accident. *We* know that. Will banged on the wall

every five minutes, just like he said. But that doesn't mean someone wasn't playing around with the dagger while he was doing it.'

'Did he tell you who his visitor was, when you went in to see him later?'

'No. He was upset about something though. I asked him to cough up, but he wouldn't. That was unlike Will.'

'And you didn't hear them through the wall?'

'No. Only voices.'

'Male or female?'

'I think one of each, but, as I said, I wasn't concentrating on that. I had a visitor too. The woman might have been the Portuguese tart.'

'Mariella Gomez?'

'Correct, Mr Didier. It was her got poor old Will here in the first place.'

'Not Mr Jowitt?'

'I don't know whose idea it was, but I do know it was that Jezebel who persuaded him. Will told me she'd come to see him.'

She remembered Harry had boasted that it had been his idea to get Will back at the Old King Cole. She grimaced. That's who her visitor had been, and it had not been pleasant. Threats, whines, and more threats. And not just against her, she recalled uneasily. Still, Harry wasn't so daft as really to be jealous of Will, was he? He must know how keen Will was on Mariella. Just what had Harry been playing at? It wasn't in Mariella's interest to kill Will, but Harry – if he was crazy enough – just might have thought it in his.

Violet and Marigold sniffled inelegantly into

handkerchiefs. 'Now we've missed our turn at the Shadwell Grand,' Violet sobbed. 'We'll be blacklisted. What's going to become of us now Will's gone?'

'How does that affect you?' Egbert Rose asked mildly.

'He was our *friend*,' they cried in unison.

'Enough of a friend for you to pop in and see him before the performance tonight?'

They regarded him in astonishment. '*That* was last night. Mr Didier was there.'

Egbert lifted an eyebrow at Auguste, who nodded.

'Did you notice where he kept the dagger while you were there?'

'No,' very firmly. 'Anyway, why should we want to kill darling Will? He was going to help us. My sister is expecting a little foreigner,' Violet added in hushed tones.

'Gomez?' asked Rose.

'A baby,' Violet explained impatiently.

'And Will was the father?'

'Oh no!' Marigold looked horrified. 'But he was going to give us money to keep us all, and get Violet a turn at the Tivoli and the Alhambra and the—'

'Might I ask who is the father, then?' Rose cut in. You never knew, it might be relevant.

'One might not,' Marigold replied tartly.

Evangeline was not quite such tough meat – metaphorically speaking, at any rate. The large handkerchief at her eyes proclaimed her grief.

'Did you visit Mr Lamb in his dressing-room before the performance began, Mrs Yapp?'

'I did not. That man –' she looked scornfully at

Auguste, '– refused to let me in. Yesterday he came between Will and me. I think he did this terrible thing himself.'

'Mr Didier was only trying to do his best for Mr Lamb.' Egbert kept a straight face.

'I loved him, and he adored me.'

Auguste kept a discreet silence.

'Mr Lamb?'

'Certainly I speak of Mr Lamb. I am the reason he returned to the Old King Cole. Did you not realise that?'

'No,' said Egbert simply. Nor did he believe it.

'My husband naturally was –' Evangeline grew a little pink, torn between the excitement of being fought over and practical self-survival which told her that in the unavoidable permanent absence of Will Lamb, she would once again be needing the services of Thomas Yapp '– very fond of Will,' she finished lamely.

Mariella swept graciously into Rose's makeshift office with the air of a tragic heroine.

'I understand Will Lamb was a friend of yours.'

'A dear, *dear* friend.'

'Did you see him before the performance tonight?'

She hesitated fractionally. Auguste could almost see her weighing up pros and cons. 'Yes,' she said brightly. 'I fear my husband was not pleased, but Will and I were *great* friends. Will was a kind man, but I could not give him the love he so desperately sought.' She opened large blue piteous eyes. 'Find his murderer,' she ordered.

'Oh, we will, miss. So you had no plans to – er – deepen that friendship here?'

'I am a married woman.' She spoke with dignity.

'Was it you suggested he come here?'

'No, Chief Inspector.'

'Yet Mr Didier tells me you were the one sent to ask him.'

'Oh *yes*,' she agreed fervently, casting Mr Didier a filthy look, and then a second, less antagonistic one. 'I believe it was felt I might have most influence. His landlady was present, naturally. It would have been most improper otherwise for me to have visited him in his rooms.'

'And naturally, there was nothing improper in your relationship with him?'

'Oh *no*, Inspector.' She raised shocked eyes to him. The eyes that lingered appraisingly on Auguste did not display shock at all.

'Then I won't keep you from your birthday celebrations any longer,' Rose cordially informed her.

She rose with great alacrity, only asking in some puzzlement, 'My *what,* Inspector?'

The rumpus outside the temporary office grew too loud to ignore. Shouting men was one thing, a bawling youngster was quite another. Especially one that Auguste recognised all too clearly. Outside he found Little Emmeline, squaring up pugnaciously to Grey's best men, and not, for the second time, getting her own way. Miguel had been extremely reluctant to buy her a bust improver, when she proposed this in return for her silence. Six fairies were prudently keeping a discreet distance away.

'What's this all about, little girl?' Rose inquired impatiently.

'Little girl' were not words likely to fly straight to the heart, if deep down one lay buried, of Little Emmeline. She fixed Rose with a vicious eye. 'You're really a copper?'

'I am.'

'Then tell these geezers I want my property out of there.' She jerked her finger towards Will's dressing-room.

'And what property do you have in there, might I ask?'

'None of your business.'

'Then you can't have it.' Rose prepared to close the door, and Emmeline hastily reconsidered and changed tactics. She wept.

'It's something I hid in there, something private.'

'What?' Rose asked.

She sobbed unrelenting. 'A red corset.'

Rose guffawed, and not knowing the reason, Emmeline naturally took it amiss. She reverted to character and screamed with temper.

'You're a silly old man, and I know something you don't know.'

'You must tell the Inspector, Emmeline,' Auguste said firmly, 'if it's about Will Lamb.'

'Only if I get my corset back,' Emmeline crowed in high glee.

'Tell us what it's doing in Will Lamb's room first. Did he borrow it?'

Emmeline stared at him in amazement. 'Whatever for? I hid it there, silly.'

'Why?'

'I needed a hiding-place. No one would look there.'

'Now tell me what you know about Will Lamb.'

'He was running away at the end of the week with Mariella,' Emmeline said impatiently.

Rose glanced at Auguste. 'You're sure? How did you know?'

'Everyone knows,' Emmeline replied innocently.

'Auguste,' Rose said briskly, 'go and get this nice young lady her corset.'

The Old King Cole by drab early morning light was shorn even of the distancing mystery and excitement lent to it by the lighting flares that beckoned so enticingly on the theatre front by night. Even the Shadwell fish market had lost its appeal this Thursday morning, as Auguste finished ordering his modest requirements and returned to the theatre to meet Egbert. Silent and grey, the building smelled of stale tobacco and unwashed plates, a fact Lizzie was already busy rectifying, cheerfully singing 'Beautiful Dreamer' while she did so. Auguste's arrival brought an instant halt to her song as she guiltily remembered Mr Lamb.

'I told me dad,' she greeted him. 'He was ever so sorry; he remembered him here in the old days. And Miss Turner. But he said it was no more than could be expected 'ere on the old 'Ighway. There were this sailor,' she explained lugubriously, 'who started killing folks. A poor old draper and his wife and tiny little baby, and then other geezers. Everyone locked their doors and there were lots, lots more 'orrible murders. They got him,' she finished with relish.

'As we shall find the murderer of Will Lamb.'

151

'I 'ope you're a better rozzer than cook,' she said lugubriously.

'Lizzie, I am indeed a cook, even though you do not approve of my pies. We are both artistes, you and I, in our own way. But I also assist Inspector Rose in some of his cases, like this one. So I cannot be present to assist you,' he put it diplomatically.

'Mibow will.'

'Who?'

'Me beau. I'm allowed to have followers, ain't I?' She stuck her chin out aggressively. 'I'm a woman.'

Auguste looked at Lizzie, the new dress nowhere to be seen, the new apron carefully shielded by the ragged old one. Hair stuck out in lumps under the cap and above the shining hopefulness of Lizzie's eyes.

'You are indeed a woman, Lizzie,' he informed her. 'And if the follower is the gentleman you met last evening, you have my full approval.'

Lizzie giggled. 'Garn.'

Horace Brodie and Harry Pickles glared at each other outside what had been Percy's office, and was not commandeered by the law. The rapport of the previous evening was over. They had virtually collided on the doorstep, summoned by Grey's men to attend the Old King Cole this morning. Brodie took it as a natural tribute that his presence was requested. He had seen the news of Will's death blazoned in his morning newspaper, and was thus hardly surprised at the summons.

'My movements, Inspector. Certainly. My humble turn is usually fourth on the bill here, but due to exceptional rowdiness last night, I decided to play earlier.'

'Isn't that Mr Jowitt's decision?'

Brodie frowned his displeasure. 'Normally, yes. At the Old King Cole, however, we tend to fix such matters ourselves. Old Jowitt tends to have money on his mind,' he added confidentially.

'So you were at the theatre early?'

'I usually am. It is my first engagement of the evening. I then leave for the Lyle in Cable Street immediately after my turn.'

'Did you have any reason to see Mr Lamb in his dressing-room before or during the performance?'

Brodie looked surprised. 'No. I remained in the dressing-room so far as I recall.'

'Anyone see you in there?'

'I've no idea.' He looked supremely bored. 'Various people wandered in and out. You could ask Mr Pickles.'

'I will.' Rose didn't take to Brodie. 'And you weren't here when Mr Lamb was killed?'

'No. Usually I take a cab to my next engagement, timing being right, but with more time at my disposal I decided to walk. This is my good-bye to the dear old place, my last week here. Percy will see me no more. The thorn in Mr Pickles' side is about to be removed.'

Rose began to see Pickles' point of view.


Until he talked to Pickles. He'd met the type many times before. Hail fellow well met, but a shifty look in the eye that made you hang on to your wallet.

'Did you go to see Will Lamb before the show started, Mr Pickles?'

'How could I do that?' he snarled. 'I were on first.'

'He was alone for some time before the curtain rose.'

'What would I want to see him for? Couldn't stand the bloke.'

'So you weren't in favour of his coming back here?'

A silence while Pickles mulled this over. 'I was,' he said at last. 'Thought Nettie'd come too.'

'She was very friendly with Will Lamb, then?'

'She weren't that friendly,' her loving husband snarled, 'and he's a liar that says so.'

Rose changed tack. 'And what time did you leave yesterday?'

'Same as normal. After my turn. Or a bit later, maybe. In time for my turn at the Shadwell Palace, anyway.'

'Anyone *vouch* for your movements before the curtain rose?' Rose asked mildly.

'Yus. Nettie.'

'For all the thirty minutes or so Will Lamb was alone?'

'Probably.' He grinned.

Fernando was a refreshingly straightforward change after Brodie and Pickles. 'Me no like Will Lamb,' he told Rose confidingly.

'Why's that, Mr Fernando?'

'He take Mariella away.'

'Only with her consent, I'm sure.'

Fernando's face darkened as he grappled with this idea. 'No,' he decided.

'Did you visit Will Lamb in his dressing-room before the performance yesterday?'

Fernando stared at him, puzzled, and shook his head. 'Fernando no remember.' He thought about Will Lamb with some pleasure. Now he was dead, Mariella would stay here where he could see her. That was all he cared about.

Down below, Percy Jowitt sat miserably in his new temporary office, which he was sharing with a ventriloquist's dummy left behind by some performer years before and never reclaimed. He left it there, because it might come in useful some day, you never knew. That's if he had a theatre left, which looked increasingly unlikely. No Wednesday takings and no Will Lamb on the programme tonight. Suddenly there came the sound of the stage door opening and a booming female voice shouting. 'Anyone here?'

He had to play butler in his own theatre now. Percy gloomily went out to investigate. From outside came the sound of a carriage rattling away, having disgorged its occupant. But the sight before him occupied his whole attention. Waving a threatening umbrella was a tall middle-aged woman of commanding physique, richly dressed in a Worth gown, covered in expensive furs. Moreover she was a familiar-looking woman.

'Where's the manager?'

He pulled himself together and straightened up. 'At your service, ma'am.' Didn't he know that voice? 'Percy Jowitt.'

'Well, Mr Jowitt, I've come to step into the breach, as you might say. I shall do Will Lamb's turn.'

His eyes glazed over. 'Very good of you, ma'am,' he said weakly. One Evangeline was enough; as he would hardly expect this grand lady to do a comedy act with a dagger, it seemed likely grand opera was her forte.

'Don't you recognise me, man?' she asked impatiently.

'Naturally, madam, but my programme is full,' he ad-libbed hastily.

'Nonsense. It's got a huge hole, you're going bankrupt, man, and I'm stepping in. No two ways about it.'

'But who—?'

'I'm the Magnificent Masher.'

Percy's rheumy eyes almost wept at his good fortune, as he speedily vacated his office, ceding it to Lady Westland. He bounced with every excited step, as optimism returned. Almost dancing, and certainly humming in his joy, he set out first to find himself a new office, and then instantly to design a new poster: The Return of the Magnificent Masher. At last, the true potential of the Old King Cole would be appreciated by the press. He spared a passing thought for the unfortunate occurrence that had given rise to this happy event, and salved his conscience by persuading himself that Will, as a man of the theatre, would be spurring him on. He *owed* it to Will to make the most of the increasing presence of newspapermen outside his beloved theatre.

Now, where should his office be? A small props cupboard somewhere? The water closet? He stopped abruptly. Standing inside the front door were two gentlemen identically clad in brown bowler hats, green checked trousers and jackets, and brightly coloured spotted waistcoats. His mouth dropped open.

One swept off his hat. 'We're your new turn,' he growled.

'I don't need any new turns,' Percy cried faintly.

'Yes, you do, laddie.'

Percy Jowitt gazed at them. What was the world coming to?

'We're bailiffs, you see,' his companion added.

Percy Jowitt saw immediately. 'I'm delighted to welcome you to the Old King Cole,' he told them despairingly.

# Chapter Six

Auguste sniffed the air appreciatively. It was not, he admitted, the best air in London, being rather full of the less inviting riverside smells, but after the gloom of the Old King Cole this morning, it was like Escoffier's Carlton kitchen. Moreover, as he turned into a narrow street leading to Cable Street, enticing smells of luncheon from the terraced houses on both sides of the street beguiled him. Were he to investigate further, he consoled himself, those smells, once traced to their source, would probably be of far less interest. When he returned last night, he had not been hungry – fortunately. John had not left a *fricassée*, nor even his soup *de Crécy*. He had left a selection of cold meats, left over, he suspected, from the servants' roast luncheon. The Duke of Davenport had obviously been a long-suffering man.

In Cable Street, he passed a small Italian eating-house in which, as he peered curiously in, Signora was doing the cooking, and the array of ingredients lined up suggested a visit might well be worthwhile – if unconducive to detection work. Egbert had once again left the Old King Cole, and this was a good opportunity

to follow up an idea of his own. True, Twitch would be
on the same trail too in the course of routine, but this
did not concern him greatly.

The Lyle was built on a grander scale than the Old
King Cole, its imposing turrets promising much that
its interior failed to provide. It had obviously buried its
ambitions and was content with the same standard of
clientele as the Old King Cole, judging by the
shabbiness, and, more importantly, its inferior eating-
room. Auguste averted his eyes from the unappetising
array of cold pies and tired sausages, and concentrated
on his task. The system of music-hall bookings, and
the lack of anyone at the Old King Cole, at least, to
monitor arrivals, together with the chaotic comings and
goings backstage meant that it was going to be difficult
to work out who had and who had not been at the
theatre in time to tamper with the dagger before the
performance, and also be there to carry out the search
of Will's dressing-room while he was on stage. As difficult
as disentangling the ingredients of a *tapenade* sauce
from its taste.

The owner of the Lyle, a jollier version of Napoleon,
Auguste decided, seemed to think it perfectly normal
that a French cook working for Percy Jowitt should be
dropping in for a chat about last night's show.

'Poor old Will Lamb.' He shook his head. 'Great loss,
great loss.'

'It is indeed.'

'Leave a grieving widow, did he?'

That hadn't occurred to Auguste. He supposed Egbert
and Twitch would have it in hand, unlikely though it
seemed that a widow would suddenly appear. Will's life

was supposedly well known. A double-shuffler and patterer in the Canterbury music-hall queue until he was discovered by a young Nettie Turner who took him to Percy Jowitt, where she herself was relatively unknown. Nettie would surely have mentioned it to him if Will had a wife or family, even estranged.

'I daresay Jowitt wants you to pinch another of my turns to fill the gap, eh? Cook, did you say you were? You're not after a job, are you?' Hope sprang into Napoleon's voice.

'No, sir. I—'

'Or are you a turn? Funny cook on stage, that sort of thing. Tossing pancakes and missing.'

'I am not a funny sort of cook.' Auguste tried to keep indignation from his voice. 'I am a very serious sort of cook.'

'Oh.' Napoleon's face fell. 'Don't think I could use you. Pity. A cook *comique*.' He considered. 'Might be something in that. I could ask old Bodge if he'd like a go.'

'If Mr Bodge is your current cook, I think he would be excellent. Juggling pies, perhaps,' Auguste suggested innocently.

Napoleon clapped him on the back. 'Not a bad idea at all. Pity to waste the pies, though. They could go back on sale afterwards, I suppose.' He ruminated, then recollected Auguste's mission. 'Can't spare old Jowitt any of my turns, I'm afraid.'

'He does not need one. In fact the Magnificent Masher has decided to return to the stage for a few appearances only, and has chosen the Old King Cole.' Auguste had been surprised, to put it mildly, when Lady Westland swept into the eating-room. She had explained she felt she had a duty to support him and the theatre, having persuaded Auguste to come there. He had been extremely gratified.

The manager was silenced with shock, obviously wondering what magic powers Jowitt possessed.

'I believe the Great Brodie has a place on your bill this week? Did he play as usual last night?'

'No one reported any hiccups to me,' Napoleon told him without apparent surprise. 'I heard him from the bar. He seemed to be going down rather well, I thought. Don't wait up, don't wait up,' he trumpeted. 'Good man that.'

'He arrived on time for his appearance?'

'Must have done. It's always tight for him but he was there. A real pro. I'll be sorry to lose him. They all seem to go in the end. Can't think why.'

'Are you sharing other performers with Mr Jowitt this week?'

Napoleon considered. 'Max Hill – he's a regular here. Just before the interval.'

'And he appeared as usual last night?'

'Must have done, my dear chap, or I'd have heard about it.' He paused. 'There's Gherkin, of course.'

'I beg your pardon?'

'Harry Pickles. Gherkin is what my wife calls him. Green and skinny. We put him on in the second half to avoid trouble. Not much love lost between him and Brodie. But he's a good man.'

It said very little for the Lyle if Pickles was a good man, Auguste thought, as he made his way back to the Old King Cole. His visit eliminated Brodie and Hill at least, since Brodie could not have ransacked the dressing-room and arrived at the Lyle in time for his turn, and Hill would have been at the Lyle at the time the ransacking took place. Pickles, not on till the second half, *could* have done it.

A most delightful smell suddenly hit his nostrils. He could detect basil in it, and found he was passing the Italian eating-house. The plump signora within looked invitingly at him. He followed his nose.

It was a long and delightful luncheon. The use of basil with aubergine and tomato was exciting, more used as he was to the *herbes* of his native Provence. The slice of polenta with mushrooms was equally enjoyable, and the ravioli was a revelation. It danced to his stomach rather than dropping as so often with a heavy thud.

Auguste poked his head guiltily down in to the Old King Cole kitchen, fearful of Lizzie's reproachful eye. No Lizzie. True, everything seemed ready. The luncheon debris had vanished and the evening food appeared ready for cooking. A swinging lady's leg of eel swayed gently in the breeze he himself made in descending the steps to the basement. Otherwise all was still. Postponing the desire to experiment immediately with the bunch of basil he had acquired from the signora, Auguste put duty first. He should report to Egbert immediately, who should surely be back by now.

He hurried through to the entrance to the music hall and up the stairs to the first-floor at the front of the building, once Percy's hideaway and which had now been commandeered by Egbert. Suddenly he stopped. The same intuition that came to his aid in cooking came now. Something was not right, and he advanced more cautiously. The door to Egbert's office was open, yet somehow he sensed Egbert was not within, and nor was Twitch. There was, however, a low murmur of voices. Stealthily Auguste moved forward, puzzled. The door would surely be locked if Egbert were not there, so whoever was within either had his permission to be there, or had broken in. He crept to the door and peered through the small gap by the hinges. He could not believe such villains were there by permission. There were two of them, in loud checked trousers and waistcoats, bowler hats, and gaudy scarves round their necks. What he noticed first, however, to his horror, was that one Bowler Hat, the plumper, taller of the two, was clutching the package containing the cross of Prince Henry the Navigator.

They were turning to come out. Auguste stiffened. He had no chance to get away; he could only try to pretend he was just arriving. There was a sudden silence from within, and he applied his eye once again to the crack.

They were reading Egbert's notes! No time now for subtlety. Auguste rushed into the room indignantly, shouting the while for Egbert. Even Twitch would be a welcome arrival.

Something hit him across the head; to Auguste it felt as if he were falling into a vast bowl of black soup which he welcomed eagerly. When he next opened his eyes, and managed to struggle to a sitting position, he saw four pairs of feet surrounding him, two clad in boots, two in shoes. The shoes were Egbert's and Twitch's; the latter were guarding the door, Auguste noticed, wincing with pain and deciding not to touch his head incautiously again.

'Fools rush in, eh, Mr Didier?'

'Enough, Stitch,' Egbert cut in sharply. 'Anyone care to tell us what the blazes is going on and why my assistant was out cold on the floor?'

Auguste distinctly heard Twitch snort.

'This ruffian attacked us,' the plump Bowler Hat said sullenly.

'And who might "us" be?'

'New turn for tonight. This is the manager's office, ain't it?'

'They were stealing the cross,' Auguste almost squealed in indignation.

Rose studied the check-suited turn. To Auguste's surprise and indignation, he suddenly grinned. 'Fine turn you are. I've seen your ugly mugs before. Special Branch, aren't you?'

'Special Branch?' repeated Auguste and Stitch together.

'Now, what could you be doing here? Didn't know my report was as fascinating as all that,' Rose mused thoughtfully. 'Couldn't at long last be in pursuit of anarchists, could you?'

'We've come for the cross,' plump Bowler Hat announced. 'It's in here, you told us.'

'I found it. Suppose I say I want to return it direct to His Majesty?'

'We can make life difficult for Chief Inspectors,' thin Bowler Hat unwisely threatened.

'I'm going to make it even more difficult for you,' Rose retorted amiably. 'Open that package you're clutching.'

Bowler Hat number one looked at him suspiciously, and reluctantly began to unroll the package. Inside was a copy of Dan Leno's memoirs.

'Early Christmas present for His Majesty,' Rose chortled. 'Wish I'd let you take it.'

'Where is it?'

'What you're after is here.' Rose opened a brown carrier bag and tipped its contents unceremoniously on to the table.

'Egbert!' Auguste scrambled to his feet, wincing but shocked at this treatment.

Bowler Hat lunged for the cross and held it piously to his chest.

'Sure you want to take it to His Majesty, are you?' Rose inquired gently.

'Yes.'

'That won't get you the Order of the Garter.'

'Why?'

'It's a fake.'

'Fake?' four voices cried together.

'This is what we found in Will Lamb's dressing-room. I thought it wise to check it this morning. A pretty bauble but a fake. And I don't run a fake-shop in my cellar at home, if that's what you're thinking.'

The Bowler Hats almost blushed. And no wonder, Auguste thought. After all, the fate of the true cross must now be in doubt. The newspapers had screamed their disapproval of the reckless gang who had stolen the cross to return it to Portugal. What would they say when they knew that the cross could be anywhere in this country, Portugal, any part of their far-flung Empire, or in a cooking pot in a South Sea Island?

Auguste, still dazed, wondered idly whether such pots might contain herbs and spices as yet unknown in the Western culinary world.

'From now on,' – plump Bowler Hat had decided on menace – 'stay out of this, Rose. You and your men. And that fellow, Grey's. And whoever this bloke here is.'

'Mr Auguste Didier. And I have a case to solve,' Rose informed them.

'Not any more, you don't.'

'Oh yes. Next I'm seeing Miguel Gomez.'

'You've been warned off,' Bowler Hat said injudiciously.

'Have I? I've got two murders to investigate, including that of Will Lamb. You taking responsibility for that?'

A pause as they considered this matter. 'All right. We'll work with you,' plump Bowler Hat said reluctantly.

'Very good of you,' Rose said cordially. 'Keep that fake, and find out who made it.'

A tentative knock at the door was followed by Percy Jowitt's face appearing round it. 'Ah. I thought you gentlemen might like to show me your turn.'

'No,' came both Bowler Hats' reply.

Percy was shocked at such lack of professionalism. 'I am afraid I must insist, gentlemen. The Old King Cole is used to a certain standard of performance. Music hall may not be your main profession, but all the more reason for me to see it.'

'What is your main profession, gentlemen?' Rose inquired with interest.

'We're bailiffs.' They glared at him. 'Remember that.'

'What names do you work under?' Percy asked briskly.

'We don't.'

'*Really*, gentlemen. This is hardly good enough,' Percy bleated.

'Cherry and Black,' plump Bowler Hat offered at last.

'Not very euphonious,' Percy commented severely. 'But I suppose it must do.' He scuttled away, taking them with him – or so he thought. Footsteps were heard returning, and Cherry came in again, grinning. 'You say his name was Didier?'

'Yes, and I am,' Auguste said firmly, 'not accustomed to being hit over the head.'

'If that's the worst that happens to you, you'll be lucky,' Cherry chortled.

'You threatening him?' Rose asked sharply.

'Me? No.' He roared with laughter. 'Fellow called Gregorin is, though.'

Gregorin? Auguste paled. Pyotr Gregorin, member of the Czar's dreaded secret police, the Okhrana, and, more importantly, half-uncle to Tatiana, whose sole mission in life now appeared to be to kill the cook who had dishonoured his family by presuming to marry into the Romanov family, albeit a remote member of it. In other words, Auguste Didier. 'He left the country a year ago,' he pointed out.

'Thought you'd like to know he's back,' Cherry crowed as he left again.

Stitch wisely took the smirk from his face.

'How are you feeling, Auguste?' Rose asked gravely.

'Like a salmon stunned by a poacher.' He made an effort at levity.

'Take care, Auguste. We'll keep as many eyes on Gregorin as we can – no use leaving it to Special Branch

– but he's as slippery as an eel.'

'May be hard to *collar* him.' Stitch could restrain himself from mirth no longer.

'If you've no need of me, Egbert,' Auguste said coldly, 'I shall return to look after my own collared eels.'

'Not yet. Stitch, be a good chap and do me a list of everyone's precise movements yesterday, together with who they remember seeing and where in the first half.'

Stitch glowered, and unwillingly retreated.

'Anything strike you as odd, Auguste?' Egbert asked, when they were alone.

'It seems to me there is more in this soup than vegetables and meat. There is a murky stock whose ingredients you would do well to discover.'

'It begins to make a pattern,' Egbert said reflectively. 'I get information too late to search the ship. Special Branch gave me the information, I'm told to keep Special Branch informed of progress though the case is all *my* responsibility, whether the villains are Portuguese Royalists, Republicans, anarchists, Charlie Peace, or Jack the Ripper come back to haunt us. Until I find the cross, when all of a sudden instead of gratitude, I'm treated like yesterday's gravy. Why do you suppose that is?'

'And why do you suppose, Egbert, Will Lamb had a *fake* cross in his room? I could understand someone giving him the cross to hide, assuming he would be above suspicion, but why a fake?'

'Perhaps the beautiful Mariella pinched it from Gomez and hid it there, not knowing it was a fake, hoping to make off with it at the end of the week when she eloped with Lamb.'

'If she were going to elope with Lamb, she wouldn't

be needing the cross. He must have been a rich man,'
Auguste pointed out. 'Perhaps the ransacking of Will's
room was not to steal something, but to plant the fake.'

'You've got something there, Auguste. Seems a bit
far-fetched, though.'

'And why plant a fake? The thieves can't have thought
it would deceive the Palace for long.'

'Perhaps it was the fake that was stolen from
Windsor?'

'HM's little game? Have a fake made in case it's
stolen? Why not tell me? And why were Special Branch
so upset at the news it was a fake? *They* thought it was
genuine.'

Auguste caught Egbert's eye. 'This is an even murkier
stock than you thought, Auguste, if what we're thinking
is true. And *how* do we find out?'

If he were capable of such brilliant detective work after
being hit over the head, Auguste thought wearily as he
returned to the kitchens, what shouldn't he be capable
of under normal circumstances?

He went down to the basement, hoping that Lizzie
had either returned or that there was nothing for him
to do. He was disappointed on both counts. He realised
to his horror it was five-thirty, and that the food had to
be cooked if it were to be ready in time. Never had he
felt less enthusiasm for pursuing his vocation. He
removed potatoes from their water, and placed them
on a tray to take upstairs. One dropped on the floor
and he had to crawl under a table to retrieve it. His
head was aching miserably, as he emerged, and saw
before him a pair of feet daintily shod in kid shoes. Not

Lizzie's. His first thought was: where is she? His second was to wonder whose feet they were. His eyes travelled up the woollen skirt, and his head jerked painfully. *There was nothing above it*. Nothing, that is, but two perfectly formed women's breasts on their naked chest, only too eager, apparently, to make his early acquaintance. He could manage only horror, as his eyes flew further up to see the lustrous red hair of Mariella Gomez and her blue eyes smiling down at him.

'Here?' was all he could manage to croak. He was thinking of the inappropriateness of such a scene in something that he temporarily thought of as his beloved kitchen, however undeserving of the name.

'My dear Auguste – I may call you that, may I not? – you are very eager. I'm so flattered.' The breasts were thrust out a shade more aggressively and he quickly clambered to his feet, eager for escape. 'Where had you in mind?' she asked. 'The table?'

He stared at her, hypnotised. Was the woman mad? The kitchen *table*? If anything were guaranteed to ensure that desire remained firmly under his control, together with all parts of the body connected to it, that was. It would be sacrilege; a desecration of furniture devoted so intimately to his art of cuisine. The kitchen table, whether used to create the finest achievements of an Escoffier, or the humblest eel pie, was nevertheless in the relationship of temple to devotee. In his indignation, Auguste could speak nothing but the truth, forgetting his French diplomacy due to a lady in such an embarrassing situation. 'Madam' – why did his voice suddenly emerge as a squeak – 'I have to attend to my potatoes.'

'Oh, do let me help.'

What did the woman mean? Her arms were thrust out, not to embrace him but to— Auguste backed away in horror, forced against the table, finding himself trapped. Was he going to have to use brute force to defend his honour? Obviously, yes.

'Sorry I'm late, Mr Didier. Mr Didier, where are you?' Lizzie came galloping down the steps, and stopped short as she took in the scene.

''Ere,' she shouted indignantly, 'what d'yer fink yer doing in my kitchen. Get outa it.' Startled, Mariella turned round, and Lizzie gawped. 'Blimey, so that's what a mermaid does.'

Mariella looked her up and down acidly as she donned her clothes. 'I'd rather be a mermaid than a filleted fish bone, dear.' She stalked away, her plan to combine pleasure with self-interest in opening an avenue to police thinking, shattered.

Left alone, Auguste and Lizzie faced each other.

'Don't worry, Mr Didier,' Lizzie announced consolingly. 'You're just getting too old to run fast enough. She's always doing this sort of thing, if she can get away from the Jaunty Juggler. That's why the cooks are always leaving. She thinks he won't catch her down here.'

Relief that she had not misjudged the situation was mingled with hurt pride. 'Too old?' Auguste repeated, picking on the salient point. 'I'm only forty-three.'

'Forty-three?' There was amazement in her voice. 'Me dad's only thirty-seven, and he's past it. No wonder you was running away from her.'

'Lizzie, the eels, if you please.'

Lizzie giggled.

* * *

'Well?' Rose looked up eagerly as Twitch came in.

The latter shook his head dolefully. 'Nothing. The men have crawled all over this place. Not a thing. And we covered their home again, too. Not a cross in sight. The only thing the men got excited about were some naughty postcards of Mrs Gomez. There was one in a bath –' Stitch reddened, as he saw his Chief's ironic look and decided not to elaborate further.

'Too much to expect, I suppose,' Rose grunted. 'Gomez is hardly likely to have hidden it in his own home knowing we might search it.'

'A risk,' Twitch pointed out rather obviously, unconsciously taking in that the Chief was talking to him like a human being for once. 'Of course, we don't *know* they're mixed up in it.'

'Far too smug not to be, if you ask me. But what were they planning to do with it? My money's on their sending the fake to the Portuguese royal family by the next ship, and selling the true cross to the highest bidder.'

'Selling it, sir?'

Rose looked at him. 'You're right to pull me up, Stitch. Not much market, except, of course, to those Republicans.'

'So it's probably sold already,' Twitch deduced pompously. 'They were holding the fake until the ship arrived, didn't want it at home because they guessed we'd be searching it, so Mrs G sweet-talked Will Lamb into holding it for her.'

Rose thought this over. 'Doesn't explain why they bothered to have a fake at all. Why not just a straight theft?'

Twitch surpassed himself. 'It would take the heat off them if the Portuguese royal family believed they'd got the real thing.'

'But if Gomez is our man, and he pinched the loot from Windsor, why bother to go to all the trouble of hiring a casual in Limehouse and murdering him?'

To this Twitch had no reply.

'Is Gomez in the theatre yet?' Rose continued.

'I'll find out, sir.' Twitch escaped thankfully. At least this was a task which would produce a firm yes or no.

'Send him up if so. And Mr Didier, if you can find him.'

Twitch departed with a slightly less light heart, but brought back both with the air of one much tried. Auguste was only too thankful for a reason to escape Lizzie's conspiratorial sympathetic eye.

'Why you want to see me *again*?' Miguel demanded passionately.

'Not for the delightful company,' Rose replied curtly. 'A nice silver cross with garnets turned up in Will Lamb's dressing-room, you see, and not long before we found it, someone tampered with his dagger and he died. Murdered. Remember now?'

Miguel shrugged. 'Why me?'

'You were hanging about in the wings while he was on stage, which you don't do normally. That a good enough reason?'

'Will was a great artiste,' Miguel muttered.

'And a *bon ami* of your wife,' Auguste amplified.

'Enemy?' Miguel looked startled.

'*Ami*. A good friend of your wife. Forgive me, I speak and think still in French, as you no doubt in Portuguese,'

Auguste continued meaningfully. 'We remain what we were born.'

Miguel's face darkened. 'What does it matter where I was born? I am from Europe, from the world. I travel since I am born.'

'No great allegiance to Portugal?' Rose asked mildly.

'Not where crosses are concerned,' Miguel replied, pleased he had not fallen into this cunning trap.

'Funny how rumours fly around a place like this,' Rose said conversationally. 'You should hear what goes on at the Yard. All sorts of stories about me being a hard man. Don't believe a word of it. And those about your wife about to run off with Will Lamb are nonsense too, you say.'

Miguel smirked. 'Of course. We are never parted.'

'Just rumours,' Rose reflected. 'Of course, if you had happened to believe them, you being a passionate man, you might have wished harm to come to Will Lamb.'

Miguel glared. 'I did not.'

'Or perhaps your wife? Had Will changed his mind about running away with her?'

'She did not. We did not. We are nothing to do with murder!' He went into a flood of Portuguese. 'Look for the ghost. It was the ghost he said did it.' He stopped suddenly, and stared at them.

'Where were you last Saturday?' Rose asked.

'At home. With Mariella,' Miguel replied quietly, his voice oddly flat.

'Anyone see you?'

'Mariella.'

'Where were you before the performance yesterday?'

'On my way here from the Britannia. I did not arrive till after the performance had started.'

'Not earlier?'

'No.'

'That's odd, Mr Gomez. You usually do, your wife was, and you said you were never parted. Especially on her birthday. Only it wasn't her birthday yesterday, like you told us, was it, Mr Gomez?'

'Are you cooking tonight, Auguste?'

Auguste eyed him. 'If you can spare me, Egbert,' he said cautiously. This was too good a chance to miss.

'I'm coming too. I want to see Ma Bisley's sword-swallower.'

It was just as well. Auguste's presence was not only desirable but essential. He was aware of Egbert's sardonic eye on him from the fastnesses of his secluded window seat. The hastily trumpeted return of the Magnificent Masher, not to mention Nettie Turner performing on the very stage where Will Lamb had died, was enough to draw the entire population of Wapping, Shadwell and Limehouse, not to mention most of the newspapermen in England. Auguste gazed panic-stricken through the window. Demand was obviously going to outstrip supply despite his increased orders that morning. That Mob had a lean and hungry look, and tonight it was not merely for barracking, it was for sensation.

'Can we obtain more pies?' he asked desperately.

Lizzie looked doubtful. 'Not from Mrs J's, we won't.' This was double-Dutch to Auguste. 'Joe could try Mrs Mount's . . .'

'The pie shop?' Auguste clutched at this straw. 'The establishment by Tobacco Dock with the rather large lady in charge?'

'That's the one.' Lizzie dived under the counter to extract a new box of catsup bottles.

Auguste regarded the soles of her feet contemplatively, struggling with his integrity. Could he so compromise his standards as to buy and sell produce *under his name* purchased from the large lady with the dirty cap and apron at Mount's Pie Emporium? Her beaming grin made no difference. The haphazard displays that suggested a large hand merely tumbled new offerings from the oven on top of those unsold from previous bakings, the unappetising bowls that lay around all too conspicuously as a new batch went in for baking, the greasy pole that was kept handily on the floor for prodding food into submission in the ovens, the dead bluebottles in the window, feet upright in surrender (had they tasted the pies?) – all these things convinced him honour should reject this solution. Another glance at the Shadwell Mob outside suggested honour should be conveniently lost for this evening, and that in any case, Lizzie's usual supplier, this Mrs J, was no doubt equally repulsive.

'What an excellent idea, Lizzie,' he agreed hollowly.

A raucous rendering of 'Two Lovely Black Eyes' outside suggested the Mob was limbering up. He could see Frederick doling out potatoes, so quickly it looked like a juggling turn by Miguel Gomez. No time for sword-swallowing this evening.

Egbert patiently sipped ale, eyeing Auguste as he rushed from cellar to eating-room and back again, bearing plates, and fresh supplies ready for the onslaught. Outside the voices grew louder, and more raucous, song giving way to demands for admittance.

Percy Jowitt pattered past the entrance to the eating-room *en route* for the front door. To open five minutes early was a surrender of his power, but tonight, any price was worth it. Frederick, sensing the tightening of muscles ready for the surge, quickly infiltrated the front ranks, swept aside by the surge and the peeling off into the eating-room, breathless and bruised. He went straight to his post, greeting his pile of fresh potatoes as a challenge to be welcomed. His eyes gleamed as he realised the hot-plate was unattended, and that tempting offerings awaited him. Egbert was there before him.

'Ah, Mr Wolf, allow me to present you with a chop.' Egbert flipped one over on to a plate with all the expertise of one evening's experience.

'How very generous of you, sir.' Frederick's eyes lit up.

Goodness knows how a throat rasped with so much sword-swallowing could cope with a mutton chop, Auguste thought, as he rushed by to take his place by the fish hot-plate. He was even more impressed that Frederick managed to consume his chop while juggling potatoes to early comers already thrusting eager hands over the counter.

'Allow me to present to you one of my best potatoes, sir,' Frederick bawled to Rose over the rabble. One hand pursued his chop, the other expertly opened a potato over a plate with one hand, buttered, peppered and salted it and pushed it proudly to Egbert.

'Very good of you.' Rose eyed the crumbs without much enthusiasm, and retreated to devour it, one eye on his intended prey. 'Tell me,' he began half an hour later after the performance had begun, 'you ever heard of a lady called Ma Bisley?'

'No,' said Frederick simply, devouring a second chop thrust under his nose as an inducement.

'She's heard of you.'

'Naturally.' Frederick took this as a tribute to his art. 'The Wolfs have a long tradition of sword-swallowing.'

'Cast your mind back to last Saturday, Mr Wolf, if you would.'

'Certainly.' Frederick was eager to oblige, especially if another chop came his way.

'Nightingale Lane mean anything to you?'

'Indeed it does. My mother, a splendid lady, six foot three, you know, always told me, "Frederick, never go near Nightingale Lane. There are goblins down there. And pirates. And ghosts." I have obeyed her. She—'

'What were you doing last Saturday afternoon?' Rose cut in. Frederick's mother was unlikely to be relevant to the case.

'Let me think. Ah, yes, the day of my *commission*. I earned two shillings.'

'For what?'

'Net.' Frederick ruminated on his triumph. 'It was a *secret* mission, so I thought carefully as to how to perform the task. I decided to take the package to a third party and to pass on part of my fee. I made this sacrifice out of duty, you understand.'

'What was it?'

'It was secret.'

'Want another chop?'

'How kind.'

'To the docks, wasn't it?'

'How percipient. Yes. North Dock. I selected a likely courier, pulling my muffler down over my face as disguise.'

Disguise? Auguste, hovering unashamedly, wondered how anything could disguise that lanky frame.

'From the Three Tars in Limehouse?'

'And some of that delightful catsup, if you please, sir. Yes.'

Auguste noted the stickiness of the bottle, the elegant way in which Frederick wiped the excess catsup from the lip with his finger and licked it appreciatively and wondered if there might be hygiene disadvantages in his scheme for regular catsup bottles on tables.

'Who gave you this mission?' Egbert asked.

'A gentleman also with a muffler. The day was not inclement, though wet, and I deduced he did not wish to be recognised. That's what gave me the idea of following his example.'

Auguste repressed a grin as he saw Egbert's face.

'Very helpful, Mr Wolf. You've no idea who it was?'

'Oh yes.'

'You have?'

'Naturally. Throats are, after all, my profession. I recognise the wrinkles and creases, much as I understand horticulturists recognise lines in tree trunks. A mere muffler is a rather insignificant disguise to a sword-swallower. If carelessly arranged it covers the mouth and nose, but not the throat. I remember my dear mother saying, "Frederick, you recall Mr—".'

'Who was it?' Egbert cut across reminiscences.

'In my mother's case, it was—'

'The man in the muffler,' Rose demanded patiently.

'The Great Brodie. Horace, I believe, to his many friends.'

Auguste hurried to the back of the *fauteuils,* behind the pit, craning his neck to see what was going on. It was hard to tell from the noise. He was determined to see Lady Westland, as Tatiana would demand a full report on her return, when she knew what interesting developments were taking place, and it would distract her from inquiring what precisely *he* had been doing at the Old King Cole. His presence in the kitchens was not going to be divulged to her. It briefly crossed his mind to wonder why Tatiana had asked Lady Westland, of mature years and figure, to keep an eye on him during her absence, and not, for example, darling Maisie, who was a friend of both of them – though particularly, he was forced to admit, of his, owing to earlier intimate acquaintanceship.

The board showing seven, once Will's, now the Magnificent Masher's number, was up and it was hard to tell from the roars and flying objects whether the number was meeting approval or not. Certainly the 'footles', the *fauteuils* of his native language, were in favour, and the circle; whether the pit and the gallery were preparing for adulation or war was difficult to determine. He need not have worried. The sight of the upraised silver end of a walking stick appearing from the wings then pausing, followed by a tall top-hat similarly extended brought an immediate howl of approval from members of the audience who could remember that well-known entrance. True, the morning suit that followed it was somewhat broader in the beam

181

than of old, but as the Magnificent Masher strolled languidly down the footlights, studied her audience through a monocle and declared in bored tones: 'I'm a Piccadilly lounger, though some would call me scrounger . . .' he relaxed. The audience was held, and by the time the Masher left the stage, to the tune of 'A Romano's Romeo', was captive. Little Emmeline, usually a prudent judge of her career, had elected to change bill position till after the interval. Orsini, once more finding himself catapulted into an unwelcome spot, flatly refused, and Jowitt rang the curtain down on the Masher's triumphant note.

Auguste returned to the eating-room for the interval to find Lizzie and Frederick in full, silent concentration on their respective tasks, as the audience began to flock in. Egbert had disappeared. Auguste collided in the doorway with an out-of-breath Joe, bearing a huge bag whose contents were already leaking grease. Auguste seized it, thrusting the objects on to the hot-plate. At first sniff he recoiled. All he could smell was grease oozing through the pastry. Then something caught at his nostrils, and he sniffed again. It was curry powder, and worse, the smell of curry powder with a purpose – to cover that of bad meat.

'Ere, mate, giv' us one of them, will you?' An indignant customer recalled him to duty.

Mrs Mount's pies, the chops, the herrings, all melted into a terrible stew of eating smells, and the result was far from fragrant. Gas lights flared and hissed before him, oven heat assaulted him, customers' yells, shouts – and occasionally fists – did the same from behind. As the last customer drifted back to barrack Little

Emmeline, Auguste sank down exhausted. Surely Escoffier would never go through this hell? Why should he, Auguste Didier, have so foolishly offered himself as a herring to the slaughter?

Orsini had a fortunate escape this evening, thanks to Little Emmeline, who had unwisely usurped his after-the-interval spot. The interval had in no way diminished the Mob's desire for revenge – and they wreaked it. This time Little Emmeline had no reserves, and retired with six fairies in tears, and her own grim expression, as she planned her response. Evangeline lasted less than a minute, and then Percy saw his chance.

'You next,' he told his bailiffs amiably. 'Turn eight, the Cherry Blacks,' he bawled to the stage manager.

Mr Cherry was in the habit of entertaining his aunts at Christmas, Percy had been given to understand; Mr Black had always fancied himself as a pierrot. They were both therefore attired in gleaming white costumes, with red pom-poms and perky little white clown's hats. Their appearance stunned the audience into silence, and thus encouraged they advanced confidently to the footlights:

'Who was that lady I saw you with last night?' Cherry inquired coyly.

'That was no lady, that was—'

Black got no further as the entire audience bawled out their own pet variations of 'my wife', and the red pom-poms were amplified in the form of squashy tomatoes. Special Branch, unused to meeting their public at such close quarters, reconsidered their position. Half an egg only partly de-shelled arrived smack in Cherry's mouth and decided it for him. He fled, with Black at his heels, as Percy Jowitt giggled helplessly into the wings.

'Glad you find it funny, Percy,' said Nettie caustically, as she sailed past to the rescue, one turn early. Orsini did not seem disposed to argue the point. She strode down to the footlights, put her hands on her hips, planted her feet firmly and belligerently, and roared at her loving audience:

'Whoa, there, you donkeys.'

They whoa'ed.

Egbert Rose, knocking at Nettie's door, was surprised to find himself faced not by Miss Turner but by Lady Westland, now back in suitable attire for her position, with Max Hill. His surprise showed.

'Max and I are old friends. We met over twenty years ago,' Lady Westland replied. 'At the Canterbury, wasn't it, Max?'

'The Cyder Cellars,' Max supplied readily.

'You may go back that far. I don't. No, the Canterbury. You were doing your W.G. Ross turn.'

'Damn your eyes,' Max snarled.

' "Sam Hall",' exclaimed Rose appreciatively. 'That takes me back. I was only a nipper when my father took me to see Ross. I always said that's what made me join the police force. An acquaintance with villains from an early age.' He could still hear the great Ross singing his famous chilling song of the murderer on his way to execution. 'And Sam Cowell. Remember his "Ratcatcher's Daughter"?'

'Anyone who remembers Sam Cowell's a friend of mine,' Max declared. 'And of Gwendolen's, too.'

Lady Westland grinned. 'Max, you're too much of an old villain yourself to go courting the law.'

'Blimey, I'd almost forgotten,' Max replied. 'I'll do me best Lord Fauntleroy act for you, velvet knickerbockers and all.' He paused. 'Who did it, eh? Who'd want to kill Will Lamb?'

'You knew him well?' Rose asked.

'As well as Nettie. As well as Gwendolen here. And it wasn't right, killing Will,' he said hoarsely.

'We'll find him,' Rose said shortly.

'Music hall's a funny old world,' Max continued. 'There's the golden hearts, like Nettie, Gwendolen here, and Will. And then there's the spongers, in it while the going's good, the fly-by-nights – and the bad eggs. And once they get behind those lights you can't always tell which is which.'

'And offstage?' Lady Westland asked him bluntly.

'Sometimes, Gwennie, not even then.'


'What are you doing still here, Miguel?' Mariella stopped as she rushed into the wings to check the fish tank, dragging her little doggies in frills and hats with her. They were well-trained. They didn't dare bark. Auguste wondered whether perhaps she dosed them. Perhaps they spent the day in an opium smoking-room, or in a gin palace? He was wrong. Mariella looked after her doggies, not through great love of them, but through the zealous regard of the artiste for her tools.

Miguel disliked dogs, particularly little ones whose grasp of household etiquette was incomplete. He had long discovered, however, that there was little point in protesting. Mariella did as she liked in such matters.

He did the planning, but if she didn't agree, she didn't co-operate. Recently, she had been very good, however – too good, perhaps. Was there something he didn't know?

'What are you doing here?' she repeated crossly.

'I got someone to cover for me at the Shadwell Palace.' He could not stop himself. 'You didn't have any plans *really* to leave with Will, did you?' he demanded.

'What foolish ideas you get in your head, my darling,' she replied lightly. 'I did as we agreed, that's all.'

Miguel had foolishly assumed that his own masculine charms were so greatly superior to Will Lamb's that there was no need to worry. Now, he was beginning to wonder, and badly shaken, both by Will Lamb's death and other matters, blurted out: 'I'm sorry, Mariella. I had a shock.'

'What?' she asked without great curiosity.

'I have realised who killed Will Lamb.'

Her eyes narrowed, as she thought hard for a moment. 'I thought it was you,' she answered him simply.


At the end of the performance Auguste returned to the eating-room for the last shift. That would be tiring, but not hold quite so much pressure. He seemed to be in some kind of lift constantly shuttling between the unreal world of police investigation, murder and Special Branch, and the equally unreal one of theatre life. Sometimes, it kindly stopped to allow him to step out into this all-too-real eating-room. No matter what happened, people must eat and there must be those who can cook, whether they be servants, wives, or professional cooks like himself. Food was real, whether it was *filets de perdreaux à la Marena* or pie and mash. Even in the midst of the soberest realities, like Will Lamb's death, food and eating must continue.

The room was crowded now with jostling good-humoured bodies, even some of the performers joining in. Bright lights, relaxing drinks, food stuffed into mouths, everywhere catchy songs from the evening's entertainment being whistled or sung. Was it right that Will Lamb should be so apparently quickly forgotten? That the warmth of tonight's raucous music hall should so quickly paper over the memory of the still body on last night's stage? Surely not; and then he glanced at some of the couples, regulars probably, and knew he was wrong. Will Lamb's performances would be securely lodged in their memories, to be brought out and appreciated in years to come. Nettie, Max, Gwendolen and others who were Will Lamb's friends, had given of their best tonight, for Will, and for music hall, and Will could have no better memorial.

The barman, waiter and Frederick stared at him reproachfully as he went to help them. It was some time before he realised that Lizzie was absent, and even longer before he could discover the reason why. When he at last descended to the cellar, he found tomorrow's eels as yet unprepared, their bodies looking every bit as reproachful as the waiter's eyes. From outside, through an open door, came the low murmur of voices, one clearly identifiable. Crossly, Auguste strode to the door. Outside in the dim light from the distant highway, he could see two figures, not locked in each other's arms, but at least a foot apart. The man held the woman's hands, quite silent now. He was gazing at her lank hair, thin face and sharp eyes as though she were a Galaxy Girl, and his eyes shone in adoration.

'I'm going to kiss you, Lizzie Brown,' Joe said softly.

Lizzie promptly shut her eyes, leaned forward, and put out her lips.

Auguste knew he should retreat, but he did not.

Joe touched them gently, then drew back. 'Lizzie—'

'Yes.'

'What do you do when you eat one of Mrs Jolly's pies?'

'Open me mouth quickly.'

'Pretend you're eating one now.' He drew closer, and this time the kiss took longer.

'Did you like that, Lizzie Brown?' he asked after a while.

Lizzie made an attempt at nonchalance. 'Ma Jolly's pies are better.'

'Don't say that, Lizzie.'

She looked at him, and uncertainly drew him to her.

This time Auguste did retreat, partly because there appeared to be tears in his eyes. For young love, or for self pity, he wondered? Or for his own empty home, however temporary. He stomped upstairs to find himself alone in the eating-room, and to his surprise found he was hungry. He searched in vain for food, until at last he came across one solitary pie over a chafing dish, obviously put aside for Lizzie's own supper. At least it did not smell of Mount's curry powder, so it must be one of Mrs Jolly's. With a sense of justice done, he picked it up and chewed into it.

Chewed? It slid in like the first oyster, indeed it was

the finest oyster, coupled with the tenderest beef, the most succulent gravy— He examined the half-eaten pie in wonder – was that a sliver of carrot? Of onion? No, not the latter, far too strong. Of mace perhaps, or orange itself? He could not stop for his brain to work it out, but let sensual pleasure seize him to the last succulent morsel.

A happy man, and thus greatly daring, he rang his own door bell in Queen Anne's Gate at gone half past twelve. He and his butler eyed each other, but greatly to Auguste's surprise there was no reproach in the Great Man's eyes.

Something was different. He caught at an elusive atmosphere, but could not define it. It was not until he crept into bed he knew what it was. The bed was different, the house was different. The house was alive again, for the bed had Tatiana in it.

# Chapter Seven

'What,' Tatiana paused for a moment in her kilometre by kilometre account of her race from Paris to Cannes, as they descended to breakfast, 'is that large bruise on your head?'

'I acquired it in the course of being looked after by Lady Westland, your friend,' Auguste replied innocently. His head had not yet recovered from the previous day, but his spirits seemed to have lifted remarkably.

'And I had thought she would be safe from your attentions,' his wife replied worriedly, with equal innocence.

He laughed in sheer pleasure at seeing her again. 'I will tell you the entire story,' he assured her. 'After, of course, you have completed the exciting tale of why you are home early and of the three hundred and thirty-seventh kilometre.'

'I burst the right front tyre cover,' she began, 'but fortunately—' Tatiana eyed him suspiciously. 'You really wish to hear this?'

'But of course.' He placed a suitably shocked expression on his face.

'Then I will tell you *before* we take breakfast.'

'Perhaps *while* we are eating, *ma mie*.' Time was important. So was the choice of breakfast from the vast array of chafing dishes that John saw fit to provide for breakfast each day. In vain, he had pointed out that the stomach must be gently wooed and comforted at such a time, not assaulted by sausages, kidneys and chops. Both contenders in this battle had entrenched their positions, and as usual it was Tatiana who negotiated a truce by gently pointing out to Auguste's soft heart that uneaten food from upstairs undoubtedly found a happy reception downstairs where it was a welcome addition to diet. His counter request for poached fish – most reasonable in his opinion – had not met with the same generosity in his opponent. Kedgeree was grudgingly provided, but its consistency varied from cloggy lumps of rice bound together by starch and processed curry powder with the occasional whisper of over-smoked haddock to a passable (by Auguste's exacting standards) light concoction of rice, cream, and delicately smoked fish and eggs with a mere hint of Indian spices.

Today was one of the latter. Could this be anything to do with Tatiana's return? Auguste was aware that he was not the most popular member of his household to his own kitchen staff, but it did not worry him unduly. High standards engendered not affection but respect in those destined to achieve them for others. Dedicated as both he and John were to the temple of gastronomy, Auguste saw no reason to lower his own standards. If pushed he was forced to admit he might possibly be persuaded to give way graciously over the matter of how to prepare gravy, but he would stand firm on the blancmange. This ancient and delicate savoury dish should not be allowed to sink forever into the tasteless sugary porridge of a Mrs Beeton nursery.

'Red corsets,' Tatiana commented thoughtfully some time later as he finished both his kedgeree and his account of the events of the Old King Cole, and was distracted by the realisation that once again only marmalade had been provided on their table. French recipe it might be, but his French palate required something sweeter at this hour.

'Delightful,' he agreed absently. 'You are wearing one?'

Tatiana laughed. 'If I sat in a chafing dish, you would pay more attention to me, *mon amour*.'

Guilty, Auguste jerked back to full attention. 'Ah, *red* corsets.'

'Why did this child possess one, and why did she hide it in Will's room?'

'As to the first, I cannot guess.'

'I can. She was forbidden to wear them at home. With me, it was the opposite,' she said ruefully. 'Useless armour.'

'And on the second, she told me it was because no one would ever look there.'

'Now why should a child think of that? I would think something or someone put the idea in her head.'

Auguste tried to concentrate. The smell of the Old King Cole's greasy food must be pickling his brains, as well as his clothes. His valet was not impressed, but again Auguste was indifferent to his suffering. His previous acquaintance with valets had been on equal terms at upper servants' dining tables, and he had managed perfectly well to dress himself for forty years, minus two or three when his mother performed the service for him. He had seen no reason to change the status quo on his marriage, just because he was storming the green baize door into high society.

Tatiana had agreed with him. Society was humbug. *All* society, was it not? It was. Then why, she inquired, had he so passively submitted to the hierarchical self-imposed practices of the upper servants when working in large houses? Was it not because it was accepted practice? It was, he admitted (reluctantly). 'Then why cannot you and I, Auguste, accept the practices of the world we live in, and yet live *our* lives, not theirs? You cook, I teach motoring.'

He had opened his mouth to protest, and then found that he had no argument to make. In theory, that was. Practice had proved a little more difficult, but over a year of marriage had made him impervious to disdainful expressions on the faces of his staff.

'I know something you don't know . . .' Little Emmeline's voice seemed to be piping in his head, insisting she took precedence over valets and marmalade. She implied she'd merely overheard general gossip, but he'd seen that look on her face on those of countless parlourmaids and footmen. The look of the smug keyhole-listener. He leapt up from the table.

'You are going already, Auguste?'

'My job, my love.'

'Does His Majesty know you have a job?'

'Of honour,' Auguste added hastily. 'And merely investigation. *Nothing* to do with cuisine.' (This was of course true – how could the Old King Cole aspire to *cuisine* – it merely provided food). 'Moreover the job was given to me by a lady whom you chose – as I shall inform His Majesty, should he ever inquire.'

Her eyes gleamed. 'Very well, Auguste. I trust he never discovers – although I understand from you he *is* somewhat involved through the stolen cross.'

'I must leave. I am going to see a young lady.'

'I am so glad.'

'Of thirteen years old.'

Little Emmeline's home in Holloway was surprisingly modest. Either Little Emmeline's fees were equally modest, or her parents were industriously investing them in 'the Funds' against a rainy day. And with Little Emmeline that rain was already threatening, in Auguste's view. Her dancing talent would not outlast her curiosity as a child performer.

When Auguste confessed he was neither prospective agent nor manager, her parents speedily lost interest and left Auguste alone with their precious offspring in the bleak Sunday parlour, which they now obviously regretted opening up merely for the likes of him. Emmeline was unusually subdued, which he put down either to her being alone with him, or to a guilty conscience – until he realised that this might possibly be Emmeline's normal self in her home surroundings. Only away from Holloway and her parents did she take vengeance on them by launching herself aggressively at her fellow players and audiences. Here, clad in a somewhat longer drearier pinafore dress than her stage costume, she looked a model, if somewhat forlorn, young girl, no longer a child.

'Emmeline, were you a friend of Will Lamb's?'

'No.' She eyed him with scorn. 'Not likely, is it? He took all my applause, his turn coming before me like that. It wasn't fair. I was glad –' she hesitated, and finished weakly '– he was going to be unhappy.'

'What do you mean?' Auguste asked sharply, the hesitation duly noted.

'He was going to run away with that woman, wasn't he?'

'Now how *did* you come to know that?'

'Everyone knew. I told you that.'

'Did she mean it?' he asked lightly.

'How should I know?' Emmeline said guardedly. 'Women say things, don't they?'

'They do indeed,' Auguste agreed. For a moment, there was accord between them. Now was the time. 'Did you overhear Mariella and Will Lamb talking from Miss Turner's room, or from the props room on the other side? You must have been very clever not to be noticed.'

'I *am* clever.' Emmeline looked complacent as she considered whether or not she needed more admiration from Auguste. 'It was easy. No one thinks children are doing any harm when they just hang around doors like I do.'

'And you were doing harm?'

'Who says so?'

'You did.'

'No, I never.'

Auguste gave up this dead-end trail. 'Did they talk about anything else interesting?'

She shrugged. 'Perhaps.'

'You'd like to help find who murdered Will Lamb, wouldn't you?'

She considered this. 'Why?'

Auguste tried to keep a pleasant smile on his face. 'It could bring you to the attention of lots of people. You'd be famous.'

'I'm famous already.'

'Only in this part of London. You would be known all over the country.'

'In Northumberland?'

'Even there,' he assured her readily. Why Northumberland, he wondered? He could not know that Little Emmeline had a fantasy life in which she played the role of Grace Darling, and had decided her future lay in her heroine's birthplace, clad in a red corset or otherwise.

'I remember she was asking him whether he'd changed something in the last few years.'

'His love for her?'

'I don't think so.'

'His shirt?' He tried a light-hearted joke, which she did not even bother to answer. She was frowning, trying hard to remember.

'I think there was something else too.'

'What?'

Such eagerness was unwise with Little Emmeline. 'Aha!'

'You must tell me,' he said gravely.

'Why?'

'It could be important. Very important.'

'I'll think about it,' she said delightedly, power in her hands.

'Emmeline, do more than think. *Tell* me, and tell no one else. No one.'

197

'Why not?'

'Because,' he hesitated. He did not wish to alarm her, but one person had been murdered. The punishment was the same for two murders as for one. 'Because if anyone else knows, it could be dangerous for *you*.' Her eyes lit up with excitement.

He continued quickly: 'And you will never get to Northumberland.'

Left alone, Emmeline went on frowning. If only she *could* remember.

Cherry and Black, clad in smart suits and bowler hats, arrived via the stage door to see Egbert Rose early on Friday afternoon, as though they wished to distance themselves as far as possible from yesterday's pierrot humiliation.

Percy, passing them in the backstage area on his way to his boot cupboard office, stopped in dismay. 'You're still here.'

'So's your debts,' growled Bowler Hat quickwittedly.

'How true, alas, but another few nights like last night and you may depend upon it, it will be a different story,' Percy burbled happily, but tactlessly.

Their faces darkened. 'You put 'em up to it, that's why they booed and threw things.' There was hope in Black's voice.

'What?' Percy looked at them in astonishment, then realised his *faux pas*. 'Oh, dearie me, indeed not. It is quite the tradition at the Old King Cole to barrack new performers; you must not take it personally. The more they boo, the more it means they like you.'

'Want us to go on tonight, do you?'

Percy gazed at them, caught in his own trap. 'Do I hear my name? I am summoned,' he cried wildly, rushing on to the stage.

Something that might have been a sad grin crossed Cherry's face. 'I wish I had been a bailiff,' he remarked wistfully. 'It seems like fun.'

Fun was not uppermost in their minds by the time they had stalked through the corridors, up the stairs and reached Rose's office, save perhaps the fun of guerrilla warfare, so recently demonstrated by the Boers.

'We have some good news for you,' Black informed Rose lugubriously.

'Good.' Rose settled himself down again. He was going to need all his wits about him.

'Co-operation, like we said.' Black rammed the point home.

'Splendid.'

'We've tracked down the bloke that did the fake of the cross –' Cherry's impressive note of triumph implied that they had been trailing the streets since dawn.

'– In return for a promise your lot won't nab him –' Rose's eyes narrowed, '– over this. We 'ad a lot of hard work, my colleague and me, to get him to talk.' Black looked suitably modest. In fact the hard work had been only comparative. The faker hadn't objected to talking since it wasn't for a regular customer, only to the minimal sum being offered for his so doing.

'Who was the customer?'

'Sir Henry Irving. What do you think of that? England's greatest actor involved in this treasonable affair.'

Rose kept his face under control. 'Have you followed this up with Sir Henry yet?'

'No.'

'You'll be lucky to do so. England's greatest actor has been ill in bed, unable to talk or move much, what with all the to-do over the Lyceum closing down. Still, he might have made a big effort, whipped down to Windsor, pinched the cross, putting on a Portuguese accent, and then gone to have a fake made down East, all in order to have a last stab at raising funds to buy his dear old theatre.'

Bleak faces met his theory. 'Bluff.'

'On my part or his?' When Cherry and Black made no answer, Rose continued evenly, 'What have you done with the fake?'

The quick glance between them was ample proof that it was his turn for the dark again. 'None of your business,' Bowler Hat informed him kindly.

'Of course not,' Rose agreed. 'I'll just report to the Assistant Commissioner then that I found it, and perhaps you'll sign a receipt to the effect you've taken it. Just keep the paperwork tidy, eh?'

Greatly to his surprise, Bowler Hat produced a pen and did so.

Rose was still reflecting on this odd turn of events, after they had left, when the Great Brodie marched in, lovingly tended by Inspector Stitch.

'I suppose there must be some urgent reason why I am summoned to attend you, Inspector?' Even in the daytime he seemed to keep up his swell appearance, Rose noticed, as he peeled his kid gloves off with great ceremony.

'Hope I haven't interrupted you in the middle of anything important?'

'Indeed you have. Newmarket is almost upon us.' Brodie laughed.

'Let's hope poor old Will Lamb wasn't hoping to place a bet. Or Henry Irving. You'll be seeing him soon, no doubt.'

Brodie gazed at him blankly, then took this as a tribute to his genius. 'It is true that I am to grace the stage up West. I had not heard Sir Henry was to tread the same boards. One of his Shakespearean monologues, perhaps? It all makes for a varied show.'

'Something you haven't told us, Mr Brodie?'

'About what? My career up West?'

'No. Your movements down East. Last Saturday, to be precise.'

'Not to my knowledge.'

Rose had interviewed too many men, however, not to be aware of tensing muscles. For all his nonchalance Brodie was wary, he decided.

'Frederick Wolf known to you?'

'Not that I am aware.'

'A sword-swallower.'

'Good gracious me, Inspector. How should I know a circus performer?'

'He entertains the queue outside the Old King Cole.'

'Ah, my queue days are over, both as prospective audience and entertainer thereof. We all have to start somewhere, Inspector, and many start with queues. Those of us who are sufficiently talented quickly move inside to warmer climes and seated audiences.'

'Very nice too, sir. So if I asked why you gave Mr Wolf

a parcel to take to North Docks last Saturday afternoon, you'd be able to tell me nothing?'

Horace Brodie gazed at him. 'Do you know, Inspector, I haven't the slightest idea what you are talking about.'

'Mr Wolf recognised you.'

'Then he is lying.'

'He don't strike me as the lying sort.'

'And I do?'

'If so, we'll find out.'

'How very reassuring. I'm glad I'm moving from here, Inspector. I'm terrified.' He laughed loudly, and by the time he left, Rose noticed, he didn't seem at all tense, nor had he asked what the parcel contained. Nor why the police should be quite so interested in it.


'Ah, Auguste, you're earlier than I expected.'

'Tatiana has returned.' Egbert raised an eyebrow. 'Naturally, Egbert, that is *not* the reason I am early.'

'She approves of you broiling chops, then?'

'I have not mentioned that yet, Egbert. There are, after all, more important issues. However, Tatiana wishes me to help find who murdered Will Lamb, not least for Lady Westland's sake, so it comes to the same thing.'

It didn't with Edith, Egbert had found. The means rarely did justify the end, particularly in the case of her cooking and Mr Pinpole's meat.

'A couple of odd things, Auguste, you might be interested in. Sir Henry Irving, for one.' He briefly recounted Special Branch's triumph and Brodie's not unexpected denial of knowing Frederick Wolf. 'And then there's our chaps from Special Branch itself. I could swear they're not crooked themselves, like Meiklejohn and his chums that set the Yard rocking some years back, but they're up to some game or other.'

'Not cricket,' Auguste remarked.

'Very funny. And now, what have *you* got to tell *me*? You're as jumpy as a lobster who sees a pot of boiling water.'

'Have you found Will Lamb's solicitor yet?'

'Stitch has just tracked him down. Not easy. No trace of any will at his home, even of correspondence with a solicitor.'

'I believe you should see that will as soon as possible.'

'Why?'

'It may be the key to his murder.'


Jasper Sprinkle, of Messrs Poslethwaite, Sprinkle & Curlie, looked like a Bath bun, Auguste decided, round, cherubic and of little flavour. His office in the large Bloomsbury house spoke not so much of Mr Sprinkle's personality (whatever it might be) but of the age-old creakiness of Poslethwaite, Sprinkle & Curlie. Mr Sprinkle, he decided, could not be the first Mr Sprinkle, but was more likely the third or even fourth. Perhaps the first Mr Sprinkle had skipped into these Georgian offices the moment the builder's last trowelful of mortar had been deprived of its load.

Gathered round in eager attentiveness to Mr Sprinkle's every word were (besides himself and Egbert), the oddly assorted mix of Evangeline Yapp, Max Hill, the Misses Pear, Percy, Mariella, Nettie, Lady Westland, a Mrs Jones, and an aged gentleman who was, Egbert informed him, a retired clog-dancer. He was also Will's uncle, and his only living relative. This was the selection Egbert had decided should be present. Mrs Jones, who turned out to be Will's landlady, was quietly sobbing, the clog-dancer looked bewildered, and Nettie and Gwendolen Westland were very quiet. Mrs Jones, Auguste decided, might feel Will's death most. Devoted though Nettie was to Will, she was of the stage, and its world was forced to move quickly from new face to face; the inner woman would continue to grieve for Will but his memory would be stored sadly away.

'Who did this terrible thing?' wailed Mrs Jones, appealing to the law in the form of Mr Sprinkle.

'One of his dear friends murdered him,' Nettie said tartly. 'Somebody still running loose round the dear Old King Cole.'

'Bailiffs!' Percy offered lugubriously. 'Those two thugs that keep wandering around. They did it.'

'Why should they?' Rose asked.

Percy looked surprised. 'They knew they wouldn't get their commission if the theatre was saved, of course. So Will had to be got rid of in order to empty my theatre again. I'm surprised you hadn't *realised* that, Inspector.' There was reproof in his voice.

'Thank you, Mr Jowitt,' Gwendolen retorted. 'May I take it you are assuming that Miss Turner and I have abandoned you to your bankrupt fate, or are you still expecting us to appear on your boards this evening?'

Percy realised his second major *faux pas*. 'Forgive me,' he gabbled. 'No, no, I mean, yes, yes.' He abandoned subtlety. 'You've got to be there tonight.'

Nettie laughed. 'Never changes, the old scrounger,

does he?' she observed to Max with no fondness in her voice.

'Dear Percy, what would we do without you?' Max yawned.

Percy looked at him. 'Starve.'

'Possibly,' Max agreed unperturbed. 'I prefer to think, die of thirst.'

Mr Sprinkle, sitting upright to take command, began to feel he was already unsuccessful. He coughed and tried a glare. It worked. 'Mr Lamb's will is not a simple one, though straightforward.' (More so than Mr Sprinkle's sentences, Auguste thought irrelevantly). 'He was, as you can guess, a rich man by most standards. It is, of course, far from usual to discuss such matters before the funeral, but in view of the circumstances and at the request of the police, and lack of objection from Mr Lamb's family, I have agreed.' The clog-dancer did not appear to recognise himself under this description.

'This will was made some time ago, and to my knowledge Mr Lamb did not make another, though it is always possible he did so, lodging it elsewhere.' His expression suggested such a course of action was unthinkable, given the expertise of Poslethwaite, Sprinkle & Curlie.

'This will provides for bequests of fifty pounds to Mr Jowitt, twenty-five pounds to Mr Hill and Mr Brodie, fifty pounds to Mrs Jones, and to Miss Turner. Mr Wilson,' he glanced at the clog-dancer, 'receives one hundred pounds.'

'And the rest?' Mariella asked hoarsely.

'You, Mrs Gomez, are his residuary legatee for personal possessions, income from his estate on publications, copyrights, and phonograph recordings, and,' he paused, 'the balance of his other liquid assets amounting at a rough estimate to about eleven thousand pounds.'

'Is that all?'

'It is a considerable sum,' Mr Sprinkle said reprovingly, and turned away. 'There is one last bequest. This was originally a codicil, but the whole will was replaced five years ago, when his career and wealth were improving rapidly, and it was then incorporated in the main body of the will.'

'How much? Who to?' screamed Mariella.

'About thirty thousand pounds. Mr Lamb had excellent financial advice.' Mr Sprinkle looked modest.

'*Who?*'

'Mr Thomas Yapp.'

Evangeline was the first to break the astounded silence of her colleagues. 'Why *him*? Why not me?' she cried heartrendingly.

'I am not at liberty—' Mr Sprinkle began, only to be interrupted by another shriek from the lady.

'Will was being careful of my reputation. He wanted no one to know of our great love.'

'He didn't love you, you old fat,' Mariella informed her coldly.

'Of course he did. But I am a *respectable* married woman. Unlike *some*,' Evangeline retorted, holding her own.

'You've got *plenty* of Will's money, Mariella,' Marigold pointed out in a trembling voice. 'And any income to come. Isn't that enough?'

Mariella didn't bother to reply.

'Poor old Will,' Nettie said harshly. 'Generous to a fault, but he did so hate to be put on. And look what happens, swindled by an auburn-haired cock-teaser.'

Mariella stood up trembling. 'I loved Will,' she declared vehemently. 'I think it's sweet of him not to have changed his will although I was forced to marry another.'

'Perfectly sweet,' agreed Nettie. 'I wonder who persuaded him not to change it?'

'Thomas Yapp obviously had a good try,' Mariella said viciously. 'I'd not seen Will for years. How could I have influenced him?'

'Yes, you have,' Mrs Jones cried indignantly. 'I recognise you. You're the lady came upsetting him a few months ago, and that weren't the first time.'

'I was asked to by Mr Jowitt, wasn't I, Percy?' Mariella shrieked, caught out. 'He wanted me to persuade Will to come here.'

Jowitt did not reply; he was wondering how far fifty pounds would go in paying off the debts of the Old King Cole.

Mariella, cornered, looked round for someone to kick. 'Why isn't old Yapp here? If you ask me, he knew all about it and is keeping out of the way.'

'Why should he?' snapped Evangeline, a lioness ready to defend her unexpectedly rich cub.

'I'll tell you why. In case our Inspector here gets in into his head that our Thomas might have wanted to hurry his fortune along.'

'Not half as much as you,' Nettie declared forthrightly.

'Miss Turner,' pink spots of anger flushed Mariella's cheeks, 'I don't know what you mean, I'm sure.'

Egbert decided to intervene. 'She's implying that the only reason you agreed to run away with Mr Lamb after the performance tonight was that you knew very well he'd be dead by then.'

'That's slander or something, isn't it?' she shrieked.

'That depends,' Mr Sprinkle said brightly, 'on whether it is true or not.'

'Here, what is this?' Mariella demanded, looking round the assembled company, seeing nothing but condemnation in their eyes. She saw only one possible ally. She hurled herself across the room and knelt dramatically at Auguste's feet, resting her red-gold head in his lap. He regarded the head with less than aesthetic admiration, his nose deducing that the Koko hair oil so liberally adorning it was not of recent application. 'You'll save me, won't you, Auguste?'

He looked in appeal at Egbert, who folded his arms, cast his eyes upwards and gave him no help whatsoever. 'There, *ma belle*,' he murmured ineffectually. 'The innocent need fear nothing.'

This did not appear to soothe Mariella at all.

'Thomas Yapp, the dark horse, eh?' Egbert remarked thoughtfully to Auguste as their cab jolted its way to Wapping.

'But he was out front all the while.'

'He could have hurried in before the performance. Will, we know, had two visitors before the curtain went up. One was most likely your beautiful lady-friend Mariella—'

'She is not,' Auguste interrupted fiercely. 'And how could the other be Yapp? He could not have carried out the ransacking of Will's dressing-room.'

'True. But we don't know that it was the murderer
did that. If Yapp's our man, then money must have
been the motive, and whoever went into the dressing-
room was looking for the cross.'

'Then why, *mon ami*, did he not find it? And why,
incidentally,' Auguste added, '*did* Will leave the bulk of
his fortune to Mr Yapp?'

There were others anguishing over Will Lamb's will.
Once she had recovered from the shock of discovering
she was not the major beneficiary, Mariella applied her
mind to how she could break the news to Miguel that
she was a beneficiary at all. It was a delicate situation.
He might now well believe she had really planned to
leave with Will after tonight's performance. Miguel
always was a fool. Both of them were, he and Will. She'd
been taken in by Miguel's dark looks and passionate
eyes. She hadn't known then about his meanness and
stupid jealousy. Now was her chance of freedom, of
taking her rightful place in Society – without her
doggies, without ever singing on stage again. Of course
she'd never have run away with Will, but equally she
wasn't going to stay with Miguel. She considered a
moment. She would stay with him till she got the money
through and then leave before he could get his hands
on it. Unfortunately this prudent course of action meant
being nice to him – temporarily.

By the time she reached home after an extended visit
to Gamages, she needed to be very nice indeed. Miguel
had already heard the news, since Egbert Rose had
thoughtfully called in to tell him.

He faced her, trembling with righteous rage, arms

akimbo. 'You were making a fool of *me*, Miguel Gomez. You were to leave me for Will, and for that he left you all his money.'

'No, darling.' Mariella adjusted her smile and came close to him in order that he could smell her new attar of roses. 'Of course not.'

He flung her dramatically away. 'After all we had planned for ourselves. *I* was to make you rich,' he shouted. 'You did not *tell* me about the will.'

'I didn't know about it,' she wailed from the carpet which she had hit with an alarming degree of force. 'It was a complete surprise.'

'I don't believe you. You *were* going to run away with Will.'

Mariella was beginning to get very tired of those words. She wondered how many more denials would be needed before she could have the cup of tea she was longing for. She made a major effort to suppress irritation, as the quickest way to her objectives. 'Just think of all we can do with this money. And there'll be an income too from his books and songs and—'

'Who knew?' he demanded suddenly. 'Who knew Will Lamb was leaving all this to you?'

She shrugged. 'Will and I referred to it a few days ago in the Old King Cole. That awful child might have realised what we were talking about.'

'Emmeline? Then everyone might have heard,' he said thoughtfully, glad he hadn't wasted money on a bust improver.

'Does it matter?'

'Will Lamb is dead, so of course it matters.' He frowned, then laughed. 'Me, I shall be your manager,' he crowed. 'You think I am just your pimp, but now I shall *manage* you.'

'For my money, yes, not lovers—' she shouted crossly, tired of the same old merry-go-round of accusations.

'So you *do* have lovers.'

This had not been a good idea, Mariella belatedly realised. She had gone astray and every sacrifice had to be made, even if it came before cups of tea. 'Only you, my beloved.' She threw off her cape, ripped off her blouse (Mrs Whatever-her-name-was could sew the buttons on again, she didn't charge much), tore off her skirt, petticoats, and posed invitingly in stays and drawers, then her hands went to the *bébé* blue ribbon that supported the latter, pushed them down, stepped neatly out of them, and seeing she had gained his attention, slowly undid the corset and daintily lifted the long chemise.

Now she had his *full* attention. He was hardly able to blurt out, 'Where's your mermaid's tail, Mariella?' and join in her merry laughter before the cup of tea was inevitably postponed for at least ten minutes.

The day's dramas had not ended for Mariella. Miguel, secure in the afterglow of possession, had for once left her alone in the theatre while he pursued some mission of his own. Mariella went out to the shed behind the Old King Cole where her little doggies were left during the performance. (Jamrach's animal trainer who also had his turn in the second half insisted on it.) Conscientiously she counted the doggies as they dutifully hopped out of their baskets and crept into the somewhat larger baskets that were their temporary home. Tonight something else awaited them, or rather their mistress, as Mariella opened the door and went into the dark shed. The doggies were delighted to find extra company but she was not, particularly since it took the large angry form of Fernando. He, too, had heard the news of her fortune.

'He leave you all his money?'

'Some of it. You are pleased for me, Fernando?' Mariella tried to say brightly, but aware from the grip of his hand on her wrist that he was far from pleased.

'You were going to run away with him.'

'No.' Exasperation seized her. 'How many times do I have to say it?'

'Everybody tell me. I do not believe them. They think me stupid. You too.'

'Of course not. I'm very fond of you,' she said wearily.

This was usually a guarantee of arousing Fernando's ecstatic devotion, but not, she realised to her alarm, tonight. Even in the dark, his eyes held more savagery than devotion. She was uncomfortably aware of his angry face and his enormous strength.

'You fond of your husband.'

'Yes.'

'And you fond of Will Lamb.'

'Yes.' Cautiously now.

'And you very fond of me.'

'Of course.' She began to be frightened.

The doggies yapped delightedly, as he seized her in a bear hug with both arms, though not precisely where a bear would traditionally clutch. His intentions were made all too obvious by his tugging at the second blouse which was going to need the attentions of Mrs Whatever-her-name-was, and the large hand was questing around her skirt in places no self-respecting bear would pick as his first mouthful. Fernando's mouth, clumsily over hers, stopped any hope of her screaming for help.

Fortunately, Auguste, hearing a noise in the shed and suspecting Lizzie and Joe of yet more philandering when the eels remained uncollared, interrupted them, much to his own surprise. Mariella's wildly flapping hands made him instantly realise that this was not another of her own seduction attempts.

'That's enough, Fernando,' he said firmly and pleasantly.

Reluctantly Fernando disengaged, sank on to the floor and began to cry. Mariella threw herself into Auguste's arms. While soothing her and helping her to straighten her clothes, Miguel arrived in search of his wife and misunderstood the situation. Taken by surprise from the rear, Auguste found himself yanked by the collar and sent spinning across the yard to collapse in a painful heap by the fence. He scrambled to his feet, and faced with a maniacal Portuguese outraged husband hastily reacted in his own defence. Mariella's shriek of 'It was Fernando, Miguel,' bought a quick response, which unfortunately left Auguste's punch without a home. He was precipitated off balance and into another heap on the ground.

'Mariella, Fernando is dangerous,' Miguel roared, administering a kick to the sobbing strong man. 'Please remember that. *Especially* now. Remember the mermaid's tail.'

Whatever he might mean by these incomprehensible words, Mariella appeared to understand them,

Auguste observed, painfully picking himself up. Sobbing, she promised she would.

By the interval, the Saturday performance bade fair to be a lacklustre anti-climax. There were no catastrophes, but fire and sparkle were noticeably absent. It affected all performers as though each one caught the mood on arrival, and left dissatisfied and petulant. In compensation, barracking too was merely half-hearted, a fact which gave Jowitt great pleasure. Only Nettie's caustic comments reduced the situation to its true perspective.

The malaise even reached Lizzie, whose beaming smile had been replaced by a scowl. What, Auguste asked her anxiously, was amiss?

'Love,' she replied curtly, slapping an innocent herring down on the gridiron with unnecessary force. Auguste winced. 'Men,' Lizzie amplified, following suit with the next one.

'Here you are dedicated to your work, Lizzie. You must put other matters aside if you are to be a true cook.'

'Man's love is of man's life a thing apart,' Lizzie intoned dolorously. '''Tis woman's whole existence.'

Auguste looked at her in astonishment. 'When did you become acquainted with the works of Lord Byron, Lizzie?'

'It was written on a picture me ma had. Daft, innit?'

'Apparently not, if you continue treating God's gifts of food in such an abominable manner,' Auguste retorted crossly. 'Kindly take care with that pie. You have flaked off one corner of the pastry.'

'Pies!' she cried scornfully, and burst into tears.

'*What* is the matter now, Lizzie?' he asked in exasperation.

'I told Joe off for pinching me pie last night. Now he's not 'ere no more.'

'Was it by any chance one of Mrs Jolly's pies?'

'You don't think I'd eat Mrs Mount's stuff, do you?'

'So, you have quarrelled with Joe?' he deduced guiltily, though it took no great detective skill. The situation was serious, not least because there was no one to pick up the pies from Mrs Jolly's. He instantly considered the choices for relief pieman. There could, in the circumstances, be only one. Himself.

'Do not cry, Lizzie,' he said with relief. 'I will collect the pies myself.'

Oddly, Lizzie howled the louder. 'I don't care who gets the bloomin' pies. I wants Joe.'

Mariella's tribulations were not over. Violet and Marigold seized the opportunity of being left in the dressing-room alone with her, after Dolly declared her intention of 'having it out with Horace'.

'Dear Will, how you will miss him,' Violet cooed.

'Oh yes,' Mariella replied mechanically, still shaken from her encounter with Fernando.

'Marigold and I are so pleased for you over your good fortune, and do share your grief.'

'Thank you. What for?' asked Mariella absently, still worrying lest Fernando crash in.

'His death,' Marigold said, shocked. 'He was . . . he was going to help us, you know.'

'Who? Fernando?'

'No. *Will*!' Violet tried to keep impatience at bay with

a bright understanding smile. 'Marigold has a little problem, you see.'

'We all do,' Mariella replied dismissively.

'A little foreigner,' Marigold dispensed with subtlety.

'Little *what*?'

'Baby!' Violet followed suit.

Mariella was suddenly all attention, studying Marigold's outline carefully. 'You've been put up the spout?'

'He promised us money – so that we could live. He said he might come to live with us and the baby.'

'What on earth can I do about it? He's dead.' Mariella was frantically wondering whether the will could be overturned if the baby were Will's. Surely not for a bastard. A sudden alarming thought. Will hadn't been so foolish as to marry the girl, had he? 'How sad,' Mariella said brightly. 'Your baby's father dead.'

'No, he's not.' Marigold was bewildered.

Mariella stared at her. 'But, Will—'

'Will wasn't the father. He was a friend,' Marigold said, shocked.

Mariella relaxed. No need to be polite any longer. 'Who was it – or don't you know?' she sneered.

Violet looked meaningfully at Marigold. 'I think we should tell people. He hasn't been very nice to us.'

'It wasn't Miguel, was it?' Mariella asked in sudden hope. She would have a real excuse for leaving then.

Marigold looked aghast. 'No. Surely you didn't think we were telling little tales on him—'

'Or trying to blackmail you into giving us money,' Violet finished for her, smiling brightly.

'No,' Mariella replied curtly, disappointing them.

'It was Horace.'

Mariella grinned. 'The old lecher. Does Dolly know?'

'Dolly?'

'You don't think she really is an innocent maid up from the country, do you?'

'We have no idea,' Violet said coldly, returning briskly to the matter in hand. 'So you do see our predicament? We need money, and Will didn't have time to give us any before he was murdered. We thought you might help.'

'Then you're as crazy as he was.'

'There's no need to be rude.'

'Go away, dear. Bring the little bastard up to sing "Never go as far as Flo",' Mariella giggled.

'I shouldn't laugh too much. We know who gave Will the cross.' Violet was quietly indignant as she and Marigold prepared to wipe the dust of the Old King Cole off their feet. Will had told them of 'Auntie's jewellery' and they could not resist a tiny peep when he wasn't watching.

Did they indeed? Mariella sat thinking for some time after they had gone.

Dolly too left, hot in pursuit of Horace at his next engagement at the Lyle. He found her waiting for him as he came offstage.

'You're off to the bright lights then, Horace?'

'I am. Look after yourself, my dear.'

'Is that all you can say to me?' she cried.

He considered. 'I believe so.'

'That wasn't what you said to me that night at the Britannia.'

'You're a lovely girl, my dear.'

He still had power over her. She blenched. 'I can come and see you sometimes, Horace?'

'Of course,' he agreed generously.

'You heard Will left you twenty-five pounds?' Dolly was anxious to keep the conversation going.

'I did. I heard *all* about it to the point of boredom.'

'Did you expect more?' she asked, slightly maliciously.

'That my dear, is one of the sadnesses of life. We always expect more.' He patted her cheek and walked away laughing.

Harry Pickles was not laughing. He was one of those who had expected more – anything, in fact. He was an old friend of Will's, wasn't he? Everyone had been left something but him. There was only one bright spot.

He threw open the door of Nettie's dressing-room without bothering to knock. 'I hear your old pal only left you a pittance. One in the eye for you.'

'At least you'll stop this nonsense of thinking Will and I were lovers, Harry.' Nettie, affected by the general malaise, dropped her guard to speak quite naturally to him.

He took full advantage. 'He obviously didn't think much of you, gal, but that don't mean you didn't fancy him, eh? Perhaps you found out he'd left the lot to Mariella and old Yapp?'

'Perhaps I did, Harry. Perhaps I did,' she said quietly.

When he had gone, disappointed in her reaction, she leaned her head in her hands. The game had to go on. Night after night, while she could still totter on to a stage. That's what the halls did to you. Took you over, wore you out and demanded your life. And what for?

For a few minutes of knowing you'd lit a flame inside yourself so strong it felt like you were burning up. The flames flared as the music stopped and you heard the roar of your audience, or even during the song, as you hit a note that reached its heart as well as its ears. But how often would it flare now, now that Will had gone, and taken the best of her with him?

Evangeline for once had given herself time to think. At the end of the performance she barred the way as her husband went to follow the audience to the bar. 'Thomas,' she said quietly, in the now silent auditorium, 'he left me nothing. He left it all to you. Why?'

'What?' Yapp raised the glass that he, as Chairman, insisted on having by him. 'Who? Left me what?'

'My beloved Will. He left all his money – well, over half of it, thirty thousand pounds – to you. Why? When he loved *me*?' Evangeline was by no means sure that her private interpretation of his motivation was correct. Thomas was very odd about Will Lamb and always had been.

Thomas gazed at her, gazed at the glass, found life too much for him, and sat down. 'How nice of him,' he said vaguely.

'I think,' Evangeline found a solution to satisfy her, 'that it was his form of revenge, because I would not, could not return his love. I was after all married to you.'

'I daresay that was it, my love.'

Thomas drained the glass. After all, he could afford all the whisky in the world. He need never work at the Old King Cole again. He could get as drunk as a lord. He almost was a lord, with that money. New horizons flashed temptingly in front of him. He could even leave Evangeline.

'Why didn't you tell me he'd left it to you? You must have known.'

'I don't think I did, my love.'

'I could have lived like a queen all these years,' she wailed. A short pause. 'I can do so now though.' Another pause. 'I won't tell them, Thomas.'

'Tell who what?'

'The police.'

'Tell *them* what?'

'That it was you got Percy to ask Will Lamb to come here.'

Auguste had spent, in contrast to most of those at the Old King Cole, a rewarding evening. He had a feeling that one of the great passions of his life had begun. Let Egbert continue his relationship with Ma Bisley. For himself, Mrs Jolly was the doorway to new and exciting fields. Or, more accurately, pies. He had set forth to Neptune Street, fearing to find another Mount's Pie Emporium, for one pie was but flimsy evidence.

Oh, how wrong he was. If smell alone had not seduced him, one look into her gas-lit windows would have made him her slave for life. One window was dressed in what he had learned was the traditional manner for an eel-pie shop: eels displayed on a huge bed of parsley surrounded by the products they were privileged to make. The other window contained not only the other traditional pastries associated with such shops, cranberry tarts, and apple tarts, but some of Mrs Jolly's other specialities: beefsteak pies, hot apple fritters, meat puddings, mutton pies, fish pies— His eye could take in no more beauty, and Auguste marched inside.

And met Mrs Jolly.

Mrs Jolly was not a tall woman, hardly reaching Will Lamb's height. Nor was she fat. Bustling was the word Auguste chose, not in an inquisitive, irritating sense, but with the decisive movements that spoke of a woman who knew where she was going. Her pink cheeks were full, her eyes bright like a robin's, her hair swept back Queen Victoria style, under a spotless cap. She was not over-generous with her smiles, and her approval, or the opposite, he sensed, would be conveyed by those considering eyes.

He took a deep breath. 'I have come from the Old King Cole.'

Mrs Jolly did not waste words. She entered a note in her record book, she bent down, extracted two large boxes, and handed over her produce.

Auguste bowed, and took paradise within his arms.

# Chapter Eight

'And very nice too.' Egbert looked approvingly at the glass of champagne cup which Tatiana handed him. Sunday at the Yard was not so hard if it involved luncheon at Queen Anne's Gate. This should by rights have been his fortnightly day off, but not on this case. A momentary twinge of remorse at the thought of Edith alone with Mr Pinpole's tough beef was dispelled. 'Where's Auguste, if I might ask?'

Tatiana pulled a face. 'I regret to inform you, Egbert, he is in the kitchen. He claimed your presence at Sunday luncheon was sufficient reason for him to check what was going on in the kitchen. I rather fear it might not be going *on* so much as going *out*, so far as John, our chef, is concerned. Auguste is not—' She broke off and laughed.

'The soul of tact?' Egbert finished blandly.

'He says two artistes should be dedicated to the achievement of perfection and John will understand.'

Auguste walked in, still wearing an apron, and a flushed expression that suggested the achievement of perfection had not been without difficulties.

'*Eh bien, chéri?*' Tatiana greeted him cautiously.

'John,' Auguste remarked airily to the room in general, 'quite saw my point of view over the caper sauce.'

'I am so glad.' Tatiana stood by the window, her attention suddenly caught by the street below.

'A little diplomacy is all that is required. English mutton requires larding, parboiling and broiling, whereas John seems quite determined to ignore such elementary procedures. I am afraid there he is a little obstinate and has *boiled* throughout. The very least one could do to achieve a satisfactory result is to provide a soft sauce *soubise* to complement its blandness, but no, he would maintain a butter caper sauce was preferable.'

'But you persuaded him in the end?'

'Naturally.' Auguste took his glass of champagne cup.

'Then why, Auguste, is John walking across Bird Cage Walk into St James's Park with a very determined stride and his hat and overcoat on?'

Auguste leapt up and joined her hurriedly at the window, guilt creeping over his face.

'Go after him, Auguste,' Tatiana suggested sweetly.

'*Mais*—'

'Please, *chéri*.'

Egbert studied his drink with great interest, as Auguste, the epitome of injured pride, hurried out, and he and Tatiana watched from the window as Auguste, running by now, went in pursuit of his errant cook, and after a few moments' consultation, the two figures walked back, if not in harmony, at least in the right direction.

'Leaves are changing colour in the park, I see. Fine sight, eh?' Egbert remarked, on Auguste's somewhat crestfallen re-entry into the drawing-room.

'It is,' Auguste replied shortly.

'Wish I could have a stroll myself, but duty calls. You'll forgive me, Tatiana, but this ain't entirely a social visit.'

'Naturally, Egbert. You have two crimes to solve, both of great urgency and national importance.'

'Two murders, and *perhaps* two separate crimes,' Egbert reminded her.

'Prince Henry the Navigator's cross is an icon of national honour.' Tatiana sighed. 'Such symbols become a burden, and heritage a duty, not a pleasure.'

'Still has to be done.'

'Indeed, yes, Egbert. My third cousin, the Czar, is a man of simple tastes, and his wife also, but they have inherited the trappings and riches of a family and must look after them for the nation's sake. Or that is the way he sees it. No one stops to ask *why* or at what cost to that nation.'

'With all due respect to your other third cousin, Tatiana, King Bertie doesn't seem to have the same attitude. Careless, letting two thieves walk off with a priceless relic.'

'You think so?' Tatiana looked directly at Egbert, and Auguste, catching the glance between the two of them, felt for a moment he had missed an idea that was communicating itself between them.

'His Majesty, Egbert, is not such a straightforward case as the Czar. He may seem to be, but he has had a long time to wait while his mother occupies the throne. He may have spent it with ideas of his own. Now that he is King, he may feel he has not a great deal of time to put them into effect.'

'Ideas on what?'

'The future of Europe, for instance,' she answered soberly. 'Did you know there are those who believe the Great Pyramid foretells the future of the world if only one can interpret it correctly? Those that so far think they can do so believe that Europe's future trembles in the balance at this very moment, and that there is the shadow of a great war approaching which will affect the whole world. Whether this is so or not, His Majesty has strong views on the need to preserve the unity of Europe.'

'Some say, *ma belle*,' Auguste joined the conversation suddenly, 'he merely wishes to keep France sweet so that he can continue to enjoy the pleasures of the Can-Can, and Gay Paree.'

Tatiana laughed. 'I fear Auguste is not altogether an admirer of some of my relations.'

'Not those who divide an artiste from his craft.'

'You and cooking, Auguste?' Egbert asked, amused.

'You were talking about pies in your sleep, Auguste,' Tatiana revealed. 'I wonder why that could be? I suppose the Old King Cole does not by some mere chance have a restaurant?'

'It does not, my love,' Auguste replied firmly. This was true. How could its abominable eating-room be termed a restaurant?

'And you cried out to a Mrs Jolly. It seems this is a lady you love with great passion,' Tatiana continued inexorably.

'I believe,' Auguste said hastily, 'we are being summoned to luncheon.' The door had providentially opened to reveal their butler, Jones, with the welcome news.

Enjoying himself hugely, Egbert held out his arm to Tatiana, leaving Auguste to bring up the rear of their small procession, as they descended the staircase to Sunday luncheon.

The Old King Cole took on the unreality of a Grimm fairy-tale, as they discussed the case over luncheon. Auguste's face darkened as he realised the sauce was indisputably better than *soubise*. Moreover, the mutton had been nowhere near a gridiron. But with Tatiana's eye on him, and Egbert's loud praises at John's efforts, he managed to turn his thoughts from luncheon (so far as this was possible) to Egbert's problems.

'If Will Lamb was murdered for the sake of the cross, it doesn't make sense for the murderer to leave it behind.'

'Suppose someone stole the true cross and substituted a fake?' Auguste suggested, trying to subdue a sneaking feeling that discussion of the cross was as helpful as John's rehashing of yesterday's baron of beef. It kept the problem alive without striking the slightest spark from the tinder-box of cuisine (or detection).

'Sir Henry Irving had the fake made, and Will Lamb went to Windsor to nab the cross. That what you believe, Auguste? You'll be telling me next that HM played a part in this too.'

'It so happens I am to visit the Palace tomorrow,' Tatiana remarked innocently. 'His Majesty asked me to make some purchases in Paris on his behalf.'

Again a glance between Egbert and Tatiana. *Was* he missing something? Auguste wondered. 'I believe the cross is a red herring, Egbert, so far as Will's murder is concerned, and the cause of it must lie in the Old King

Cole. Will gets letters warning him off, the raven is released to frighten him away, he sees ghosts everywhere. Perhaps someone thought the will might be changed because of the cross business.'

'Or maybe the will was the reason someone was anxious to get him there in the first place. My word,' Egbert's attention was suddenly diverted, 'you've got a good cook here.' He plunged further into the apple charlotte.

Auguste gulped, refraining from comment with great effort. 'We do not yet know who.'

'I wonder what old Jowitt's doing this afternoon?' Egbert said resignedly.

Old Jowitt had put on his carpet slippers, determined to ignore the bright sunshine of the Sunday afternoon, when the rest of the East End of London was disporting itself, children in sailor suits, husbands and wives in Sunday best, strolling round Victoria Park. He favoured the newspaper, a bottle of whisky, and a pipe. A stuffed parrot glared at such indulgence from under his glass jar, the dark-coloured curtains were eagerly awaiting the moment when they could be drawn, a small fire burned in the grate. A plate of crumpets, butter and toasting fork lay on the hearth. Percy was a remarkably happy man. The bailiffs seemed to have vanished, he had had fifty pounds bequeathed to him and he had found friends in high places: Scotland Yard, Magnificent Mashers, Nettie Turners – all had the good of Percy Jowitt at heart. None of them would let poor Percy starve. He was, nevertheless, painfully aware that next week's programme did not display the same élan and flair of the performers of the week before. Percy believed in looking on the bright side, however, and the bright side told him that there was unlikely to be another murder to upset the proceedings, even if the programme did include Little Emmeline and Evangeline, and now lacked Nettie, Horace, Will Lamb and the Magnificent Masher. It suddenly occurred to him that now Thomas was a rich man, he too might desert the ship, but he comforted himself that Thomas would never do such a thing, for he was far too loyal. Even if he did, there would be compensations: at least he would take Evangeline with him.

The unexpected knock on the door disturbed his afternoon. He remembered with annoyance that he'd given the girl the afternoon off and that meant he'd have to open it himself. He was not pleased. He was even less pleased when the reality intruded in the form of his ex-bailiff and his cook. It took some moments for him to recall that they were in fact something to do with the police.

'Cosy little den you have here,' Rose remarked as Percy grumpily led the way into his living-room. The parlour hadn't been opened since Maud died twenty years earlier.

Gratified, Percy cheered up. 'It is, isn't it?' He shifted a pile of newspapers on to the floor to free a second chair and looked round helplessly for a third. If cooks ever sat. Did they sit? He had a vague idea that they stood all the time, waiting for orders. Still it was Sunday, and Percy was an obliging man. He spotted a piano stool submerged under the summer curtains which had been taken down by the girl last month and left there, presumably for spring. He tipped the pile on to the floor and dragged it forward.

'Cast your mind back, Mr Jowitt.'

Percy tried to look helpful. 'To when?'

'To when you decided to ask Miss Turner and Will Lamb down here. Which of them was your first choice, for example?'

Percy looked scared. 'I really cannot recall.'

'Try again.'

Percy cast wildly around in his memory. 'Do you know,' he cried, well pleased, 'I do believe it was Will. What do you think of that?' Well satisfied, Percy placed his hands on the paunch that might have been there if he ever remembered to feed it properly.

'And it was *your* idea? That right?'

'Naturally.' An air of hauteur replaced satisfaction.

'Even though he's been murdered?'

Percy grasped the point. 'Perhaps it wasn't entirely mine. I believe someone or other mentioned the name which gave me the idea.'

'Try to remember exactly.'

'During our little celebration.'

'For what?'

'I found it was forty years since the Old King Cole music hall opened. Magnificent day. So I said why don't we all have one of Mrs Jolly's pies – no disparagement to Mr Beezer our then cook, naturally – and a bowl of punch. The punch was extraordinarily good. Mr Brodie got quite carried away, indeed we all became a little tipsy.'

Rose's eye went to the whisky bottle, but he said nothing.

'Yes, I do remember,' Percy continued. 'It all began as a joke.'

'*What you need is Marie Lloyd and Dan Leno, Percy,*' Horace Brodie roared.

'*Percy couldn't afford to pay Leno for a half a minute,*' Pickles jeered.

'*The Great Chirgwin?*' twittered Dolly.

'*Not while I'm here,*' Horace roared again, smacking her bottom affectionately.

'*Hope that won't be long,*' Pickles shouted.

'*You're right. I'm off to Gay Paree, fellows.*'

'*And I know who's coming with you,*' trilled Dolly dancing on the table, not taking him seriously.

'*Don't wait up, don't wait up for me, Dolly,*' Horace hiccuped, entirely seriously. '*Who are you going to replace me with, Percy?*'

'*I'd like to meet Dan Leno,*' sighed Mariella.

'*I'm sure you would. You like short men, don't you?*' her husband informed her.

'*Like Will Lamb?*' Pickles giggled. '*What about Marie Lloyd or Nettie? I notice you don't want to meet them again.*'

'*Dear old Will,*' Thomas Yapp tossed back his second glass of punch, surprised it had such a delightful kick in it. Percy wasn't usually that generous. '*Why don't you invite him?*'

'*Dear old Will,*' chorused Pickles. '*Yes, let's have him down, Percy. Invite Nettie too, and Will can cheer up the box office, and all our bloomin' wives, Nettie, Mariella, and even Evangeline here.*'

Evangeline attempted to draw herself up with dignity. '*Do not,*' she said with dignity, '*speak like that of the man I love.*'

Thomas's hands tightened on his glass, as Percy looked

*blearily around. 'I've had a good idea,' Percy told them
importantly. 'It's just come to me. I'll give Will Lamb a
week's booking.'*

'It was most odd. Suddenly everyone was talking about
Nettie and Will. So the idea came to me – I think.'

'*Who* was talking most?'

'Pickles, I believe, Thomas, perhaps others.' He looked
appealingly at Rose. 'Somehow, though as you know
I'm not a fanciful man,' he admitted humbly, 'I felt my
regulars were very, very eager that Nettie and Will
should come. An artiste like me is sensitive to
atmosphere.'

The atmosphere here was getting overpowering, and
Auguste was glad when Egbert got up to go.

'Ah well.' Percy brightened. 'Pity there are not enough
crumpets for three.' He had a sudden thought. 'Mr Er –
er, I must tell you, I'm not impressed. You should
improve your herrings. I had a complaint only the other
day – only one, it is true—' he added hastily as he saw
the thunderclouds gather on Auguste's face.

'You'll have to find yourself a new cook,' Rose told
him, quickly averting trouble. 'I'm going to need Mr
Didier's help.'

'He's a bailiff as well as a cook?' Percy asked, muddled.

'I'm a *detective*.' Rose was irritated. 'You've had a
murder here, remember?'

'I remember,' Percy agreed gloomily.

Egbert cast a look at the crumpets and took his
revenge. 'And I'll ask you, Jowitt, to be so good as to
accompany us to the theatre *now*.'

'Is that really necessary?' Percy asked plaintively.

'It is.'

'But I have to find a new cook.'

'Appoint Miss Lizzie,' Auguste told him firmly. 'She is untrained save by experience, but she has the right instincts.'

'Who's Lizzie?' her employer wailed.

'The young lady who assisted me last week.'

'You mean the girl?' Percy looked puzzled. 'Can she cook herrings?'

'Much better than I.' Self-sacrifice was well worth it in the interests of Lizzie's career.

The Old King Cole on a Sunday smelled of stale air, of stale food and greasepaint, of human sweat on costumes from which their owners had temporarily departed.

'What do you want to see?' Percy asked complainingly, lumbering through the stage door.

'This.' Egbert flung open the door of the props room adjoining Will's dressing-room. 'You two go next door and have a chat, will you?'

Auguste shivered as he went into the still untouched room, with Percy reluctantly following. The Old King Cole seemed infected by evil, not just by the stillness of a Sunday. It was more even than that a death had taken place. It was as if there were undercurrents here that divided each of these performers in suspicion and hate.

'She can't manage,' Percy pronounced loudly.

'Who?'

'The girl.'

'Get Miss Lizzie an assistant.'

'*Pay* someone you mean?' Percy asked, horrified.

'Mr Jowitt, if you pay good wages your trade will improve.'

Percy thought this over. 'My niece's husband has just lost his job as a coalman, he could do it.'

'Coalmen are not cooks. *I* will arrange it.' He would begin by asking Mrs Jolly if she knew of someone suitable.

Jolly – what odd names people had in this country. In China he had heard people had names like Night-of-the-Shining Moon. Perhaps he could institute such a system here. Auguste of the *Cailles Farcies*. Monsieur Auguste Eel Pie—

'Auguste,' Egbert was shouting sharply. 'Come here!'

When Egbert used that tone of voice, Auguste ran. He found him, not next door, but in the wings looking into the corner.

'Look at that fish tank.'

Auguste did so.

Mariella's fish tank contained more than its usual rocks and chute. It contained a human body. Eyes staring, black hair streaming, it was Miguel Gomez and he was dead.

Auguste felt cold and sick. Some hours later the oppressive evil of the Old King Cole had not yet lifted, although the body had now been taken away. It had turned out to be one of the most unpleasant afternoons of his life. He and Egbert had had to haul Gomez's body with great difficulty out of the tank to establish what they both already knew – that he was dead. Washing in the inadequate facilities of the theatre, and drying themselves and their clothes in the trapped warmth of

234

the dark kitchens had resulted in even lower spirits. A police doctor, photographer, and fingerprint sergeant had busied themselves at their tasks. Stitch had been despatched to break the news to Gomez's widow, and Percy abandoned hope of crumpets; they remained a far-off ideal only to be contemplated when the horrors that afflicted his beloved theatre had vanished.

'Stunned and then drowned.' Egbert came over to Auguste at last. 'Dead a few hours when we found him.'

'Not last night, after the performance?'

'Possible, but unlikely. We'll know more after the pathologist has had a look. His wife will tell us, anyway.'

'Unless she—' Auguste broke off.

'Did it,' Egbert finished for him. 'Not the easiest of methods to murder your husband.'

'And if it was because of the cross, why should she murder Gomez so soon after Will Lamb's death and draw attention to herself?'

'Mariella inherits under Lamb's will so you wouldn't think she'd want Lamb involved in the cross affair at all, for fear he'd change his mind over the will. He seems to have been an old-fashioned sort of chap, Will Lamb. He wouldn't take kindly to robbing England to pay Portugal. So it must have been planted on him.'

'Except that if the Gomezes did involve Lamb, he would provide some protection, would he not? Scotland Yard would hardly put *him* in the Tower, and that would shelter them too.'

'Especially if Henry Irving ordered the fake.' Egbert sighed. 'This is a madhouse, Auguste.'

'No, *mon ami*. A theatre, the home of illusion. There is a carefully planned script somewhere.'

'That fish-tank murder didn't come from a script. It looks like panic, to my mind.'

'By a man. No woman could do it.'

'Not alone, maybe. She'd need a helper.'

'Someone strong,' Auguste agreed slowly, memories of yesterday coming back to him. 'Very strong.'

'Not,' Egbert said, following his thoughts, 'necessarily. It could be a matter of balance, if the body were tipped over to fall by its own weight, head over heels.'

Auguste shuddered. The picture in his mind became even more vivid at the thought of such callousness.

'We found this stuffed in that wooden house the dogs come through to slide down the chute.' Egbert flourished an odd object, which Auguste identified after a moment as Mariella's mermaid fish tail.

'Ask the widow what it was doing there, Auguste. You can relieve Twitch. I'm going to get hold of Special Branch, and tell them their chum is dead.'

'I think your presence is necessary too, Egbert,' Auguste said quickly. 'After all, you believe Mariella is implicated in the theft of the cross.'

'This is about her husband's death.' Egbert eyed him curiously.

'I think you should be present, or the Inspector remain.'

'Why?'

'She attacked me,' Auguste told him unwillingly. 'Although I realise that with her husband dead, she will not be feeling in need of love—'

'In need of *what*?' Egbert stared at him, as he gradually took in his meaning, and the shadow of a grin came to his face. 'Well, blow me down, it's lucky Twitch hasn't your charms.'

Whether he had them or not, Twitch was extremely uncomfortable, physically and mentally. For once he was more than glad to see the arrival of that blasted Frenchie, not to mention the Chief behind him. Auguste and Egbert Rose found him sitting bolt upright on the sofa, with Mariella's arm clamping him to her, her auburn head on his shoulder – making his jacket all soggy, as he later explained to a, for once, less than sympathetic Mrs Stitch.

'Why kill Miguel?' Mariella wailed as they arrived.

'When did you see your husband last, Mrs Gomez?' Rose wasted no time. Not too much sympathy was needed here.

'This morning.' Tears filled her eyes again. 'We were going to have whelks at the George, but Miguel said he had to meet someone.'

'Did he say who or where?'

'No.'

'Usual for him to meet people on a Sunday, was it?'

'Yes. He had lots of business friends.'

'In juggling?'

'Yes.' Mariella glowered, caught out.

'In the jewellery business too?'

She opened her blue eyes wider. 'Jewellers? Whatever do you mean?'

'I mean Prince Henry the Navigator's cross, ma'am, as you know full well.'

'The one you keep thinking Miguel stole?'

'That very one. Now there's been three murders. Don't

you think, you being a clever lady, it's time you told me about it?'

'About what?'

'About how you weren't involved with that cross business at all. Or how you were forced by your husband to do what he commanded.' Her eyes flickered. 'Otherwise,' Rose continued, 'we might think you yourself were mixed up with the cross and the murders, or even that it was all to do with wills.'

'What's my legacy to do with it?' she asked sharply.

'Did I say that, ma'am? You mistook me. I meant Will Lamb's murder. Him being involved in this nasty cross business too. Political reasons, I expect, above your pretty little head.'

She sat bolt upright, eyes flashing with anger now. Stitch leapt eagerly off the sofa, and retreated to the door. For a moment, Auguste thought Egbert had gone too far, but he underestimated him. He had the measure of Mariella.

Mariella suddenly smiled, the fragile smile of a woman who had been through the distressing experience of learning of the tragic death of a husband drowned in her very own fish tank.

'I didn't know about it,' she pleaded. 'Miguel was a proud man, and so proud of his country's great heritage. He was determined to avenge its wrongs, so he decided on this stupid plan to steal the cross. Only it wasn't stealing, he said, because it rightfully belonged to Portugal. But the captain of the ship with whom he had arranged to take the cross to Portugal was frightened and left early, so that Miguel missed him. He was so worried about being left with the cross so he had the brilliant idea of asking Will Lamb to keep it until the ship returned. If anyone found it, Will was such an important person no one would investigate further and it would be hushed up. He forced *me* to ask Will, because Will,' she looked modest, 'liked me. I didn't want to, but he *made* me. I told Will it was Auntie's jewellery, wasn't that funny? Miguel made me suggest to Will that we ran away together at the end of the week, too.' She looked at them to see how this was going down. 'And it wasn't unkind to Will. It was just fantasy. He would have been terrified if I really had eloped with him.'

'But he might have changed his will if you hadn't,' Rose pointed out reflectively.

'Never!' she said promptly, prepared for this one. 'But then someone killed him,' she added.

'And left the cross behind. Odd.'

'No. They *took* the cross,' she replied promptly, 'and left a fake. Wasn't that nasty?'

'It was indeed, ma'am,' Rose agreed. 'Did your husband happen to mention to you he killed a man in Nightingale Lane?'

'*Kill*? Who?' She displayed great astonishment.

'A casual hired by Frederick Wolf to take the cross to the ship for your husband.'

She shook her head. 'You go too fast for me, Inspector. *Who* is Frederick Wolf? Miguel took the parcel himself.'

'Then there seem to have been a lot of parcels making for the *Lisboa* that afternoon.'

'Isn't that a coincidence?' she murmured. 'I do hope you can make sense of all this, Inspector, and find my darling's murderer?' Whether darling was in the singular or plural was not clear from the spoken word.

'Don't worry, Mrs Gomez. By the time I've finished, this case will be as firmly welded as the stones in that cross.'

Had he forgotten the loose garnet, Auguste wondered? Or did Egbert realise it was still to be some time in the welding?

There was no reprieve. Egbert had wanted him present at the Old King Cole on Monday morning. In vain Auguste had pointed out the importance of his own mission.

'Twitch can do that,' was all Egbert replied.

The thought of Twitch being told where he was to spend the day almost reconciled Auguste to his fate. 'May I tell him, Egbert?' he asked hopefully.

Rose eyed him, tempted to agree. 'I will,' he had answered regretfully.

The stage of the Old King Cole was now hosting a large gathering of its performers and management, some more willing than others to be present. Brodie was highly indignant at being recalled so speedily from his new London home, Max was annoyed at appearing in the morning at all. Little Emmeline was excited even under the guardianship of her forbidding parents. Dolly was delighted at seeing Horace again so unexpectedly. The twins had their eyes fixed on Horace too. Fernando looked in vain for Mariella, but was disappointed. No one seemed to notice Miguel's absence, which had not yet been reported in the newspapers.

'Any of you come to the theatre yesterday?' Egbert inquired.

He was answered by looks of astonishment. They were professionals, and Sunday was Sunday. A travelling day if you were unfortunate, but not a theatre day.

'Apparently not, Inspector. Moreover we would prefer not to be here this morning, since poor Will's inquest is this afternoon. Why are we?' Brodie asked mildly.

'Miguel Gomez was murdered yesterday. *Here*.'

'Here?' was the first reaction, from Pickles. An odd one, thought Auguste, as though the fact that he had been murdered presented no great surprise.

'Who by?' asked Max hoarsely, but Rose did not answer him.

'Why?' screamed the twins. Not that they had any great admiration for Miguel, but it served as one more dark episode in their rapidly blackening existence.

'He was not nice to Mariella,' Fernando replied.

'So you think she murdered him, do you?' Dolly asked brightly.

He stared at her. 'Fernando not know.'

'I think you're all being stupid,' was Emmeline's contribution. 'I know why he was killed. It must have been because he heard what Mr Lamb said when he died,' she boasted importantly. 'All murder stories are like that.'

'By golly, she's right,' Rose said to Auguste.

'The ghost?' asked Auguste.

'Of course,' screamed Marigold. 'Will told me about it. The ghost sent a raven to keep Will away from the theatre, but it didn't work. So Miguel must have seen the ghost, like Will. Or the raven. Anyway, the ghost came again when Miguel died.'

'There'll be a third. Never two without three. That's what they say.' Dolly rose to her feet, and flung her arms round Horace. 'Take care, my darling, take care.'

'Do sit down, Dolly.' Horace sounded bored.

'No ghost threw Miguel into the fish tank,' Egbert said bluntly.

'The ghost might have frightened someone into doing it, though,' Marigold said obstinately.

'Somebody,' Violet amplified breathlessly, 'very simple – and very strong.'

Slowly Fernando got to his feet. 'Fernando go now,' he announced. Egbert made no attempt to stop him.


No one had seen Miguel here yesterday, no one knew of anybody who had planned to see Miguel here yesterday. No one apparently had any evidence to connect Miguel with Will Lamb. Everyone was interested only in their own turns. There was, and could be, no corporate unity here, Auguste realised. Whatever secrets the performers held, they shared with themselves alone, not with their fellow artistes.

There was very little unity in the kitchen either. There too, solus turns were favoured.

'I don't need no one to help,' Lizzie yelled at him crossly. 'I can manage.'

Auguste looked meaningfully at the piles of unscrubbed vegetables. Love was affecting Lizzie's work, that was clear. He cared a little about her heart, but the work he cared a lot about, and Lizzie needed an assistant. He set out forthwith to Mrs Jolly's pie shop. Mrs Jolly, unknown to her, had taken on the role of Mother Earth, and Auguste for one ready to worship at her shrine, as the answer to all problems.

'Three dozen of your eel and shallot pies, if I may, Mrs Jolly. And I wonder if your delicious mutton pies are available?'

'Katt.'

'I beg your pardon.' Auguste misinterpreted this ambiguous word, wondering if he had been mistaken in the excellence of the ingredients.

'Mr Katt's recipe, that is.'

'Of the late Kit-Kat club?' Auguste was dazed. The mutton pies of its host, Christopher Katt, had gone down in culinary legend. Never had he heard mention of a recipe having survived. 'You know its secret?' He held his breath.

'Mine. For me grandchildren.' She saw his face and relented slightly. 'Eels is different. I drowns 'em in sherry.'

How simple – of course. That was the taste he had sought to identify.

'Animals don't drink sherry liquor,' Mrs Jolly commented indisputably.

'That is true. Nor do they have the pleasure of appreciating your pies.'

Mrs Jolly brooded. 'They don't worry about things like we do.'

'That too is true.' Auguste was happy to agree with anything so long as the Queen of Pies continued her craft.

'That's why they don't drink.'

He gazed at her. 'I believe Brillat-Savarin made the same observation, Mrs Jolly. In different words, of course.'

'You tell 'im to come along 'ere, then,' Mrs Jolly offered generously. 'I'll give 'im one of me muttons.'

'I'm looking for an assistant cook,' Auguste began.

'He's not here.'

'I thought you might know of a young lad or lass awaiting employment – of a modest kind,' he added quickly.

She shook her head. 'No. There's me nephew, of course, me late husband's, that is. He's bone lazy. He's not doing nothing. Never does. His heart's in the right place, I'll say that for him.'

And so was his stomach, Auguste saw, as his aunt yelled for him to descend from the upper floor. He was a veritable Dickensian Fat Boy. He grinned, but the twinkle in his eye suggested more good-humour than dedication to work. Nevertheless, a nephew of Mrs Jolly's must deserve serious consideration.

'Charlie Jolly,' his aunt announced disparagingly.

'Good morning, Mr Jolly. I have a job for you,' Auguste announced briskly.

'Don't know that I want one.'

'I do, however,' Auguste told him briskly. 'Carry these. You're the new assistant in the eating-room of the Old King Cole.' He thrust the huge box of his purchases in his arms, and he and a reluctant Charles Jolly made their way back to the Old King Cole.

'Lizzie, I have brought your new assistant. Perhaps you would show this young gentleman what to do.' Auguste injected a note of authority.

'Where?' Lizzie peered suspiciously at what appeared to be a walking box. 'I don't see no man. Anyway, men is trouble.'

'For this evening, Lizzie, men is *help*.'

'Deceivers, that's what they are.' Lizzie paused as the box slowly descended to the table, and Charlie's girth appeared in its place, followed by his grin. A grin of confidence.

'What you grinning for, Fatsie?'

'I likes the looks of you, Miss Lizzie.'

' 'Op it. I'm spoken for.' There was bravado in her voice.

'I'll stay.'

' 'Oppit!'

'Staying.'

'*Out!*'

'Lizzie—'Auguste began to plead, but Charlie needed no advocate.

'Miss Eliza, you're a corker.'

She bridled, and her eyes slowly fell. 'Just this evening then,' she agreed modestly.

'You should have told us at once, not after your lads had been sniffing around.' Cherry sounded hurt. Egbert had gone back to his office in the Old King Cole and found his *bêtes noires* waiting.

'Why? You haven't proved any connection between Gomez and your cross, have you?'

A pause. 'Co-operation, we said.'

'Where's the cross, then?'

'The fake?'

'Either of them.'

'We've found the real one.'

'Where?' Rose asked sharply.

'At the bottom of the Thames.'

Rose whistled, sheer astonishment making him relax.

Heartened, Cherry amplified. 'A lad called Joe Bisley went fishing for eels, and come up with it all wrapped up in sacking. His Majesty is going to be pleased.'

'And what have you done with the fake?'

A silence.

'Well?' Rose said grimly.

'Haven't you got it?' Cherry asked weakly.

'I gave it to you.'

'And we gave it to Gomez,' Black gabbled. 'So you should have it back by now.'

'You what?' Rose shouted incredulously.

'There's factors you don't know about,' Cherry said portentously.

'I can see that.'

'So now Gomez is dead – where is it?' Cherry clearly thought offence was the best method of defence.

'Tell you what,' Rose said furiously. 'You find me Gomez's murderer and I'll find you the fake.' He paused. 'This cross you found in the Thames. How did you know it was the real one?'

'Because we gave the fake to Gomez.' Cherry failed to see the fallacy of this argument.

'Excellent. Well done, gentlemen.' Rose returned cordiality. 'He probably gave it back to Sir Henry Irving. All right, was it, your cross? Not harmed in any way?'

'No.' Cherry's confidence had returned. 'His Majesty's going to be very pleased.'

Rose did not comment. In his trouser pocket was a red garnet.

Auguste arrived at the Old King Cole early, after the inquest on Will Lamb. It had been a depressing

246

experience, packed with newspapermen and the prurient, together with, it seemed, half the theatrical world of London. The proceedings themselves seemed to have little to do with the dancing clown that would live in Auguste's memory. The verdict had been murder by persons unknown, which had provided a climax as melodramatic as any in the theatre, given that the press were still working on the lines of its having been a tragic accident.

The cast, such as it was, was also ready early, simply because none of its members had other engagements that evening. The other local music halls had suddenly dropped them, fearing that murder might well stalk in their wake. Even the improved houses at the Old King Cole did not encourage them. And these improved houses looked doomed to fade rapidly if a better programme than tonight's could not be found, Percy thought despairingly. No Nettie, no Magnificent Masher, no Will Lamb, not even Miguel Gomez – Max Hill had been promoted to the first half at a moment's notice, but old Max could hardly compensate for all the gaps.

Auguste found Lizzie rapt by the attentions of her new-found love, rather than attending to customers. Trusting that the stars would rub off from her eyes and scatter themselves over her cooking, he tore himself away, and found a desperate Percy assessing the mood of the crowd as they pushed in. Thomas Yapp, with the stage between him and inquisitive questions about his inheritance, was already out front, pondering whether his good fortune would improve his status with the Shadwell Mob. There was no sign of Egbert, and Auguste hurried upstairs to find him in the front office.

'Did I tell you they've found the cross?' Rose was standing at the window, watching the last of the queue disappearing into the hall, and the flying hands of Frederick Wolf, as he handed over one last potato. Fifteen minutes ago he had just watched him swallow half a sword, and on the whole potatoes looked preferable.

'The real one or the fake?' Auguste asked.

'I'm getting tired of those words. The real one, they think. The idiots gave the fake to Gomez, and are convinced I've found it. I told 'em Gomez probably gave it back to Irving.'

Auguste laughed, just as Twitch burst in, eager to impart news.

'I thought you should know immediately, sir.'

Below at the music-hall entrance, there seemed to be some kind of disturbance. Cries of pleasure – or horror were they? Auguste could distinguish Jowitt's voice and he was certainly pleased about something.

'I've done as you asked,' Twitch told Egbert loudly, ignoring Auguste, 'and went to Somerset House. And you, sir, were quite right. There *is* a link.'

Auguste's attention was torn between his desire to discover the meaning of the commotion below, and to hear Twitch's news. Once before he had been instrumental in sending Twitch to Somerset House, with far less dramatic success.

'Lamb must have been a stage name,' Twitch continued. 'When I tracked back – hard work it is, sir – there's no doubt. Thomas Yapp is Will Lamb's *brother*.'

'Well done, Stitch,' Rose said cordially.

'You've worked hard, Inspector Stitch,' Auguste said.

He meant it. The transitory world of the stage impersonated real life and could successfully bury its secrets. Disinterring them could be difficult. Impersonated real life? *Impersonated*? 'Egbert,' he cried, 'what did Sir Henry Irving and the Great Brodie have in common?'

'Is this a riddle?' Twitch asked, annoyed his great news had not had the reception it deserved.

'No, Stitch. I think,' Rose replied after a moment, 'Mr Didier means they were both probably recognised by their voices.'

Before Stitch could frame his come-back, the door was flung open once more and Lady Westland swept in, with Percy pink with excitement at her heels.

'The Magnificent Masher has returned to help me again,' he cried with jubilation. 'Lady Westland insists on telling you the good news herself.'

'No, I don't, you old fool,' Gwendolen said crossly. 'Nettie wanted me to play here this week to keep houses up. And now I find Max Hill's not here yet, and he should be. Percy told him he was playing number two spot.'

'Don't worry, Lady Westland. We'll change the order,' Percy offered eagerly. 'You go on just when you wish.'

'Never mind about the order. Where's Max?' she demanded.

Rose looked at Auguste. 'Impersonators. *Where's Max*, Auguste?'

# Chapter Nine

Too late. Why did he always have his best ideas too
late? Like adding the ginger to the *écrevisses à la Maisie*
just as the sauce was ready to serve?

'Max might just have been delayed or be ill,' Auguste
pointed out.

'Max is a trouper, Mr Didier,' Gwendolen said. 'He is
never ill. Or if he is, he would send a replacement, or at
the very least ample warning.'

'I heard nothing,' Jowitt wailed plaintively. 'It is too
bad of Max, and I will tell him so. I will dock his wages.
No, I can't. I haven't paid him recently. He's a good chap.
He hasn't complained.'

No, merely worked for Gomez instead, Auguste
thought, with sinking heart. All so obvious, now he
thought back. Max the Portuguese ambassador, Max
who took the cross to have the fake made, Max who
took the cross to Frederick Wolf. 'Surely he is not a
murderer, Egbert?'

'It's hard to see him in *that* role, I grant you,' Egbert
agreed reluctantly. 'But he hasn't wasted much time
making himself scarce, has he?'

'Nonsense.' Lady Westland decided to intervene. 'Of

course Max is not a murderer. Nettie and I have known him for years.'

'Perhaps he'd never had occasion to murder anyone before, ma'am,' Egbert pointed out. 'Surprising what people will do when they're scared.'

'Scared of what?' she asked.

'Discovery, perhaps. Any idea where he might have gone?'

'I do not.' Gwendolen said stiffly. 'That is your task, Inspector. And *mine* is to do something about that terrible rumpus in the auditorium.'

'Rumpus?' Jowitt repeated plaintively. 'I heard nothing.' He listened. There was certainly noise, and it was certainly growing. Evangeline must be on. She and Orsini were the natural targets for the Shadwell Mob's mirth. They hadn't given up. They seemed to be good-humoured at the moment, but working up to something else.

'We should have closed the place down after Lamb's murder,' Egbert said to Auguste, as Gwendolen marched purposefully downstairs to her dressing-room.

'I would doubt if that would have saved Miguel, *mon ami*.'

'Perhaps it would, and perhaps saved Max too.'

'Max? You think he's in danger? But from whom once Miguel was dead?'

'It might be connected with Miguel's death.'

'You mean you think he might have done it?'

'He could have fallen out with his old pal.' Auguste was silent. 'I know you like him, Auguste,' Egbert added kindly. 'But that's not relevant, you know that.'

Auguste did. It underlined the difference between

them, Egbert the professional, himself the amateur. In the last resort, Egbert played with chessmen on his board; friend or foe had to be immaterial. Auguste had the privilege – if that was the word – of choice, but not if he were playing in Egbert's team.

'Max did not leave when Will was killed,' he said at last.

'He liked Will. He didn't care for his being murdered and believed Miguel had done it. That's my theory.'

'So Max then killed Miguel?'

'Any proof to the contrary?'

'No,' said Auguste unwillingly.

'Who are his chums round here? You've seen more of him that I have.'

'He was often in the eating-room with Clarence Bishop, lightning sketcher and ventriloquist.'

'One of those lads who draws you in two ticks of a puppy dog's tail? One of them got Edith to the life. She didn't like it because he left two of the cherries off her new hat.'

'Clarence Bishop is not a pavement artist. He tells a story and does sketches of the scenes on the pad, and also sketches animals and people, using them as his ventriloquist's dummy.'

'Sounds rather high falutin' for the Old King Cole.'

'Perhaps that is why his turn is buried in the middle of the second half.'

'Then we'd better talk to him now. At least he may know where Max lodges, which is more than Percy seems to.'

Auguste ran downstairs to find the Magnificent Masher, clad in a makeshift costume of check trousers left behind by Brodie, Pickles' waistcoat (too small for the Masher's now ample bosom), and Percy's battered top-hat, striding purposefully past him. She did not notice him, not did it occur to him to wonder why she had not brought her costume with her. All her energy was concentrated on the stage and the need to woo an audience that was quite sure it had already won whatever battle it imagined it was fighting tonight.

From his vantage point in the wings, Auguste saw the tip of the cane shooting on to the stage, its owner, back to him, out of sight to the audience. Things were bad. The well-known signal made no difference. The noise paused, then redoubled. Gwendolen took a deep breath, signalling to the orchestra to strike up with 'I'm a Mayfair masher . . .'

She strode on to the stage, then rested, bored, on her cane. She twirled it idly. She made no attempt whatsoever to quell the audience, but let them roar away. When a well-aimed potato hit her, she removed her gloves, and examined her hands, then replaced the gloves with great care. Finally in sheer astonishment at her indifference, the Shadwell Mob ceased their shouting and waited to see what would happen next.

'You may be wondering where I got these trousers . . .' She glanced down at the check in disgust. 'Well, I'll tell you – if you listen.'

It appeared, eventually, they would; and by the time they had been told a rigmarole of money-lenders, betting gentlemen, drinking bars and Newmarket, they were laughing and singing with her.

Clarence Bishop was not singing. He was shivering in his shoes in the eating-room at the thought of being thrown to the lions in the increasingly near future.

Auguste caught him by the arm, and led him firmly upstairs. 'When people are in that mood, anything will set them off. There's nothing you can do to avert it. You will not believe this, but one evening last week some came into my eating-room and threw tomato catsup everywhere. I did not take it personally, however.'

That is not what Lizzie would have said, had she been privy to this conversation, as she had been to the hurt pride of Auguste Didier that evening. He had, after all, put the catsup (his own recipe) on the tables himself and had not expected it to be literally thrown in his face.

'It's hard not to take it personally,' Clarence said dolefully, 'when a rotten tomato arrives smack in the face of your hippopotamus.'

'*Je m'excuse?*'

'Hippopotamus. I do an excellent hippopotamus roar when I do my sketch of exciting adventure in Africa. They didn't seem to like it on Saturday, however.'

'You are destined for better things.' Auguste clapped him heartily on the back. It was all he could think of to say.

Clarence brightened. 'Do you think so?'

'I do,' Auguste confirmed quickly, as he ushered him up to Egbert's office.

'Ah. You're Max Hill's chum,' Rose greeted him.

'I'm not responsible for his not being here,' the chum squawked quickly. 'All artistes are responsible for their own timekeeping.'

'It's not timekeeping we're concerned with. It's where he is.'

'I don't know, I'm sure. How can I?' Clarence looked even more alarmed. 'Am I my brother's keeper?'

'You're related to Max Hill then?'

'No!' yelled Clarence.

'Live with him?'

'No . . .' There was some hesitation this time.

'But you know where he lives.'

'Yes.'

'Where?'

Clarence looked for escape and found none. 'In the same lodgings as myself. Bethnal Green is very nice. We all lead separate lives. Mrs Bistle will tell you that.'

'And who might Mrs Bistle be?'

'Our excellent landlady. Sometimes we go to the theatre together, sometimes we don't, depending on our engagements. Max and I, that is. Not Mrs Bistle. She doesn't come to the theatre, of course,' he ended in a nervous whinny of laughter, 'unless we invite her.'

'Did you see Max Hill today?'

'Of course. He was there while you were telling us about Miguel. I was to meet him in Mr Didier's excellent eating-room afterwards,' he added ingratiatingly.

Auguste, relishing appreciation of whatever standard of sincerity, suddenly realised it was no longer *his* eating-room. It was Lizzie's eating-room, and whether her burgeoning talent would be up to it it was too early to say. Good teacher though he was, he could hardly flatter himself he had instilled enough technique into that young lady in a week to set her up for life. Moreover she was showing distressing tendencies of being distracted by young love.

'Did you?'

'Did I what?'

'Meet him in the eating-room?'

'I met him, but he wanted to go to a pub,' Clarence was forced to admit. 'So we went out and had a drink together, and a pie.'

'One of Mrs Jolly's?'

Clarence regarded Auguste doubtfully, looking for a trap. 'The Cock and Dragon doesn't have any ladies. Not ladies, if you see what I mean.'

Auguste did. A peep into some of the nearby pubs had quickly told him that the only ladies present were those in hope of immediate employment supplying the needs of seamen coming off the ships.

'And what then?' Rose asked, impatient with pies.

'We parted. He said he'd see me tonight as usual.'

'Did he say where he was going?' Rose asked urgently.

'He said he had one or two things to do.' Clarence was only too well aware he was, not for the first time, disappointing his audience. He looked alarmed. 'He's all right, I suppose? You don't think he's had an accident?'

'What sort of accident?'

'He might have been murdered,' Clarence cried shrilly. 'A lot of people have, you know.'

Rose did know.

The Shadwell Mob were recklessly risking their earnings from the managers of rival music halls by abandoning barracking for cheers of approval. Gwendolen was coming off the stage, bathed in triumph, as Auguste came backstage to meet her. 'Nasty crowd,' she said gleefully. 'I had to work hard, remembering all my old tricks. I've been away too long, and there's not much call for music-hall technique in the peerage.' She paused. 'Tatiana returned, has she?' she asked, apparently inconsequentially.

'She has, I am delighted to say.'

'I'm in the doghouse, am I, for bringing you down here?'

'She has no objection at all.' Lady Westland's eyebrows arched in surprise. 'Naturally,' he added, as if it hardly mattered, 'I have not mentioned to her that I was a cook here.'

'I do understand,' she replied gravely.

'Tatiana visited His Majesty this morning,' he added, to underline his point the more heavily.

'What about?'

It was not the reply he expected, but he saw no harm in telling her. After all, thanks to the efficiency of the Harmsworth Press the whole of England knew about the theft of Prince Henry the Navigator's cross from Windsor Castle, though, it occurred to him, few people at the Old King Cole yet seemed to.

'His Majesty is naturally eager to hear about Tatiana's motor races in France,' he began diplomatically.

'Of course,' Lady Westland murmured, then briskly said, 'Do not let me keep you from your great love, Mr Didier.'

'Madame?'

'Your eating-room, of course. Were you not intending to visit it to ensure everything is in order for the after-performance diners?' She marched off, swinging her cane and chuckling heartily, though for the life of him he could not see why. Suddenly, she stopped and returned to him, and said to him seriously, and incongruously in her check-trousered outfit, 'I want Max found, Auguste. I've known him for a long time, and I can't afford to lose a friend.'

Auguste, somewhat puzzled, hurried back through the corridors to the eating-room, telling himself he must remember he was no longer in a position of power. He merely wished to see whether Lizzie required extra assistance, but if one of Mrs Jolly's pies were by chance still available . . . Also, he admitted to some curiosity as to whether the new-found love of Charlie and Lizzie had survived the testing ground of the evening.

The latter point was soon settled. Auguste's eye immediately fell on the plump, reasonably white-uniformed shape of Charlie, offhandedly turned the odd chop with one hand and cuddling Lizzie with the other. As Auguste hurtled through the door, agonised as to what the diners might find – if anything – when the performance ended, Charlie turned a slow warm intimate smile on his beloved. A technique surely far beyond his years, Auguste thought enviously. He himself had not perfected it until he met Violetta, and then had been at least twenty-six. He had first attempted it, he recalled, while demonstrating a *cailles aux raisins*. Six months later they had parted over a *crêpe Jeannette*. She had mistakenly taken the latter to be a rival. (There had been one, but her name was not Jeannette.)

He coughed gently. 'Lizzie, is everything in order?'

She spun round, her face red – either from love or guilt. 'Naturally, Mr Didier,' she said fervently. 'Charlie is wonderful. You're going to stay, aren't you, Charlie?'

'Try and keep me away, Miss Eliza. You spice an eel as good as Auntie, and that's saying something.'

Lizzie flushed at this over-lavish praise, and wriggled modestly.

'There's a lady waiting for you, Mr D,' she sang out, as belatedly she recalled her duties and fled down the stairs. She jerked a thumb as she went. 'Over in the corner,' her disembodied voice cried.

'Lady?' Auguste turned round curiously, and was startled to see Tatiana, as out of place here as an ortolan in a pile of mutton chops. Her dark coat and hat did not stand out from those around her, her bearing and lively face did.

'You don't mind my coming here, do you, Auguste?' she asked innocently as he sat down.

'*Ma mie*, I am delighted to see you.' He glanced nervously at his surroundings, and relaxed. After all, he could be here for some totally innocent purpose, not for cooking purposes. True, a certain familiarity with the cook might be misinterpreted, yet he was a detective, he reminded himself, and entitled to speak to everyone.

'I have been enjoying the performance.'

'Enjoying?'

She laughed. 'Parts of it. Gwendolen was superb, and there was someone else—'

Auguste thought quickly through the other artistes – if that was the right word, and could not immediately think who she had in mind. 'Our Pickles?' he asked doubtfully.

'No. That child.'

'*Emmeline*?'

His astonishment was so great, she giggled. 'She is a

terrible dancer, but talented all the same. She is a natural comedienne, and no one has realised it. I shall tell Gwendolen.'

'Why?' Auguste asked faintly, horrified at the thought of Emmeline's beady eyes intruding into his life.

'I wonder if she can sing.'

'Gwendolen?'

'*Emmeline.*'

'I doubt it. Where would she buy songs?'

'That's where Gwendolen might help.'

Auguste decided to relegate this minor matter to the back of his mind. 'I feel sure Little Emmeline is not what brought you here, *ma fleur*.'

'If I have something to eat and a glass of ale, I might remember what brought me. A chop?' she asked hopefully.

'A *chop*? But, *ma mie*, I could prepare you a delicate *omelette aux truffes* with a *petite salade*—'

'I would so like a plain chop,' she interrupted wistfully. 'Gwendolen's motor-car passed several Russian restaurants nearby – we could go there if you prefer.'

'If you are determined to eat here,' Auguste said hastily, 'I will get you a pie.'

'But—'

'A very *special* pie.' He ignored her protest and began to vie for Lizzie's attention. It took some time.

"Course you can have a coupla pies, Mr D. You know where they are, swelp yourself,' she told him grandly. "Ere,' she added, 'I showed Charlie how to do them chops just like you showed me. Never mind about them pies – I'll get 'em. You can have them on the house.'

'*Showed*?' Tatiana queried, after Auguste expressed his gratitude for this munificence.

'He's not a bad cook, is he, ma'am?' Lizzie asked her, one woman to another. 'Must be a help at home. All the regulars took to him. I didn't think they would, him being a Frenchie, but he understands grub, I'll say that for him.'

'Oh yes, he does indeed, Miss – er?' Tatiana agreed.

'Lizzie. I'm his assistant, or was. Now I'm cook and Charlie there –' she looked at her plump swain with pride, '– 'e 'elps me. All thanks to Mr D, eh?' She dug him gratefully in the ribs.

'Lizzie, that gentleman there is trying to attract your attention,' Auguste said firmly, looking at a particularly belligerent member of the Mob. She exclaimed and rushed off.

'Cook?' asked Tatiana politely.

'Detective,' he explained firmly. 'The cooking was essential as part of that job.'

'I understand completely.'

'*And* it was Lady Westland who arranged it for me.'

'Indeed. Auguste, does His Majesty know about this?'

'No. But surely he cannot but approve if it results in the return of the cross.'

A plate with a large pie suddenly shot in front of Tatiana, followed by one for Auguste. These were followed rapidly by two jugs of ale sliding across the table in their eagerness after being slammed down by old Jacob's drinks waiter.

'The cross. Ah yes. That is why I am here tonight.'

'Evening, Tatiana.' Egbert materialised at their side. 'Mind if I join you?'

'I am delighted, Egbert. Now I can tell you both together.'

'My word, those pies look good,' he said meaningfully.

Auguste sighed, pushed his plate over to Egbert, and hurried to the bar to obtain a replacement. There was none. Resentfully, he returned to the table, trying hard to restrain envy of their enjoyment.

'If that lady called Mrs Jolly made this pie,' Tatiana said approvingly, 'I realise why Auguste has such a passion for her.' Auguste enviously watched a crumb lying on her plate. Even a crumb should not be wasted of that delicious feather-light pastry. 'Egbert, His Majesty has told me the truth about the cross.'

'And what might that be?' Egbert asked sharply, relegating pies and Edith's inadequacies in the preparation thereof to the back of his mind.

'You did not fail in your task, Egbert. You were too good at it.'

'Explain, if you please.'

'His Majesty was caught,' she began, 'in a difficult situation. The King of Portugal, as you know, is to visit him in less than two months, and next year Bertie will return the visit. He is, as you also know, a firm believer in the need for unity in Europe, and standing between him and accomplishing this ideal was the cross, since it has become the subject of so much controversy. If he retained it, Portugal would be very upset; if he returned it, half of England would never forgive him, and nor would much of Europe – not on Portugal's behalf but because it feared the same principle being applied to many of their so-called national treasures.'

'So His Majesty had the fake made?'

Tatiana shook her head. 'No. He had the brilliant idea, as it then seemed, of arranging for the cross to be stolen; he would seem to be very upset, but in fact would ensure the cross was sent back to the Portuguese royal family. If it seemed to the public that it had been stolen, he reasoned, whether for financial or political motives, he could not be blamed after the initial uproar had died down. The idea was good, but he made one mistake. His Special Branch personal detective, Mr Sweeney, was naturally the first person he turned to, and Sweeney naturally suggested Special Branch handle this delicate operation for him. They did, but with unfortunate results. The Portuguese footman they planted at Windsor Castle in order to allow the theft to happen, was a Republican sympathiser, who chose his friend Miguel to carry out the actual theft. Once the theft had taken place, the plan was that the CID should be brought in. You, Egbert, would be kept in the dark, and naturally you should have no chance of actually regaining the cross. The newspapers, however, would see that you were trying to do you best, but failing.'

Egbert's face was black with anger.

'I can see you are annoyed, Egbert, and rightly so,' she continued anxiously, 'but consider His Majesty's position. You could not be told, or you might not play your part correctly.'

'That's all that's important, is it?' snarled Egbert.

'No. There is the future peace of Europe to consider.'

Reluctantly, Egbert's feathers were persuaded to be soothed. 'What went wrong?'

'His Majesty does not know, except that he had been told there is a fake in circulation. He is very anxious about it, for if the fake reaches Portugal, even greater damage could be done to international relations.'

Egbert found sympathy hard. 'Tell him he'll be getting good news from his beloved Special Branch.'

'Are you sure?'

'As far as the CID knows, *yes*. And I'll have another of those pies, Auguste.'

'There aren't any more.' Auguste was still smarting.

'Eaten them all, have you? You'd better brush up your ordering skills.' It was rare for Egbert to be in such ill-humour.

'*Oh*!' Tatiana, who from her seat had a view into the corridor where the audience was still flooding through from the auditorium, had suddenly cried out.

'It's only the Shadwell Mob,' Auguste said soothingly. 'Do not be alarmed.'

'No – yes. Auguste, for a moment I thought I recognised someone.'

'Who?'

'Gregorin,' she answered soberly.

In a flash, Auguste had rushed into the corridor to join the crowd, and was swept along with them on to St George's Street. Could that slim figure disappearing into the darkness be Gregorin? It was impossible to tell, yet a certain shiver in his spine that had nothing to do with the chilly autumnal air told him it was all too possible. There was no hope of catching him, even if there were any point, and he returned slowly to the table.

Egbert looked up anxiously. 'I told Special Branch to keep an eye on him.'

'I think one eye is not sufficient where Gregorin is concerned,' Auguste replied quietly, and tried to

concentrate on crosses, or pies, or anything but Gregorin.
It was difficult until another familiar figure pushed its
way through the crowd into the eating-room. It was Lizzie's
long-lost love (for two days at least), Joe. He made his
way behind the counter, and watched belligerently as
Charlie cuddled Lizzie by the fried herrings.

'Oy,' he yelled grimly.

Lizzie turned, and screamed. Charlie cast an
indifferent eye, and then resumed his occupation. Joe
tore his rival's arm away from Lizzie, and spun him
round, with some difficulty owing to his girth.

'*My* girl,' he said meaningly.

'Miss Eliza can choose.' Charlie was unperturbed.

'She chose me.'

'You went orf,' sobbed Lizzie.

'I had to. A man has to work. Same as you. Ma had a
fishing job for me.'

'You never said.'

'I did.'

'You never.'

'I'm back.'

'Too late,' said Charlie, grinning.

He was ignored. 'You loved me, Lizzie.'

'She loves me now.'

'Which one of us, Liz?' Joe asked heavily. 'You've got
to choose.'

A large dirty hand was thrust over the counter and
between them. 'Do I 'ave to get me own bleedin' chop,
then?'

Charlie put a hot chop in the hand without the benefit
of plate. The man's yell was outdone by Lizzie's, who
burst into tears. 'I dunno, do I?'

She ran down the steps to the basement, howling. Joe and Charlie looked at each other, and with one accord walked outside to settle the issue, purposefully followed by the aggrieved chop purchaser.

Charlie shrugged, and grinned at Auguste. 'Women,' he said as they passed.

Tatiana tapped Auguste on the arm. 'Don't you think, Auguste, for the good of the Old King Cole, you should sacrifice your scruples and become their very temporary cook?'

By Tuesday morning, his guilt over his illicit cooking had almost entirely vanished. The power of a sunny morning was great. After all, he pointed out to Tatiana, the King had not been entirely without fault himself.

'Does he know you are involved in this murder case?'

'No.'

'I thought not.'

'Just as I forgot to mention that I was cooking,' he added blithely. 'Which I am now doing with *your* agreement – though only to keep an eye on Lizzie's progress.'

'In romance?'

'She is only sixteen, a child.'

'Her problem seemed quite an adult one to me.'

Auguste had a brainwave. 'You look after the affairs of Miss Emmeline, I will protect Miss Lizzie.'

Miss Lizzie, however, had to come second to Egbert's demands, and by the time their hansom arrived at Max Hill's Bethnal Green lodgings, he had forgotten all about her.

Mrs Bistle leaned on her broom and eyed them suspiciously. 'Mr 'Ill?'

'Is he in?' Egbert asked.

'I don't hold with folk always having visitors. I never said I'd be a parlourmaid when I took 'im in.'

Just as well, Auguste thought, averting his eyes from her dirty apron and, more importantly, face and hair.

'You'd better follow me,' she said grudgingly.

In silence, they followed her aggrieved rear up four flights of steps, until she rapped on a door. 'Mr 'Ill?' Her raucous shout received no reply.

With little ceremony, she flung the unlocked door open to reveal a room crowded with photographs, clothes, old newspapers, and ill-assorted china.

'Have you seen him go out this morning?'

'Nah.'

'Yesterday?'

'Might have.'

'Endeavour to remember, please,' Egbert said mildly, but she heard the undertones, and no doubt thinking it was imprudent to get on the wrong side of the law without cause, became remarkably voluble.

'Now I comes to think of it, yes, I did see 'im.' She waited for congratulation, but none came. 'He went out in the morning. Came back and went out in the afternoon.'

'Did he say where to?'

'He was in a hurry.'

'No idea where he went?'

'He said he wouldn't be back for a few days, but to keep his room and he'd send money. I wish I'd a sovereign for every one of them as says that,' she

remarked scathingly. 'Uncle Sam pawnbroker sees more
of me than the old man.' She shrugged. 'Not much here
for Uncle Sam. Still, it ain't my business where he goes,
is it?'

'Did he have a suitcase with him?'

She thought about this. 'Yes. Not a big one, mind, or
I'd have wondered what he was up to. He often takes
one – for his – what d'yer call it? – impersonations.'

'You've seen him perform?'

'Poor old chap. He were past it, but not bad. I done
all the halls, so I know.'

'And you've no idea where he went?' Egbert ploughed
on relentlessly.

'Oh yes, why didn't yer ask? He tells me to tell Mr
Bishop he could find him at the old Canterbury.'

'Why, if he wishes to vanish, does he tell his landlady
where he's going?' Auguste asked, as they left. 'Perhaps
there's some innocent explanation for his disappearance
after all.'

'The Canterbury's more a place for swells and
mashers now, not for Max's usual audience. More likely
he threw that in to keep us off the scent. Still, it's worth
sending Twitch to watch the place, in case it's a double
bluff.'

'And what do you wish me to do now, Egbert?'

'You can come with me to see the lovely Mariella. I
don't want her taking a fancy to me.'

Mariella, smartly dressed in deepest black for Will's
funeral that afternoon, had obviously been spending in
advance of her legacy. Auguste wondered irreverently
whether she had ordered a black spangly mermaid's
costume, but decided he was being unfair. Her eye for

an attractive man, he told himself modestly, did not mean she had not been sincerely fond of her husband. And even if her eye for money were stronger than for men, it did not mean she did not sincerely grieve for Miguel – or for Will Lamb, if he were being generous. Perhaps generosity did not stretch as far as that.

'I have been writing,' she said in a low voice, 'to Miguel's family in Portugal. I have told them I will do all I can to help them. Miguel would wish me to.'

'Very good of you, ma'am. Of course, with your fees from the Palace, you'll be able to help a great deal sooner even than that. If you get them, that is.' Egbert sat on the edge of an armchair, with his hands firmly on his knees.

'Fees from the Palace?' she repeated innocently. 'I don't perform there.'

'Come, come, ma'am. I've heard all about it from the one witness no one would question. His Majesty himself. So now you need not feel obliged, as you obviously did earlier, to keep me in the dark for reasons of national security.'

Mariella looked at him sharply. 'Oh, I'm so glad you *know*. It has been a great burden. And what do you mean,' she added, alarmed, '*if* I get them?'

'That's the part you're going to explain to me, ma'am. I know what Special Branch ordered your husband to do, and I'm sure you know it too. Now you're going to tell me what *his* plan was. And I'm sure you know that too.'

'No—' She broke off suddenly.

'I thought you'd manage to remember it was you gave

270

the cross to Will Lamb. That wasn't in His Majesty's plan, was it?'

'No. We had to improvise after it all went wrong,' she said sullenly.

'And you're British too, of course. That makes it treason, to betray the crown. Still, it's not often we put people in the Tower now. Even Captain Blood managed to wangle a pardon after stealing the Crown Jewels. Not often we hang people down at Execution Dock either nowadays.'

Mariella took the point rapidly. She burst into tears. 'Oh dear,' she sobbed, 'I only wanted to help Miguel. He was so upset when the plan went wrong, and he had to think what to do.'

'Try again, ma'am. Begin with the Republican sympathisers in Windsor Castle, who got in touch with Miguel to ask him to do the job.'

She glared. 'You're sure you won't think I was involved?'

'Not *sure*, no. But there's just a chance, if you can convince me you know nothing about a murder or two, as an accessory before the fact.'

'Oh *no*. I could not have condoned murder. It would be far too dangerous for one thing. You police are so wonderful at finding murderers.'

The tops of Egbert's ears went slightly pink, Auguste noticed with amusement.

'Miguel had always planned to steal the cross back from Frederick Wolf, you see, so that he could pass it to his political contact.'

'Why give it to Frederick in the first place?'

'Because it would look very suspicious if he said he

was robbed himself. He was going to make sure there were witnesses to the attack – er – the theft of the cross from Frederick.'

'But it went wrong because Frederick decided he'd hire someone else.'

'Yes. Miguel was upset, and had to take this man to a quiet place to steal it back, so that the ship would sail without it. Miguel then got a fake made, so he would be paid by the Republicans for the real cross, and he could send the fake to Portugal when the ship next docked. He *made* me ask Will to keep it for me. I didn't want to because—'

'Will had left you a lot of money and you didn't want to risk anything upsetting that.'

'Because I was *fond* of Will,' she retorted with dignity. 'I tried to warn him, so you can tell that was so. I knew he was superstitious, so I sent letters to him to frighten him into keeping away. Miguel would have killed me—' She stopped short and smiled brightly. 'And I released that horrid dirty raven to scare him too, because I was afraid Will would get caught up by accident in their plans. Miguel had made me promise to tell a story to Will that I would run away with him at the end of the week, and the parcel with the cross was my auntie's jewellery. He thought it was very funny when everyone in the theatre seemed to know about us running away, but then he began to be worried that I really *was going* to go.'

'So you think he killed Will Lamb for that reason?'

'I don't know,' she whispered. 'He could have done. He was a strange man.' Like all the men in her life, she was thinking viciously. Miguel, Will, Fernando . . . Why couldn't she have a nice straightforward man like this Frenchman? She looked shyly at Auguste, and wondered whether she should have another try. Surely he could not resist twice?

'And what happened to the cross? The real one. Did he give it to the Republicans?'

'No. He was going to, but Will died first, and he couldn't keep the appointment.'

'Where is it?'

'It was in my mermaid's tail. There was room for it even with my legs in it, if I took my petticoats off.' She managed to convey this latter was a thrilling experience.

Egbert sighed. 'The blunt instrument, eh? The one that killed him. And only you knew about it.'

'No!' she shouted. 'Anyone could have seen. *Anyone.*'

'That you'd got a priceless cross in there? Unlikely.'

'It wasn't me,' she sobbed.

'What happened to the fake cross?' Egbert continued inexorably.

'I don't know. Miguel said that man in the bowler hat took it after Will died.'

'That man in the bowler hat gave it back to your husband. Where is it?'

'I don't know,' she shouted.

Egbert seemed to believe her. 'Tell me about Max Hill.'

'He's an impersonator.'

'We know he's more than that, ma'am. Don't waste time.'

'He went with Miguel to the Castle,' she said sulkily, 'and he pretended to be Horace Brodie while he handed the cross to Frederick.'

'Why Brodie?'

'Why not? Max doesn't like him, that's all.'

'Why do you think he's disappeared? Do you think he murdered your husband?'

'Oh *no*.' She thought for a moment. 'Though Max did get very upset when Will died. Perhaps he thought Miguel had done it. I did myself sometimes.'

'Only sometimes.'

'He was a very *jealous* man . . .' She tweaked a strand of her red hair that was easily pulled free from its artificial fashionable moorings. Now she could afford to have Mrs Thing come in and do it as often as she wanted. Oh, the joys of being nearly rich.

The funeral of Will Lamb, organised by Nettie, was a still calm centre in a whirlpool. The whirlpool consisted of newspapermen, the theatrical world and devoted admirers. Its centre was small, of those that loved him for himself, as well as for his art. And it was Nettie led that small band.

That evening Auguste and Egbert donned tails and white waistcoat, and Tatiana and Edith their prettiest dresses, and sat in the *fauteuils* of the Old King Cole. Here Will had begun, here he had finished. In music hall had lain his life. What better place for them to remember him?

# Chapter Ten

Inspector Stitch smarted. He had a distinct feeling that the Chief had known all the time that he was on a wild-goose chase, and furthermore he was aggrieved that he was late on duty through no fault of his own. Mrs Stitch had taken a different view. His head felt like a bowl with lots of nasty things swimming around not nearly as innocent as goldfish. With powers worthy of his position of CID inspector, he had deduced that the ginger beer which had been pressed upon him in the famous Long Bar at the Canterbury Music Hall last night, had not been so innocuous as he had thought. Why should anyone want to lace the drink of a complete stranger? It beat him. No one could have deduced he was a police officer, thanks to the curly moustache that he had carefully gummed on and the top-hat pulled well down over his forehead, not to mention the knitted scarf Mrs Stitch had made him for last Christmas, which he had drawn closely round his chin.

Stitch rapped on the Chief's door, happier now that they were back in civilisation, in other words not at the Old King Cole, but in the familiar surroundings of the Yard. Normally the Chief's door was open, but this morning it was not. Anyone other than Stitch, who remained blissfully confident the Chief would be eager to see him at any time, would have taken this as a warning.

'No one turned up, sir.'

'I take it,' Rose said not bothering to glance up, 'you're referring to our vanishing impersonator?'

'Old Hill, sir. Yes. I was there the whole blooming evening, and not a whisker. He wasn't performing, he wasn't watching, he wasn't drinking.'

'He might have been in disguise.' There was irony in Rose's voice.

'Couldn't fool me, sir,' Stitch said, ignoring it. 'My own disguise was impenetrable.'

'Someone warn him, do you think?'

'Might have,' Stitch agreed dubiously. 'But the fellows in the bar didn't look his sort, if you know what I mean.'

'Toffs and mashers?'

'Yes, sir. I don't see Max in those surroundings.'

'No more do I, Stitch. No more than I believed Max's shouting out to Bishop exactly where he was going. Still, we had to cover it.'

Stitch, with some effort, remained silent. In theory the Chief was right, but in practice he noticed it was always him that did the covering. Still, it showed how reliable he was, he supposed, and cheered up.

Rose grinned at him; if Stitch had been a connoisseur of grins, he would have termed it shark-like. 'No one I can trust like you, Stitch,' reading his thoughts perfectly.

Stitch glowed, though only for a moment. The sudden appearance of Special Branch removed all satisfaction.

'Where is he?' Cherry demanded without preamble. 'He wasn't at the Canterbury.'

Rose glanced at him speculatively. This was not the Old King Cole, but his office at the Yard, and he didn't like unannounced visitors, particularly these two.

Twitch, however, also had a grudge. 'You bribed that fellow to stand me that drink,' he cried indignantly. 'What did you do it for?'

'*In vino veritas*,' Black piped up proudly.

There was precious little *veritas* in Stitch's head, whatever that might be. But he was full of something. Stitch thought savagely – a burning desire for revenge.

'You tipped him the wink, didn't you?' Cherry said heavily.

'I never tip winks.' Stitch recovered his equilibrium.

'Just a minute. I'd like a hand in this,' Rose interrupted sarcastically. 'I'm feeling left out. Who are you talking about, Cherry?'

'Max Hill. We want him.'

'Got the hounds of Buckingham Palace after you, have you? How's getting hold of Max going to help you?'

'Never you mind. The cross affair is ours.'

'I'm investigating a trifling matter of three murders, which may or may not be connected with your blasted cross.'

'You think Max Hill did them?'

'He's involved,' Rose answered shortly.

Cherry thought about this, and decided to play heavy. 'We want him more.'

'Why's that?'

Rose's voice was mild enough, but even so one look at his face and Cherry decided co-operation might get him further than a lone hand. 'He's got the cross.'

'Has he? How do you know that?'

'Fairly obvious, ain't it?' Cherry asked complacently. 'So where is he?'

'Not the least idea. Could be anywhere in England.'

'Not too good for the CID. Better consult Sherlock Holmes, eh?' At this witticism, Cherry burst into roars of laughter.

Rose was not going to be guffawed at by Special Branch, and he decided to play his ace. Edith had often remarked on his excellent timing in a hand of whist. 'I thought His Majesty had it? You found it in the Thames, didn't you? He hasn't lost it again, has he?'

Cherry's eyes bulged viciously, as he flushed the colour of his name. 'He says it's a fake.'

Egbert seized his opportunity to laugh. 'Fake, eh?'

'That's why we want Max Hill. *Before* you get him.' Cherry did not take humiliation lightly.

'I'll try to remember that.'

Good humour restored, Egbert Rose shortly made his way across Horse Guards' Parade and St James's Park where he stopped to watch bread being thrown to the ducks. With the tip of his umbrella he rooted up a mushroom which had evaded the eyes of an army of His Majesty's public servants on their morning march to work, and proceeded to Queen Anne's Gate.

He found Auguste at work in his second favourite room. The first was the kitchen, but he was banished from this all too often, and Egbert found him in his second-floor study. Two walls were lined with an impressive array of books, and the other two with prints. They all had a common theme: food. Egbert had looked at the books once. Grimod de La Reynière's *Almanach des Gourmands*, Brillat-Savarin, Mrs Glasse – he remembered seeing an old copy of that on his mother's shelves. Belonged to her grandmother. Or great-grandmother. He couldn't remember which. *The Closet of the Eminently Learned Sir Kenelm Digby, Knight, Opened* – nothing like blowing your own trumpet. *The Cook's Oracle* and even, he grinned to himself, Alexis Soyer's *The Gastronomic Regenerator*.

'I see Soyer isn't giving you much inspiration today,' he remarked, seeing Auguste listlessly staring at a blank sheet of paper.

'There is a large gap, *mon ami*, between this pile of blank paper and those shelves of bound books,' Auguste remarked sagely and sadly. In his imagination, all ten volumes of his *Dining with Didier* already resided on those shelves where they would remain for centuries to come, a monument to his achievements in the culinary field. Unfortunately even Volume I was far from completion. All because of John.

'I am barred from my own kitchen,' he declared passionately. 'How am I to ensure all these recipes are at the peak of perfection if I am excluded from my own kitchen?'

Privately, Egbert sympathised. 'Ask him to test them for you?' he suggested, with a straight face.

'Ask John to test a *chaudfroid* of chicken? He could not judge a plate of bubble and squeak. My reputation would be lost for ever. Look at this delightful recipe for marrow. How can I tell whether thyme or marjoram should predominate without testing it *now*? I am a Johnson in need of a Boswell, *mon ami*.'

'How about Tatiana?'

'And ask her to forfeit her own interests?'

'Where is she now?'

'At the School, in the motor-garage. A particularly interesting 40 hp Panhard is arriving today. She had to be there, just as I have to be present at the first tasting of the season's claret, or the first arrival in Covent Garden of the new season's potatoes. I must look elsewhere for my Boswell.'

'No use looking at me,' Egbert replied quickly. 'I've got crosses on my mind. In fact, I had more in mind you helping *me* out.'

Auguste brightened at the prospect of a valid excuse for abandoning the dispiriting task in front of him. 'How?' he asked hopefully.

'Special Branch are after our friend Max.'

'There is no sign of him?'

'Not at the old Canterbury.'

'Then let us try the other one.'

'I'm not following you.'

'Perhaps Max was trying to convey to Clarence Bishop where he would be, without stating it. In other words he has gone to the *city* of Canterbury.'

Egbert stared at him. 'Auguste, you're wasted messing around with suet and ox-liver.'

'They are not my favourite working materials, but the true artiste can create from the poorest base provided he suits the end to the means, and does not try to create—'

'A silk purse out of a pig's ear?'

'A pig's ear has its uses also, *mon ami*,' Auguste told him seriously. 'Take a boar's head, for instance—'

'It's an old English saying, Auguste.'

'Oh.' Auguste regarded him doubtfully, wondering whether the sacred name of cuisine was being treated too lightly. He decided to ignore the slight, intended or not.

'I'll give you more than a pig's ear to chew on if you come to Canterbury with me.'

'Very well.' Auguste brightened at the thought of luncheon. Would they reach Canterbury in time, though? It was already eleven o'clock. He firmly dismissed such thoughts, telling himself that Egbert's mission must take precedence.

Robbin's Music Hall, a run-down establishment on the northern outskirts of Canterbury, had almost as few pretensions as the Old King Cole. Its paint was peeling and the man in the box office was picking his teeth with a programme, hastily put down at the appearance of two gentlemen, as he saw a prospect of selling two expensive *fauteuils*, rarely patronised by the local soldiery.

It had proved a fruitless afternoon for Auguste and Egbert, save for an excellent luncheon of roast duck and cucumbers at the Fleur de Lys hotel near the Cathedral. No hotel, boarding house or music hall had heard of Max Hill, leading them to the depressing realisation that either Max was not in the city at all, or that he had changed his name. They were now combing the halls for the second time, and the Robbin's programme did not look promising. Written out in chalk on a board was a list of twenty-odd names, ranging from Tom Wilkins, the Amazing Wizard, to Fred Fox and his Dancing Fleas.

'Scratching the end of the barrel, you might say,' Egbert guffawed.

'But this is not, Egbert. Look – the Magnificient Mount.'

'What of it? Our chap's an impersonator, not a lion *comique*.'

'But Mount, Hill – they are very similar. It is worth staying to make sure.'

Picturing Edith's doleful face, if they failed to return that night, Egbert wasn't so convinced. It took three-quarters of an hour of bad jokes and worse songs before the familiar strains of 'Don't Wait Up' from a top-hatted bushy-bearded lion *comique* put the question beyond doubt.

'Magnificent Max becomes the Great Brodie, eh?' he said grimly. 'I thought there was a little matter of ownership over these songs.'

'Only, as in so many other things, when there is a risk of discovery.'

'He's about to be discovered *now*.' Egbert got up, ignoring the protest of the young lovers next to him, and with Auguste following, made his way to the exit. 'No need to announce our arrival, I think.' There wasn't, for news had travelled quickly.

No sooner had they reached the main entrance than they saw their prey run into the street from the side of the building and half walk, half run, towards the city. Somewhere a cat yowled, perhaps in protest at being disturbed by pounding feet in its night-time contemplation of the starry heavens.

'That's all we need.' Rose took off like an elderly greyhound with a new lease of life, with Max's fleeing figure periodically bobbing into sight in the yellow pools of the gas lamps. They ran past the Archbishop's Palace, and then skirted the Cathedral itself, a dark mass looming above them. Auguste yelped as his foot slipped on the cobbles of Sun Street, thinking sympathetically of pilgrims approaching on their knees.

'He's gone,' Egbert cursed.

'Into the Cathedral?' panted Auguste. 'There are many exits to it, and he could double back the way he came.'

The Cathedral, dimly lit for late worshippers, was quiet. No movement, little sound. Before them rose the piers and arches of the graceful nave, ahead of them stretching into infinity, the choir, altar and Trinity Chapel, around them the heavy silence of the centuries. Worshippers seemed as still as the monuments that surrounded them.

'There.' Auguste clutched Egbert's arm, pointing to the south aisle.

'Making for that exit on the right,' Egbert said. 'Remember?' They had walked round the Cathedral that afternoon, slightly conscience-stricken in that it could not be classed as 'work'. Now unexpectedly, work it had become. They walked, as quickly as they dared, trying to keep their eye on the figure that half-merged with the shadows.

'He's not going out. He's going up the steps,' Egbert hissed, and rushed on towards the Trinity Chapel. Murmuring an apology to *le bon Seigneur*, Auguste hurried to the far side to await Max's arrival. He waited in vain, for only Egbert rounded the far corner of the chapel and came down to join him.

'He must be hiding somewhere. He can't have slipped out.'

The silence seemed even heavier here, where the lighting was dimmer than in the nave. Auguste forced himself to concentrate. He brought to his aid the skills his father had taught him while hunting in the Cannes hills: to be still, to listen, and to understand what the prey was doing, thinking and feeling.

Somewhere he knew Max was waiting, probably watching them. Or was it Max? Here, in this vast place, it was all too easy to imagine that not Max, but Pyotr Gregorin might slink round a pillar, pounce like the animal of prey he was and fell him regardless of place. Auguste shivered. Just so had Thomas à Becket died at the hands of four murderers, only a few steps from where they were now standing.

'There he is!'

Max suddenly shot out of a side chapel, running back up to the steps to disappear into the Cathedral precincts, and as they followed him outside an indignant cry floated back to them: 'I'm too old for this sort of lark.'

The receding footsteps in the night air left little doubt which way he had gone or that they would not now catch up with him. In the darkness the remains of the old monastery surrounded them, and a left turn took them the way that Max had undoubtedly gone – down an arcaded passageway with one dim light. Beyond was a large open space, with buildings all round.

'He could be anywhere,' Egbert said in disgust. 'We're as like to see him again as Old Nell the cook.'

'Who is this lady?' Auguste asked, puzzled. As he had good reason to know, Edith, with the help of their one maid, was in charge of cooking at Highbury.

'One of the Ingoldsby legends. Learnt it by heart at school. That passage we've just come down is the Dark Entry, and that house on the corner is where the Canon lived. His cook was the jealous sort and killed him with a game pie.'

'This woman was no true cook,' Auguste declared indignantly. 'No true cook could *poison* what should be a work of art.'

'She seemed to have agreed with you, for she poisoned herself with a bit too, and her skeleton was found underneath here tucked up with the remains. She comes back on Friday nights from time to time.'

Auguste glanced at the cold, dark, suddenly inhospitable passageway. Today was Wednesday, but suppose she was making an exception tonight? The splendours of Mrs Jolly faded as pies loomed before him in all their most unappetising forms. His footsteps quickened.

Only the wondrous invention of the telephone had soothed Egbert's annoyance at Max Hill's escape. Baiting Auguste was hardly compensation. But the telephone had enabled him to have Thomas Yapp waiting for him in his office by the time he arrived. Even so, he was not in good spirits. Edith was an exacting mistress where ironing was concerned, and the lack of a fresh shirt sorely affected his temper. Overnight sprees were for sergeants, not chief inspectors.

Thomas Yapp was seemingly unsurprised at his

summons. 'It is rather sudden, Inspector,' he began pleasantly. 'Not that I mind, of course.'

'I'm glad,' snarled Rose, sitting at his desk peremptorily pointing Auguste to a corner.

With Stitch also present, Thomas began to appreciate he was firmly wedged into a quartet which was probably all hostile. 'What can I do for you?' he asked, a little less confidently.

'Quite a lot, Mr Yapp. Why didn't you tell us you were Will Lamb's brother?'

'Ah.' Thomas looked vaguely around. 'I was afraid if I did you might believe I had something to do with his death.'

'And you didn't, of course.'

'Naturally not.' Thomas looked shocked. 'He was my brother. Anyway,' descending to practicalities, 'how could I? I was out front all the evening.'

'You could have doctored that knife before the performance began.'

Thomas considered this. 'I didn't.'

'Your wife had the opportunity to do the same.' Rose was in mean mood.

'But Evangeline did not *know*,' he yelped. 'That was the whole point.'

'What point?'

'I did not want her to know about my relationship with Will or—' He stopped.

'The money?'

'My relationship with Will,' he repeated defiantly.

'Why not?'

Thomas Yapp hesitated. 'My wife,' he began, 'is a much misunderstood woman.'

'In what way?'

'In every way. She is warm-hearted, impulsive, lovable—' He broke off, aware he might be overdoing things. 'She has a great need for affection. I sometimes fear I disappoint her,' he added sadly. 'She fancied she was in love with Will, and I decided not to spoil these daydreams. Especially the one that he loved her. It seemed the least I could do. How could I tell her that I was actually Will's brother, when I discovered it? She would have been in love with her brother-in-law, and it would have spoiled the dream if it had no possibility of a happy ending.'

'But it might have given her another one,' Rose pointed out.

'And what is that?'

'Will was a rich man.'

'You mean she would have had hopes of Will's giving us money. But I would *never* have allowed it. She would realise that.'

'Did she know he'd bequeathed so much money to you?'

'No,' he said sharply. 'I had no idea myself, so how could she?'

'Suppose she found out?'

'How?'

'Will might have told her to keep her quiet.'

Thomas Yapp rose in wounded dignity. 'I shall go now.'

'Sit down.'

Thomas obeyed. Very few would have the nerve not to, faced with Egbert Rose in this mood.

'Kindly explain how you and your wife had no idea of your kinship to Will for so long.'

'That's easy,' Thomas said, relieved. 'I'm older than Will was. Our parents were clog-dancers, but my mother ran off and took Will, being a baby, with her. I was left with my father. He gave up clog-dancing and became a chairman instead. The first time I saw him I knew that was my role in life too. He never mentioned my mother or my baby brother after that, and I forgot all about them. The name Lamb meant nothing to me since it was the name our mother took when she left.'

'How did you find out?'

'Mr father told me just before he died.'

'And what did you do about it?'

'Nothing.'

'*Nothing*? Your brother is the famous Will Lamb, and you did nothing? You expect us to believe that?' Stitch decided to take part.

Thomas looked anxious. 'Yes. It's the truth.'

'So Will came to find *you*?'

'Yes. Well, not quite like that. He came to my father's funeral. It's very simple really,' Thomas said apologetically.

'Too simple.'

'Some things are.' There was a touch of defiance in Thomas's voice.

'And what happened then?'

'Will got me a job at the Old King Cole. I was very pleased for it was my first regular assignment. And only one, of course,' he added sadly.

'Didn't Will tell your wife he was your brother?'

'No.'

'Why the need for secrecy now?'

'I've told you. Evangeline. You wouldn't tell her, would you?'

'Are you aiming to give up your inheritance? Won't she think it a little odd?'

'No. Evangeline thinks it was really for her, and given to me merely to save her reputation.'

Rose's good humour was restored. The corners of his mouth twitched, but were controlled. Thomas was not getting away quite so easily. 'You were one of those suggested Will Lamb was invited back.' There was no query in his statement, and Thomas looked alarmed.

'I wanted to see my brother again.'

'You could have seen him any where. Why here?'

'I used to meet him in London sometimes, but I never dared suggest the notion. He was *famous*. I thought if Percy asked, it would be good for the Old King Cole.'

'Although it would stir up your wife?' Rose asked grimly.

Thomas did not reply, and Rose, to Auguste's surprise, did not press it.

'Believe him?' he asked Auguste after Thomas had left. 'Think he's capable of murder, of frightening Max into running away?'

'I think many people are capable of murder if the incentive is strong enough,' Auguste said gravely. 'But Thomas was out front before the performance. He saw Will on Tuesday, not Wednesday. It's unlikely he could have tampered with the dagger.'

'And Max?'

'No one saw him at the Old King Cole early on.'

'True. Doesn't mean he wasn't there, though. Pickles?'

Auguste shook his head. 'He could have done it, but has little motive.'

'Fernando?'

'That is more likely.' He thought of the scene he had witnessed.

'Mariella?'

'She has the ruthlessness.'

'If Max is innocent, Auguste, why doesn't the blighter tell us what he knows to protect himself? He didn't run away for nothing.'

'Perhaps he feared he would incriminate himself in some way.'

'But we already *know* he's implicated.'

'He doesn't know we know.'

'Why on earth would we be chasing him otherwise?'

'He thinks we believe him guilty of murder.'

'So he ran for sanctuary like Thomas à Becket, eh?'

'And hasn't found it.'

Egbert considered. 'If I were Max, where else would I seek sanctuary?'

'Only one place, *mon ami*.' There was no need for Auguste to say more. There was only one place to which Max Hill would run.

'How do you fancy a night at the halls, Auguste? I'll treat you.'

# Chapter Eleven

The Alhambra was as far removed from the music-hall
world of the Old King Cole as the Empire. Its Moorish
architecture and large auditorium would have quelled
the Shadwell Mob before they were over the threshold,
for all the Alhambra's long-standing Bohemian
reputation. As Auguste craned his head upward to gaze
at the enormous sun-burner in the domed ceiling, he
recalled it was here that the acrobat Léotard had
inspired audience and song as the daring young man
on the flying trapeze flew above the audience's heads.
From their seats in the dress circle he and Egbert had
an excellent view of the stage, and the audience was
both large and excited. Music hall might be less
prominent now at the Alhambra than ballet and
spectacle, but when the programme boasted Nettie
Turner a full house could be instantly guaranteed. The
rest of the programme was almost immaterial,
especially when it included the dubious attractions of a
young lady called Emmeline. There was, hardly to their
surprise, no Max Hill featured on the programme,
though the Great Brodie appeared early in the first half.

His turn had not changed greatly since they had last

seen it at the Old King Cole, and perhaps his cross between the coarse and the ambitious masher was pitched even better for West End audiences than for Stepney. He launched himself on to the stage, immediately starting with 'Don't Wait Up'. Hearing its by now familiar strains, gave Auguste a strange feeling as though one of Soyer's soup-kitchen meals had had the temerity to present itself under an Escoffier silver salver. But the audience was responsive, and his airy confidence made them more so. The Great Brodie could well be on his way to top of the bill, Auguste decided without enthusiasm. Doubtless he was being unfair, for the man had had a long struggle to get where he now was. Auguste's attention began to wander, and was only recalled to the stage as the Great Brodie launched into a song apparently about fish.

'Why is he singing of skate?' he whispered to Egbert, as the Great Brodie took his bow and sauntered from the stage.

'Skate? You've got food on the brain. It's called "Hooray, Hooray, Hooray".'

Auguste looked puzzled, then laughed at himself. The trouble with being brought up with two languages was that they mixed all too easily. He had fastened on the syllable 'ray', but heard '*raie*'. He had purchased some delightful skate at Shadwell. Its flavour—

'Here she comes,' Egbert said gloomily, easing his bow tie with his finger. It was warm in here.

At first Auguste hardly recognised Emmeline. If not dressed in a red corset, at least she was allowed to be her age, instead of a precocious eight-year-old. Emmeline had been transformed into a cheeky thirteen-year-old, dressed in school uniform. Her former fairies, looking rather frightened in their new role, were similarly clad, their eyes glued to their leader as she barged around the stage, full of bewilderment and patter on the ludicrous doings of 'grown-ups'. Particularly Ma and Pa. These self-same respectable bodies in real life were in fact sitting further along in the front row of the dress circle, as out of place here as they were in the Old King Cole. Auguste could not find it in himself to be sorry for them as Emmeline launched into a catchy song, howled with an effective tunelessness, on the peccadilloes of Ma and Pa in kissing milkman and parlour-maid respectively, with a chorus catchphrase of 'Emmeline, that isn't very nice!' This was the former fairies' sole opportunity to shine, as drilled into unison they bawled the last line with her.

Nettie's vitality which poured out over the footlights during her turn was just as it had been at the Old King Cole, but her style had been tailored for her audience. They approved it, and it made it all the harder for Auguste and Egbert to fight their way in past the guard at the stage door after the performance. None of the happy-go-lucky ways of the East End here. The guard was obviously a former soldier who took his duties very seriously. He looked dubiously upon Chief Inspector Rose's credentials and was ostentatiously surprised when a message came back via the messenger boy that Miss Turner was willing to see them.

Nettie was already in evening dress, awaiting them, and her face, devoid of greasepaint, was still showing that curious empty look that Auguste remembered from his days at the Galaxy Theatre; it lingered for a while after greasepaint was removed, as if the mask torn off, the real person needed time to step back into its face. Nevertheless her eyes looked more lively than Auguste had seen them since Will's death. 'What did you think?' she demanded.

'You were magnificent.'

'Not me,' she interrupted impatiently. 'Young Emmeline.'

'A remarkable transformation. You have worked hard.'

'It was worth it to see the look on her parents' faces,' Nettie said with glee. 'You should have heard what they had to say to me after the first performance. "Oh, Miss Turner, we do admire your style," she whined, "but we regret we cannot approve of your songs." "What song had you in mind?" says I. "That lewd one about the animal." "My Donkey Song?" says I indignantly. "Nothing wrong with that. Listen. 'Whoa, Nelly, don't you go too far'." '

She sang it for them now with tears in her eyes for the dear old donkey's health; the body that had wriggled so suggestively, now trembled with emotion. 'That got them,' she said complacently. 'Loud, maybe. Never lewd. Now what was it you want to see me about? Caught Will's murderer, have you?'

'We're smelling the fox,' Rose told her.

'Anyone I know?' she asked steadily.

'Probably, yes.'

'Pickles,' she burst out. 'That's why you're here, isn't it?'

'No. Max Hill.'

'Max?' she repeated, startled. 'What's the old geezer

been up to? You're not telling me *he* murdered Will, are you?'

'It's possible. He's disappeared. We thought he might have come to you for help,' Auguste explained.

'*Me*? Why?'

'You're part of his old circle of friends. You were all at the Old King Cole together. You were Will's friend and his. If he were going to contact anyone, it would be you. You or Brodie, and I wouldn't count much on Brodie having a sympathetic ear for old friends. He couldn't go to Mariella Gomez.'

'I've not set eyes on him, and I don't think Horace has. He'd have told me – if only to protect himself.'

'You don't like him?'

Nettie shrugged. 'He's all right. Good fun, provided you agree to put Mr Brodie first. Can't blame him for that, but I'm getting too old to be made a stepping stone of.' She paused. 'Why did Max disappear?'

'Because of Miguel Gomez's death.'

'I don't see him doing it.'

'Tell us about Max Hill's background, if you would, Miss Turner.'

'There's not a lot I know. Only as much as one knows of those you worked with on and off over a long period. He was a middle-aged man when Will and I started at the Old King Cole, and as high in the tree as he was going to go, so he had time to help us both. I don't think we knew anything of what he was like outside the halls. He was just there, part of the scene. With some people you get to know a lot about their private lives, and with others, like Max, you don't.'

'A mystery man?'

'Far from it, I'd say. We just never asked. How much do you know about that inspector of yours, Stitch, isn't it? You work with him, you don't go to the zoo with him.' Egbert grinned. 'Max is a kind man, that's what I'd say. Always willing to do you a good turn – without overlooking a chance of doing one for himself. That help?'

'Even if it were against the law?'

She nodded. 'Probably. Especially if there were a laugh in it.' She paused. 'The halls are hard taskmasters, Inspector. We need our laughs. Look at this face of mine. What has it got?'

Auguste looked at her, first the bright lively eyes, then her round, almost homely face. 'Character,' he said firmly.

'A nice way of saying I've got a lot of deep lines. No Ellaline Terriss, am I, all soft pink and white baby face? This is what the halls do to you. It's all right when you're young, but you don't age well. Mine's a hard face, and so are all of those you see in music hall. First comes the illusion on the stage and offstage, when the greasepaint's off the painted gargoyle, you see the truth. We wouldn't have it any other way, though. Underneath Max's devil-may-care character is a tough man.'

'Romanos.' The Great Brodie looked round in satisfaction. 'You know, gentlemen, I've waited twelve years for this, and by Jove, I'm going to enjoy it twelve times as much.'

Auguste began to warm towards him. In the light of what Nettie had said, he saw now how great a leap Brodie had made from the Old King Cole. Supper at Romanos, even if enjoyed in the company of a Scotland

Yard Chief Inspector and a half-French chef, represented an achievement. He was almost sorry he had not taken them to his old *maître*'s beloved Carlton.

Brodie puffed his cigar after the meal in pure satisfaction. 'And now, gentlemen, you may be permitted to tell me why my company is so desirable this evening.'

'Max Hill. He's disappeared. We thought you might have seen him.'

'I have not. Max and I are old colleagues, but hardly bosom friends. Why do you think he disappeared? Guilt?'

'Possibly.'

'Of Gomez's death. Will Lamb?'

'Unlikely the second.'

'Why?'

'He has no motives, and he wasn't at the theatre at the time the dagger must have been tampered with.'

'Ah. I believe it is common knowledge now that Max was concerned with this unfortunate cross business and that Will Lamb was also. Does that not constitute grounds for a motive? And as for the second – Inspector, Nettie is an admirable person, but in her loyalty is so strong, her usual integrity may occasionally be compromised.'

'Meaning?'

'As you will, Inspector.'

'He was appearing at the same halls as you, wasn't he, the week of Lamb's murder?'

'The Old King Cole and the Lyle, yes.'

'Was he with you?'

'Did he accompany me, do you mean? No. However, last week he should have appeared, I recall, at the end of the first half of the Lyle, and in the second half at the

Old King Cole. I appeared in the first half at both, and at a third hall late in the second.'

'Should have?' Rose picked up sharply.

'Managers change order to please themselves from time to time, or to cover for non-appearing artistes. Max and I, for example, have a long-standing arrangement whereby he would from time to time cover for me, if I have a particularly tight schedule, or on occasion, I confess, an affair with a young lady.'

Auguste promptly unwarmed towards him, thinking of poor Dolly Dadd.

'Did this happen the day Lamb died?' Rose wasn't feeling overwarm either.

'Oddly enough it did. I didn't mention it, since I could not see how it would affect the timing of the murder, but Max did ask me to change for the Wednesday performance. He asked me the evening before. Said he had to meet someone in a pub and didn't think he could get there in time. Could he do my spot, and I his? I agreed.'

'And you thought this didn't affect the murder?' Rose said grimly.

'There is no way it could have done, Inspector. I understand the dagger was tampered with before the performance, or some time up to the point where the stage manager collected the dagger.'

'Which was during your own turn that night, the second spot. I saw him!' Auguste agreed.

'Max would have had plenty of time to reach the Lyle to play my turn, or his own, if he'd come in to see Will before the performance. However, I think you will find he had other business afoot, and that was during and after his usual appearance at the Lyle. You must look elsewhere for your murderer, I fear.'

'But not your impersonator, Mr Brodie.'

'My what?'

'Max Hill may have impersonated you in a little crooked business on the Saturday, the twentieth.'

Brodie was suddenly guarded. 'What crooked business?'

'The Windsor cross.'

Brodie threw back his head and laughed. 'In this case, I am only too glad to pin the blame on Max. He is an excellent impersonator.'

'We're missing something, Auguste,' Egbert remarked gloomily, over a last drink, once they were alone.

'What?'

'If I knew that we wouldn't be missing it. Too much of a coincidence, surely, that Max asked to switch the very night of Lamb's death?'

'Perhaps it was to do with the cross.'

'You mean he'd found out that Gomez was double-crossing Special Branch, and that it was something to do with that?'

'Yes.'

'And if he found out Gomez had been intending to murder Frederick, then he, Max, he reckoned, could be next on the programme. So he killed him and decided to take an even closer interest in the cross. Like running away with it. A lot of ifs, but they all add up to the fact that Max Hill is no innocent man. I'm beginning to think you've provided the missing factor.'

'But Mariella probably has the cross,' Auguste quickly

pointed out, aware he didn't want Max to be guilty.

'Not her. The lady would be doing something about it if she had. My men have followed her on a good few trips to Bond Street, but nothing more.'

'These ingredients do not yet make a recipe, Egbert,' Auguste maintained defiantly. 'I am *sure* there is still some flavouring we are overlooking.'

'Only your imagination, Auguste. The ingredients in my larder taste all right to me.'

Auguste forbore to say that with Edith's cooking, the results of Egbert's larder were seldom of the happiest.

When he arrived home, he found Queen Anne's Gate ablaze with lights. Tatiana blithely ignored cost. She enjoyed electric light so much it seemed every single one had to be on to be enjoyed to the full in case this new and marvellous source of energy disappeared again.

'Some friends of mine dislike it,' she had told him. 'It is too harsh for their complexions. But I find it is most useful for studying the underneath and insides of motor-cars.'

'Here?'

'In the booklet. I wish to study the details of the new Panhard.'

'Then why are you sitting eating that horrible-looking eclair?'

'Because John has made them today.'

Auguste eyed her with great suspicion. 'They are edible?'

'Certainly. Auguste, you must get over your distrust of our chef.'

'Why?' he asked belligerently.

'He will leave.'

'That will be a disaster?'

'Yes. He will be the *eighth* to do so, and we have only been married just over a year.'

'I could take his place.'

'You could not.'

'*Ma mie*, we are quarrelling.' There was reproach in his voice.

'Sometimes married people do,' she replied darkly. '*When* it is justified.'

'But you are being unreasonable . . .' Auguste stopped. Tatiana with a whisk of skirts was departing. Unwillingly, she hesitated as she remembered what she had to tell him. 'We are going out tomorrow.'

His heart sank. He had looked forward to a quiet dinner discussing John's inadequacies.

'We are taking luncheon at Hampstead,' she continued.

'We are driving out to the *country*?'

'It is not far.'

'But the horses . . .'

'We'll motor there,' she said reassuringly.

His heart sank even further. Suppose Tatiana insisted on driving the machine herself? Her style of driving was far from suitable to ensure calm nerves and restful eating.

'Where are we going?' he inquired with no great hopes of a welcome answer. The talk would no doubt be focused either on motor-cars or on the latest doings of King Edward and Mrs Keppel. Both subjects tested his endurance.

His wife regarded him kindly. 'To the home of Lady Westland.'

The mansion in Hampstead overlooking the Heath cheered Auguste immediately. It was large, comfortable and inviting-looking, like the Magnificent Masher herself. He began to wonder what kind of cook she had.

'Is it a large party?' he asked Tatiana.

'Just us. She and her husband and one family friend, she told me.'

Auguste looked round the entrance hall while the business of divesting themselves of hats and cloaks took place. This appeared to be a strictly equal marriage. Half of the prints and paintings reflected a regimental career (Lord Westland, he remembered, was a retired general) and the other half were prints and paintings of the Magnificent Masher at the peak of her career. Auguste began to approve of the so-far unknown General Lord Westland. Many such gentlemen on marrying into the world of the stage went to great pains to hide all trace of their wives' former career. Dear Maisie, for example, had suffered in this way, though she had gained revenge by starting her own business. It was through her he had met Tatiana again, and yes, he had much to thank Maisie for, besides their halcyon days together in times long past.

'My dear Tatiana.' Lady Westland, looking as unlike the Magnificent Masher as it was possible to do, advanced to meet them. 'And Auguste, how good of you both to come out at such short notice.'

Short notice? His antennae quivered. Why short notice?

'Lord Westland.' Tatiana bowed in acknowledgement of his greeting. This was not the tall ramrod figure of Auguste's imagination. He was a general of Napoleonic stature and build, not as short as the nation's beloved Bobs, but no dominating presence. Or was he? One glance at those keen eyes, and Auguste began to realise he was greatly mistaken in his snap judgement.

'And, of course, you know our friend.' Lady Westland led the way into the drawing-room – no friend was in sight. 'Do come out, Max,' Gwendolen boomed.

Slowly, cautiously, Max Hill's head appeared over the back of a sofa. He looked extremely nervous.

'There you are,' cried Tatiana delightedly.

'This ain't my idea,' Max informed Auguste crossly, as he emerged. He edged nearer the door.

'I'm sure it is not.' Auguste looked questioningly at Lady Westland. 'It was you, then, to whom Max ran for sanctuary.' Not Nettie, as they'd assumed.

'You have a quaint way of putting it, Auguste, but in fact it was to my husband he ran.'

'You, Lord Westland?' Auguste was totally puzzled now.

'My wife is correct,' the General said. 'If you would allow me to explain, we can then all take luncheon.'

It sounded so reasonable, so normal, that Auguste's head spun. He wondered feverishly whether he should insist on telephoning Egbert immediately. Or should he himself take Max in charge? In the event he adopted neither course of action and reminding himself of a Brillat-Savarin aphorism that the most essential attribute for a cook was punctuality, and telling himself that generals must adhere to the same rule, he put his confidence in the luncheon arriving at the time set and not a moment later. It was merely a matter of adapting the time of his stomach. Max at last, with his eyes fixed firmly on Auguste, followed the example of the rest of the company and sat down. His ill-fitting morning-dress suit was evidently dredged up from the General's wardrobe judging by the length of the trousers, Auguste saw, and was making him even more ill at ease.

'We enjoyed your performance in Canterbury, Mr Hill,' he began meaningfully.

'Glad to hear it,' Max replied nervously.

The General took command. 'You will have heard that I have retired from His Majesty's army. It is not correct, Mr Didier. I have retired from active service, but I now have another role which cannot be discussed further.'

'I understand.' They seemed the right words to say, but Auguste was not at all sure he did.

'You will not have heard of Section H. It was created in response to the communication needs of the South African war, and then expanded its role.'

'Spying?' Auguste asked eagerly.

Lord Westland frowned. 'That is one word certainly. Intelligence-gathering is perhaps a better. Before Section H there was only one office responsible for secret-service work, with a team of outside informants who were paid for their information. Now Section H had taken over its work and is rapidly expanding it. And so, of course, is its partner, or as some have it, rival.'

'In other words, Special Branch,' Lady Westland put in.

'As Gwendolen has so frankly put it, Special Branch.

I concede there is a certain rivalry between our departments. Formed to cope with the menace of the Fenians, which they did excellently, they were then eager to expand overseas. While we, being more recently formed, co-operated during the war, we are less enthusiastic about its continuing. When it was reported to me that His Majesty had been so unwise as to entrust Special Branch with the delicate mission of returning Prince Henry's cross to Portugal and that they had chosen Mr Gomez as their key man, I was extremely concerned, since we knew all too well Gomez was of Republican sympathies. However, we did not know whether his politics exceeded his love of money, and Gwendolen had the excellent notion of calling on her old friend Max to keep an eye on the situation.'

Max looked up as if being a dear old friend was not always a position to be cherished.

'He played the part of double agent most effectively, I am sure you will agree, Mr Didier,' the General continued. Max looked modest. 'He inveigled himself into being Gomez's partner, and as soon as he realised Gomez was playing a double hand of his own, he let Gwendolen know so that we could keep an eye on what was going on.'

'And myself?' Auguste inquired coldly.

'My dear Mr Didier, a double precaution. Quite genuinely, Nettie, knowing nothing of this, was worried about Will and told Gwendolen. What better than to have you as an unknowing but stalwart ally in the theatre, especially when poor Will Lamb was murdered and it seemed Gwendolen should be there herself?'

'And Will? You involved Will in the cross affair?'

'I did my bloomin' best, begging your pardon,' a nod towards Tatiana, 'to keep him away,' Max shouted indignantly. 'I couldn't tell him the truth, about the Gomezes' plan to make use of him, so I tries to scare him. I did one of my impersonations of old Bill Terriss. Whenever Will came to West End theatre land, there was yours truly just whisking away out of sight in the cloak and hat or booming out behind him. I scared the living daylights out of meself, let alone him.'

'So it was you on the Saturday night who shouted out from the audience,' Auguste exclaimed.

'Yes, and a fat lot of good it did.' Max was aggrieved. 'One flash of that red-headed tart's b— eyes,' he amended hastily, 'and Will was down there slobbering. Wild horses couldn't have kept him away, let alone Bill Terriss.'

'Mariella was trying to keep him away too, she told us. She was writing letters to scare him.'

'She wasn't trying half as hard as me. Anyway, no wonder. She had her inheritance to think about. I was more interested in old Will not getting dragged into anything nasty. Poor old devil. Then that happened to him.'

'Why did you run away, Max, if Lord Westland was protecting you?' Auguste inquired.

'What else could I do?' he said plaintively. 'Those Special Branch boys can't wait to pin something on me, and it won't be the Victoria Cross *or* old Prince Henry's.'

'Such as what?'

'Gomez's murder.'

'But where is the cross?' Auguste asked. 'You know it's disappeared?'

'I haven't the slightest idea, me old darling.'

'Come on, Max, you must have,' Gwendolen said encouragingly. 'You can tell us now.'

'Look here, the last I knew Gomez was taking it to his Republican chums; he was going to take it after his turn that Wednesday, and I had it all lined up to be there too incognito. But he never turned up at the pub he was going to meet them at. Because of Will's death, I thought then. But he didn't go out of his way to get it to them Thursday, Friday or Saturday, either.'

'How do you know?'

'I know, old chum, because his mob descended on me when they heard he was dead and used a few tough methods to tell 'em where it was. Not nice at all. I went to Madam Mariella and told her to take care. You should, me darling, I said, because you'll be the next on the list. That frightened her. Better talk to her. Me. I'm guiltless as a new-born whelk. Where's that grub, Gwendolen?'

The drive back to London was almost pleasant, considering it was by motor-car. Tatiana was talking technical nonsense (or so it seemed to Auguste) to Manners, whom to his pleasant surprise was driving, and so he was able to dream. Dream of the delightful luncheon they had just eaten, dream of Egbert's face when he told him of Max's whereabouts, dream of a time when John no longer reigned in his kitchen, dream of the time that Will Lamb's murderer was safely behind bars and he could resume *Dining with Didier*. Suddenly the prospect no longer seemed so appealing. He tried to stimulate his interest by reciting (silently) every kind of fish he could think of, allotting the perfect sauce to each. *Brochet à l'Orly, Cabillard à la Provençale, Carp à la Choucroute* – or perhaps *à la Chambord? . . . Morue au Gratin, Moules à la Villeroy, Raie au*— He remembered his earlier mistake and laughed.

'Don't you think so, Auguste?'

'I do,' he agreed quickly, only belatedly wondering what he was concurring with, and intent on his own line of thought.

'I'm so glad. Manners can investigate then.'

Tomorrow morning he would see Egbert. He wondered whether by chance Egbert kept a Portuguese dictionary in his office.

'That's all I need. Army Intelligence mixed up with this case. A case of too many cooks, or crooks in this case. Did you believe Hill, Auguste?' Egbert asked irately, when Auguste went to report the next morning.

'Yes, but if not he, then who?'

'Well, I don't. A bloke can get hungry waiting for your missing ingredients.'

'I have brought it with me, Egbert.' Auguste placed a small book on his desk. 'I bought this Portuguese dictionary at Mr Bumpus's excellent establishment this morning.'

Egbert sighed. 'What makes me think I'm in for one of your fancy ideas?'

'Not fancy at all. Will Lamb's dying word as reported by Gomez was "Ghost".'

'That's right. Now we know Max was playing the ghost Will saw. Lamb had realised who was playing Terriss *and* who his murderer was. He was telling us.'

Auguste stared at him, horrified. 'I never thought of that.'

'Lucky I did, then. Wraps up the case nicely.'

'Perhaps not.'

'Make this quick and make this good, Auguste,' Egbert threatened.

'Suppose Gomez heard what he thought was the word ghost in Portuguese, just as I did *raie* instead of "Hooray"?'

'Any evidence?'

'It's a line of thought.'

'What is it?'

Auguste turned open the page. He had resisted doing so in the hansom, so sure he was right. Staring at the page he was less sure. 'S-O-M-B-R-A-' he read out.

'Chap in a sombrero hat, eh?' Egbert was not amused.

Auguste looked up the pronunciation. 'O-m is a nasal sound, as in French.' He tried it.

'If that's all, I'll collect Twitch – we'll be off to arrest Hill.'

'No, it's not all.' Something else lingered. The smell of a dish not quite cooked recently. Which dish? Max Hill? His talk with Egbert, with Brodie, with Nettie? Little Emmeline? Something came to him, the detail that would not digest, like *sombra*, it was only one word, but it was odd in the circumstances.

'Right, you've had your chance,' Egbert said briskly.

'No, one moment,' Auguste said sharply. Please, please, he told his brain, *work*. Bring together all the ingredients and tell me how these words fit. He began to talk to Egbert, eager to get his thoughts into the world. If he could get Egbert to listen, to gain his attention, that might be the catalyst he needed.

Egbert listened. As usual, he cut through the ideas, and came down to fact. He could cut clear through the spongiest cake down to the strong base beneath – if it existed.

'If you're right,' he said, 'you can tell me what the blazes the case was all about, *if* you can puzzle it out.'

'And then?'

'Then we all meet down at the Old King Cole tomorrow afternoon. Percy, Max, Emmeline, Nettie, Brodie, Pickles, the twins, the Yapps, Fernando, Mariella, Old Uncle Tom Cherry and all.'

# Chapter Twelve

Max and breakfast were not a beautiful sight, at least, not linked together. To Auguste, coming in from his own unfortunate start to the day, Max looked an incongruous figure at the Westlands' elegant table, as he sat in solitary splendid state with a napkin tastefully tucked under the dirty red scarf round his neck. Both seemed to be contributing to the mopping-up of unconsidered trifles from Max's mouth. The Westlands' footman was studiedly fixing his attention on the middle air somewhere over Max's head, as Max scraped back his chair, and stalked grandly to the sideboard for what, judging by the footman's amazed face, must be at least his third plateful of herrings.

'You moving in here too?' he grunted, seeing Auguste.

'Perhaps. Those eggs look magnificent.' He spoke with feeling. This morning the all-important day for Egbert and himself, had begun with a domestic crisis. It was too much. How was a man expected to work? Worst of all, Tatiana had appeared to blame him, merely because he had ventured to observe to his own cook that the eggs were too hard to be eaten *au beurre*.

'That's how *I* cook them, sir.' Emphasis on the 'I' did not go unremarked.

'In that case I suggest your technique could be improved.'

'Ten minutes was good enough for the Duke of Davenport, sir.'

'The Duke of Davenport is dead,' snapped Auguste, patience exhausted. His tone, he conceded, possibly implied this was due to his cook.

'He enjoyed his eggs—'

'Then let him pay your wages.'

It was at this point Tatiana had entered the room, instantly taking in the situation – as did John.

'Are you asking me to leave, sir?' There was a distinctly artificial quiver in his voice.

Auguste gritted his teeth, infuriated by the man's hypocrisy. He must stick to his principles, despite Tatiana's reproachful eye. 'I am sure you are not, *are you,* Auguste?' his wife said.

What on earth had possessed him? Some age-old recollection of man's need to be master in his own household. 'If you cannot cook a simple egg correctly, then I am.'

This, he had prided himself, would be the subtle answer. Give the man a challenge, put him on his mettle. It had been greatly to his surprise that John had immediately replied: 'Very well, sir. It's been a pleasure working for *you*, madam.' And that was that.

If husbands could be so instantly dismissed, Auguste realised he would rapidly be following in John's wake.

'Now,' Tatiana remarked, *'all* our staff will leave.'

'You blame *me*?' He was hurt beyond belief.

'No, yes – oh, Auguste, how *could* you? You know how difficult it is to find good servants.'

'He was *not* good. Leave it to me. I will solve this problem.'

'When?'

'Have I ever let you down?' Sometimes the general was preferable to the particular in reply.

She thought about this rather too long for comfort. 'Not intentionally,' she said at last.

This was not the answer he could have wished, and it aggrieved him greatly on top of a bad indigestible egg.

'I will find the answer.'

The last sight he had was of Tatiana's despairing face. He covered guilt by telling himself now he was a detective. Such disputes belonged to his former life as chef, one he had been forbidden to follow by his wife's family. He was not fairly treated. He stomped to the motor-car. He had the feeling from Manners' stiff back that news had travelled fast in the servants' hall, and he knew only too well just how fast that could be. John had been no more popular with the staff than with him, he told himself, though he knew Tatiana was right. A criticism of one member of staff was a slight against all, in the unofficial trade union of the servants' hall. It was for this reason that the sight of Max calmly enjoying what looked like an excellent breakfast was hardly likely to endear him to Auguste.

'I have come to escort you. Now.'

'You're going to lock me up,' Max said gloomily. 'I'll never be seen alive no more.'

'Nonsense. Inspector Rose has a few more questions, that is all.'

It took much persuasion, wailing, and more persuasion, before Max condescended to accompany him, and it was eleven o'clock before Auguste delivered his charge into the loving arms of Inspector Stitch, who greeted them at the front entrance of the Yard, managing to convey somehow he had been working since five in the morning.

Max was silent as he was led higher and higher into the far reaches of the Yard, and once installed in Rose's office, folded his arms, and looked as nonchalant as though this venue would be his first choice for morning chats.

'Horace Brodie tells us you asked to switch turns at the Lyle, the evening Lamb was murdered, Mr Hill. That correct?' Rose asked him.

Max nodded cautiously.

So much for theories. Auguste's hopes subsided quicker than a soufflé. If Brodie had been lying . . .

'And why was that?' Rose pressed on.

Max took his point immediately. 'Not because I killed poor old Will. Look, Brodie's turn at the Lyle was *before* mine, not after. So that proves it. Why would I want to do an *earlier* turn if I had plans to kill Will and burgle his dressing-room?' he said triumphantly.

'To give yourself an alibi, perhaps,' Rose suggested irritatingly. 'No one said the chap who burgled the dressing-room tampered with the dagger too.'

'Now look here—'

'Did you simply change places in the programme, or did you impersonate him and then do your turn much later in the programme, say the second half?'

'What would I want to do that for? Not then I didn't.

I won't say I haven't, mind, but not then,' Max agreed.

'You're sure?'

'Course I'm sure,' Max roared indignantly. 'I had somewhere to go.'

'Ransack Will's dressing-room?'

'Blimey, how many more times? *No.* I was trying to find out what Gomez was up to. The bleeding State should be grateful to me, not trying to put a rope round me. You coppers are all the same. Nick the first innocent that comes along. And it had to be me.'

'Yes, Mr Hill, you're right,' Rose agreed cordially. 'And it'll still be you unless you play your cards right.'

'I've played 'em straight into your loving hands, it seems to me. Like I said, I was out following Gomez.'

'Dressed like the ghost of William Terriss? Will cried out "Ghost" as he died.'

Max regarded him with scorn, and didn't bother to answer.

'Does the word *sombra* mean anything to you?' Auguste asked hopefully.

Max sniggered. 'Going on the streets as a Dr Cure-'em-all, are you? One of them quack remedies? I've had my whack of that. Liver pills was my line. Could have made a fortune if it hadn't been for my lumbago. No, it don't.'

Egbert was meanwhile making a telephone call. 'All right,' he told Max, 'the manager of the Lyle confirms you both performed that night, and for all he knows you might have changed position.'

'Thanks,' said Max sarcastically.

'So now we just need to know exactly where you went after you left the Lyle.'

'It wasn't to the bleedin' Old King Cole,' Max said firmly. 'I weren't there till the second half, and no one can say they saw me, 'cos I weren't there.'

'There's such a things as back windows.'

'There's such a thing as lumbago, mate,' Max rejoined fervently. 'Look, the reason I ran was I thought you and those Special Branch johnnies were all in it together. Can you blame me? I thought you were going to bump me off so you didn't have to tell His Majesty you'd gone and lost his cross. That one in the bowler hat killed Gomez, I reckon.'

Rose considered this entrancing theory and reluctantly discarded it as unlikely. 'No, but I still think there's something you know we don't. That's why you're coming down to the Old King Cole this afternoon.'

'Why?' Max asked suspiciously.

'We're going to play jigsaw puzzles, and to make sure you're right there, playing with us, you're going to have luncheon in a nice warm cell.'

'With Inspector Stitch as waiter,' Auguste added.

'So that's the red herring squashed,' Egbert said to Auguste, when Max had been led away. 'Pity. I fancied Horace Brodie in preference to Max.'

'Are you sure?' Auguste said wistfully, reluctant to see his theory vanish.

'Not me. The manager. I reminded him he told you he hadn't actually seen Brodie, only heard him singing his blinking song, and was he quite sure it wasn't Max? He said he was quite sure Brodie was there to do his turn, whether in Max's position or not, because he went backstage and found him fondling his wife.'

'Oh.'

'He said there's no way she'd mistake Max for Horace.'

'Oh. But he still—'

'Could have done it? So could lots of them, including Max. Too many cooks, like I said.'

'Please do not mention that word.' Auguste winced.

'Trouble in the kitchen, eh? Lizzie?'

'No. Tatiana is not pleased with me, but it is *not my fault*,' he declared passionately.

'Love's old sweet song, eh?'

'Precisely, Egbert. And that, I still think, is the sauce for our goose.'

Mariella was not as happy as she might have been, considering her purchase of six new frocks from Madame Latour of Bond Street, not to mention her legacy. There were two reasons: firstly, she had discovered that solicitors did not work as quickly as legatees might desire, and secondly, that wretched cross was still hidden somewhere, a fact of great interest to a group of gentlemen who had made it clear to her they were prepared to abandon claim to this title if she failed to find it for them. In a way, therefore, she had no objection to spending the afternoon at the Old King Cole. Much as she dreaded meeting Fernando, she had to talk to him, and the presence of Scotland Yard as well as her fellow artistes should ensure that neither Republicans nor Special Branch could openly attack her. Nevertheless it still meant putting her head in a definite lions' den, and the risks were high. The doors might close on her before she could escape. And lions were not as biddable as little dogs.

\* \* \*

'I've come to give you a ride in style, Harry,' Nettie said shortly.

'You're a wonderful woman, Nettie.' Pickles adopted his old caressing voice, attempting to leap up nonchalantly to the carriage, but failing at his first attempt.

'Forget all that. It's too late.'

'You don't seem able to. Why else do you come?' The smiling caress in his voice grew more forced.

'Because I've a reputation to think of, and you're still my husband in name,' she told him briskly. 'It's not going to do me any good if you're carted off to prison.'

'What for?' His face grew pale.

'What have you been doing?'

'Nothing.'

'Then you've nothing to worry about.'

'You still think I killed Will,' he said suddenly.

'Someone did.'

'Not me.'

'And they're still looking for that cross. I wouldn't put it past you to have had a hand in that.'

'Wouldn't you?'

'Come on, Harry. If they're after you for that, I'll help you all I can. But not if it's for Will's murder.'

Our loveable Pickles did not reply, but whistled a merry tune, as though he had not a care in the world.

The Misses Pear obeyed their summons to the Old King Cole, both on the whole happy ladies, for Marigold had just discovered it had all been a horrible mistake. A result of too many acrobatics and too little cabbage, her doctor had told her. Dear Mama had always told them to be sure to eat lots of suet every day, and that an apple a day kept the doctor away. If only it kept the Horaces of this world away too . . .

There was only one dark spot about coming to the Old King Cole this afternoon, and it made them a little uneasy.

'Marigold?'

'Yes, Violet.'

'After today, shall we go away?'

'Do let's, Violet.'

'I suppose we should do it?' There was hope in her voice. If only Marigold suggested they needn't talk to anyone about anything.

'Will would want us to,' Marigold said.

'Yes, of course,' Violet agreed bleakly.


Blackguard Horace was returning to his alma mater, the Old King Cole, with mixed feelings. He was, he told himself, an established star now and could gloat over lesser lights. He had achieved eminence solely through his own efforts. He grinned. However, there were problems. One of them was Dolly, who was still for some reason out for his blood. The twins hardly entered his calculations, so distant was their memory. Scotland Yard and Special Branch's presence worried him slightly. He had no opinion of their brain power and *that* was the problem. They might pick on anyone, even in sheer stupidity on *him*. The sooner he could get out of this and back to the fleshpots of the Alhambra, and the flesh of that delightful lady in the green tights, the better. Odd, it had been ladies' legs started it all. He'd had a passion for legs in tights ever since he fell in love with the darling of the gods, Nellie Farren, when he was eight. In her days as principal boy in burlesques, Nellie had been far removed from his orbit. She was long dead now, but that had never lessened his determination to join the galaxy of the great, just as she had done. So it was all the more important that the police did not accidentally blunder their way to him.

Fernando left his lodgings with one thought in mind. Mariella. He would see her, apologise, and everything would be all right. He had assumed it would be, once Will Lamb was dead, and it was only his foolishness in approaching Mariella too soon that had upset her. Now she was happy because she was going to be rich, so it would be all right to talk to her, just as he'd planned.

Emmeline was humming. Underneath her pinafore dress nestled the red corset, and her mother hadn't said a word when she told her. Emmeline felt she'd made an important discovery: money controlled the world. The fees that the Alhambra paid had quickly quelled her parents' opposition to the reborn Emmeline, and the lesson would not be lost on their daughter. If money could so quickly influence *them*, what else might it not achieve? She might only be thirteen, but nevertheless it seemed to her this might be a sound rule to apply to her future life.

Then she thought of Nettie Turner. Nettie had been good to her. Nettie was famous and rich, *and* she was nice too, so perhaps life wasn't as straightforward as Emmeline had imagined. Perhaps she would set out to be another Nettie Turner. She cheered up and practised smiling in the mirror. She was intrigued by the difference it made to her face. Perhaps she should go round smiling at people, and not bother learning their secrets at doors. That wasn't much fun anyway, since things that grown-up people kept as secrets tended to be dull. True, she had obtained her red corset by this method. She had a sudden memory of that time. She'd been so eager to get the corset it had gone right out of her mind. But now it was clear, so perhaps she'd start off her new career of being nice by telling that funny French chef. Perhaps she'd get a reward. Emmeline hastily reminded herself that money was not going to be all important from now on.

Percy Jowitt reluctantly took off his carpet slippers, pushed them under the armchair in case his housekeeper made yet more disparaging remarks about their condition, and put on his shoes. Normally this was a delightful task that implied their owner was about to launch them in the direction of his beloved theatre. Today, however, it was not quite so pleasant since memories of murder would be resurrected by, it seemed to Percy, the entire security establishment of the British Isles. They would want his office again too.

Box-office receipts were so good now that there had been no threat of bailiffs for a week. Until this morning. Most unreasonably, one creditor – a powerful one, His Majesty's Government – had grown abusive. This seemed to Percy entirely unreasonable when he was doing his best for his country by providing such wonderful entertainment, but in black and white His Majesty's Government had threatened a visit from their representative. Beside this spectre the prospect of sitting next to a murderer this afternoon was small beer indeed. Percy had his own ideas about this murder, and they had nothing to do with crosses. He hadn't bothered to tell anyone about them because (a) it was police business and (b) it wasn't likely it would happen again. At least, he hoped not. These things happened in music hall from time to time. Anyway, nothing untoward would take place this afternoon. Not with Scotland Yard present.

Inspector Stitch was keeping a close eye on Max in the hansom, in case Max plunged out into the traffic chaos of Ludgate Circus as off a diving board. This fellow was not going to think he could fool Stitch; he could tell he was looking for ways to escape. He wouldn't. Not while in Stitch's custody.

'Ever been in the Tower?' he asked Hill genially, as they passed the fortress.

'No.'

You will, laddie,' Stitch sniggered. 'Under Traitor's Gate for you, eh? That's what you get for double-crossing the crown.'

Max looked unimpressed, and decided to get his own back with a fair impression of Egbert Rose. 'You allowed to terrorise witnesses, Twitch?'

'That's my job . . . Blimey, you sounded just like the Chief.'

'That's *my* job.'

Stitch did not quite follow this, but did realise he was dealing with a very slippery customer indeed, and was relieved when the cab drew up to the front of the Old King Cole. He paid the fare (without tip, since that was never reimbursed), and firmly took Max by the arm. 'No slip 'twixt cup and lip,' he informed his captive.

'If there's a drink in it, I wouldn't let it slip.' Max was suddenly inclined to be jovial. 'How about it?'

Stitch was shocked.

'I'm on duty,' he choked. 'My job is to deliver you to the Chief.' He had a sudden feeling that this was going to be easier said than done as Max pushed his way through the crowd in the eating-room with Stitch grimly clinging on to his arm from behind. Max was an artiste carefully trained in the art of timing; Stitch was not. Two plates of pie and mash rushed by on Lizzie's tray, and somehow Max was on one side of her with Stitch caught on the other. A lesser man than Stitch would have let go. He did not.

It was Lizzie who landed up on the floor, with Max falling on her, and Twitch on him, and the mash squashed between them. Nevertheless, it was a triumph for law and order. Max Hill was safely delivered to the Chief.

There was only one place large enough to accommodate them all and that was the stage itself. This afternoon its equipment and props were sparse in the extreme. Two Tee-pieces and a standard yielded a meagre glow, and chairs, summoned from all quarters, gave it the air of waiting for a second audience to face that in the auditorium. Egbert Rose eyed his audience. The old familiar faces: Fernando (who had been delighted when Mariella was so sweet to him, and horrified when she suddenly grew angry, all because he didn't know anything about that stupid cross); Mariella (who was

beginning to realise just who Miguel had gone to meet
that Sunday morning, and wonder how much it was
worth to her); the Tumbling Twins (who were very
surprised at the reception of their news); Dolly (who
had at last seen the light about Handsome Horace);
Percy (who was mentally budgeting future box-office
receipts); Pickles (who was beginning to grow uneasy);
Nettie (who had finally come to the conclusion that Will's
death freed her from all obligation to Pickles); Emmeline
(who was rather frightened at the results of her little
talk); Thomas Yapp (who was in a panic of indecision);
Brodie (who was beginning to think women were more
trouble than they were worth) – and Max. Max was
considering his position. It could hardly escape his
attention that Special Branch was hemming him in:
Cherry was on one side of him, Black on the other. He
wondered if he was being set up. And that wasn't the
only problem he had. He needed to do a bit of thinking,
then he might be in a position to trade.

'You're all holding bits of this jigsaw puzzle, and none
of you has bothered to wonder if they fit,' Rose began.
'So now we're going to do the puzzle together. We've got
two separate puzzles here. You've all heard about the
missing Windsor cross; it unfortunately landed up here,
and caused one murder, and we've got another puzzle
in Will Lamb's murder, which in turn caused another
murder. Our mistake was to think there was only one
puzzle. There wasn't, and we *know* it now.' He
emphasised the 'know'. No one commented, one or two
still trying to assimilate the news that the Old King
Cole had links to royalty, albeit illegal ones.

'My friends here from a different department at the

Yard have cleverly worked out what's happened to the cross,' Rose continued graciously. 'All we have to do is find it. It's still here somewhere, otherwise I don't think Mrs Gomez would have been so eager to come.'

Mariella stiffened but decided silence was the better part of valour.

'So we'll concentrate on Will Lamb's murder, and that of Miguel Gomez – if that doesn't distress you too much, Mrs Gomez. We think Gomez was murdered because he guessed who murdered Lamb.'

'*What*?' Mariella shrieked.

'Probably he was blackmailing the murderer,' Rose continued unperturbed.

'Nonsense,' she shrieked again.

'Or perhaps he murdered Will Lamb himself, and someone took revenge.'

'No!'

'Now, there are only a few of you who could both have doctored the dagger and ransacked the dressing-room.'

'But that was to look for the cross,' Mariella objected. 'You said that had nothing to do with Will's death.'

'Ah yes. But suppose it was to make it look as *if* the cross, or to be more accurate, what the murderer thought was a bundle of your auntie's jewellery, was the motive for the murder. It wasn't, of course. It was quite different, and Miguel Gomez knew it. Now how could he have known? He would have known that his wife, for instance, had no motive for murder, nor probably Fernando, nor anyone who was not involved with the theft of the cross in the first place.'

'I was involved with the cross,' shouted Max, seeing a way out.

'Certainly you were, so you had a motive to murder Will Lamb if it *were* committed for the sake of the cross.'

'But you said it was for something else,' Max cried, alarmed, wondering where he'd gone wrong.

'True, but—'

'I'm getting out of here,' Max roared suddenly. 'It's too bloomin' dangerous.'

He sized up Cherry and Black's positions, pushed his chair back, and then over, and with the expertise of the elderly acrobat, and showing no signs at all of lumbago, somersaulted out on to the stage with a clear passage to the wings, before Cherry and Black could move from their chairs.

'Get him,' Rose shouted at Twitch.

Unfortunately he too failed to clarify to whom his order was addressed, and the whole company responded on behalf of law and order, and regardless of Rose's later countermanding calls, milled into the wings in search of Max. Only Nettie and Auguste remained with Rose.

'This is a real old pantomime,' Nettie laughed. 'Talk about Clown and the stolen sausages.'

'Only in this panto Clown might be murdered?'

Nettie changed in an instant. 'Max?' she asked sharply. 'More belly-laughs than brains, he's got.'

'I'll go, Egbert,' Auguste told him.

'Find Stitch. Get support. You'll need it.'

The hounds had spread out now. All around him was quiet, though elsewhere in the theatre he could hear faint far-off sounds of movement. Outside or inside. Auguste swallowed, trying to suppress instinctive fear, and replace it with reason. Rational thought told him that this place had a dozen or so people moving through it, all intent on finding Max, but that it might not be Max who was in the greatest danger. Outside, Egbert would have men posted on every approach to the theatre, back and front. There were too many people around for harm to come to anyone – to Max or to himself. Fear told him that his quarry was beyond reason now, that he was guided by primitive urges, of which the uppermost now would be self-survival, the most powerful of all.

He, Auguste, must find Max, therefore, for where Max was, so would be the person he sought. Max was an elderly man. That somersault must have exhausted him. As an old fox, he'd try to find a lair now.

And where, even in this dark barn of a theatre, would he find that? He heard a distant shout, a woman's, and stopped. Mariella's? If she had found Max there would be more noise, more shouts, but there were none. Would Max have gone under the stage? No, too dangerous, for there were no escape routes from it. If he stayed within the theatre he would have made for the auditorium or the pub end, either on the ground or first floor. Yet the corridors and stairs linking the two parts of the building, sandwiching the auditorium in between, were long; would Max risk being caught in a chase along them? No, if he were Max, he would hide outside until the hunt had died down a little and then double back inside to seek a better hiding-place. He could not have gone far since the alleys leading to the roadways were guarded, but he could climb walls on to that waste land, or, if he could reach it, hide in the old churchyard.

Convinced he was right, he ran outside, where the

light was rapidly fading. There was enough to see no one lurked behind the wall facing him. He pulled open the doors of the earth closets – nothing. If Max had been out here, he had already gone. Not to left or right, but back.. Not into the theatre, but towards the steps leading down to the basement areas of the kitchens. Heart pounding, as he pulled one door open after another, he realised he was wasting time. Max would never hide in such a confined space. He would be at large where, if cornered, he could run. And that meant the auditorium.

He pulled at the door used as an exit for the gallery. It was locked. He rushed into the kitchens to take the longer way round. Now there were people: Lizzie staring in amazement as he rushed by. Twitch working his way through the pub area, Mariella quarrelling with Fernando in the passageway, even Pickles. Down or up? Up surely, where there was greater choice of hiding-place.

Auguste advanced into the dark silent corridor, intent – too intent – on finding Max. The doors to the auditorium were open, but within all was dark. The stage which showed the merest dim glow of gas light served only to emphasise the blackness around him. Max could have gone anywhere. Behind the circle or gallery seats? He gulped, prickles burning at the back of his neck. No, there was someone closer than that. In this corridor? In one of the two boxes opening off it? He shut his eyes, since they were of no use in this dark, putting out his hands in front of him, ridiculously thinking this might ward off evil. He could almost hear evil breathing.

There was a scream. Not Max, a woman's, no, a *child's*, and it was a scream of terror. Then he knew for sure that Max was not the hunted fox. It was Emmeline, ahead of him in the dark, in one of the boxes, trapped with a murderer.

He shouted out, to draw attention to their plight. 'Here, Egbert, *here*!' and plunged forward. Surely he must be level with the boxes now. He was, his left hand made contact with the door jamb, his right feeling for his path.

Then the door opened, he felt the draught hit the sticky warmth around him, and a hand seized his, doubling it back excruciatingly, then, as he collapsed, the hands moved round his throat, choking him. Surely people must come, they must have heard, they were running – or was it the drumming in his head? Was the life quietly being choked out of him? Would he die too soon? Then a relief, a trickle of light, flailing bodies, and a merciful chance to lie gasping for air on the ground. Gradually he recognised the familiar form of Twitch, blessed Twitch, strong and *here,* who ignoring the temptation to let the Frenchie suffer a bit, had won the struggle and was handcuffing Horace Brodie with the full majesty of the law.

Egbert Rose pushed his way through the group of chattering people surrounding Auguste, back on the stage, where Emmeline was efficiently rubbing butter into Auguste's tender neck. 'I told him I knew,' she said with satisfaction. 'I forgot all about seeing him in the props room because of my corset, and I only just remembered.'

'Did it not occur to you he might have been a murderer?' he asked painfully. It was so obvious looking back. Brodie had been listening in too, had heard about 'Auntie's jewellery', had heard or deduced about the will, and that, to him, had meant he must act quickly to eliminate Will.

Emmeline considered. 'No,' she said at last. 'Not until he came into the box after me.'

'You're a brave girl, Emmeline,' Auguste said in surprise.

Emmeline blushed. Apart from Nettie, no one had ever paid her a compliment. 'Yes, I was,' she said aggrieved. 'It wasn't fair. I'd said I'd keep quiet if he gave me a bust improver.'

Egbert pushed his way through to his friend. 'You're alive, then.'

'Thanks to Inspector Stitch.'

Something that might have been a reluctant grin hovered on Egbert's lips. 'I'm off to the Yard with our chum. Come in, as soon as you're able. I've—'

He was interrupted by Percy Jowitt, striding importantly up to them, and pushing Fernando to one side in order to have space for his dramatic announcement: 'I've got the villain.'

'Yes, yes, I'm going off to lock him up,' Egbert said testily.

'Excellent!' Percy beamed.

The case was over, Auguste had survived, his days at the Old King Cole were at an end, and he was not sorry.

'What had he done, exactly?' Percy inquired hesitantly, after Rose had left.

330

'He murdered Will Lamb and my husband,' Mariella replied viciously. 'So Mr Didier says.'

'So it wasn't you, beloved,' Evangeline cried, throwing her arms round a stoical Thomas.

'Are you sure?' Percy asked, surprised.

'Yes. Once we realised *why*, everything was clear. It was the song.'

'Song?' Nettie repeated sharply.

'Yes. You remember you told us Will was always generous with his work and handed out songs to anyone who wanted to sing them. I suspect Brodie had sung several over the years, but then "Don't Wait Up" caught on. On the strength of it he was going up to the Alhambra. People would be humming it, singing it, whistling it, everywhere, and Will would have undoubtedly heard it. But the difference with this song was that he had sold the publication rights in it, and handed over copyright to the publishers as usual. Will's copyright.'

'What?' Mariella's ears caught the magic words. 'But that's *mine*.'

'I'm sure he realised that. He might hope to talk Will round, but if you, Mariella, heard about it, as future holder of his copyrights, you would have insisted not only on your right, but—'

'Exposing the swine for what he is,' agreed Mariella without hesitation. 'And I'm going to.'

'Will didn't like being taken advantage of,' Nettie said pointedly. 'By *anyone*.'

The innuendo passed Mariella by.

'Brodie had no choice, as he saw it,' Auguste continued. 'He had to prevent Will hearing that song.

And once he got to London that would be impossible, so he had to get Will to the Old King Cole. With luck Will wouldn't hear it, but it didn't really matter since he had to die anyway.'

'All for a bleedin' song,' Nettie said angrily.

'Like your Donkey Song, Nettie,' Mariella said coolly. 'That was Will's too, wasn't it?'

'That's right,' Nettie agreed readily. 'I nicked all the money and gave it to a Society for Fallen Women. So you ain't lost it.'

Mariella opened her mouth to reply, and changed her mind.

'Will did hear the song,' Auguste went on, 'because he arrived early on the Tuesday night. He had it out with Brodie, and suffered the penalty.'

'My poor darling Will!' Evangeline cried.

Thomas cleared his throat, his eyes beseeching Auguste to keep silence on his relationship.

'Poor Will indeed,' Auguste said soberly. 'Everything must have seemed to be going well for Brodie. He arranged to meet Will before the performance and must have doctored the dagger then. Max asked him to change turns, which gave Brodie the idea of ransacking the dressing-room, since he had more time to play with. Then it would appear that Mariella's jewellery – as he thought – would be a motive. Instead, he was nonplussed to find the cross, and recognising these were uncharted waters, decided to leave it behind.'

'And Miguel?' Mariella asked offhandedly.

'I think your late husband realised, for whatever reason, that Brodie was the murderer. Perhaps he thought again what Will had said and realised the word was in fact two words, of which the first was "song", and the second "Bro—". I doubt Will realised what Brodie had done, but was muttering what was uppermost in his mind. Gomez was greedy, however. His plans for the cross had gone awry. If he wasn't careful, he'd lose the fee for stealing the cross, *and* his wife. So he decided to make money where he could, and thus lost his life. Brodie found the fake cross tucked in the mermaid's tail, and as a red herring threw it to join its fellow fish in the Thames – where it was found, thanks to one of Ma Bisley's team who saw a suspicious splash, and her nephew's fishing abilities.'

'Why set Brodie after me?' Max asked, aggrieved. 'I never knew about his bloomin' song.'

'He wasn't after you. It was Emmeline, though doubtless he could be forgiven for thinking you knew who Miguel's murderer was.'

Max sighed. 'I ran away because of all you geezers. There's only one lot can murder in this country and get away with it: the bloomin' government.'

'Hear, hear,' said Percy brightly.

'Moreover,' Max continued, 'who was it Brodie decided to have a go at murdering first just now? Emmeline, me, or you?'

There was a silence.

'Me,' said Auguste reluctantly.

'Well, then.'

'I think,' said Marigold reluctantly, 'that he may just have misinterpreted something I said. It has worried me a little.'

'What?' Auguste asked grimly.

'I merely happened to mention to Horace that he

should be careful about little foreigners, and if he didn't watch out, one of them would soon be his undoing.'

'I,' Auguste fixed on the insulting point, 'am not *little*. I am five feet ten inches.'

'I meant my baby, only I didn't have one. Isn't that nice?'

'Delightful!' said Auguste savagely.

The Old King Cole murders were solved, and its life could return to normal. Already the backstage area was filling with both familiar and new faces. Auguste had waved Emmeline off to the Alhambra, together with Nettie and Max Hill.

'You never know, Max,' she'd said, 'they may just need a turn at short notice tonight. Could be your lucky night.'

Here at the Old King Cole he could still see the stalwarts. Dolly was talking to the Misses Pears, no doubt with mutual claims that they had always known there was something odd about Horace, and shivering delicately at the idea of having been in a murderer's arms. He was more or less right. Marigold was mentally informing her womb how lucky it had been, Violet was making plans to tell their story for money. It could be entitled 'Ladies in Pink Tights' were she to sell to a gentlemen's magazine, or 'How We Were Deceived by a Villain', if to a ladies'. They were also congratulating themselves on having accepted Horace's generous gift of twenty pounds after their little talk about that song Will was so upset about.

Auguste saw Evangeline emerge from the dressing-room in full warpaint for the stage. Fernando was feverishly hunting for some missing prop, Mariella was leading out her dogs, with a fish tail tucked under her arm. Thomas and Evangeline were in front (Thomas having decided to tell his wife that he was Will's brother and been happily surprised at her reception of his news, and Evangeline wondering whether Percy's new warmth towards her turn meant he was in love with her or with her husband's money — she decided the former).

Percy was contemplating his stage contentedly. All was well at the Old King Cole. It appeared the trouble had all been due to Brodie's song. He could have told them about that a long time ago. It never occurred to him. That kind of thing was always happening in music hall.

Life was returning to normal, Auguste decided, watching the Old King Cole gather itself together. The stage door opened and a short fat man half-hidden by a one-man-band staggered in. He eyed Auguste strangely, obviously sizing him up as to what kind of turn he might be.

Auguste decided to go to the eating-room, and return later perhaps. There, in the form of Mrs Jolly's pies, would be comfort. Unfortunately there was not. There was only Lizzie, in tears and with no sign of either Charlie or Joe assisting her, and a very rowdy crowd of would-be customers.

'Lizzie,' he asked despairingly, as he rushed to see how great the catering problem was, 'is this the fault of your love life again?'

She peered round the corner of the apron she was using to dab her eyes. 'Oh, Mr Didier. No. It's me career. I'd decided to go in for that Raine's Charity. You gets lots of money in St George's when you marry if you've done five unblemished years in service. But how can I? No 'elp. No pies.'

'Where's Joe?' asked Auguste briskly.

'Gone back to Ma Bisley. I got sick of him always hanging round, always cheerful, "Do you love me, Lizzie?" when I was trying to work. A woman has the right to work in peace, say I.'

Auguste let this pass. 'And Charlie?'

'He had to go too, didn't he?'

'And the food for this evening?'

'Frederick and me, that's all. I ain't done 'is pertaters for the interval, or the fish, or the 'ash.'

Auguste flew downstairs. No wasting energy on words. What was needed was action. It was fully three-quarters of an hour of frantic preparation before he had breath to ask: '*Why* did Charlie have to go and –' a fearful memory came back '– why are there no pies?'

'Mr D, you are a wonder,' Lizzie said appreciatively, surveying his work. She had cheered up. 'The shop burned down this afternoon.'

'What?' he shrieked. 'Mrs *Jolly's* shop?'

'Yes.'

'But Lizzie, what has happened to Mrs Jolly? She was hurt?'

She shrugged. 'Dunno. Happens all time, don't it? They've nowhere else to go. Workhouse, maybe.'

'Do not be foolish, Lizzie. The woman is an artiste. People with genius do not go to workhouses.'

'Don't they?' she commented darkly. 'That's all you know.'

She was serious. The terrible possibilities of this fate

overwhelmed him. He promptly abandoned his post and Lizzie, in the cause of higher objectives for mankind: the saving of Mrs Jolly. He ran as quickly as he could to what remained of Mrs Jolly's pie shop.

Both shop and living quarters were burned out. Inside, moving desultory among charred wreckage, Auguste could see a plump figure, picking up black objects and letting them drop again.

'Charlie,' he yelled. 'Let me in.'

'Hop in, Mr D,' Charles shouted morosely. 'No winders left.'

He was right. Once inside, Auguste stood surrounded by destruction. In a twinkle, the shop had disappeared. Gone were the pies of wonder that this morning must have adorned that blackened marble slab, gone the choucroute, the sausages, the tempting cheeses.

'How is your aunt?' he inquired anxiously.

'Having a cup of char next door but one. It's next door, now. That one went as well.'

'What will you do?'

'No more shops, Auntie says. Washing, perhaps. Factory work.'

'Factory work?' Auguste almost screeched. 'And you?'

'Fancy being a clerk. Nice lot of sitting down,' Charlie explained. 'These lady typewriters have a nice life.'

'But the pies—'

Charlie sighed. 'Life rises and falls, Mr D. Just like them pies.'

An idea so fantastic suddenly came to Auguste, he knew instantly that it was the solution, the right solution, the *only* solution. 'Charlie, pull down the shutters,' he ordered him. 'Lock up this nightmare and take me to your aunt *immediately*.' Charlie, he noted, was in the habit of obeying orders, probably because life was easier that way.

Auguste followed his stout rear into a small terraced house, where he found his quarry sitting in front of the fire, staring at a cold cup of tea. He did not inquire after her health, that could come later. This was more important.

'Mrs Jolly,' he informed her, 'your pies are too good for the world to lose. Is the rest of your cuisine of equal standard?'

'No more shops,' she said listlessly.

'So I've been told. What are your specialities, whose recipes do you approve, can you cook a tolerable omelette?'

She looked puzzled. 'I makes me own recipes. I took a look at that Mrs Marshall. Didn't take to her.'

Auguste warmed to her. Any cook who didn't take to Mrs Marshall's recipes was after his own heart.

'You use coralline pepper?' he ventured cautiously.

'Never. Now, when I was in service—'

This was too much good fortune. Indeed the heavens were raining manna, or at least the means of making it. 'So you have not always worked in shops?'

'No more shops.'

'Quite. Now, when you were in service—'

'I worked for Mr Kettner, and then for one of them Grand Dukes—'

Sometimes there were rewards in life for those that toiled, as he had that day. Auguste sighed: 'Mrs Jolly, do you like working with people?'

'Yes, if they leave me be.'

'Would you like working for me, even if I did not leave you be *all* the time? I am married, but my wife is much more reasonable than I. She does not cook, only eats.'

Mrs Jolly looked at him, and took a long time to answer. 'You don't have a shop, do you?'

'I do not. I have a large house which has accommodation and need for a cook.'

An agonising pause. 'Maybe I'll try it. But no opening no shops, mind.'

The joy was exquisite, like the first night of love. Only one more thing remained to be settled.

'Charlie!'

'Yessir?'

'I have a job for you also. It involves a lot of sitting.' Charlie looked interested. 'And eating.' Even more interested. 'I, Charlie,' Auguste continued, 'am a Johnson in need of a Boswell.'

'What's a Boswell?'

'A Boswell is you, Charlie.'

'What would I tell Lizzie?'

'Leave Lizzie to me.'

'Lizzie, I have bad news to impart. I am to take Charlie from you. Will it break your heart?' He had gone straight back, finding Lizzie about to eat her own supper.

'Tell you frankly, Mr D, I'd be glad of it. Sick of 'im hanging round me. I'd like to get on and do the cooking myself.'

'You do not mind the loss of both your swains?'

'Who needs men?' she observed scornfully, tucking into her mutton chop. 'Besides,' she gulped down an inelegant mouthful, 'that new waiter on the beer has his eye on me.' She giggled. 'Frederick's jealous. Wotcher, Mr Jowitt.'

Percy arrived simultaneously with Egbert Rose. Auguste flushed guilty, remembering belatedly he had been asked to call at the Yard.

'So this is where you are, Auguste,' Egbert said, annoyed. 'Couldn't believe you'd still be hanging around here, but Tatiana said you weren't back yet. I came here to tell you our lad is safely locked up and—'

Percy interrupted. 'That reminds me. I thought you said you were going to do something about that villain.'

'We have.'

'No, you haven't. He's still here.'

'Which villain?' Rose asked impatiently.

'The one you were after.'

'He's locked up, Mr Jowitt.'

'I know he is, but he won't be much longer because I didn't hit him very hard, because the club broke, and I heard him moving just now. Don't you think he ought to be let out?'

'Who?'

'I don't know his name. The one you were after. I told you I'd got the villain locked up,' Percy said, aggrieved. 'He is in the cellar outside, where I usually lock bailiffs.'

'I remember,' Egbert said grimly.

'Perhaps—' an awful thought occurred to Percy, 'he *is* the bailiff. I thought he was your murderer, otherwise I wouldn't have hit him. I daresay if he's a bailiff he won't be too pleased.'

'No doubt about that. Let's go and unlock him,' Egbert said resignedly, leading the way with Percy, Auguste and Lizzie following behind.

'I hit him with this,' Percy said proudly, picking up an object from the ground.

'Fernando's club,' said Auguste, laughing, taking it from him. 'This must have been what he was looking for this evening. I should keep out of his way – *aaayee*!'

Percy had unlocked the shed, the door had been violently thrown back from within, knocking Egbert sideways and leaving Auguste face to face with the occupant – and his knife.

The occupant was Pyotr Gregorin.

Catlike with murderous eyes which had lit up as they saw their prey, he launched himself forward as Auguste instinctively raised the club, fortunately deflecting the first blow. Percy scuttled out of harm's way, the club was seized and thrown away, as Auguste, still in the grip of shock, was locked to the enemy for the fatal jab. Egbert, caught on the wrong side, was only now recovering his balance and moving. Lizzie was on the right side. As Gregorin's arm moved, she jumped lithely on to his back, hauling up his arm, then biting his ear with all the relish of a mutton chop. Auguste, recovering his wits, hit him first in the ribs and then in the place that proved Gregorin's main case against him, that Auguste was no gentleman.

He collapsed with Lizzie tumbling after him, and Egbert and Auguste diving for him simultaneously, knocking the knife from his hand. But immediately Gregorin with vicelike strength wriggled from underneath the pile of bodies and out, vaulted over the wall and disappeared into the darkness.

'Er, is he a friend of yours?' Percy cautiously inquired from behind the door.

'No. Just one of the family.' Auguste helped Lizzie up, supporting her as she staggered slightly. 'You are hurt, Lizzie?'

"Course not. Only a bruise.'

'Then what,' he asked quietly, 'are you crying for?'

'It's me dress,' she wailed. 'It's torn.'

'I will get you twenty new dresses, Lizzie.'

'No, you won't. You promised that before, but you never did.' There was no rancour in her voice. 'This is me only dress. A manageress has to look smart, don't she?'

'The day after tomorrow, Lizzie, we shall go shopping. Your new staff will look after the restaurant.'

'What new staff?' yelped Percy.

'The new staff that I shall be appointing and *you* will be paying for, Mr Jowitt.'

'Oh. How?' he asked nervously.

'Out of the reward you will get.'

'For locking up His Majesty's bailiff? I hardly think—'

'No. For this.' Auguste picked up the broken club, and twisted off its top.

Inside was Prince Henry the Navigator's cross.

# Epilogue

His Majesty King Edward VII beamed at his three visitors in the Buckingham Palace audience chamber. Chief Inspector Egbert Rose, who was bearing Prince Henry's cross, dearest Tatiana, his favourite cousin, and—

'You again,' he said jovially to Auguste.

'Yes, sir.'

'Mixed up with crime again, I hear.'

'Not intentionally, sir.'

'I should hope not.' A silence. 'Not cooking, anyway.'

'Only in my own establishment, sir.'

'Auguste has found us the most excellent cook, Bertie,' Tatiana informed him. 'She can even cook Russian dishes.'

'I should give them a miss if I were you, Tati. A lot of beetroot. Turns your skin red. That's for me, is it?' turning to Rose.

'Yes, Your Majesty.' Egbert handed over his charge. The King examined it closely. 'And here is the garnet that fell out, sir. I thought your own staff might wish to replace it.'

'Quite right. That's that, then,' the King said.

'It presents a problem to you, Bertie, I fear,' Tatiana observed sweetly.

'What's that, Tati?'

'Now that it's back, you have the problem of whether to return it to Portugal again,' she pointed out.

Auguste glanced at her curiously. He knew that look on her face. The last time had been driving back from Lord and Lady Westland's home, when he had, apparently, eagerly agreed to the purchase of a new motor-car. This time he paid more attention.

'Ah.' The King thought for a moment. 'Luckily no one knows it's been found. It can stay missing and turn up after the King of Portugal has come and gone from here in November.'

'But what of the reward?' Auguste asked.

'Reward?'

'To the finder of the cross. One Mr Percy Jowitt.'

'Ah.' The King fidgeted. 'I suppose— Very well, I'll see it's done.'

'Generously, Bertie, as you always do,' Tatiana said innocently.

'This reputation the British crown has for hoarding is entirely undeserved. The crown is always generous. Or,' the King added hastily, 'it will be in this case. That satisfy you?'

Auguste looked at Tatiana. She nodded slightly. Strange, how wives and husbands come to think alike. 'Not entirely, sir,' he said.

'What?' The King stared at this impudent upstart.

'We'd like to know the true story,' Tatiana told him.

The King stopped fulminating. 'About what?'

'The cross,' Auguste said quietly.